Duty to Kill

A Novel by

J.W. Stone

WARRIORS PUBLISHING GROUP
LOCKHART, TEXAS

PROLOGUE

Most Marines thought the assignment of Second Lieutenant Evert Easterday as 3rd Platoon Commander was a mistake, but today he led the platoon in the largest battle since Chosin Reservoir. He stood in the middle of the street watching Corporal Reggie Miller's blood flow across the pavement to a pool where it joined the blood of a dead Vietcong. The Vietcong had raised the manhole cover, crawled out of the sewer tunnel, and shot Miller in the back. Although severely wounded, Miller somehow managed to kill the Vietcong. The corpsman shoved his hand up towards Miller's groin, trying desperately to stop the bleeding.

Easterday shouted at Miller's squad leader, Corporal Franklin, "Go get Carson and Jones, ASAP!"

Easterday then bent down towards the sewer entrance, smelled the foul odor, and listened for sounds inside. He thought about Cpl. Miller and tried to control his anger. The best in the platoon, Miller could hump more gear than any other Marine, could move silently through the jungles of Vietnam, could hear the faintest noise, and could see the slightest movement. He always volunteered for point, and without fail, he spotted the enemy first. Due to Miller, most of the Marines in the 3rd Platoon would go home.

Searching for Carson and Jones, Corporal Franklin waded through the mud of the narrow streets, scaled an ancient stone fence, and ducked inside a bombed-out building, then ran out the back door into the next street. Hue City looked like a scene from a World War I movie, with almost every building destroyed or burning. The Marines of Bravo Company were pinned down by Vietcong bunkered inside a house perfectly situated to block any northward movement.

Over the years, the Marines had honed their skills as jungle fighters, but they had difficulty adapting to the close-quarter street fighting inside Hue City. Dozens of Marines would die taking a house, only to find it empty because the Vietcong had crossed to the next row of buildings or ducked back down one of the manholes and into the sewer tunnels.

Franklin found Carson and Jones crouched behind an abandoned French Citroen sports car and yelled over the noise of the battle: "Charlie, Lieutenant Easterday wants to see you and Jones, ASAP!" At that, he motioned for Corporal Charles Carson and PFC Kenneth Jones to follow, and the three worked their way back to where he had left Easterday.

"Corporal Carson, the enemy came out of this manhole, I need this cleared. Find out what is down there." Easterday spoke in a loud, but calm, voice.

Without speaking, Carson and Jones handed Cpl. Franklin their rifles, 5.56 ammunition pouches, Alice packs, and canteens, and stripped down to their green T-shirts. Each carried only a Colt 1911 pistol, .45 caliber ammunition, bayonets, and flashlights.

"PFC Jones, I will take point. Stay as far back as possible and do not move forward unless you hear shooting." Carson carefully slid face-first down the manhole entrance. Then he crawled down, stopped, and listened for a long time. As he stared intensely into the pitch-black sewer tunnel, he saw and heard nothing, and smelled only the damp stench of fresh sewage. While he mentally debated whether to feel his way along or turn on his flashlight, his pulse started to race, and panic grew inside his stomach. With his senses kicked into overdrive, Carson inched forward, listening, smelling, and watching for anything in the dark.

After 15 minutes, the top of his head touched the bricks of the antiquated tunnel wall in front of him, and he made out the intersection of tunnels to the left and the right. With his stomach in his throat, and the fear increasing, Carson turned to his right. In a short distance, he could feel another intersection. This time there were three choices, straight, left, or right. He chose left, still sneaking along in complete darkness, and ignoring the raw sewage flowing on the floor. He walked and crawled for another half an hour, a distance he estimated at 400 yards.

Although Carson had cleared many Vietcong tunnels in the Que Son Mountains, he sensed something different about the old Hue

City sewer tunnels. The intense blackness now horrified him, and he desperately wanted to turn on his flashlight, but he realized that at this point it would be suicide. Each step produced a growing sense of impending doom. He saw nothing and heard only his heavy breathing, but his heart pounded. An intense tremor racked his right hand, and he could barely hold on to the Colt pistol. His right leg was unsteady and shook violently every time he stopped to listen for sounds.

A noise! Faint, muted.

As he listened to make out what he had just heard, Carson's fear started to overwhelm him. His instincts were screaming at him to haul ass back towards PFC Jones and the tunnel entrance. But for some reason, he could not move. He just stood with his arms and legs shaking. His hair stood on end in panic.

For an agonizingly long time, Carson wrestled with his duty to stay and the guilt of leaving. Finally, he did something he had never done before—he turned and started sneaking back towards the entrance. He felt beaten.

At first, he crawled along in the darkness. But then he jumped to his feet, turned on his flashlight, and ran as fast as he could move in the small tunnel. He ran to the intersection and then to the left. He ran for another 100 yards to another intersection, turned right for 10 yards, stopped, and turned off his flashlight. He sat down in the black, ignoring the filth, and pointing the Colt pistol towards the tunnel intersection. He just sat there shaking in terror. After five minutes, he saw a light and someone coming down the tunnel to the left of the intersection. Carson fought not to vomit and now shook so violently that it took both hands to hold on to his pistol. The light grew stronger.

In one instant, the person stepped out into Carson's tunnel and turned the bright light on him. Although paralyzed by terror, Carson managed to pull the trigger, and the Colt pistol flashed and fired its 45-caliber bullet. The burst of light destroyed Carson's night vision, and the ear-splitting boom disoriented him. Gradually, Carson recognized a flashlight laying on the floor shining through the liquid at the opposite wall. He slowly crawled over to pick it up.

To his horror, he identified the flashlight as a Marine Corps' issued MX-991/U. He grabbed it and pointed it toward the body. There was not much left of the face, but Carson recognized the body of PFC Jones.

Carson almost collapsed but managed to pull Jones out of the effluent and propped his back against the wall. The blood flowed on Carson and soaked his T-shirt, but he did not care. His eyes teared. He started to wail in pure terror, like a child crying out for their mother. Loudly bawling, he did not care if a Vietcong heard him or came to kill him. He wanted to die. He just sat in the dim light of the flashlight, sobbing and sobbing.

After half an hour, Carson stopped crying. He turned off the flashlight and sat in the dark, just trying to think for another ten minutes.

Suddenly, Carson was blinded by another muzzle blast and explosion and fell backward. He felt the intense pain where the bullet had ripped through his stomach. He instantly fired the Colt 1911 pistol toward the attacker, heard the moan, and saw the body fall to the floor.

Again, Carson found himself sitting on the tunnel floor staring at the light from a flashlight pointed at the wall. The warm wetness of his stomach wound soaked his pants. His sight stayed blurry. With each breath, pain seared its way through his body. As the cloudiness engulfed his mind, he thought about giving up, just curling up and dying.

After an hour, Carson opened his eyes and listened. Drawing on the last fumes of his reserve strength, he crept towards the second flashlight. It was not Marine Corps issued, and he felt a surge of elation beyond anything he had ever known. A Soviet nine-millimeter Makarov pistol lay next to the dead Vietcong.

Carson started crawling down the tunnel and back towards the entrance, gently and reverently dragging Jones's body.

Part 1

"These are the times that try men's souls. The summer soldier and the sunshine patriot will, in this crisis, shrink from the service of their country; but he that stands now deserves the love and thanks of man and woman."

Thomas Paine
1778

Chapter 1

"I can't believe Sergeant Jones was a no-show!" Corporal Jacobs repeated for the third time in the last hour.

The lack of a turret and numerous antennas made the amphibious tractor parked ramp down between two camouflage nets easily recognizable as an AAVC-7A1 command vehicle. The radio-intercept aerials sprung from its roof-like spines on a sea urchin. Manufactured 18 years earlier by FMC Corporation, this one had been extensively upgraded, and improved, through the years. It now had a 400-horsepower Cummins engine, enhanced armor, and a desert yellow paint job.

Parked in the Mohave Desert, just outside Camp Wilson, Marine Corps Base Twentynine Palms, California, three Marines sat cross-legged on the amtrac's ramp, like a cowboy, and two Indians smoking a peace pipe. Instead of a pipe, they passed around field manuals for the PRC-105 UFH radio, encryption units, and other components of the amtrac's communications system. White salt rings from sweating caked their tanker overalls, and dark crescents of fatigue circled beneath their eyes. A five-ton truck lumbered past them, covering them with another layer of dust.

"God damn it! I sure wish Sergeant Jones was here; he would know what to do!" Cpl. Jacobs continued with his unmistakable Ozark drawl.

As acting communications chief, Cpl. Jacobs, as well as the other Marines in the battalion, felt a sense of betrayal that Sgt. Nathan Jones failed to report for the unit's recent mobilization. A near-mythical figure, popular and respected, to have Sgt. Jones not report for duty deeply touched everyone in the communications section. His motive remained so incomprehensible that no solid rumor emerged to address it. Instead, everyone hoped that any day he would show up, have a good reason for missing movement, and go back to work as the communications chief. No one wanted to deploy for combat without him.

Lieutenant Colonel Evert Easterday, the 4th Tanks' Commanding Officer, ignored Jacobs' remarks. Easterday was an infantry officer with extensive combat experience in Vietnam. He won the Bronze Star at Hue City. He was now a civilian attorney but continued to serve in the Marine Corps as a reservist.

First Lieutenant Bob Ward, the Communications Officer, also ignored Jacobs' whining and kept his face buried inside the field manuals. Lieutenant Ward was prior-enlisted, a big man—simply mountainous—with a perpetually shaved scalp and huge body-builder arms. Unfortunately, since the unit arrived last week for mobilization training at Marine Corps Base Twentynine Palms, California Lieutenant Ward had done nothing but play with his radios, turning them on and off, cleaning the microphone terminals, and endlessly trying to contact the Air Operations Officer.

The radio repair manuals were difficult to comprehend. LtCol. Easterday would ask Lt. Ward or Cpl. Jacobs to clarify a paragraph or diagram, and from time to time, he would also read out loud a section from a manual that earlier in the day generated discussion. But at this point, Ward and Jacobs simply met his readings with blank stares and continued to bitch about Sgt. Nathan Jones' absence.

"It has to be the encryption override switch," Jacobs stated positively. Ward remained silent for a moment, as he thought about Jacobs' diagnosis.

"Corporal Jacobs, do we have a replacement switch?" Easterday asked.

"No, sir."

"How long to get one?"

"A long time, maybe ten days… maybe a month."

Lieutenant Colonel Easterday did not have much time; he had to get communications up before the battalion training exercise the next morning.

"Any other ideas?"

For a moment, Cpl. Jacobs pretended to be thinking, then looked over at Lt. Ward, hoping he would volunteer an answer.

"I guess not," Jacobs finally responded.

"Damn it! Does nobody have a workaround? I remember Sergeant Jones came up with a fix during the Pinnacle Advance Exercise last year. But you're saying you don't have one?" Easterday yelled with anger in his voice.

"Maybe we could call Colonel Wick over at Fourth Division?" Cpl. Jacobs responded. Easterday, with a blank expression, gazed out across Camp Wilson.

"What do you think, Ward?"

"I hate to bother Colonel Wick again, but we've been running rabbits down holes for three days. Corporal Jacobs, you make that call." Ward answered.

"Sir, if I try and call, I know Colonel Wick is going to be pissed. Yesterday, he told me to stop calling him and to keep reading the manuals. He has no replacement switches."

"All right; let's get him on the horn. I'll do the talking," Easterday said.

At that, all three stood up and moved inside the cramped space of the amtrac which was packed with flickering computer screens and radios. The closed air of the amtrac smelled rich with the heat of the radios like a hot clothing iron sitting on an ironing board. Garbled chatter hissed from the overhead speakers, and the other amtrac crewmembers crouched over the steel bench and strained to hear incoming reports.

Ward, Jacobs, and Easterday strapped themselves into one of the eight canvas-covered seats, slid on tanker helmets, and adjusted their microphones. The hot afternoon air mixed their body odor with the smell of radios, diesel fuel, dust, and hot steel. Jacobs turned on one of the RT-442 radios, pulled out his laminated frequency card, and changed the frequency to the non-tactical administrative net for 4th Division. Static crackled in the headset almost immediately. He listened for a moment, then looked at Easterday, and gave him a visual thumbs up.

"Romeo Three Tango, this is Yankee Nine India, over." Easterday spoke clearly and slowly.

"Yankee Nine India, this is Romeo Three Tango, over."

"This is Fourth Tanks' Six, can you put the Operations Officer on? Over."

"Wait one."

"Go ahead, Easterday." Col. Wick announced unenthusiastically.

"Lieutenant Ward and I are making no progress on our radios. We are possum-fucked. Can you help us?"

"Sorry, Easterday, everyone is having problems with the PRC-105 UFHs. It's the encryption override switch. We can't get replacements."

"Colonel Wick, I know the manual says no workaround, but last year, during the Pinnacle Advance Exercise, our communications chief, Sergeant Jones, came up with a solution."

"Yeah, I remember that. What has happened to Sergeant Jones? Still UA?"

"No word yet. But like you, I believe Sergeant Jones may show up any day," Easterday answered sadly. "But until we get these radios up, we're dead in the water for tomorrow's exercise. What am I supposed to do?"

"Sorry, Easterday, I don't have an answer. Without communications, I am expecting the exercise to be a complete cluster fuck."

Easterday looked towards Ward and Jacobs, holding the key off the mike.

"Anything else?"

They shook their heads, and Easterday keyed the mike.

"Colonel Wick. Thanks for your time. If anyone comes up with a workaround, please let us know ASAP."

"Roger that. If things change, I will be in touch immediately."

"Out."

The three pulled off their helmets, spun their chairs, and frowned at each other. Jacobs looked at the PRC-105 UFH radio in front of his position as though it were the first time he had ever seen it and started reading the manual again.

"All right, Corporal Jacobs, keep trying. Lieutenant Ward, we better get some chow. Patrol brief at the S-3 tent at 1800."

Chapter 2

The roar of the Ford V-8 engine died down as Nathan Jones pulled in the clutch and applied the brake. Black crude oil covered Nathan's face, work shirt, gloves, and boots. His derrick hand, Vertis Smith, threw in the pipe vice and grabbed the sucker-rod end. As Vertis aligned the rod over the hole, Nathan eased off the pulling unit brake and let the rod down with the perfect amount of tension to start the threads. Vertis cranked the wrench, and Nathan could see his rod-man, Ernie Johnson, stumbling back to the end of the rod basket.

Oil Well #26 stood on the Baker Lease located in the Wabash River Bottoms five miles southeast of Caryville, Illinois in the middle of a harvested corn field blanketed with a foot of snow. Crown Oil Company completed the well in 1957 and set the casing pipe at 2,700 feet, a fairly deep oil well for Southern Illinois, and one that took eight hours to pull the pump from the bottom, repair it, and run it back down. Nathan Jones had been at this well site in all kinds of weather—summer heat, fall rain, and winter snow. However, Nathan could not remember a day as bad as today's blizzard.

Ernie Johnson liked to drink whiskey, especially on cold days. At three o'clock, he declared that he felt sick, stopped working, and crawled inside the truck cab. Nathan remained silent. The old man appeared drunk, but nothing could change that now. Normally, the loss of a crewman would shut down a pulling unit, but both Nathan and Vertis could run rods with just a two-man crew. It slowed their progress considerably, but they kept adding sucker rods and lowering the string back into the hole.

"Holy shit!" Vertis exclaimed at the sight of Curley Harris' pickup truck. Nathan considered getting Ernie out of the truck and on his feet, but it appeared too late. Curley parked, walked to the truck, and spit out his wad of chewing tobacco. He opened the door, grabbed Ernie's coat collar, and drug him out, throwing him on the frozen ground.

Ernie stumbled to his feet, pleading: "I am sick, Curley! Real bad sick!"

Not saying anything, Curley swung at Ernie, hitting him in the face and knocking him down again. He then started kicking and stomping Ernie with cruel expertise that scared Nathan and Vertis. Ernie curled up in a ball and pleaded with Curley.

"Please stop, Curley. I am an old man. I get sick in the cold."

"Where is it, you son-of-a-bitch?" Curley shouted and continued to kick Ernie on the ground.

"Where is it?"

Nathan dove between Curley and Ernie. He stood over Ernie. A pinched look formed on Curley's face, and he moved towards Nathan until their faces were only inches apart.

"Get your ass out of my way, Nathan. I am not putting up with this bullshit. Ernie knows he has an ass-kicking coming."

Nathan did not answer but continued to block Ernie from Curley. Curley's eyes went wild. He spun back and to the right and swung hard; the right uppercut connecting with Nathan's jaw. In Curley's lifetime that punch had knocked out a dozen other men, but Nathan stood there, seemingly unhurt, not hitting back, but not moving. Curley started to throw another punch but somehow marshaled his anger. The two men glared at each other for a long time, neither backing down. Finally, Curley spoke, slowly and carefully like he was instructing someone to disarm a bomb.

"Either get your fists up or get out of my way."

"I won't hit you, Curley, but I can't just stand by and watch. Vertis and I can finish this well without Ernie, no problem."

Curley's anger left, replaced by confusion. Ernie managed to stand and raise his hands.

"It's under the driver's seat, Curley. I'll get back to work."

Out of breath, Ernie bent over in pain. Curley gave Ernie a long-disgusted look, moved to the driver's side of the pulling unit, opened the door, and pulled out a half-empty bottle of Four Roses whiskey. He poured it on the snow.

"You old bastard! You're lucky to have a friend like Nathan. Now get your ass over there and finish this well." Curley walked back to his pickup, stopped, and yelled back. "I am warning you, Ernie, if you get one of these men hurt, I will kill you myself."

"OK, Curley," Ernie replied as he hurried over to the rod basket.

"Nathan, I want to talk to you when you get back to the shop. You let Ernie do thc cleanup."

⋘⋙

The shop building at Harris Well Service looked like a shack, but the coal stove kept the place warm. Three framed walls, one with a large window, separated Curley's desk from the rest of the building. Nathan knocked on the glass, and Curley motioned him in. Nathan hurried inside and sat in the dilapidated chair. Curley pulled out a stack of cash from the center drawer.

"Here's everything I owe you through today, plus one thousand dollars for your vacation time," Curley said nervously. When he spoke, he slipped his chewing tobacco against one cheek, and that side of his face bulged out.

"You have a right to fire me, but you don't owe me vacation time? I ain't taken it."

"Look, Nathan," Curley growled. "You take this for Emma Lee. I am trying to help you, God damn it. I saw the newspaper this afternoon."

"What newspaper?"

"The *Evansville Press!* The picture of you burning your draft card?"

"I didn't burn a draft card. Hell, Curley, there ain't no draft."

It took a moment for Curley to settle back in his chair, and start chewing again, thinking. "Well, I don't know what the hell you call it today, but your picture is on the front page at some peace rally in St. Louis. You are burning something."

Nathan nodded weakly.

"It won't take long for that red-neck Sheriff to come looking for you. That bastard would love to have any excuse to shoot a black man. Please, son…go home right now, keep your eye out for the Sheriff, and leave Caryville as soon as possible."

"Curley, I didn't expect this," Nathan said, speaking with difficulty.

"I sure didn't plan on leaving you shorthanded this winter."

"Listen, there are plenty of good hands looking for work. Now get moving."

☙❧

By the time he left Harris Well Service, the sun had set, the temperature had dropped, and the roads had iced over. Soon, it started snowing again. Nathan drove the moss green 1976 Dodge D100 very slowly. He did not want to go off in a ditch or get stuck in a snowbank on the way home. As he maneuvered in the snow, he thought about what he could tell his grandmother and began to regret his decision not to report for mobilization.

A half-mile out, Nathan decided he needed to avoid the steep front driveway leading to his grandmother's house. He turned into the south gate of their farm onto the old oilfield lease road. He concentrated on keeping the Dodge exactly centered in the road to avoid the grader ditches. The clouds blocked the moonlight, and the snowflakes swirled in front of his headlights and windshield. Nathan began to doubt whether he would make it to the house and struggled to find the cattle guard located at the fence line. Finally, he felt his tires rumble over the cattle guard, and soon he was at the house.

At one time there had been a sea of oil under the Jones' farm, but the Jones family never owned a drop. During the boom in the 1940s, the original owners severed the mineral rights from the surface rights, moved to Chicago, and lived off the royalties. Granddad Jones had the hassle of dealing with the oil company destroying his land but none of the benefits. It did not much matter anymore, because almost all the oil wells had played out.

After parking his pickup as close to the house as possible, Nathan opened the door to a flurry of snowflakes that pelted his face. He hurried to the back porch and pulled off his rubber boots, jumper, and overalls before stepping through the back door into the warmth of the kitchen. His Grandma, Emma Lee Jones, had supper on the table, fried deer steaks from a buck Nathan shot, mashed potatoes, gravy, and green beans canned from their garden. A thick, meaty aroma filled the house. Nathan sat in the chair closest to the door and slipped on the pair of cowboy boots he left there that morning. Emma Lee sat down, said grace, and they started the meal. When they had finished eating, Emma Lee stood to clear the table.

"Grandma, can you sit back down for a minute? I gotta say something."

Nathan's grandmother looked frightened, and Nathan tried to speak but couldn't for a long time.

"I failed to report to the Marine Corps for active duty. I have to leave. Jeremiah will take care of you."

Nathan then saw the look of confusion and the tears well up in his grandmother's eyes.

"Nathan, I've never understood why you, or your dad, wanted to join the Marines. But it's too late now. You should turn yourself in tomorrow. If you do that, Nathan, it can't be that bad. If you run away, they will kill you."

"As a Christian, I can't be a part of this war," Nathan said sadly.

"Of course, Nathan. But please don't do this. Stay here. We can pray together for peace. That's all a Christian can do."

"My unit shipped out of St. Louis last weekend. They are at Twentynine Palms, California, getting ready to go to Saudi Arabia. What if there's war? I would have to kill another person. I can't risk that."

Emma Lee's mouth dropped open, her shoulders slumped, and tears rolled down her cheeks. "Oh, Nathan, please don't leave. Stay here with me. God will take care of us."

"Maybe I can figure out a way to go back to the Marines. But I can't do that right now. I need to pray on it. I cannot say—just cannot explain it right now."

Emma Lee walked unsteadily to the kitchen sink, grabbed the edge with both hands, and stared out the window into the snow. Her head dropped forward, and a shudder went through her body. Nathan heard a helpless moan. Then she started to sob, deep sobs, that shook her shoulders. Nathan watched his grandma cry. He rushed over and held her close.

"I am sorry, Grandma. I never meant to hurt you. Please forgive me, but I have to leave. Curley says the Sheriff will come looking for me tomorrow."

Emma Lee continued to weep and started washing the dishes.

Chapter 3

Colonel Earl Cahill, U.S.M.C., stood and gracefully assumed the position of attention in the same manner he had practiced 26 years ago at Marine Corps Recruit Depot, San Diego, and watched the Deputy Secretary of the Navy, Williby Holt, take the seat at the head of the conference table. Col. Cahill had left his office over an hour before because Marine Corps Headquarters was not located in the Pentagon. The largest office building in the world had room for Air Force lieutenants, Navy chiefs, and Army sergeants, but most Marines, including Marine Corps colonels and generals, had to commute from the Navy Annex two miles down Lee Highway in Arlington, Virginia. This morning Col. Cahill arrived ten minutes early, while Williby Holt strolled in ten minutes late.

"Please have a seat, ladies and gentlemen," Holt mumbled while staring at a folder placed in front of him by his assistant. A dozen admirals resumed their seats at the conference table and waited to receive their copy of the folder.

At age 53, Colonel Cahill stood at six feet and weighed 186 pounds, with broad shoulders and a slim waist. He enjoyed sharp features and intelligent eyes and wore his brown hair in a moderate Marine Corps cut. He preferred a "high and tight," but short haircuts for senior officers were frowned upon in Washington. Today, he wore the Alpha Uniform: olive-drab wool blouse and trousers, long-sleeve khaki shirt and tie underneath the blouse, and ribbons and badges. His expert badges for rifle and pistol were pinned to his left pocket flap, and above the badges he wore ribbons from his many years of service.

An infantry officer who had spent his career in the field, Cahill did not enjoy attending these meetings in the Pentagon. Like many grunts, he remained skeptical of any officer that never served in combat and loathed Marines that spent their entire careers at Headquarters. Cahill realized that his promotion to colonel had been offered only as a reward for his service in Vietnam and the Medal of Honor awarded him for action at Hue City. He guessed the members of his promotion board expected him to do the honorable thing, serve a couple of tours as a colonel and retire promptly on being passed over for brigadier general. But instead, after being passed over, he accepted this tour at Headquarters, Washington, D.C.

Not surprisingly, Cahill received an utterly meaningless assignment, Deputy Assistant to the Commandant on Executive Affairs, and spent his time attending meetings of various committees, arguing with the members and getting out-voted. His boss, the Deputy Assistant Commandant, Lieutenant General John Reynolds, and the rest of the Marine Corps, ignored his lengthy memoranda on the actions taken at the meetings and seemed to prefer that he do nothing. Today, Cahill promised himself he would do the smart thing—keep his mouth shut, vote with the majority, and send Reynolds a half-page memorandum summarizing the action of the committee.

"Ladies and Gentlemen, the first item on our agenda this morning is the replacement of the Colt 45 ACP M1911A1 pistol with the Beretta 9mm M9 pistol. The issue has been thoroughly briefed, and you all have had an opportunity to submit written comments. We have discussed the issue at previous meetings, and I believe it is time for a formal vote. However, I will allow further discussion."

The Deputy Secretary paused and glanced around the conference room. Col. Cahill mentally debated with himself. *The decision won't be changed. Why say anything? Don't embarrass yourself and piss everyone off. Just keep quiet.*

"All right; the committee agrees. Let's move to the next item on today's agenda …" Williby Holt returned his attention to the folder.

"Mr. Deputy Secretary, I believe the suggested course of action is a mistake for several reasons." Col. Cahill heard the words spout from his mouth, but his mind questioned whether he had spoken them. His eyes saw the scornful stares of the rest of the military officers in the room, resentful of Cahill's frequent objections.

"You were a little slow today, Colonel Cahill." Many of the officers chuckled. The Deputy Secretary smiled and continued.

"Frankly, I know this decision does not sit well with you. Go ahead and make your points. Just keep it short, please."

"Thank you, Mr. Deputy Secretary." Cahill looked around the room before continuing.

"Ladies and Gentlemen, I understand the advantages of standardization with the Army, Air Force, and NATO on offensive weapon systems. But pistols are not used in general warfighting and are rarely used to inflict enemy casualties. The choice between the Colt and Beretta will not impact any unit's firepower. Instead, we are talking about a strictly defensive weapon carried by Marine officers and senior NCOs. Standardization regarding personal sidearms is pointless.

"The Colt has won its place in the Marine Corps as a legendary, reliable, and trusted sidearm. It has seen service in World War I, World War II, Korea, Vietnam, and every other conflict since its adoption in 1911. I can tell you unequivocally that Marine Officers love and treasure their Colts and will hate adopting an Italian pistol over an American pistol designed by John M. Browning.

You say that technology moves forward, that the Beretta is a modern pistol, and that the Colt is outdated. But the Colt is a better pistol than the Beretta. The Colt shoots a powerful cartridge, the .45 caliber ACP with a 230-grain bullet, while the puny 9mm Beretta fires a 124-grain bullet. For this reason, the fact that the Colt's magazine holds only eight rounds versus Berretta's fifteen-round capacity is not important. Marines rely upon their marksmanship, not popping off a dozen rounds toward the enemy.

"In conclusion, if it ain't broke, don't fix it! The Marine Corps has issued over 150,000 serviceable Colts, and when the Marine's inventory wears out the Army will have over 600,000 available to the Marines. We are already trained to shoot the Colt, with some Marines having fired thousands of practice rounds. Why spend the money on purchasing Berettas and re-training our officers and NCOs?

"As the only infantry Marine on this committee, and only officer with combat experience, I respectfully object to your decision to replace the Colt with the Beretta."

Earl Cahill looked at the Deputy Secretary.

"Thank you, Colonel Cahill. Is anyone else opposed to the replacement of the Colt with the Berretta? Very well, I will report to the Secretary of the Navy that the Committee recommends adopting the Beretta. The next item on the agenda is very important." The Deputy Secretary announced with an unusual degree of enthusiasm.

"We will start with a short brief from Lieutenant Watson…Lieutenant." A woman sailor stood at the end of the table, checked to make certain the door to the conference room remained secured and faced a PowerPoint screen at the other end. She looked 30 or so, with short brown hair, attractive, and no-nonsense eyes.

"Ladies and gentlemen, this brief and all sources of information are classified as top secret. The subject is desertion. As you know, desertion is a military offense under Article eighty-five of the Uniform Code of Military Justice. Any member of the armed forces who without authority remains absent from his unit with intent to remain away permanently or quits his unit with intent to avoid hazardous duty, is guilty of desertion.

"Recent historical analysis confirms that desertion is a critical element, maybe the most important factor, in securing victory over defeat.

"The Revolutionary War was nearly lost as a result of high desertion rates. The Civil War was won because of the mass desertion of 300,000 Confederate troops in the spring of 1865. In World War II the European campaign was crippled by, and almost lost, because of the desertion of 50,000 U. S. servicemen. There were 13,790 desertions during the Korean War. In the view of many, the U. S. military lost the Vietnam War because of its failure to adequately address draft evasion and desertion. During the war, the rate of desertion doubled. A total of 40,227 service men and women deserted in 1967, 53,667 in 1968, 89,088 in 1969, and 98,324 in 1970. In the end, a total of 423,422 men and women were classified as deserters. Another 102,000 avoided the draft by various means, mostly by fleeing to Canada. Of the 423,422 deserting after enlistment, over 390,865 were apprehended, administratively discharged, or court-martialed. At the time President Carter granted unconditional amnesty in 1977 it is estimated that over 32,000 deserters remained at large.

"The Defense Department recently completed a survey of 800 Vietnam War deserters. At the time of desertion, ten percent faced court-martial for criminal offenses. Another forty percent offered a reason to have left some pressing family crisis. The remaining fifty percent claimed that they left because they were opposed to the war on moral and political grounds. Significantly, forty-three and a half percent of the deserters admitted to actively opposing the war after leaving the military by participating in protests, marches, strikes, and base blockades. Thus, Vietnam deserters not only degraded the fighting ability of the military through the reduction of needed manpower but also strengthened the anti-war movement.

"This weekend the largest anti-war rally to date expressing opposition against United States' participation in the Gulf Conflict took place in downtown St. Louis, Missouri. The number of participants is estimated to be between 150,000 and 200,000 people. The event was unprecedented not only in terms of the size of the demonstration but also in terms of the close coordination of dozens of anti-war coalition groups across the country. The size of the crowd forced most businesses to close on Friday.

"Most organized events took place on Saturday when the crowds were urged on by international peace activists, religious leaders, actors, and musicians. The rally ended with a march through the streets of St. Louis. Some marchers wore costumes and masks bearing President Bush's image, and most carried signs with slogans such as 'No Blood for Oil,' 'Act Now—Stop the War,' 'What would Jesus do?' and 'No to U.S. War in Iraq.'

"The crowd's excitement peaked when a Marine Corps Reservist, four Naval Reservists, and six Army Reservists appeared on stage and symbolically burned their mobilization orders—reminiscent of the draft card burnings during the Vietnam War.

"Unfortunately, several news organizations covered the rally, and it is believed that many photographs were produced. However, as sometimes happens, all newspapers choose the same lead photograph—the one of the Marine, Sailors, and Soldiers burning their orders. Versions of this photograph have appeared in at least twenty-five major newspapers and magazines.

"Ladies and gentlemen, that concludes this brief."

Lieutenant Watson turned, sat down, and the Deputy Secretary looked around the room before speaking.

"I met with the President and the Secretary of the Navy on this issue. The last thing we want is for the public to think this will be another Vietnam. Obviously, something must be done about these reservists who are refusing to report for active duty."

Holt paused to allow everyone to review the summary.

"The war has not started, and we already have a bunch of our reservists refusing to serve. Ladies and gentlemen this must be stopped!"

The conference room remained silent, and Cahill focused on the summary sheet until Holt continued.

"We are going to make an example of the people in that photograph." The Deputy Secretary proclaimed in his most forceful voice.

"We are starting with the senior ranking member. His name is Sergeant Nathan Jones. Even though a sergeant with six years of service, he now claims he is a conscientious objector." The Deputy Secretary went silent and looked at Colonel Cahill, the only Marine on the Committee. "Colonel Cahill, what have you got to say on this issue?"

"Mr. Deputy Secretary, in every war there are a few cowards. Shirking a dangerous assignment is an infection that spreads more quickly than the plague. The thought of a Sergeant of Marines abandoning his unit to participate in a peace rally is disgusting. We should not allow a photograph of a Marine Non-Commissioned Officer appearing at a peace rally to be published all over the United States without also publishing the fact that he will face severe punishment. Whatever it takes, Sergeant Jones needs to be arrested, prosecuted, and severely punished," Col. Cahill answered in a voice full of pronouncement.

"Good analysis, Colonel Cahill. For once we agree on something. The Navy Criminal Investigative Service will do whatever it takes to immediately apprehend Sergeant Jones. He will be prosecuted to the full extent of the law. Now, we will move on to the next agenda item."

Chapter 4

In a small office in the Kenneth Gray Federal Building, Benton, Illinois, Marshal Shelia Collins slid the rubber band off the end of the St. Louis *Post-Dispatch* and leaned back in her chair. The time was 4:00 p.m. and at this point in her career, Shelia Collins felt at ease quitting work early. For 26 years she worked at a feverish pace, ten or twelve hours a day. She earned the reputation of an intelligent, methodical policewoman, who went into every situation with a plan. Now, she could spend an hour or so each day just drinking coffee and reading newspapers.

The front page of the St. Louis *Post-Dispatch* read "PEACE MARCH SHUTS DOWN CITY," with a photograph underneath of a group of servicemen burning their mobilization orders. The article stated that one of the servicemen resided in Caryville, a small town about 25 miles from Benton. Marshal Collins headed upstairs to find the bailiff and found him flirting with the young courtroom clerk.

"Orville, have you seen the Post's front page?"

"See it every day."

Shelia Collins ignored the smart remark. "Did you know that there are anti-war protestors around here?"

"Just because we drive pickups, drink beer, and fry everything, doesn't mean we're warmongers. The unions' trouble with the coal mines taught us about big government and big corporations shitting on little people. When they temporarily shut down Southern Illinois University in 1969, believe me, not all those demonstrators were students. A lot of the people marching against the Vietnam War were from around here."

"Did you recognize anyone in the newspaper photograph?"

"Nope."

When Marshal Collins returned to her office, she could hear the telephone ringing inside. She hurried to open the door and grabbed the phone.

"Shelia, did I catch you at a bad time?" Collins recognized the voice of the Chief Marshal for the District of Illinois in Chicago, Mac Brenner.

"No boss, just upstairs in court. What can I do for you?" The telephone went silent, then a slightly plaintive voice.

"Just calling to give you a heads up. I got a call from Washington. There is a Marine Corps Reservist from your neck of the woods, Sergeant Nathan Jones, who did not obey his orders to report for active duty and later participated in the peace rally in St. Louis. Apparently, it's a big deal for a sergeant to go UA and the Naval Criminal Investigative Service is flying in an agent as soon as possible. But time is of the essence, and they have asked for our help. As soon as possible, I want you to drive up to Caryville and attempt to apprehend Jones. We will fax down the details."

"Mac, I have to tell you, I've never had a desertion case."

"Well, that's not surprising. When servicemen fail to report for duty, the military sends out a message that they are in an unauthorized leave status and are to be delivered to military authorities. The U.S. Marshal doesn't go looking for them. If we discover a UA serviceman, or arrest them for something else, we transport them to the nearest military installation and turn them over to military authorities."

"It's snowing here, and all the roads are Level 3—closed to all traffic. There is no way I can make it to Caryville tonight."

"Well, I guess if you can't move, Jones can't either, so just get up to Caryville as soon as you can."

"Sorry, but I still don't understand. What am I doing with this case?

"This guy is part of a group that stirred up some trouble in St. Louis yesterday, and someone requested that the United States Marshal in Washington assist in his apprehension. Obviously, Washington is confused because that should be a job for the FBI, but we can do what we can until they figure it out…As I said, an NCIS agent should be there late tomorrow or the next day."

"Judge Brady has a full calendar this week. He depends on me, and he won't be able to conduct hearings. Why don't you send Marshal Keys from Bellville?"

"It's a hundred and twenty miles from Caryville to Bellville. You are a lot closer."

"Call Washington and tell them to send it to the FBI."

"Look, Marshal Collins, this conversation is finished. I'll ask for an opinion from legal, but right now, I want you to go to Caryville and apprehend Nathan Jones. You got it?'

"I got it, but Judge Brady is not going to be happy."

⋘⋙

What a bunch of crap! Marshal Collins kept telling herself. *But I shouldn't have spoken that way to Mac Brenner.* Her guilt made her give up trying to sleep. At 3:30 a.m., she eased out of bed so as not to wake her partner and quietly dressed.

Last night, she reviewed the military records on Sgt. Nathan Jones and planned to apprehend him at the address listed as his home of record. With all the snow, she was not sure she could make it to Caryville but figured she had to try to satisfy Mac Brenner.

At 4:30 a.m., Emma Lee Jones knocked on her grandson's bedroom door. She did this every weekday at 5:30 a.m. so that Nathan could make it to work by 6:30. Today, Nathan wanted to leave before daylight.

Emma Lee returned to the kitchen and finished fixing Nathan's breakfast. Nathan hurriedly put on his clothes, stopped at the bathroom to wash his hands, and sat down at the kitchen table. At a quarter to six, he started loading his pickup. At the same time, Marshal Collins was entering the big curve outside Caryville. Tired from fighting the snow, she slowed for the four-way stop, then pulled into the Shell station and parked on the side.

The snow forced Collins to maneuver through the gas pumps to find a clear path to the station door. She pushed the old door open and heard a loud clanking sound from the bell attached to the inside. A big, broad-shouldered man, dressed in greasy overalls, gazed at her from behind the glass case next to the cash register. The two examined each other closely.

"Good morning. Can you tell me how to get to the Emma Lee Jones' house?"

The attendant continued to stare at Collins, grunted, and finally answered. "Nope."

Marshal Collins placed her badge on the rickety old countertop.

"Do you know Nathan Jones?"

"I used to know Nathan. We went to school together."

"Where does he live?"

The gas station attendant smiled a crooked smile and answered, "I don't know where he lives now."

"Where does his mother live?"

"Out in the country somewhere, I guess. She used to live up past Evert's Garage. I don't know."

"Which direction is Evert's Garage?"

The attendant's face contorted in defiance. He pointed out the window towards the four-way stop. "Down the road. But you'll get yourself stuck in this snow. Better wait awhile"

Collins turned to walk out, and the attendant spoke up.

"Better take one of those cards so you can call me for help when you get stuck."

Collins headed west. She kept the Suburban in four-wheel drive and drove at ten miles an hour. After five miles, she pulled over to check her map at the intersection of the first road.

Meanwhile, Nathan finished loading his pickup. It remained dark but the sun had started to light up the eastern horizon. He rushed inside to say goodbye to his grandma.

"Goodbye, Grandma. You know I love you."

Emma Lee did not answer. She just looked sad. With tears in her eyes, she followed Nathan outside wearing a winter jacket over her housecoat. Nathan spoke loudly as he hustled back to the pickup.

"Don't worry, Grandma. Cannot tell you where I am headed, but I will be all right. I will call when I get a chance."

"Nathan, please! The snow is too deep. Stay here, and we can figure this out. Don't leave me. Please."

"Sorry, Grandma. I need to get going before the Sheriff shows up."

ಀ

Marshal Collins turned left at the four-way stop at Evert's Garage, then took a right at the first road west, drove north, and struggled to read the name on every mailbox she passed. After two miles she found one with the name "Emma Lee Jones." She turned into the steep driveway. The Suburban's tires spun, and the vehicle violently fishtailed from side to side. Collins slammed down the accelerator and fought to keep it out of the ditch.

When Nathan closed the door on his pickup, he looked in the rearview mirror to turn around. He vaguely saw headlights coming up the driveway. He stopped backing up, threw the transmission in first, and floored the old pickup. He gripped the steering wheel, white-knuckled, and raced down the oilfield lease road, heading back to the south gate of the farm. This morning, covered with the deep snow, the lease road could not be seen at all, and Nathan sped along just guessing at its location.

When Collins topped the ridge, she saw Nathan's taillights, turned on her flashing lights, and gave chase. The Government Suburban accelerated quickly. The vehicles raced down the lane, Collins bouncing in and out of the bar ditches on each side. When Collins closed within 50 feet, she decided to wreck Nathan's pickup by ramming its rear end. She floored the Suburban.

Of course, Collins did not know that the oil company had installed a cattle guard at the fence line. The oil company used two-inch steel pipes, spaced about three inches apart, and placed perpendicular to the road. If a cow tried to cross, its hooves would slide through the tubing into the pit underneath. After 20 years, the steel pipe rusted away at each end, leaving the cattle guard about three feet narrower than the road.

This morning the cattle guard lay underneath the snow, but Nathan guessed exactly where the ends were, and when he crossed the cattle guard, he hugged the left side. Marshal Collins had no clue. She drove over the cattle guard on the right side where the end had rusted away. The front of the Suburban dropped into the cattle guard pit and slammed to a stop.

The airbags exploded, and a piece of the steel tubing broke through the vehicle floor and narrowly missed Collin's foot. After a moment, Marshal Collins slowly pushed the door open, unbuckled her seat belt, got out, and watched Nathan's pickup disappear over a hill. The Suburban sat in the middle of the cattle guard.

Collins tried to telephone for help but had no reception on her cell phone. She painfully and slowly followed Nathan's tire tracks in the snow, headed southeast, back towards Caryville.

After walking an hour, Collins' cell reception returned at the top of a hill. She called Marshal Mac Brenner in Chicago and reported that Nathan had left Caryville. Out of embarrassment, she did not disclose to Marshal Brenner anything about her attempt to stop Nathan's pickup. She could not provide Nathan's plate number or a description of his pickup. She just reported that she slid off a road and crashed into a cattle guard. Marshal Collins then used the business card from Caryville gas station to call the attendant she spoke with earlier that morning.

"This is Marshal Shelia Collins. I met you early this morning."

The attendant broke into a half-suppressed horse laugh.

"Are you stuck, Marshal?"

"Unfortunately. Yes."

"Where you at?"

"About a mile southeast of Nathan Jones's house. My Suburban is stuck on a farm road. I can give you the directions."

"Don't need directions. Know where you are at. I'll be there in an hour."

With his stomach in knots and riddled with guilt, Nathan kept driving the Dodge pickup south towards the old New Harmony Bridge. He felt positive that he had made a lot of mistakes. He should have reported for duty. He should not have attended the peace rally. *I should just turn around, go back, and surrender myself.*

Chapter 5

Lieutenant General John Reynolds sat at his desk reading Colonel Earl Cahill's 20-page Objection to the Special Committee's Decision to Adopt the Berretta pistol. After reading the Objection, Reynolds wadded up the memoranda and tossed it in his trash can. He thought, *What a dinosaur. The Colt should have been replaced years ago. I will have his ass for this shit.*

When Col. Earl Cahill entered the Headquarters Building, he noticed the hollow feeling in his stomach. Widely known for his nerves of steel, many Marines believed that nothing could shake Cahill's iron composure. But this morning, he felt apprehensive about this meeting with Reynolds. Cahill expected that Gen. Reynolds wanted to discuss Cahill's dissenting memorandum on the adoption of the Berretta pistol, but he hoped they could also discuss Cahill's request to command an infantry unit in Saudi Arabia.

Before entering Gen. Reynold's office, Col. Cahill stepped inside the men's room. He carefully dampened a paper towel and wiped the dust off his dress shoes. Next, he unbuttoned the coat on his dress Alpha uniform. He pulled his trousers down and went through a practiced maneuver of "re-blousing" his shirt so that it fit perfectly tucked into his pants. He inspected himself in the mirror to make certain that his belt, zipper flap, and button lines remained perfectly aligned. He checked the six rows of ribbons to make certain they were all properly aligned. Satisfied with his appearance, he proceeded to the office of General Reynolds.

After cooling his heels for an hour sitting in Reynold's secretary's office, Col. Cahill marched into the office of Gen. Reynolds and stopped exactly three feet in front of Reynolds' desk. He snapped to attention and waited for Gen. Reynolds to offer him a seat. Instead of looking up, Reynolds studied documents on his desk, as though some emergency required his immediate attention. He did not extend any courtesy to Cahill that might indicate respect. *Now things are going to get nasty; he is going to start treating me like a second lieutenant.*

General Reynolds looked to be about the same age as Cahill, but was more than a few pounds overweight, with a tough face and gray hair that appeared too long for a Marine. He let Col. Cahill stand at attention a full minute before he even looked up. When he finally glanced at him, he only grunted, and continued to ignore Cahill.

"Have a seat, Colonel," Reynolds said sternly.

Colonel Cahill seated himself in one of the chairs, still appearing to be at a position of attention.

"I've read your dissenting memorandum on replacing the Colt with the Beretta and your request for transfer," Gen. Reynolds barked.

"You consider yourself some kind of special field Marine. Is that right Cahill?"

"I consider all Marines to be field Marines," Cahill answered, the pride in his voice completely open. He knew that his answer would piss off Reynolds.

"You are too good to be with us Pentagon pogues?" Gen. Reynolds continued, ignoring Cahill's answer. "I've served three tours at Headquarters, and I have never seen a field-grade officer make as big an ass of himself as you have done, Cahill. From what I have seen you are a hopeless alcoholic, an inept administrator, stubborn as hell, and a hot head," Reynolds continued.

Cahill stared straight ahead and did not speak.

"The Navy and Marine Corps have already entered contracts for the purchase of the 9-millimeter Beretta Pistol. Also, my endorsement of your request for transfer to command an infantry unit recommends denial. I am not sending a Tyrannosaurus Rex into combat. You are too old and incompetent.

"We will defeat Iraq with superior technology, like the Berretta pistol, that you cannot understand. Our precision-guided weapons, computer-driven logistics, satellite communications, and modern armor will win without casualties.

"The Marines in Saudi Arabia need educated and intelligent commanders that know our new weapon systems, and our new technology, and leaders capable of cooperating with the Army, Air Force, and allies. They do not need you, Cahill. Your old blood and guts approach to warfare is ancient history.

"It's sad that I am the only Marine at Headquarters willing to take on a Medal of Honor winner like you, but I will do it. I am not going to let you get Marines killed. Do you know what you are, Cahill? You are a constant source of embarrassment for the Commandant," Reynolds yelled angrily.

"If I had my way, the Commandant would convene a board of inquiry and have you retired." Reynold's anger grew with each word.

"That is what I recommended to the Commandant. Well, luckily for you, the Commandant has a different solution, Cahill. He is offering you a reassignment as the Commanding Officer of the rear element of the Fourth Marine Division."

Cahill took the news with notable silence, processing the sad reality with a military instinct. "Did you say 'Rear?'" Cahill heard himself mumble.

"Of course, I said *Rear!*" Reynolds bellowed.

"I just fucking explained!" Reynolds yelled, completely losing his temper. "You should be damn grateful the Commandant is giving you this. I am not the only officer that recommended a board of inquiry into your DUI. I guess he thinks we are all too busy to deal with your bullshit, and he does not want to answer to some misguided Congressman for fucking with a Medal of Honor winner." Reynolds studied Cahill contemptuously.

"I don't have all day. What is it going to be, Cahill—Fourth Division (Rear) or a board of inquiry?"

For the first time in his life, Earl Cahill felt the pain of failure. He sat stunned. Unable to think clearly. "What exactly does the Commanding Officer, Rear, do?"

"Well, you see, that is the beauty of the Commandant's plan. You won't be doing a fucking thing of any importance—you have fucked up everything here at Headquarters, but even you cannot fuck this up. The Commanding General Forward, Major General Lenard, may ask you to do a few simple things, but pretty much there is nothing to do. Just stay off the skyline, do not be seen drunk in public, and wait for your retirement orders."

Reynolds's eyes looked at the papers on his desk and then settled on those of Cahill. They stared at each other for a long time, neither blinking. Cahill tried to remember the location of the 4th Division concluding that it might be in New Orleans.

"I asked you a question, Colonel. Answer me." Reynolds prodded.

"General Reynolds, will I be transferred to New Orleans?"

"No, we are not sending an alcoholic to New Orleans. The flag for Fourth Division (Rear) will be at Marine Corps Air Station, Yuma Arizona. The Commandant wants you, and the Fourth Division (Rear), as far away from Washington D.C. as possible. Yuma is as far as you can go. So, I am going to ask you one more time—board of inquiry or Yuma? Which is it, Colonel?"

Colonel Cahill sat silently staring at his shoes. Finally, he looked up at General Reynolds, "The answer is Fourth Division (Rear). Will that be all?"

"No! That is not all. I don't want a single phone call about you, or from you, at Fourth Division. I am specifically ordering you not to communicate directly with the Commandant, and he has approved this order. No more of your fucking memoranda to the Commandant. We do not want to hear from you about any fucking problems. This time you better follow my orders. Don't try and change a damn thing. Just disappear. You got that Colonel."

"Aye-Aye. The Colonel understands." Cahill answered mimicking a boot camp voice. "Is that all, General Reynolds?"

Reynolds looked Colonel Cahill directly in the eyes.

"That is all. Get the fuck out of my office."

Chapter 6

Twenty miles southwest of Karber's Ridge, Illinois, Jeremiah Jones reached the end of the logger's road and parked his worn-out 1972 Chevrolet Pickup. He got started late, and the trip from Caryville had taken over two hours, much longer than he planned.

After Nathan left home, Emma Lee Jones called her oldest son, Jeremiah, and begged him to go find Nathan and bring him back. She felt certain that Nathan would be killed by the police. The Methodist Church preacher, and most of the church members, spent the day at her house praying for Nathan.

Everyone said Nathan Jones had gone to Mexico, but Emma Lee and Jeremiah were not sure. They knew that even after joining the church in Mt. Carmel, Nathan continued to love the Marine Corps, and they believed that sooner or later Nathan would voluntarily return to the Marines.

By the time Jeremiah stepped out of his pickup it had gotten very late, and Jeremiah worried that it would be dark in less than two hours. Dressed in faded blue jeans, a khaki shirt, and work boots, he retrieved the gunny sack from the rear seat, then instinctively analyzed the fresh deer tracks crossing the road. Jeremiah concluded the tracks were made by six does and a very large buck. He hurried west on the ancient Indian trail, now used mainly by horse riders from the camps surrounding High Knob Ranch.

At age 40, Jeremiah Jones had a bad limp from a work accident, carried an extra 40 pounds on his six-foot frame, and had not exercised in 20 years. None of that slowed him down in the woods. He moved swiftly and silently down the trail. After 200 yards he stopped, ran back to the Blazer, and retrieved a can of sardines from the glovebox. Nathan and Jeremiah believed that packing a can of sardines brought good luck, and Jeremiah carried this can on numerous successful hunting trips. He crammed the sardines in his pocket and returned to the trail.

After an hour Jeremiah turned south on the abandoned—and barely perceptible—One-Horse Gap trail. The ascension of the sun lengthened the shadows of the tall hickory trees, and he felt the air growing cooler; still, he enjoyed the slight breeze filled with the clean smells of the forest. Jeremiah's brain seemed to glow in the wilderness, and he saw, smelled, and heard everything in the woods. He navigated the abandoned trail like a trucker following an interstate highway. Soon he spotted One-Horse Gap, a narrow crevice cut into a limestone ridge that ran between the Ohio and Mississippi Rivers, and the only way over the ridge for 20 miles in each direction.

Through the years, the rocks near the gap had shifted and thick trees grew in the narrow opening so that today no horse could make it through the gap. Indeed, it appeared nearly impossible for a man to make it through, so Jeremiah paused to rest at the base and to make certain he had not been followed. Then he carefully headed up the side of the ridge, moving over the boulders. Several times he lost his footing but always kept one hand free to grab a rock or tree, and by this method, avoided injury from falls. After another half-hour, he reached the top of the ridge. He left the old trail and changed to a westerly course following the southern crest of the mountains. He gaged the sun, calculating a half-hour before total darkness, and raced through the woods with a new sense of urgency. He hoped to find the cutoff point before dark.

Soon, the descending sun levered the light rays over the hills so that the tops of the western slopes remained bright while the eastern slopes slipped into darkness. Jeremiah slowed his pace and stopped frequently to examine the contours and test his memory, or to watch whitetail deer sneaking through the timber. Finally, he recognized the rounded rock cliff that marked the drop-off for the boxed canyon. He used a wild grapevine to repel down the side into the black depression. It was now completely dark, and Jeremiah had to stumble down the slope until he sensed he stood in the rock-strewn creek. He continued to follow the creek down into the expanding gulch, inching his way along in complete silence, watching for the light of a fire. He stopped frequently to listen for any sound.

Then he smelled the smoke, just the faintest, most intangible of odors, and he paused in midstride, moved under the trees, and waited, scenting the wind. In a moment he caught it again, and then he moved towards it, very slowly. Ghostlike, he moved among the trees, stepping over dead falls, avoiding the path. From time to time, he hesitated, waiting for his senses to pick up some scent, some sound. He heard nothing.

"Are you lost, old man?" A voice, only a few feet away, whispered out of the darkness.

"How could I be lost? I smelled your camp an hour ago." Jeremiah answered sarcastically.

"Well, see if you can keep up."

The figure raced up the side of the draw to a group of boulders and seemed to disappear into the rocks. Jeremiah extended his arms, prodding and probing like a blind man. Eventually, he felt the tiny crack in the rocks, attempted to squeeze inside, and sucked in his big belly. After pushing himself through the opening, Jeremiah heard the crackle of logs burning and saw a fire in the center of the cave. The faint light gave the cave an eerie, shadowy feel, and it felt stuffy with the odor of smoke.

"Maybe I should name this place *Fat-Man's Squeeze*." Nathan laughed.

"Yeah, and maybe I should kick your ass," Jeremiah replied.

"I brought you some supplies."

"Any whiskey?" Nathan asked.

Jeremiah opened the sack and reverently removed a fifth of Old Grandad bourbon whiskey. He pretended to hand it over, then abruptly pulled it back, slowly opened it, and took a large swallow before passing the bottle to Nathan.

"Don't tell Grandma I brought you whiskey. She's pissed enough." Jeremiah spoke jokingly.

"Well, I never told her about the beer you used to buy me, so I don't think I will mention the whiskey either."

Nathan felt for a cup inside his pack, poured two fingers, and returned the bottle to Jeremiah. The men sipped their whiskey and let a moment pass.

"It is good to see you, Jeremiah. Thanks for the supplies. How's Grandma?"

"It's good to see you, Nathan." Jeremiah said, pausing to find a better place to sit inside the cave, and then continuing. "What do you expect? Grandma is a mess. She asked me to find you and bring your sorry ass home." Jeremiah's voice turned serious, and the conversation died as both men sought to avoid the painful discussion, they each knew was coming.

"Hey, this place is loaded with deer! I saw a buck and four does coming in," Jeremiah exclaimed.

"Yeah, I haven't seen a thing for weeks, but it seems they moved into this area yesterday. I've seen a lot of tracks and counted three does in the canyon yesterday." Nathan agreed.

"A nice buck is hanging around…be a good place for you to hunt when the season opens." Nathan continued.

Try as they might, they could not stay off the obvious subject. After a long pull on the Old Grandad, Jeremiah spoke in a solemn tone.

"Grandma, the preacher, and the entire congregation have been praying for you since you left. Grandma keeps saying that you are going to be killed."

Both men sipped their whiskey, and Nathan did not reply. Finally, Jeremiah looked up from gazing at the small fire. "She asked me to find you and tell you to come on home. She says the Marines will go easy on you if you turn yourself in."

Nathan continued his silence, a wave of emotion rose in his chest, the weight of the world on his shoulders. The fire crackled, and the log fell, sending up a shower of sparks.

"Well, tell Grandma that you found me, but do not tell her where I am. I am fine, but I can't come home yet. Tell her not to worry, and that I know what I am doing."

"Nathan, do you really know what you are doing? I never got why you joined the God-damn Marines in the first place. What, just because our dad did? And this shit is fucking crazy, Brother." There was bitterness in Jeremiah's voice.

"Just trying to do what Jesus taught, not kill another man. It is my peaceful protest of an immoral war. Black men shouldn't spill their blood for oil."

"Damn it, Nathan. You always must take things to the extreme! You keep getting your 'itis's,' don't you?

"When you were in high school you wouldn't do a lick of work. You had Basketball. Your whole world was basketball, basketball, basketball. All you wanted to do was shoot hoops and practice, twenty-four hours a day.

"Then, your gung-ho Marine Corps shit. Boot camp. Active duty. Then the reserves—always volunteering for extra duty. Spending all your money on new uniforms.

"Next, taverns. When we were hitting the bars together, you were the hardest drinking, craziest, meanest son-of-a-bitch I ever saw. Drinking, fucking, and fighting, that's all you wanted to do. Don't forget, I know you. I have seen you beat the shit out of men just for the fun of it.

"Now, this extreme religious shit. I cannot imagine an asshole like you running an orphanage in Mexico. It's just fucking nuts! You will be fucking and fighting again within a year. It is time to grow up!"

Nathan just shrugged as if his current situation was fine with him.

"One day you will understand. I am not dying to protect oil reserves and the profits of American corporations that have ties to Dick Cheney and George Bush," Nathan replied but unenthusiastically this time.

"Was it that good-looking professor in Mount Carmel that messed up your mind this time? She looks like a great fuck, but she will get your ass killed for sure." Jeremiah's voice had become loud and disapproving. "You are going back home with me. And right now."

"No, I am not."

Both men gazed at the fire for a long time.

"OK, Brother. I fucking tried my best and I ain't going to fight you. If you want to die, and do not care about your grandma, I will leave you here."

Jeremiah reached over and emptied the contents of the gunny sack on the floor of the cave, then removed the sardines from his side pocket.

"Here, these sardines are lucky. Don't eat 'em, just hang on to them."

The two men sat in silence again.

"Soon, they'll find you, and if they don't kill you during your arrest, they'll lock you up for years." Jeremiah pleaded one last time.

"Stop worrying, Jeremiah. You always worry too much. There ain't no one can catch me in these woods."

"No one catch you! The FBI can catch anyone. And do not forget that this part of Illinois had slaves. Come deer season there'll be hundreds of hunters walking around. Some of these old crackers know every cave, and they would love to shoot your black ass and haul you in like a trophy deer. They will be heroes. I can hear them laughing now—'I got my buck. He just does not have any horns.' Don't you know that it's still dangerous for a black man around here!"

Once again, the conversation died, and the men sat transfixed on the fire. After ten minutes of silence, Jeremiah stood.

"I guess I'll be going now, Nathan. You know you can always come home. You got family—and don't forget that."

"I am sorry Jeremiah," Nathan said, tears in his eyes. "Please tell Grandma that I will be all right. Let me think some more, and maybe I will turn myself in." Nathan's voice sounded sad.

Chapter 7

NCIS Agent Norval Palmer seemed always in a foul mood, and his perpetual scowl, broad shoulders, and thick arms did not invite friendly conversation. He had sad brown eyes and a growl of a voice that made his comments sound like afterthoughts. At this point, Palmer hated his job, he hated Marine Corps Air Station, Yuma, Arizona, and most of all he hated what had happened to his beloved Marine Corps.

Even before Norval Palmer retired as a first sergeant and accepted a position with the Naval Criminal Investigative Service, fellow Marines started calling him "Brown Shoes" or "Old Corps." He made no objection to this because he loved the old days for the "spit and polish," the endless parades, the ceremonies and balls, the sea duty aboard cruisers and battleships, and the embassy duty in foreign countries. In those days, "Semper Fidelis" was not a recruiting slogan, it symbolized a way of life. Marines were the best of men—honest, hardworking, and law-abiding. Although no one thought of Norval Palmer as fatherly, in those days he maintained a certain compassion for the young Marines, and he seemed to see something good in every one of them, even the ones he arrested.

"You know, they could have joined the Navy," he often repeated. "But they chose the Marines, so right there, there has to be some good in them."

What depressed Agent Palmer today was that as far as he could see, many of the good things about the Marine Corps were gone. The Vietnam War forced the Marine Corps to increase its numbers threefold and that meant lowering standards. Recruiters camped out at court houses, and young felons were given the choice of "volunteering" for the Marines or going to prison. The drill instructors did what they could to weed out the hard-core criminals, but during Vietnam it became hopeless. The hookers, drugs, and violence of Vietnam made the new recruits worse.

Agent Palmer guessed that 99 percent of the enlisted Marines returning to Marine Corps Air Station, Yuma, Arizona from Vietnam were alcoholics, 80 percent used marijuana, half had already committed a crime (assault, theft, drunk on duty, insubordination, disrespect, or unauthorized absence), and ten percent were dealing drugs.

Still, in Palmer's view, a Marine controlled his life, and he had to make the right choices. He decided whether to abuse alcohol or drugs. He chose his off-duty lifestyle. He obeyed the laws or broke them. A Marine took his stand one way or the other.

"Ladies and Gentlemen, now would be a good time to start powering down your electronic devices. We will be landing in St. Louis shortly."

Agent Palmer returned the file on Sgt. Nathan Jones to his briefcase and removed the rental-car agreement which he placed in his jacket pocket. As soon as he walked off the plane, he stepped to the side in the waiting area and used his government-issued cell phone to call the Chief of Operations at the Naval Criminal Investigative Service at the Washington Navy Yard, Washington, D.C.

"Chief Gill, this is Agent Palmer. I have just landed in St. Louis and will pick up my rental and drive to Caryville to attempt to apprehend Sergeant Jones as soon as possible."

"Good to hear from you Norval. Listen, we asked the U.S. Marshal's office for assistance, and yesterday, one of the marshals, Marshal Shelia Collins, attempted to apprehend Jones at his mother's house in Caryville. Jones has already fled the area, and Collins wrecked her government Suburban. She spent the night at the Best Western Motel in Mount Vernon, Illinois, which is on the way from St. Louis to Caryville, and she will continue to assist in the investigation. I want you to pick her up at the motel and take charge. Her phone number is (618) 665-0283."

"I got it, Chief."

Agent Palmer telephoned Collings, picked her up at the motel, and drove to Emma Lee Jones's farm in Caryville.

Palmer then parked on a hill about a quarter of a mile away, where they could see Emma Lee Jones's tiny house wedged on the side of the opposite hill in a fashion that caused the front porch to hang five feet in the air. The main section of the house had a wooden shingled roof, rough wood siding, two windows, and a door in the middle. Another room hung to the east with a corrugated tin roof, tar paper for siding, and one small window. A chimney made from a piece of oilfield pipe leaned against the west side and bellowed out white smoke from a hardwood fire. Steps made of two-by-six boards ran off the side towards the driveway. An outhouse stood off to the side with a plank sidewalk leading back to the house which appeared to still be in use.

The rest of the day, Palmer and Collins watched the house through government-issued binoculars. No one entered or left the house, and at four o'clock, they decided to visit Emma Lee Jones before it turned dark. Most of the snow had melted in the heat of the day, and the steep lane had turned into a sea of mud. Even a four-wheel drive could not make it up to the house without getting stuck. For a moment Palmer and Collins stared at each other.

"Shelia, you wait here in the car. I'll walk up the lane to the house."

Palmer then stepped out and struggled up the driveway. He maneuvered the porch stairs and knocked gently on the door. The small vibration nearly caused one of the glass panes to fall out. Palmer heard movement inside. Without apparent fear or caution, Mrs. Jones opened the door wide and smiled. A large woman with gray hair, she had a regal bearing, with her bulk consisting more of muscle than fat. Even though home alone, she wore a long floral-pattern dress, casual shoes, a pearl necklace, earrings, and lipstick. Hard living carved deep lines into her leathery complexion. Her cologne evoked the cosmetics counter at some midsized department store. She spoke in a calm, deep voice. "Please come in."

"Thank you, Ma'am. My name is Norval Palmer, and I am an agent with the Naval Criminal Investigative Service."

Norval looked at his boots again. The mud extended over the soles and halfway up the sides. He pulled them off and set them on the porch before stepping into the house. Inside, the living room seemed compulsively ordered and immaculately clean. The pleasant smell of something baking in the oven permeated the house, while heat radiated from a stove, which appeared to be another piece of oilfield pipe with metal welded over the ends and a makeshift door. A neat stack of wood lined part of the west wall.

"Please, Mr. Palmer; will you have a seat." Emma Lee motioned towards a small recliner covered with a decorative hand-sewn quilt. Walking towards the chair, Palmer could feel the old, unlevel, wooden floor sag under his feet.

"I put a pot of coffee on for supper. Would you like a cup?"

"Thank you. That sounds nice."

When Emma Lee Jones left the room, Palmer took the opportunity to further examine the place. A large Bible rested on the coffee table. An ancient telephone sat on a waist-high table, but the room lacked a television or radio. Palmer looked but found no evidence of mail, a newspaper, or any magazine. The north wall was covered with photographs that Palmer recognized as being Sgt. Nathan Jones and some other Marine. Additional photographs included basketball teams and numerous photographs of Nathan receiving various sports awards. A photograph of Nathan in his dress blues graduating from boot camp surrounded by Marine Corps citations, medals, and awards stood as the centerpiece.

"I see you are interested in my grandson's military career," Mrs. Jones said as she offered the cup of coffee in one hand and a piece of chocolate cake in the other. Palmer accepted both and carefully set the cake on the coffee table so that he could steady the coffee cup with both hands.

"Yes, Ma'am, I am. I have been assigned the task of returning Sergeant Jones to the military authorities. I would like to talk to him before it is too late."

Emma did not speak but simply looked Palmer in the eyes. Norval could tell that Emma did not believe him, and he felt guilty for not being entirely truthful. He tried to retreat.

"Of course, I have no control over the military, but I believe that the sooner Sergeant Jones returns to duty the easier it will be for him."

It seemed to Palmer that Mrs. Jones believed the last statement, so he continued.

"I need your help, Mrs. Jones," Palmer spoke as he handed Emma Lee his card. "I need to convince your grandson to turn himself in. He can reach me at that number, and I will be working with the U.S. Marshal out of the Federal Building in Benton. I can drive anywhere he wants to meet me, or he can just call me and talk. Will you give him the message?" Norval sat the coffee on the table and took a bite of the cake.

"Sir, I honestly don't know how to get in touch with Nathan. He did not tell me where he was headed. If I can do it, I will give him your message. I got to say, Nathan is a good man and always does what he thinks is the right thing. But he doesn't do anything just because I, or someone else, tells him to. So it likely will not make much difference if he gets your message or not. Nathan will do what his heart tells him that Jesus wants him to do."

"I respect that Ma'am," Palmer answered and focused on the coffee and cake. Agent Palmer then walked over to the wall with all the photographs and pointed to the Marine he did not recognize. "And who is this?"

"That's my boy, Kenneth, Nathan's father." The reminder of her son brought tears into Emma Lee's eyes and voice.

"Obviously, he was a Marine."

"The poor boy got married and could not find a job, so he enlisted in the Marines. You know, Mr. Palmer, at one time Caryville was a boom town—drilling companies, trucking companies—and everything that goes with it. All the stores were open twenty-four hours. I think we had a half-dozen gas stations, restaurants, and taverns." Her eyes smiled from old memories. "But the oil dried up in the sixties. What Nathan does now is about all that is left of the oil industry." Emma Lee Jones grew quiet, and Agent Palmer waited.

"Could I talk with Kenneth?"

"He was killed in Vietnam on February 11, 1968, at Hue City. He never saw his boy, Nathan." She grew tearful again as she answered.

"What about Nathan's mother? Is she still alive?"

"She died five years later. Her boyfriend ran off the road by the New Harmony Bridge. That is when I started raising Nathan and his older brother Jeremiah." Emma Lee continued to study Agent Palmer's face, and that made Norval feel very uncomfortable.

"Do you mind telling me more about Sergeant Jones?"

"I guess not."

"How long has he been living here?"

"A couple of years. He moved in after his divorce."

"Are you in contact with his ex-wife?"

"No. Nathan caught Stacy in a tavern in Caryville with another man. There was a bad fight, and Nathan got arrested. After that, Nathan asked me not to talk to her, so I have not."

"Mrs. Jones, is there anything else you want to tell me about your son?"

"Well, let's see. As I said, his father was a good man, joined the Marines to support his family, but left Nathan an orphan. Somehow, I think that Kenneth is the reason Nathan also joined the Marines. Nathan still feels the pain of being an orphan and wants to spend his life helping orphans in Mexico."

"From the wall, it looks like he's quite athletic." Norval looked at the wall, then Mrs. Jones continued.

"Oh yes. He was the best basketball player in these parts. Always been mannerly, there was a while he liked his whiskey, but he doesn't go to the bars anymore since he joined his church. Never cusses and goes to Bible study up in Mount Carmel every Sunday. He's also really smart and has a degree from Wabash Valley College. If he had the money, he could get a four-year college degree without any trouble at all…got a good job with Curley Harris running a pulling unit and never misses a day of work. That is my Nathan." The fond memory returned to her face, and the two sat in silence again.

"Do you have a family, Mr. Palmer?

"Yes. My kids are grown, but I still live with my wife of thirty-two years. I am from Yuma, Arizona."

"Would you like to stay for supper?"

"Thank you, but I can't. The marshal is waiting for me, and I need to get started for Benton. I better get going."

Mrs. Jones stood first and moved to the door. When Palmer arrived at the door, she took her hand and pressed it hard between his.

"Promise me something, Mr. Palmer." Again, Emma Lee stared into Norval's eyes.

"If I can."

"Promise me you won't hurt my Nathan."

"I am not going to hurt him, Ma'am. Just going to ask him to turn himself in. That is the truth—and a promise."

Chapter 8

During his career, Colonel Earl Cahill had spent several years at Camp Lejeune, North Carolina, and knew that II MEF (Second Marine Expeditionary Force) utilized the north wing of the old headquarters building. This morning Cahill waited outside the office of the Chief of Staff, an old friend, Colonel Bob Wills. Many years ago, then-Captain Wills had served as Lieutenant Cahill's commanding officer in Vietnam. As Cahill waited the waves of introspection continued, and that feeling of impending doom grew stronger. He kept thinking that Gen. Reynolds' ass-chewing had really gotten to him. *Maybe what Reynolds said is true—I have become an alcoholic, and incompetent when it comes to desk jobs. A full-bird colonel utterly incapable of getting in line for a general's slot. My field days are long gone. My life has become as boring as a tax accountant's.*

When Cahill walked into Col. Wills' office, the intended handshake quickly degenerated into an affectionate hug. The Marines sat and Cahill noticed Wills' pale, weathered face and the flabby skin down the front of his neck. Always thin to begin with, Wills appeared grossly underweight. Cahill felt shocked by how much older the man looked since he had last seen him three years ago. *He is about the same age I am. If he looks like that, then how do I look?*

"How's Patricia?" Colonel Wills asked with a smile.

Cahill stared at him and tried to smile, one old friend to another. "I am afraid we separated last year. She took a job near Los Angeles."

"I am sorry to hear that." Wills hesitated. Married to the same woman for 30 years, marital discord baffled him, and he never knew what to say when confronted with it. But he thought to himself that many good Marines get divorced and that it was not a character flaw.

"So, I guess that makes moving a lot easier." Wills chuckled.

"Yep; packed all of my trash in my car, and from here, I am headed for the BOQ in Yuma"

Wills glanced out the window and then back at Cahill before speaking. "Earl, I am surprised that you did not pick up general in the last board. You've checked all the boxes. If a Medal of Honor winner can't make it, it makes me feel like I don't have a chance in hell of being promoted," Wills said with sudden seriousness.

"Well, at some point every Marine ends up with a commanding officer that doesn't like him. I guess General Reynolds and I have a personality conflict. But, Bob, I am shocked that you were not promoted. You are a little senior to me and way more qualified. There's just no rhyme, or reason, who gets promoted anymore," Cahill answered.

"Well, Earl, I am still having fun and plan on sticking around. They will have to either promote me or kick me out."

"Bob, did Lieutenant General Lenard request me for this assignment?"

"No, Earl. We had already assigned Colonel Young. The Commandant called General Lenard and asked if Colonel Young could switch billets with you in Washington. Colonel Young has a logistics background and is needed for planning how we will get men, equipment, and supplies to Saudi. He is just a better fit at Headquarters. The Commandant said nothing bad about you."

"Well, that's good to hear."

"I am sorry to have to tell you…General Reynolds later called General Lenard. I guess the scuttlebutt is that you have a drinking problem. You were hanging out in off-bass bars, got drunk, and wrecked your car in Arlington. You got off the DUI on some legal technicality. I told General Lenard that I had heard nothing like that and that drinking had never impaired your ability to perform."

"Thanks, Bob. Just so you know, I wrecked my car in a rainstorm. No one got hurt. Never charged with driving under the influence."

"Why is the rear element of the Fourth Division at Marine Corps Air Station Yuma?"

"Fair question. Fourth Division has seventy-eight units at reserve centers spread all over the United States, including Hawaii and Alaska. But they do not have judges, lawyers, or brigs, and no way to run courts-martial on deserters. We are only twenty-five percent through the mobilization process, and we have something over one hundred and fifty reservists who failed to report for mobilization. This number could end up in the thousands. So, we need a base where we can efficiently process all these deserters." Wills paused but Cahill had no question, so he continued.

"Our Fourth Wing is headquartered in Yuma, along with three reserve fighter squadrons and the Air Station has a large brig, space for four courtrooms, office space, BOQ rooms, and barracks. An unintended benefit is that Yuma is a long way from everything. We are hoping that the peace organizations, and news media, will not be excited to spend their summers there."

⊂⊃

From the Headquarters building, Col. Cahill drove to the Bachelor Officer's Quarters, and after checking in, he sat on the side of the bed drinking Jack Daniels and reading the instructions for charging a long-distance call to his room. He dialed in three sets of numbers.

"Hello." Earl heard his wife Patricia's voice.

"Patricia, it's me, Earl." Patricia did not answer.

"I wanted to let you know that I have been transferred from Washington to Yuma, Arizona. I will call you when I get there with a new telephone number and mailing address."

"Gosh, Earl, I didn't know there was a Marine base in Arizona."

"It is an air base. We were never there."

"So, what in the world are you going to do at an air base?"

"Actually, I will be the commanding officer for the rear element of Fourth Division…Hey, Pat, can I speak with Elizabeth?"

"Sorry, she's at band practice." The conversation ended and the line seemed to go dead.

"Earl, I talked to a lawyer. She says our divorce should be simple. There is a formula for child support and for military retirement. I thought I would keep my car, and the furniture here in California, and you would keep your car. Nothing else worth arguing about." As she spoke the emotion in Patricia's voice increased, then silence.

"I understand, Pat. I guess we should get it over with," Earl answered.

"OK, Earl. My lawyer is drawing up an agreement, and I can send it to you in Yuma. I do not want to fight, so if there is something you do not like, don't get angry, just let me know."

"All right, Patricia. I will call you guys when I get to Yuma, and we can go from there."

Earl Cahill hung up and refilled his glass with Jack Daniels. At this point, he could not sleep without a nightcap, so he sat in the chair drinking for an hour. He finally passed out, woke at 0200, struggled to undress, and made it to bed.

Chapter 9

The next morning it took Norval Palmer two hours to drive from Benton to Mt. Carmel and another 30 minutes to locate the Wabash Valley College campus just off Route 1. As soon as he parked, Norval telephoned Marshal Collins to let her know his location and that he intended to interview several key witnesses in Mt. Carmel. Marshal Collins replied that she planned to drive to Caryville and interview the Caryville police chief, Jones's boss, Curley Harris, and anyone else available.

When Agent Palmer entered the faculty office at Wabash Valley College, he showed the receptionist his badge and asked to see the dean. The offices were in a converted dormitory with narrow hallways and white concrete block walls. The building made Norval's office in Yuma seem upscale. After a short wait, the receptionist escorted Palmer down the hall, pointed at a door, and said, "Dean Novotney is expecting you."

When he entered the door, Palmer saw an attractive black woman sitting behind the desk. Probably in her late 30s, wearing a black silk skirt and a matching blouse with a high collar, she stood at least six feet tall and had a forceful presence even bigger than her height. Palmer soon noticed a scowl on Mrs. Novotney's face.

"Can I help you, Marshal?"

"I hope so…I am an NCIS agent trying to locate one of your former students, Nathan Jones. He is wanted on a charge of desertion. He left his place of residence in Caryville two days ago."

"At Wabash Valley College we respect the privacy of our students, and we don't release information," She replied with surprising anger.

"There is an apprehension order for Mr. Jones. I can have you subpoenaed to appear in Federal Court in Benton. It's up to you— save yourself a drive and answer my questions today, or I will need to see you in Benton tomorrow morning." The dean continued her disturbing stare and then picked up her phone.

"Margie, will you bring me the student file for Nathan Jones?" Novotney put the phone down and stared at Palmer. "Marshal, do you know anything about Nathan?"

"Not much, only what is in his military service record book. That's exactly why I am asking to look at his college file."

"Well, he is a very good person. Intelligent and hard working. He graduated with honors and received an associate's degree. He wants to continue his education and obtain a bachelor's in religious studies. Nathan is a member of the New Unity in Christ Church and sends a check each month to support an orphanage in Sonoyta, Mexico.

"It seems like you know a lot about Nathan."

"Yes. I am also a member of the New Unity in Christ Church, and I have attended services and Bible Study with Nathan. Nathan is not a criminal."

"Yes, ma'am. But he is violating the law."

"Our government is violating international law! The United States' planned invasion of Kuwait is for no purpose except to support the oil companies. It is clearly illegal and immoral."

"Our opinions are not relevant," Palmer answered weakly and looked toward the door. He desperately hoped that the file would arrive.

"Cops just amaze me!" Judy Novotney spoke in a loud and disgusting voice. "You talk about protecting the public and pretend you are the good guys. But you're like the Nazi Gestapo in Germany; you just follow orders. Morality is not relevant to you people!"

Agent Palmer tried to think of a response, but could not, and was saved by the arrival of the file.

"May I review this in another room? I do not want to take up more of your time."

"Obviously, meaningful dialogue with you is impossible! But I will stay and make sure you don't steal something." The hostility flowed with every word.

It did not take Agent Palmer long to review the thin file. Two years of night classes, straight As, a major in general studies, and a lot of Spanish courses. Palmer wrote down Nathan's apartment address in Mt. Carmel. All the time Agent Palmer reviewed the file, Dean

Novotney sat across the table frowning and staring at Palmer. Her hostility was palpable.

"Do you remember anything else about Nathan?"

"As I said, a wonderful young man. Something I doubt you would understand."

"Did you know he had an apartment in Mt. Carmel?"

"Yes."

"Where would you look for Nathan?'

"Why would I look for Nathan?"

"Where should I look for him?"

"Obviously, I don't know, and frankly, don't want to help you. If Nathan left his grandmother's house two days ago, he is probably already in Sonoyta, Mexico doing the Lord's work. You are wasting your time."

෧෨

After half an hour, Agent Palmer had found the apartment address. The two-story apartments were arranged in a square with a parking lot in the middle. There wasn't a single parking space open, so Palmer drove back out to the street and parked a block away. The snow continued falling. He then walked around the square twice before finding the apartment number.

The first thing Palmer noticed about the young woman answering the door was that she was not wearing a bra. She wore a man's long-sleeved shirt and apparently nothing else. The young lady had huge boobs, and the gentle swaying continued underneath her shirt long after her other movements had stopped. Her hair remained tied in a sort of knot on the side of her head, and yesterday's makeup endured under her eyes.

"Well, get inside so I can close the door! I'm freezing standing here!" she demanded in an irritated voice.

The startled Norval Palmer overreacted, brushing against her breasts getting through the door, and practically knocked Stacy Jones down. Palmer stood panting while the young lady swayed some more. The apartment looked a mess, and Palmer had to pick his way through dirty clothes, dirty dishes, old newspapers, and discarded shoes to find a place to stand.

"I am sorry. I am Agent Palmer, and I am looking for Nathan Jones. He is wanted for desertion and disappeared two days ago. If you are Stacy Jones, I would like to ask a few questions."

"Yeah. I am Stacy; Nathan and I have been divorced for about a year." She walked barefoot towards the kitchen, and Agent Palmer followed cautiously.

"Want some coffee?"

"Thanks, but I've had my fill for this morning."

"Does Nathan ever call or visit you?"

"Look, I have not heard from him since the divorce. It wasn't pleasant."

"I understand divorces, but sometimes exes stay in touch."

"Here's the deal. When I met Nathan, he was a lot of fun—so good-looking. We were crazy in love. We went out every weekend, hitting local bars, drinking, dancing, and shooting pool. The sex was awesome."

Stacy paused and smiled, enjoying the fact that her comment about sex made Norval uncomfortable.

"Then suddenly Nathan got this religion thing. I don't know why. Like I said…I thought he was happy. But he started talking about nothing but the Bible and his new church. He wouldn't go anywhere, except church. You know…only sinners go to taverns. I did not like his church, and I could not just sit at home all the time. I asked for a divorce."

"So, no communication at all since the divorce?" Agent Palmer asked, trying to sound sympathetic.

"Maybe he called me once while hunting. I kind of remember him asking about his mail."

"Can I ask where I might look for him?"

Stacy paused. Anger spread over her face. "I don't know…as I said, he got on that religious kick with his professor at Wabash Valley College."

"Which professor?"

"Dean Novotney. He thinks she's Mother Mary or some bull shit. I think she just wants Nathan. I know they were sleeping together."

"I have already talked to Dean Novotney. No help."

"Not surprised. They plan on going to Mexico together to run an orphanage. That's their plan, helping poor Mexican kids."

"Where does Nathan hunt? Always around Mt Carmel?"

"I don't know for sure. Around Mt Carmel, on his mother's farm outside Caryville, down south in Shawnee National Forest—a lot of other places."

"Who did he hunt with?

"Beats me. His brother, Jeremiah—maybe Vertis Smith—sorry, I must get ready for work."

"All right, Miss Jones. I will be going."

Chapter 10

Collins' research disclosed that Nathan's pickup, a 1976 Dodge D100, Illinois License 38T33C, was registered in his name, and she issued BOLO bulletins in five states for the police to be on the lookout for Nathan's pickup.

Every witness confirmed that Nathan wanted to work at an orphanage near Sonoyta, Mexico, and Palmer and Collins agreed that he might already be there. But if Nathan Jones was not in Mexico, he might be hiding out in the woods somewhere in Southern Illinois, perhaps in an area familiar to him from hunting trips.

On the fifth day of the investigation, Agent Palmer drove to the Illinois Fish and Game Department's main office in Springfield, Illinois. He spoke to a supervisor.

"Mr. Jones has applied for the same deer hunt unit every year for the past eighteen and with the same two people, Jeremiah Jones and Vertis Smith. Here is a copy of his most recent application, including the names and addresses of all hunters."

Palmer turned to the application. He recognized one of the hunters, Jeremiah Jones, as Nathan's brother. Palmer had already interviewed Jeremiah, and he steadfastly claimed to know nothing about where his brother went. The remaining hunter, Vertis Smith, had a Caryville address.

"May I have a map of this unit?" Palmer asked, almost smiling with the good news.

The supervisor returned with a copy of the hunting regulations including a map of Unit 35. Located in the Shawnee National Forrest, Unit 35 included one-half of Gallatin County and all of Pope County, Illinois.

⊂≳⊅

On the way back to Benton from Springfield, Agent Palmer decided to visit Vertis Smith's home in Caryville, arriving at 7:00 p.m. A huge man answered the door. He had a splotchy face, a crooked nose, and an unkempt mustache. He wore a wrinkled khaki work shirt and matching pants with a clean pair of dress cowboy boots. Agent Palmer stuck his badge in the man's face, trying to position it in the light beaming from the front room. Norval spoke loudly to be heard over the blaring television.

"Good evening. I am Agent Palmer. May I come in?"

Vertis Smith stared at Agent Palmer from heavy-lidded eyes, eyes without expression, without emotion.

"Come on in and have a seat," the big man finally replied.

"I am an NCIS agent tasked with locating Nathan Jones. I want to ask you about your deer hunting trips with Jones."

"Really?" Vertis stared at Palmer with a blank expression.

"I have checked the records. You and Nathan apply for a deer permit almost every year."

"OK . . . I've put in for a tag with Nathan and his brother, but last year he didn't even show up to hunt. Nathan is all wound up with them holy rollers up in Mt. Carmel, and I think he ended up hunting with some of them folks. Jeremiah said Nathan killed a monster buck up there, but I don't know where he shot it."

"Well, I am supposed to make sure Nathan is not still around this area. I know that you have hunted with Nathan in Unit 35. Where do you all stay?"

Vertis suddenly gazed hard at Palmer.

"Hell, Nathan told me and everybody else he wanted to move to Mexico to preach at his church's mission, and I heard that's exactly what he did when this draft thing came up. You are just wasting your time talking to me. Anyways, if Nathan is still here in the woods, there is no way in hell you will ever find him. Nobody could."

"You are the one wasting time. Stop arguing and tell me about your hunting trips, or get your toothbrush, because you are going with me to the Federal Jail in Benton!"

"All right. All right, Officer. I'll tell you about our hunting trips. Years ago, we rented an old farmhouse in Equality, but it burnt down. For the last ten years, or so, we've just camped in my little trailer."

"Where do you park it?"

"Lots of places. Anywhere we can find a wide spot off the blacktop where we won't get stuck and there aren't other hunters around."

Agent Palmer unfolded the map of Unit 35 and handed Vertis a pen. "Mark your camping sites and number them backward from last year."

Vertis drew one big circle around Unit 35.

"That's it. Go get your toothbrush. I am taking you to jail."

"Look, Marshal, I am trying to help, but I can't possibly mark all the places we have camped on this map. We've hunted all over, and I don't want to send you on a wild-goose chase. Anyway, as I said we always park right off the main road. Do you think Nathan is just going to hang out next to the road where everyone can see him? He's going to be way back in the woods."

Instead of continuing his anger, Palmer realized that Vertis was right. He paused to think.

"OK, I accept that, but at least tell me—does Nathan have a favorite spot?"

"That's not the way we hunt. The deer in these parts move all the time. Like I said, we've hunted every inch of that unit. We get up, leave camp in our pickup, look for sign, and hunt wherever we find it. I swear, if Nathan is hiding out in Unit 35, no one is going to find him in a million years. He would see you or hear you before you got within a mile. You just don't have a chance in hell."

With a sigh of defeat, Agent Palmer said, "Thanks for your time, Mr. Smith," and left.

Chapter 11

Agent Palmer and Marshal Collins sat in her office at the Benton Courthouse with NCIS Chief of Operations, Leroy Gill, and Illinois Chief Marshal Mac Brenner on the speakerphone.

"Marshal Collins agrees with me. Nathan Jones is already in Mexico!" Agent Palmer yelled loudly, his voice trembling with anger.

"How can you be so sure?" Chief Gill asked in a conversational tone.

"Have you even read my daily reports? Jones completed two years of Spanish in college. He joined a local church with an orphanage in Sonoyta, Mexico. He sends money to the orphanage every month. Over the last two years, Jones told numerous friends he wanted to move to Mexico to become a missionary. What more do you want to close this file?"

"A U.S. Passport is required to travel in Mexico. We pulled the records. Nathan Jones does not have a passport."

"Oh! I call total bullshit on that one! You forget that I reside in Yuma, Arizona. I have talked to U.S. Customs and Border Patrol agents that work the Mexican border. At tourist crossings, Mexican border agents almost never ask to see a passport. Jones could have easily crossed at the El Paso—Juarez, Yuma—San Luis, or San Diego—Tijuana crossings without a passport."

Mac Brenner spoke next. "Well, there is also no record of Jones purchasing Mexican auto insurance for his pickup. The Mexican police routinely pull over vehicles licensed in the United States to check for Mexican insurance. So how has Jones been driving around Mexico without insurance?"

"Why are we playing these games?" This time Marshal Collins shouted at the phone.

"Sonoyta is a short distance from the border, and Nathan Jones could have driven there without being checked for insurance. Hell, he could have purchased insurance under another name."

Chief Gill spoke next.

"Well, Agent Palmer, Mr. Brenner and I are getting a lot of pressure from the Secretary of the Navy to apprehend Jones. The lawyers are looking at the jurisdictional issue, but it looks like any federal agency has jurisdiction to arrest Jones and the Secretary is pushing everyone—NCIS, the U.S. Marshals, and even the FBI. I guess participating in a peace rally pissed off some higher-ups. I just wish you two could give us some evidence that Sergeant Jones made it to Sonoyta." Chief Gill spoke with a tone of resignation.

"This is Marshal Collins, and I can answer that. Here are what the facts show. It is easy to cross the border. There exist hundreds of ways Jones could be in Sonoyta without records. Norval and I can keep looking for years, and we will never find Nathan Jones even if he is hiding in Shawnee National Forest."

There was a long silence before Chief Gill spoke.

"Marshal Collins, I sincerely appreciate all your assistance in this case. You and Agent Palmer have done a great job so far, and I agree with you that the evidence is compelling. Jones is probably in Mexico. But this is political. We cannot confirm that fact. DC is still on my ass and your boss's ass. You two will have to continue the investigation."

"Can't we do something to see if Jones is at the Mexico mission?" Marshal Collins interrupted. "Could we ask for help from Mexican law enforcement? Not arrest him, just see if he is there."

"That was my idea," Chief Gill responded. "But I got shot down by both the State Department and Department of Defense. If Jones is in Mexico, he is considered a political refugee. He cannot be extradited. We cannot involve Mexican authorities, and we can't go there. We cannot do anything, official or unofficial. We damn sure don't want the news media reporting that we are chasing deserters into Mexico."

"Come on, Mac! Can't you do something?" Sheila Collins asked.

"Again, I agree that's where Jones probably is, but it has to be confirmed."

"There is no way to confirm it without going to Mexico!" Marshal Collins shouted. "I am sick and tired of wasting my time just to write meaningless daily reports. You promised that I could give Judge Brady priority. Last week he had to reschedule four hearings because I was up in Caryville interviewing witnesses. I just do not have the time to waste on a dead-end investigation. This is just political bullshit, and I will not be the Nazi Gestapo."

"Ladies and gentlemen. We don't like it either, and believe me, Chief Gill and I have been pushing back. But we all must do what our bosses in Washington, DC tell us to do, and they want daily status reports on your investigation. It's a shitty assignment, but in thirty years of law enforcement, I am sure you two have had worse. Do something every day and send me a report. Remember, you have Agent Palmer there on days that you must be in court."

Mac Brenner hung up before Shelia could tear into him again.

Chapter 12

At 0650, Colonel Earl Cahill parked in the space at the end of the circular drive marked "Commanding Officer" at the 4th Marine Division (Rear) Headquarters in Yuma, Arizona. The parking lot looked empty, but Cahill noticed a Woman Marine Officer rush across the entryway and up the stairs. A set of keys hung from a lanyard in her hand. She glanced over at Col. Cahill, then struggled to open the front door. Cahill guessed her assignment as Adjutant or the Officer of the Day, and that she had arrived late.

Sitting in his car looking at the Headquarters Building, Cahill thought, whether assigned to the front or to the rear, a commanding officer must command. But that feeling of impending doom persisted, and he wrestled with those thoughts.

From the outside, there appeared no sign of any activity in the building, but once inside Cahill could hear music. He also noticed a light dusting of sand at the entry and that the floor needed waxing. He proceeded up the stairs to the second deck. A large red and gold sign placed over the glass door stated, *Command Deck—Enter for Official Business Only*. Cahill walked through the doors, down the wide hallway towards the music, and stepped inside an open door.

Blue tile covered the floor and walls, and a gaggle of clerks sat at desks sleepily staring at paperwork. A young Lance Corporal saw Cahill and nearly fell out of her chair, recovered, sprang to her feet, and shouted, "Attention on Deck." A heavy-set Master Sergeant quickly turned off the radio and stood behind his desk holding a cup of coffee. He seemed a jovial disciplinarian who probably kept the paperwork flowing without unnecessary drama. He frowned at first but quickly smiled before speaking.

"I'm Master Sergeant Parker, Admin Chief. May I help you, Colonel?"

"Yes. Inform the executive officer that the new CO is aboard and would like to see him," Col. Cahill answered with an air of confidence.

"Colonel, the Executive Officer has not yet arrived for the day. Should I telephone him at home, or would the Colonel prefer to speak with the adjutant, Lieutenant Brown?"

"Who's in charge in the XO's absence?"

"Well," Parker muttered. "I believe the staff judge advocate is the next senior officer; he only deals with legal matters, but he is here. The G-3, Lieutenant Colonel Harris's office is on the first deck, but I have not seen him yet. He should be here momentarily."

Just from Master Sergeant Parker's reaction, Colonel Cahill suspected there might be a problem with Staff Judge Advocate. "Show me to the SJA's office."

Master Sergeant Parker looked unhappy but hurried past Cahill. "Right this way, Colonel." Cahill started to follow Parker but stopped, turned at the door, and called out: "Leave the radio off. Starting today, no radio. Starting tomorrow, the uniform of the day is Charlies. Carry on!"

At the end of the hall, Parker pounded three times on the door labeled *Staff Judge Advocate* and a soft voice responded, "Come in." Parker pulled open the door and stepped to the side. As Col. Cahill entered the room, a heavy-set and old-looking lieutenant colonel stood up, slowly moved around his desk, and cleared a stack of papers off one of the chairs. He did not look like a warrior and hesitantly faced Cahill. "Good morning, Colonel, I'm Lieutenant Colonel John Bumbaugh. Would you care to have a seat?"

Cahill noticed that Bumbaugh seemed not at all impressed by his superior rank, and instead, addressed him as an equal. He decided to let that issue slide given the fact that Bumbaugh looked at least 20 years older. Cahill accepted the chair while Bumbaugh returned to his huge desk covered with files, legal pads, and documents.

For a while, Cahill just looked around the office at the large paintings with massive frames, antique furniture, ornately carved chairs, leather couch, marble-topped end tables, shaded lamps, and oak bookcases that lined every wall. The cabinets were crammed full of all manner of old things. And everywhere, not only on the desk but also on the floor, the furniture, and the bookcases, there were stacks and stacks of documents.

"Lieutenant Colonel Bumbaugh, what is all this shit? I have never seen a Marine officer's office look this messy. Is this the Headquarters Building or an antique shop?"

Bumbaugh chuckled. A small thing, but the way he laughed told Cahill a lot. There seemed something proprietary about it. Bumbaugh was telling Cahill that he was not concerned about impressing him. Worse yet, Bumbaugh appeared slow to answer, almost senile. Cahill felt himself starting to get pissed.

"It's a fucking mess, Colonel. All this antique crap belongs to the Second Division (Forward) Staff Judge Advocate, Colonel Chinaski. He left it here when he shipped out for Saudi Arabia. I am stuck with it."

"Are you the senior officer in the Division?"

"Yes. But Major Picket is the Executive Officer and is now acting Commanding Officer for Fourth Division (Rear). I am assigned as the Staff Judge Advocate, and I do not get involved in anything but legal stuff."

"What's your background, Lieutenant Colonel?" Cahill asked in a conversational tone, hiding his anger.

"A tour in Nam, probably at the time you were in grade school. Got out, finished law school, and have twenty-six years reserve time as a Judge Advocate."

"And where's home?"

"New Orleans. I mostly do probate work."

"I guess you must have volunteered for this duty and are probably losing those big fat lawyer fees," Cahill suggested sarcastically.

"Well, yes. Colonel Chinaski and I go way back. He asked me to be here in case he needed someone with my rank to get things done, and I could not say no."

"And so far, has he needed anything?" Cahill started to think that Bumbaugh was just helping a friend.

"For a while, Colonel Chinaski tried to telephone me, but the satellite phones do not work half the time. Haven't heard from him for almost a month." Bumbaugh paused and stared out the window.

"So, what is the legal situation?" Cahill asked impatiently.

Again, Bumbaugh stared out the window for too long and seemed like he could not remember something.

"Can I ask my assistant, Major Hendrix, to brief you on what is going on in the legal department? She is right next door." Bumbaugh asked and for the first time moved quickly around Col. Cahill to open the door. He returned with a Women Marine.

"Sir, I am Major Cindy Hendrix, Chief Trial Counsel. The Marine Corps is taking all legal assets forward—Staff Judge Advocates, prosecutors, defense counsel, judges, court reporters, legal clerks—everyone except a few Women Marines. Headquarters has taken the position that the law prohibits women in a combat environment, even if serving as a judge advocate. Currently, besides me, you have six reserve lawyers and four legal clerks."

"What about deserters?" Cahill asked.

"We have a couple of active-duty Marines in the brig and another thirty-five reservists in pretrial confinement. We also have another thirty or so reservists who failed to report for mobilization then surrendered to military authority and are here on base waiting for their courts-martial but are not in pretrial confinement. The reservists who voluntarily returned are assigned to a sort of casualty platoon and billeted in Barracks Number Eight. Headquarters expects the number of deserters to increase dramatically, maybe into the thousands, and we are getting prepared for that happening. Some Marines have already joined peace organizations and apparently have decided that they really do not want to be in the Marine Corps, particularly if there is a war going on."

"Oh, yes. I know about the peace rallies."

"Our task right now is to mobilize additional reserve lawyers who can prosecute or defend the deserters. We have Marine Reserve lawyers all over the country, but many are not in legal billets. Lieutenant Colonel Bumbaugh and I spend most of our time on the telephone in a sort of good-old-boy-network getting referrals for lawyer reservists, then calling them up, and asking if they will agree to be mobilized. Surprisingly, most do agree. Then, we must get them travel orders, billeting, etc. Our target is to mobilize at least an additional ten prosecutors and maybe ten defense lawyers."

"Are there any other legal issues that I should know about?"

"None that are not related to the prosecution of deserters."

"Thank you, Major Hendrix."

Cahill headed for the office door and then stopped. After a moment, he walked back to Bumbaugh's desk, "I don't think it's funny."

Just by looking at Cahill's face, Bumbaugh knew enough to immediately stand up.

"Sir?"

"I do not think it is funny. Colonel Chinaski shipping out and leaving his personal trash in this office. He does not own this office. Call Chinaski and tell him I said to get rid of this shit, put it in storage, whatever. If he has a problem with that have him call me, but get this place squared away, immediately."

Chapter 13

Nathan Jones woke an hour before daylight and opened a can of beanie weenies, the only food he had left, and ate them cold. Thankfully, it seemed the deer had finally moved into the area. He fought a sudden chill when he stepped out of the cave, darted back inside, and put on his heavy hunting coat. Nathan threw the backpack on and carried his Browning bow to his side along with a quiver of broadhead arrows.

After crossing a ridge, he started to tiptoe towards the tree stand he had sat in every morning for the last two weeks without seeing a deer. At the tree, Nathan climbed to the old board seat, pulled his bow up, and hung it on a limb. Sitting in the dark, it felt cold, really cold, and although Nathan had on more clothes than he usually wore, he began shivering with the worst spot in the center of his back where sweat had accumulated. He fought the cold and tried to be quiet. His remaining supplies would not last long, and he desperately needed meat.

Nathan could hear the wind stirring the dry, unfallen leaves of the tree. A branch creaked in the cold. He turned on the old seat so that his back faced the wind that blew down from the ridge, not a strong wind, but chilly, very chilly. Several times he considered climbing down to move around. He even thought about going back to the cave to get warm but kept reminding himself that most deer are shot at daylight. *Just stay quiet a little longer. Maybe Jeremiah's sardines will change my luck. I need to kill a deer.*

When he reached the verge of giving up, Nathan glanced east and saw for the first time light in the still gray sky. It would be sunup soon, and streams of light started to shoot in from the morning sun and moved by the minute. The clear air increased visibility. No wind now, and no noise. As the temperature slowly climbed, Nathan stopped shivering.

Directly before Nathan, lay a grove of wild, wind-torn locust trees, so thick that a man could not enter. Year after year, however, the tree stand had proven perfectly located to catch deer exiting the grove, and Nathan refused to give up this morning. Soon, he sensed a deer heading his way through the locust grove. He carefully repositioned himself on the two-by-twelve seat. Nothing moved but the wind. But he knew how to wait and watch for movement.

Soon, the whitetail buck stepped out looking around and pausing from time to time to eat. The buck was large and seemed to be rolling in fat. Nathan thought again how much he needed that meat, needed it badly. He took an arrow from his quiver, put it in position, and then waited an instant. He lifted the bow, waiting and watching. The distance appeared about right. The buck angled slightly away from him, with its right side visible. Nathan drew back the bowstring and let the arrow go. It went true, into the deer's left side just behind the front leg. A perfect shot.

The deer let out a grunting noise, turned uphill, and started to run, but quickly went down. Nathan looked around. He waited. At last, very carefully, he crawled down from the tree and eased over to the buck. First, he knelt and prayed. Then he retrieved his arrows. He dressed the buck in a manner not to show any sign of a human, taking only the choice pieces of meat, backstrap, quarters, and tenderloin. The coyotes, crows, or possums would eat the rest before the next morning. Nathan would have enough meat to last weeks.

Chapter 14

At 0430 every morning, Colonel Cahill put on his uniform and headed to work. The closest route ran along the desert to Gate 4, commonly referred to as the "Back Gate." This morning, within 100 yards of leaving the BOQ, he spotted a coyote crossing the road. The animal's eyes caught his headlights and glowed brightly. Ghost like, it stared at Cahill's vehicle, then sauntered toward Runway 3, disappearing into the creosote bushes. The coyote showed no fear, or rush to get away, and seemed to be challenging Cahill to do something. Cahill wondered if somehow the animal sensed the weakness he still felt after receiving Reynold's ass-chewing in Washington, D.C. He had a vague recollection that Cherokee Indians considered seeing a coyote in the morning a bad omen.

At the Back Gate, and probably alerted by the blue officer's sticker on Cahill's car, the gate guard hurried out of the guard shack, came to attention, and smartly saluted. Col. Cahill passed his identification card, and the guard studied it carefully.

"Good morning, Sir."

"Good morning, Marine," Cahill replied in a friendly tone but continued to examine the guard with cool, measuring eyes.

The guard spoke nervously. "Sir, this is a restricted access gate; you need a pass to enter. You can get one from the adjutant."

"Lance Corporal, what is your unit?"

A curious look came over the guard's face. "Military Police Company, Headquarters and Service Battalion, Fourth Marine Division."

"Who is the commanding officer of the Fourth Marine Division?"

"Sir, I don't have that information."

"Every Marine should know the name of his commanding officer. Your commanding officer is Colonel Earl Cahill. The same name that is on that identification card I just handed you. The adjutant works for me. I will access through any gate, at any time, and anyplace, and I do not need a special pass. Does that make sense to you?"

The guard almost shouted. "Yes, Sir. I will open the gate."

As Cahill drove onward towards the Headquarters Building, he noticed the sign *Provost Marshal* on his left and a late model, jacked-up blue-and-white Chevrolet Blazer parked in the space. He made a spur-of-the-moment decision to stop, exited his car, and strode towards the entrance. Inside stood a tall reception counter, labeled *Duty Desk Sergeant.*

"How may I be of service, Sir?" The Gunnery Sergeant asked with a smile. Cahill read his name tag: *Tyler.*

"I'm Colonel Cahill, the Fourth Division Commanding Officer. I want to speak with the Provost Marshal."

It startled Cahill when Tyler turned and bellowed down the hallway. "Lance Corporal Glover, get in here." In a second, a Lance Corporal appeared.

"Take the Colonel down to Gunner Carson's office."

Soon, Cahill could see an open door and a bald Warrant Officer sitting behind a desk. The Lance Corporal pounded on the hatch and announced, "Gunner Carson, a Colonel is here to see you."

The Warrant Officer quickly extinguished his cigarette, jumped to his feet, and came around the desk. Cahill zeroed in on the fact that he looked less than five-and-a-half feet tall, extremely short for a Marine. Cahill also noted that the Chief Warrant Officer's military bearing and uniform were perfect. He shook Cahill's hand with a very firm grip.

"Chief Warrant Officer Charles Carson, acting Provost Marshal, what can I do for you, Colonel?"

"I am the new Commanding Officer for Fourth Marine Division (Rear)."

Cahill now peered at a man who looked only slightly younger than him and seemed almost as seasoned. Small-faced, with wild, active eyes and a shaved head, Carson projected ferocity and self-confidence. The muscular arms and shaved head were only part of it. He was the image of a Chief Warrant Officer.

"Colonel, have you had coffee yet?"

"No. I could use some."

Carson came back to the office carrying two cups of coffee and handed one to Cahill. "Welcome aboard, Sir."

"Nice to meet you."

The six rows of ribbons on Carson's uniform told Cahill a lot. Carson was a Warrant Officer who had come up through the enlisted ranks. Carson, like Cahill, had served in the infantry, probably 15 years or more, and had three tours in Vietnam. He had suffered three combat wounds. The top left Silver Star constituted the third-highest award a Marine could receive for valor in combat, ranking above the Bronze Star. In fact, for heroism in combat only the Congressional Medal of Honor worn by Cahill, and the Navy Cross, ranked above it. Gunner Carson also wore the Prisoner of War Medal.

After serving years as a Marine officer, Cahill knew the fundamental difference for enlisted Marines and warrant officers coming up through the ranks. In the case of commissioned officers, the decisive moments in combat came with the capture or loss of high ground, successful offensives, well-executed retreats, and massive battles. For the enlisted grunts, the significant events in Vietnam were personal—surviving a mortar barrage, finding shelter in a ditch, eating hot food, or losing a close friend. Enlisted Marines usually carried heavy emotional damage from those experiences.

Cahill looked across the room and noticed the photograph on the wall. Carson and two other Marines stood shirtless near the entrance of a tunnel holding flashlights in their left hands and Colt M1911 pistols in their right hands. Three dead Vietnamese lay in front of them. Cahill knew exactly what that meant.

In the war against the French, the Viet Minh created an extensive system of tunnels, which the Vietcong later expanded and improved. By the time the U.S. Armed Forces arrived, the tunnels included headquarters, hospitals, barracks, and storage areas for food and ammunition. The Vietcong made hit-and-run raids against Soldiers and Marines and then vanished into the tunnels.

Marines who cleared the tunnels were unofficially called "tunnel rats." They had to be short and highly skilled at hand-to-hand combat because they were equipped with only a standard-issue Colt M1911 pistol, a bayonet, a flashlight, and explosives. Their skill in using these weapons, as old as war itself, determined whether they lived or died. An extremely dangerous job, Marines who volunteered to clear tunnels had the reputation of being some of the toughest Marines in Vietnam.

"Looks like you were a tunnel rat?" Cahill moved closer to the photograph.

For a second, Gunner Carson involuntarily thought about the violent scenes inside the tunnels. But this morning, he quickly suppressed those memories long enough to answer Col. Cahill.

"Yes, sir. As they say, a tunnel rat is not worth a rat's ass."

"I know those tunnels were death traps. Is that how you were captured?"

"Yes, Sir."

"Did you rely upon a standard-issue Colt M1911 pistol?"

"Of course, Sir."

"Any complaints about the Colt?"

"No way. Without a doubt, the Colt is the most reliable, hardest-hitting pistol in the world. As a matter of fact, a Vietcong once shot me in the stomach at point-blank range with a Soviet nine-millimeter Makarov pistol. It hurt, but I then shot him with my Colt .45 caliber. He is dead. I am alive…" The two men looked each other in the eye and sensed a bond that could not be defined.

"Bad news, Gunner. In Washington, I sat on a Special Committee to consider replacing the Colt with the 9mm Beretta now used by the Army and Air Force. I opposed adopting the Beretta; Marines will hate it. Unfortunately, I was outvoted by a bunch of Headquarter paper-pushers impressed with the 15-round magazine capacity of the Italian pistol."

Cahill said the words *Headquarter paper pushers* like most people would say *child molesters.*

"This is a close hold, just between us, but, within weeks, the Navy and Marine Corps will announce the retirement of the Colt."

Suddenly, Carson's face contorted with disbelief. His skin started to redden with hints of purple. He stood up and paced behind his desk. Cahill could see the disbelief in his eyes.

"I just cannot believe that, Sir! The Commandant can't let that happen!" Carson unconsciously began to speak too loudly to be proper in the presence of a senior officer. He continued to pace, back and forth, while shaking his head.

"Sir, I've shot the 9 mm Parabellum. With that measly underpowered round, a Marine's going to need all 15 shots just to knock down the enemy...Respectfully, I just can't believe this shit. The Colt is part of the Marine Corps."

"I know how you feel, Gunner. I did everything I could. I guess we will just have to live with it."

Chapter 15

The night after Nathan Jones shot the buck it snowed hard, about ten inches, and that worked perfectly to hide Nathan's tracks. Nathan stayed inside the cave, gorging himself on the fresh deer meat. He kept thinking that hunting season did not start for another week, and the snow and the extremely cold weather would discourage hikers and horseback riders, so now was the time to reconnoiter the area surrounding the cave.

He exited the cave at daylight and slid down the side of the ridge wearing his military boots, trousers, and a camouflage hunting coat. He carried one of the candy bars Jeremiah had left him, his canteen, and for good luck, the can of sardines, but no map or compass since he felt confident that he could find High Knob Ranch by simple dead reckoning.

Nathan wanted to move fast, but he knew the risk of spraining an ankle in the Southern Illinois woods and hiked slowly, his eyes down, carefully avoiding rocks, fallen tree limbs, and groundhog holes. He planned to cover the 12 miles in six hours, arrive at the ranch an hour before dark, and use his field glasses to reconnoiter the place. If everything looked good at High Knob Ranch, he would use the payphone in front of the restaurant to call his grandma, and maybe Judy Novotney.

At eight in the morning, Nathan realized that he had miscalculated the difficulty of reaching High Knob in six hours. The mud and remaining snow drifts slowed his progress. Sweat soaked his clothes, and his wet boots weighed him down. Each ridge line seemed more difficult, and instead of maintaining a straight course he meandered about for less steep, and easier to cross, slopes and low points on the ridges. After four hours, Nathan intersected a gravel road. This meant he was lost since there were no roads between his hideout and the ranch. He cursed himself and backtracked in his mind each ridge and hollow crossed. He guessed the gravel road to be the one running between Herod and Garden of the Gods and figured that if he followed it south, he would hit the High Knob horse trail. He headed south as fast as he could and within an hour found the trail, then turned east on the trail towards High Knob Ranch at a run, trying to make up for lost time.

Suddenly, Nathan saw movement ahead, dove to the ground, and crawled 30 yards to hide under a fallen hickory tree. He slithered under the log on his back. The earth felt freezing cold, and his clothes were soaking wet. He bit his lip and remained perfectly still. From under the log, Nathan could hear noises up the trail but could see nothing. He thought he heard someone slapped on the back and then feet stomping. He decided there might be more than one person and maybe a half dozen horses.

At first, Nathan planned to let the people pass, but after lying under the log for over five minutes it seemed clear they had stopped. Worse, it sounded like someone kept trying to circle around him. Nathan moved out, headfirst. With his feet still under the log, he sat up and looked up the trail. Now he could see a horse and rider.

"Son, would you move over that ridge or come out where I can see you? You are scaring the hell out of my horse, and he won't pass where you're hiding."

Nathan grimaced, closed his eyes in frustration, and tried to decide what to do next. First, he started to crawl up the ridge, but soon he felt so damned stupid, he just stopped. Nathan slowly stood up, walked out to the trail, threw up both arms in a gesture of frustration, and stared at the rider. The old cowboy had a long grey beard, heavy eyebrows, and a scar across his left eye. As cold as it seemed to Nathan the rider wore nothing but a long sleeve shirt rolled up to his elbows and held a Pabst Blue Ribbon beer in one hand. A dark sweat stain circled the brim of his hat. The saddle, breast strap, and bags looked new and expensive, and the old man straddled a magnificent sorrel quarter horse. After a moment, he rode up close to Nathan. His eyes looked around the forest and then settled on Nathan's. They stared at each other for a long time, neither blinking. He then stuck out his arm, handing Nathan the beer can.

"Son, hold that while I dismount."

He then moved the horse next to a small stump. "Come on Fred, Stretch out." He spoke to the horse in a low monotone voice. "Stretch…stretch…stretch." The horse moved his front feet slowly forward leaving his rear legs in place and causing his back to lower four inches. The elderly cowboy struggled to pull his right leg over the back of the saddle, clung to the side to rest, and finally lowered himself onto the stump. He then loosened the girth strap on the saddle, dropped the reins, and retrieved another beer from the saddle bags, which he traded with Nathan for the one Nathan had been holding. Finally, he eased over to a log, rubbed his backside with one hand, readjusted his hat, and sat down. Nathan just followed.

"How you doing, young man? I'm Chinker Hopson."

Nathan popped the tab on the beer and watched it fizzle.

"I guess I am going to have to be more careful," Nathan said defensively.

"Yeah, my horse smelled you a mile up the trail," Chinker said, grinning at his beer.

"But I still don't figure how you saw me," Nathan pleaded.

"I told Fred you were not going to jump us. I knew that you were just hiding from the law, but there are some things you can't explain to a horse, even one as smart as Fred." For a long time both men sat in silence and took swigs of the beer. Finally, Nathan spoke.

"Do you know who I am?'

"Nope—just saw your face in the newspaper a couple of times. I know you are a deserter." The men sat in silence again.

"Son, will you get us a couple of full ones, I want to tell you a story."

As Nathan retrieved two beers from saddle bags, the Chinker started talking.

"You know, I deserted from the Army in World War II. Now that took some balls." He thought that funny and laughed at his own humor.

"Back then it was not like this Saudi Arabia thing. Hell, our Country was attacked by the Japanese. We expected them to invade California. I was thirty years old. Worked in the oil field and had my own construction company. Even had a wife and baby. By God, I was entitled to a draft exemption, but some dumb son-of-a-bitch drafted me anyway. Well, I reported, went through boot camp, and was transferred to El Paso, Texas. But, as soon as I got leave, I made up my mind that I wasn't going to stay. I went home and told everyone in town that I had a medical discharge. What surprised the hell out of me was that there weren't any questions asked. I went back to work in the oil field and stayed home for over two months. The worse sixty days of my life!" Chinker Hopson said with enormous conviction.

"I knew I shouldn't have been drafted, and that I was right to stand up for my rights, but I kept thinking about the poor dumb-ass dipshits in my platoon. God forgive my pride, but I considered myself the smartest man in the U.S. Army. The way I saw it back then was that the Army needed my brains, if those boys were to survive." The old man snorted a laugh.

"I finally made up my mind sitting in the chair at the barber shop. When the barber asked me how I wanted my hair cut, I said, 'Like a recruit at boot camp.' The next day I put on my uniform and caught the bus to St. Louis. At the train station, the military police started to arrest me, but I told them I didn't give a damn—if they could get me back to El Paso any faster, then By God, arrest me. They thought about that and just put me on the next train. I had no stinking idea that my unit had orders transferring us overseas. But when I showed up, my company was moving out.

"You know, son, I've always been lucky. When I reported to the First Sergeant, he just said, 'Hopson, I knew you wouldn't miss move-ment. Now, get your ass to work, and I will deal with you later.' I never even got charged with anything, and in a few weeks the First Sergeant forgot about the whole thing." Without saying anything else, Chinker hobbled over to his horse and pulled out a couple more beers.

"So where did you end up?" Nathan asked.

Chinker whooped a loud laugh. "Norfolk, Virginia; then Pensacola, Florida; then back to El Paso, Texas. Never went anywhere overseas. Never saw a lick of combat."

Chinker downed the last beer, picked up the empty cans, and returned them to the saddle bags. He caught his horse, cinched up the saddle, led him back to the stump, and laboriously climbed back on.

"It's getting close to dark, Son. I got no use for this damn President. We got all the oil we need right here in Southern Illinois. But you ain't doing yourself any good hiding out in these woods. Go back to your unit before they get shipped to Saudi Arabia. Find your First Sergeant, make up some story, and take your punishment..." Chinker paused to look at Nathan's reaction, then gave his horse the rains.

"Son, I think I will make like horseshit and hit the trail. Take care of yourself."

Nathan carefully studied the sun setting over the ridge, then headed back to the cave. He would need to scout the area some other time.

Chapter 16

Four days later, Nathan Jones stepped out of the cave into the sunlight of a glorious Southern Illinois morning. He felt a cool freshness in the air like that from the sea, not cold, pleasant. He now moved with extreme vigilance though the woods, knowing that at any time he might come across someone. He paused frequently to listen. If he heard no sound, he moved on, but every time with utmost caution.

As he eased south through the hills, Nathan topped a ridge and looked over the vast panorama of hills, woods, and valleys. Timbered ridges marched away in endless procession, with rock outcrops here and there. Nathan studied the distance with his binoculars, his eyes sweeping the country bit by bit, missing nothing, remembering everything.

Nathan crossed a deep hollow, then headed back up the other side. Trees choked a great crack up which he traveled, mostly white oak and hickory, which he recognized as "One Horse Gap." There was a lot of debris, loose rock, and thick trees. At a rock outcrop on top of the ridge, he sighted a blacktop road. He glassed it with his binoculars. He saw a few cars, but nothing that looked like law enforcement. He walked on, always staying far away from the horse trails, and keeping in the trees for cover. He found animal tracks but nothing human. He hiked through the thickest of the woods now, careful to break no twigs and leave no other sign of his passing.

At ten o'clock, Nathan turned east and worked his way along Karber's Ridge, staying under its shadow, trying to keep under cover. At last Nathan stopped, pulled off his daypack, and sat down on a rock, unable to go further without resting. He sat leaning against a leafless hickory tree, partially concealed by the underbrush. By this time, the sun had risen high, and the warmth felt good as he leaned back against the strength of the thick tree.

Nathan could not help but think about his predicament. After his encounter with Chinker Hopson, he thought a lot about going back to his unit. It would be awkward. He could not hope for the positive reception experienced by Chinker. There would be a court-martial and some of the Marines would always hate him for not reporting for duty.

Maybe Jeremiah is right. Did Judy Novotney totally screw up my mind? The Marine Corps is a big part of my life...and...I just walked away from it. The best people I know are Marines. Marines never use words like "love your fellow man," but it is somehow there all the time. Like Chinker said, maybe it is not too late. I could get out to Twentynine Palms and turn myself in.

Nathan then pulled out a copy of the Articles of the New Unity in Christ Church from his pack. Nathan had obtained the copy of Dr. Raymond Brown's Articles from Judy Novotney, and they had read the Articles together many times. Nathan read Dr. Brown's writings:

"War and armed force are contrary to the New Testament principles for Christians. Jesus has forbidden any form of murder. Christians are commanded to return good for evil, 'put the sword into the sheath,' or 'to beat their swords into plowshares' According to the Scriptures, therefore, it is inconsistent for Christians to participate in military service as a combatant, whether in defense or offense."

By the time he completed reading Dr. Brown's Article, Nathan had again convinced himself that his act of disobedience was the only thing he could do as a Christian. He could not participate in this war. He should have submitted his conscientious objector package and have been classified as a 1-A-0 noncombatant.

Next, Nathan debated with himself how long he could hide out in Shawnee National Forest. Since boyhood, Nathan and his brother Jeremiah had spent hundreds of days in the woods. At the right time, he would have no difficulty harvesting another deer near the cave. The meat would keep well in the cool weather, and each deer would last him for weeks, maybe months. Jeremiah had left him breakfast bars, trail mix, and candy—an ample supply for weeks. Indeed, living alone in the Shawnee National Forrest almost seemed a kind of adventure.

After several hours, Nathan stood and moved off along the northeast slope of Karber's Ridge, working his way towards the flat top of the adjoining ridge and into the pine trees planted years ago by the Civilian Conservation Corps. It went dark faster than Nathan expected, and he had to follow a dim game trail through the pines. A mile from the cave, he left the trail and went down a steep hill through the oak trees. Here, the trees grew so close together that he had to weave his way, often turning sideways to get through, but on the damp leaves he left almost no mark of his passing.

He hesitated several times. He stopped and carefully looked around and listened. An hour after dark, he reentered the cave. He loved being alone this way.

Chapter 17

Every day for a month, Agent Palmer and Marshal Collins drove around Hunt Unit 35 hoping they might find Nathan's pickup stashed somewhere, sometimes stopping to walk a short distance up a logging road or pulling over to check out an abandoned barn. They also visited every store, gas station, and horse camp in the area. They talked with farmers, hikers, hunters, and fishermen. At the end of the month, Agent Palmer and Marshal Collins had interviewed 57 witnesses living in Caryville, Mt. Carmel, Equality, Karber's Ridge, and High Knob Ranch but they discovered nothing of significance. Only a few witnesses wanted to help. Most witnesses insisted that Nathan Jones went to Mexico. Nathan was a "good man," from a "good family," and wanted to be a missionary. And of course, every evening Palmer and Collins filed their status reports with Chief Gill and Chief Brenner.

Today, the weather station forecasted clear skies and Agent Palmer planned to search from the air in a rented Bell 206 Helicopter.

Marshal Collins continued searching on the ground. She first staked out the Phillips 66 Station in Equality, then the Karber's Ridge Store, and then High Knob Ranch by sitting in her Suburban and using her binoculars to scan the areas.

Meanwhile, Agent Palmer boarded the helicopter and instructed the pilot to circle the boundary of Hunt Unit 35, then to continue to make loops, and each time narrow the circumference. It seemed almost impossible to spot someone under the hardwood and pine trees, but Palmer might catch Jones crossing one of the clearings.

On the same morning, the dwindling stock of deer meat forced Nathan Jones to leave the cave. He slipped out an hour before daylight and trekked to a tree stand Jeremiah had built almost 20 years earlier. At the hickory tree, Nathan climbed the two-by-four ladder to the two-by-twelve board used as a seat, sat there until noon without seeing any deer, and decided to return to the cave.

On the way back, the clear sky and bright sun forced Nathan to stop every 20 yards and scan for any police or hunter. He stayed far away from the trails and hid in the thick brush.

Around noon, Nathan repeatedly heard something he could not make out. At first, it sounded like a dirt bike or all-terrain vehicle. Then, Nathan suddenly recognized the sound of a helicopter, and he instantly decided that even the hickory trees were too open. He needed to get to the thick pine trees on the other side of the clearing. He broke and ran, but halfway across, he heard the helicopter coming over the nearest ridge, almost on top of him. Quickly, Nathan dove to the ground and crawled under a small patch of brush in the middle of the clearing. He waited, listening. There seemed no way to get to the pine trees.

The sound of the jet motor came back, closer, and closer. When it came within view the helicopter flew very low, no more than 100 feet off the ground. Obviously, the occupants were searching the clearing. The helicopter flew so low and slow that when it passed, Nathan could see the faces of the men inside. He waited. *What if they land? If they land and get out, they will find me. I am stuck.*

Nathan slowly pulled up clumps of the prairie grass growing under the brush and covered himself. His heart pounded heavily, and his mouth felt dry with fear. From the sound that the helicopter made, it seemed to be circling the clearing. It swung low, a wide, slow circle around the area. The thought of running passed through Nathan's mind. *Dear God, please help me.*

Soon, Nathan could hear the helicopter land, the blades settling down and the motor quieting. Sweat chilled the back of his neck. The *swoosh, swoosh* of the blades repeated less and less often. Next, Nathan heard a door slide open, and voices. He heard at least one man get out. Nathan did not move. The fear came in torrents, and Nathan could barely breathe. A sick feeling settled in his stomach and his legs shook violently. *Please, Dear God, I do not want to go to prison.*

Swoosh, swoosh, swoosh, the engine kept running. For a very long time, the helicopter did not leave. After about half an hour, Nathan heard voices again, then footsteps, and the door slid closed. The rotor started beating faster, and Nathan heard the helicopter lift off.

He peeked through the brush as the helicopter climbed up and over the trees. It headed towards the next clearing, its roar slowly dying away.

Finally, the noise was gone, but for a moment, Nathan could not stand. His legs were trembling too much, and he thought he would throw up. *Dear God, thank you. I see that, one way or another, it is time to leave Shawnee National Forest.*

Chapter 18

At two o'clock on another freezing day in Shawnee National Forest, Marshal Collins parked her black Suburban and stepped outside. The sky appeared cloudy, and the air felt damp with the expectant rain. She hiked up the Colder Springs trail deep into the woods.

At the same time, Nathan eased out of the cave four miles away, trudged across the creek and up the bluff on the other side. By now, he considered the cave an almost perfect hiding place. Yet after the helicopter incident, each time Nathan left the cave, he used a different route and each time with increasing care. His reconnaissance told him that the black Suburban returned to the area every day.

Today, Nathan wanted to try a new path further west on the same summit and followed the horse trail towards Colder Springs. After a few minutes, he heard something and stopped abruptly. He waited, listening.

Through the years, Nathan had spotted many hunters without them ever seeing him, and he understood how men moved through the forest. He peered through the woods, waiting, certain it was not a deer, and expecting to see another person. The sound had been ever so slight, and then he saw movement. More movement, a sly, cautious movement. Nathan remained high among the thick scrub oak on the side of the hill. There were many low branches blocking visibility, and he could see little, he could only hear slight sounds now and then. He waited.

A movement again, something black, something moving with extreme caution, something stalking.

The shadow moved again, briefly glimpsed among the trees. Finally, Nathan observed a woman with binoculars scanning the woods. He could see the holster on the woman's side—a police officer. He calculated the distance to his cave at over four miles, but the policewoman could not know that, and Nathan suspected she was looking for his hideout.

The woman moved again, crossing in front of Nathan, but at least 200 yards away. She became visible only in brief glimpses, as the trees at that distance formed almost a wall, merging one with the other. Now the woman entered a small clearing. Watching her, Nathan decided the woman was not trailing him, but simply casting about, looking for some indication of a hiding place—a firepit, foot tracks. She would find nothing where she stood, yet had Nathan been only a few minutes further along the trail, they might have met face to face.

After an hour, the woman started moving away, headed back towards Colder Springs and Grindstaff Road. Watching her go, Nathan thought to himself once more that it would soon be time to leave his hideout. At least he knew he was being hunted in the woods, not just by helicopter, but by officers on foot. After this, he must be doubly careful in leaving the cave. He remained hidden, not moving, and waiting for the woman to first move far away.

As Marshal Collins hiked down the hollow, she noticed a game trail leading up the bluff. She followed the trail as it passed through narrow cracks to the top of one of the boulders. Despite the tight squeeze, she forced her way through, glimpsing the shelf beyond. She felt dark approaching and saw only vague sunlight falling through the trees. She pushed herself through the last of the cracks and stepped out quickly. She wanted to be back at her Suburban before dark.

In the instant that she took her next step Collins saw the ice, but it was an instant too late. She felt herself falling, and wild with panic, she dropped her binoculars and grabbed out wildly for anything to stop the fall. Her fingers caught the edge, and she held on. She hung suspended above the creek 30 feet below.

Collins knew that she was no longer a strong woman. She had stopped working out years ago. But for a few seconds, she hung on, choking with fear, and then she tried to pull herself up. She could not do it. Her fingers seemed to slip, and she cried out, as loud as she possibly could: "Help me! Somebody, help me! Please!"

She tried to fight down the panic. Maybe she could get up there. She had to get up there. Using all her strength she pulled herself up several inches and then tried to get an elbow over the edge. She made it. Her elbow rested on the edge, and she pulled herself up further and swung a leg to the ledge.

She thought she had made it, but in one awful instant, she felt her elbow slip on the ice and then she was falling through the air. She braced herself for the horrible impact to come.

She seemed to fall for a long time and started bouncing off the boulders along the cliff. The pain, excruciating pain, tortured her even before she hit the ledge at the bottom. Another moment of horrible agony as her leg snapped, and then unendurable pain exploded in her side. She lay in the snow and the mud. For a moment she just stared up at the sky.

Using all her willpower, she slid over to a small tree, pulled herself up, and sat leaning with her back against the tree. She felt for her cell phone—gone. Sidearm—gone.

On the other ridge, Nathan heard the scream. Without hesitating, he moved down into the hollow and picked up Collins' tracks. He followed, scanning as far ahead as he could see. Shortly after Collins' tracks headed up the game trail, Nathan saw her leaning against the tree.

Marshal Collins looked up at Nathan Bell, instantly recognized him from the photographs but said nothing. With the dropping of the sun, the temperature had lowered to where she could see her breath. Nathan knelt and gently examined the Marshal's leg.

"Can you move your toes?"

Collins replied, "Yes," in a very weak voice cracking with pain and moved her foot. Then she suddenly shivered.

"Try to hold your arms out and move your fingers."

She complied. Nathan checked her pulse.

"Where does it hurt?"

"My leg and ribs."

Nathan felt Collin's ribs. "Spit up any blood?"

"Nope."

"I'm pretty sure your leg's broken, and you probably have a couple of broken ribs. I could build a fire and try and find a phone to call the sheriff to get an ambulance. But I'm not sure if those guys can find you in the dark, and it's going to get very cold tonight. Or I can carry you back to your Suburban, if you can stand the pain."

"You've been watching my Suburban?" Collins inquired wearily.

"Every day for weeks," Nathan answered.

"I don't want to go through the rescue scene, stretcher, ambulance, all that stuff. If you help me back to my Suburban, I can drive myself home. It's not too far."

"Fine, but the only way I can carry you is on my back. It's the way they now do it in the military. Put your arms around my shoulders and legs around my waist."

Nathan, with Collins on his back, headed down the side of the stream towards Grindstaff Road. The moon came and went behind the clouds, with its bluish light illuminating the trail, then disappearing again.

"Thank God. My Suburban is at the end of this trail."

Nathan continued in silence. Soon only the largest trees and boulders were distinguishable in outline, and the only sounds were that of the creek water trickling over bedrocks and of night birds. Collins fought to hide the pain in her side and tried to speak.

"Nathan, I'm Marshal Collins from Benton." Collins could feel Nathan's muscles tense. But she had to talk to him. "I'm helping an agent with the Naval Criminal Investigative Service look for you. His name's Agent Palmer. We talked to your grandmother, brother, and a lot of folks that know you in Caryville. We just wanted to find you and ask you to give yourself up."

Shelia Collins felt helplessly silly hanging on Nathan's back, her arms and legs wrapped around him, talking softly in his ear, and trying to sound like a policewoman. Nathan said nothing.

"My boss in Chicago and Agent Palmer will get blamed for my clumsiness, and then they will blame you for me getting hurt. This's just going to lead to a bunch of NCIS agents, marshals, or FBI agents tramping around the woods, and you, or somebody else, will get hurt."

Nathan felt himself sweating and panting, but he did not stop or slow down. He did not speak. Collins endured the extreme discomfort and did not complain. After two hours, Nathan spotted her Suburban. "You think you can drive with that leg?"

"No problem."

"If I were you, I would go straight to the hospital in Harrisburg."

"Sure, Nathan. Here is my card and telephone number. If you need anything you call me. I owe you."

"All right. I'll think about it."

Nathan watched Collin's taillights grow faint in the dark. After a moment they disappeared completely, and the woods went quiet and still. Clouds had formed, and it was now a moonless pitch-dark night. Nathan struggled to find a way through the trees, and as always, he frequently paused to listen and to learn if he had been followed. The trails he knew could not be seen in the dark. Familiar ridges looked different. It felt very cold, and he covered his face with the hood on his jacket.

It became so dark that Nathan had to backtrack several times before reaching his cave five hours later. Inside, he built a fire and tried to get warm. As always, he felt safe in his cave and would be comfortable from the cold. But he remained alone and very tired. He was both physically tired and tired of hiding.

Suppose I just stay inside the cave, night and day? I could do that, at least for a couple of weeks. But Marshal Collins is right. I will get blamed for her fall. Now that they know I am here, the search will intensify and continue until they catch me. I must either turn myself in or leave for Mexico.

Chapter 19

The snow fell soft and steady as Agent Palmer drove inside the parking lot at the Kenneth Gray Courthouse. He saw four Chevrolet sedans and two additional black Suburbans parked near the front door. The lights were on in every office. He pulled the collar up on his jacket and hurried for the front door of the Courthouse.

Inside, he discovered the office he had been using had its door standing open. A woman sat at the desk staring at the monitor on a computer that had not been there yesterday. Palmer stared at the cord running from the computer to the phone jack, and the woman sensed his presence and sprang to her feet.

"Good morning. I am Supervisory Special Agent Nancy Schuler. You must be Agent Palmer. Sorry about using your desk, but Marshal Brenner told me to move into your office."

"What's going on?"

"I better let Marshall Collins explain. She's in her office. Come on. I'll walk you down."

"No need. I know where her office is."

When Palmer arrived at Collins' office, the door stood open and she sat behind her desk. She immediately looked up. Palmer noticed the set of crutches leaning against the wall.

"Come inside and close the door."

When the door was closed, Collins started talking. "We were wrong, Norval. Jones didn't go to Mexico. He stayed here in the Shawnee National Forrest."

"Did you find him?"

"No. He found me. Yesterday, I fell off a cliff and broke my ribs and leg. Nathan heard me screaming and rescued me. Carried me back to my Suburban on his back."

"Well, that took some guts. I guess some of the good stuff we've been hearing about Jones is true. So, what's going on with the FBI agents being here this morning?" Palmer looked at Collins uncertainly.

"I called my boss last night. He contacted the U.S. Marshal in Washington, and somehow a decision was made that the FBI should take over the case. Washington is now going full field on this one."

"This is going to be a fucking circus."

"I know, I know. An Assistant Director of the FBI is overseeing from DC." Collins paused, and Palmer glanced out the window.

"Brenner told me that he spoke with Chief Gill at NCIS and that you and I are off the case."

"I wonder why I haven't heard from Gill."

"I'm sure you will shortly."

"Brenner wants us to immediately hand over everything to these folks and to brief them this morning on where they should start their investigation. Do you need to speak with Gill before we do that?"

"No. Gill will be happy to get away from this thing, and I can't stop the FBI. I just want to tell these people not to hurt Jones. He's been a good Marine, and I think he is just confused about some things. He doesn't deserve to get hurt."

Palmer, and Collins using her crutches, walked down the hall to Courtroom Three. Agent Palmer noticed that the prosecution and defense tables had been pushed together, and FBI agents sat reading documents and taking notes. There were several maps clamped onto the demonstrative exhibit stand, and the attorney blackboard stood in front of the judge's bench. As they stepped inside, Chief Marshal Brenner stood.

"Ladies and gentlemen, this is Marshal Shelia Collins and NCIS Agent Norval Palmer." Brenner made the announcement loudly so that the whole room could hear.

"Agent Palmer, if it's OK, we'll have Marshal Collins start the briefing."

"Sure. That's fine. Go ahead, Shelia."

Collins leaned her crutches against the judges' bench, turned the attorney podium around to face the FBI Agents, braced herself, and started talking.

"Sergeant Nathan Jones is a reservist and a civilian oil field worker from Caryville. He is a very religious man, and his goal is to run an orphanage in Mexico. For that reason, everyone thought he had gone to Mexico." Collins then hobbled over to one of the maps and pointed to Colder Springs.

She first explained what happened the day before, her fall, and Jones' rescue efforts. For some reason, FBI Agent Schuler wanted her to give every part of the story equal time and constantly interrupted with questions about unimportant details.

"Mr. Jones is not stupid, and I bet that he moved out during the night. He probably is now headed for the mission in Sonoyta, Mexico, and all border crossings should be on the lookout for him and his turquoise 1976 Dodge pickup, his Illinois License plate number is in the computer." Collins paused and smiled.

"We know this area is a hunting unit where Nathan hunted deer every year. If he has not left, it's a hell of a big area. Jones probably knows a dozen caves, abandoned cabins, and a hundred places to hide."

"Do you think there is a chance Sergeant Jones would show up in the daylight?" Schuler asked.

"No. Most likely he walked out of the woods last night and left before dawn in his pickup."

"How about it? Can we get night vision goggles? Or infrared cameras?" Agent Schuler directed the questions to one of the agents in the rear of the courtroom.

"They are available. May take a day to get them here," the agent responded.

Supervisory Agent Schuler then asked Agent Palmer to speak.

"Ladies and gentlemen, I am a retired Marine. I have reviewed Sergeant Jones' military record, and prior to this incident, it was exemplary. He is a very talented Communications Chief with a reserve unit out of St. Louis. Marshal Collins and I have interviewed over fifty witnesses regarding Jones' character. Everyone had good things to say about Jones. Imagine a fugitive rescuing a law enforcement officer. That doesn't happen. So, I want to emphasize again that this is a good man, maybe confused, but not a danger to others. I understand that you are under pressure to apprehend Jones as soon as possible, but I cannot imagine any circumstance that could justify the use of lethal force against Nathan Jones. Please be careful."

"All right, Agent Palmer and Marshal Collins; sounds like that is all we got," Schuler announced and continued. "I agree with Agent Palmer. We do not want Jones harmed. Lethal force is not authorized, except in self-defense. I want Agent Nelson to do the individual work assignments. Determine if roadblocks would make sense. Someone alert U.S. Border Patrol. Someone, get over to that national forest and start searching for Jones's pickup. Someone, get those NVG's and cameras here as soon as possible. Someone put out an APB on that pickup. Someone alert the Illinois State Police.

"With all these resources, we need 24-hour surveillance on his grandmother, brother, deer-hunting buddy, and former employer. I want their phones tapped." Palmer realized that all the FBI agents were nodding as if Schuler made some sort of sense.

"I want three helicopters providing surveillance of the area starting this afternoon. Agent Wilson, you write up the authorization for a phone tap this morning. I want you to walk it into court with me this afternoon."

FBI Agent Schuler then looked around, appeared to be counting the FBI agents, and continued.

"That is enough for this morning. We will meet here every morning at 0600. Agent Wilson—I want those wiretap warrants ready for me to review before 1600."

Chapter 20

The sky was full of helicopters, day and night, and the FBI Suburbans appeared to be parked everywhere now—the Phillips 66 station, Karber's Ridge Store, and all the horse camps. Clearly, the police were just waiting for Nathan to come out of the woods.

Moving very slowly, Nathan arrived at High Knob Ranch at dusk as the sun disappeared behind an icy ridge. He got a good view of the camp through his binoculars. Most of the weekender horse riders had loaded up and pulled out. One trailer remained with a small group of cowboys drinking whiskey around a campfire. Nathan figured that they were going to take Monday off work and would be up late. A black FBI Suburban was parked on a hill about a quarter of a mile from the High Knob Restaurant. Nathan drank a full canteen, curled up under a pine tree, and fell asleep.

Around 2:00 a.m., Nathan woke needing to urinate. With the cold weather it seemed unlikely anyone would be watching at this hour, but Nathan remained wary. Again, he used the field glasses to carefully scout out the ranch. The Suburban had disappeared, and this time no one could be seen. Nathan moved carefully, staying in the shadows as best he could, down the hill, and to the dark side of the restaurant. He stepped into the light and walked to the pay phone. It was an old-fashioned phone booth with a hinged, folding door. Nathan pulled it shut and using coins dialed his friend's number in Mt Carmel. The phone rang six times before a sleepy voice answered.

"Hello…"

"Hey, Judy. It's me, Nathan."

"Oh." A sleepy pause. "Nathan…Are you all right?"

"Yeah, I am fine."

"Can you tell me if you are in Mexico?"

"I haven't left yet."

"What have you been doing?"

"Hold on!" Nathan stayed on the line and carefully looked around the ranch. When he returned to the phone Judy sounded wide awake and excited.

"Judy, I've just been thinking and praying—trying to make the right decision."

"I am so glad you called tonight. What you did at the St. Louis rally was amazing. I am so proud of you."

"Well, I don't know, Judy. It could have been a mistake for me. I just cannot figure this one out."

"It's hard to figure, Nathan. The Holy Bible, Church Doctrine, and Dr. Brown agree that no member of our Church can participate in war. War is immoral. The problem is that the Church just doesn't seem to want to get involved with the peace movement. I can't even get through to Dr. Brown, and he has said nothing about the war in his weekly sermons. Did you know that last week, Students Against the War held a protest rally at Southern Illinois University with speakers from Washington?"

"No," Nathan said uncertainly.

"Well, Nathan, there were over five hundred anti-war protesters present and most of the SIU faculty joined in the protest—Nathan, it was just awesome." Professor Novotney talked so fast that Nathan could not interrupt her.

"There is a strong movement in Congress to force President Bush to withdraw all troops by withholding funds. People are starting to understand that this war is sinful. It is all about oil and big profits for rich corporations." Judy paused to catch her breath. Her voice sounded thicker than he recalled, throaty, a little broken on some of the words.

"The National Peace Coalition is organizing more peace demonstrations all over the world. Nathan, there is even a protest planned for Wabash Valley College in two weeks!"

Nathan paused. He did not want to get further involved with the National Peace Coalition, but he desperately wanted to see Judy Novotney again.

"Judy, I will not kill for oil in the Persian Gulf, and I agree that the President's actions are illegal. But if I make another public appearance, I will just end up in prison. I have thought about it, and that's not going to help anyone. I want to get to Mexico and work at the mission assisting the poor at least until this thing is over, maybe forever. But first, I need to see Dr. Brown at the New Unity in Christ Church in Columbus. Maybe he will help me and accept me for a job at the Sonoyta orphanage. Can you go with me to Columbus and then to Mexico?"

"Oh, Nathan! There's nothing in the world I would rather do than go with you to Mexico. But I can't leave right now. You go, and I will catch up with you at the end of this semester."

"Understood, but I need a ride to Columbus. Do you know anyone that will do it?"

"I will take you to Columbus."

"But don't you have to be in Mt. Carmel?"

"Look, Nathan, what you did in St. Louis is one hundred times more important than what I do her in Mt. Carmel. I will get you to Columbus."

Nathan paused and, without excitement, responded: "OK. Pick me up tomorrow night at nine. It will be plenty dark but not so late as to draw suspicion. You remember the Karber's Ridge Store?"

"I think so. I am sure I can find it."

"If you are coming through Harrisburg from Mt Carmel, you are headed south. Go through Karber's Ridge—past Karber's Ridge store and take the first road left. Keep going east for a quarter of a mile then you head down a big hill. At the bottom is the French Creek Bridge. Drive over the bridge and stop at the end. I will be waiting in the brush on the side of the road, and when you stop, I will run out and jump in the car. Keep a look out for headlights from either direction. If another car comes by, just drive on, and come back to the bridge after an hour. I will be watching from the woods."

"Yes, I can do it, Nathan. Nine p.m. this Saturday night. If I don't see you there, I will be back at the bridge an hour later at ten. Nathan, you are such a brave and wonderful person."

"I have to go."

"Bye, Nathan. I love you."

 CஜBO

It all began so beautifully. On the fourth day after the FBI took over the search, the sun came out bright and warm, and Nathan looked forward to never freezing again in the Shawnee Mountains. The walk to the French Creek Bridge was easy.

At nine o'clock p.m., he sat on the side of the road near the bridge, half asleep, with his back braced against a tree. He had been waiting an hour for Judy Novotney to show up, and he started to worry. The night air began to grow cold. Suddenly, he noticed a white sedan crest the hill and grabbed for the binoculars lying in his lap. Instantly awake, he brought the binoculars to his eyes and struggled to focus in the dark on the vehicle. The vehicle looked like law enforcement, and to be safe, Nathan rolled to his left and ducked behind the patch of prairie grass. He waited until the sound of the car faded over the next hill and looked at his watch again.

After another hour, Nathan decided to head back to his cave. *Damn it. I guess I shouldn't have eaten Jeremiah's sardines. Looks like bad luck is coming.*

He slowly eased up the hill, deeper into the woods. About halfway to the top, he saw headlights and heard the second vehicle. The Mustang slowed and pulled off to the side of the road at the end of the French Creek Bridge, just like they had planned.

Damn it, Nathan thought as he started running down the hill towards the car. He thought for sure that Judy would leave before he could get to the bridge. But even in the dark, Nathan moved with astonishing speed, jumping logs, bouncing off trees, and sliding in the mud. He made it to French Creek Bridge just as the Mustang started moving and slapped his hand on the trunk. Judy slammed on the brakes, and he jumped in the passenger seat.

"Let's get out of here! I just saw two cops!" Nathan shouted.

"Oh, my God." Judy looked terrified.

"I think they are patrolling this road looking for me."

Judy floored the Mustang and sped west towards Herod while Nathan turned in his seat, stared out the back glass, and saw no one. No headlights, no pursuit, nothing at all.

The car bounced violently on the rough blacktop, but after a few miles, Judy settled in and lowered her speed to a perfect rhythm for the sharp curves. She made a right at Herod onto Route 34, another right at Mitchellville onto Route 145, and another left north towards Harrisburg. They were moving along a dark stretch of road with endless woods around them. Judy suddenly pulled over at a farm road, stopped, and turned off the ignition and the lights. She looked at Nathan.

"I'm scared, Nathan. I don't know if I can do this."

"Judy, it will be all right. Let's get out of Illinois as soon as possible and then we can talk. Head to Carbondale, then north, and cross at the Chester Bridge to Missouri. We can think about taking Interstate 55 when we get there."

The Mustang rumbled on, climbing the steep, winding roads. Soon, the rain started falling and steadily increased its tempo. By the time they reached Harrisburg, the rain fell in slanted, violent sheets.

"So, Nathan. I believe God wants you to do the most that you can. Being a missionary in Mexico is wonderful, but God wants you to help stop this war."

Nathan's eyes searched hers in the dim light of the car, Judy glanced at Nathan, then the rain-soaked road, and she kept talking.

"Nathan, I have always been a Christian. I believe everything in the scripture. I see the falsehood in our society and our political institutions. I see the same thing in our churches. For me, my religious beliefs take precedence over everything, including political beliefs." Judy went silent for a while and drove. She carefully passed a semi-truck laboring with its heavy load on a hillside.

"I don't see a difference between Christian political action and Christian religion."

Judy went silent and neither spoke for a few minutes.

"Nathan, there are some great lawyers defending protestors. Have you heard of William Kunstler?"

"Yeah...I know he defended draft dodgers during Vietnam and the Chicago Seven."

"Yes. He was part of the anti-war movement during the Vietnam War. Before you do anything, you should call William Kunstler, and see what he has to say."

"Like I said Judy. The first thing I must do is talk to Dr. Brown in Columbus."

Judy Novotney hung a right just after a town called Grimsby, a small farming community on a two-lane highway. She slowed down to the speed limit on the main drag. The highway took them north but kept them in the hills. Safer that way, they thought. They did not want to get close to the I-57 corridor because it is heavily patrolled. Pulling into a motel in rural Southern Illinois would raise questions, so they drove on into the night, and Nathan slept, awakened, and slept again. After three hours, Nathan said, "I could sure use a shower and cup of coffee."

Before Judy could respond, he continued. "But not in Illinois. We can hit the first place in Missouri."

෬෫

They drove another hour in silence. The rain stopped. At the intersection of I-55 and Route 51, just outside Perryville, Missouri, Judy, and Nathan spotted a dinner, *Flossie's Café.* It was a greasy spoon, as perfect as anything Nathan had ever seen. Judy stopped the car with the headlights shining on the front door. She turned off the ignition, and for a moment, they sat in the car saying nothing. Finally, Nathan opened the door, climbed out, and headed for the front door of the restaurant. Inside, the checkered tiles on the café floor showed wear patterns leading from the door to the counter.

Farmers in brown Carhartt coats, horse riders in boots, and oil field hands in coveralls sat intermixed with truck drivers wearing all sorts of outfits. A waitress the size of a refrigerator made change at the register, and three other waitresses hustled between the tables and the kitchen window. The battered tables and mismatched chairs smelled of old grease and fresh coffee. Nathan chose a booth at the end of the room, out of hearing distance from the other dinners. There were no menus on the table. A waitress quickly followed with menus and a coffee pot. When the waitress came back, Nathan ordered first.

"Coffee. Three eggs over-easy, bacon, patty sausage, short stack, hash browns, cheeseburger, french fries, and a bowl of chili."

Judy's and the waitress's eyes grew large, but Nathan paid no attention. Judy ordered a Denver omelet. Then, Judy intensely looked at Nathan and in a low voice spoke.

"Nathan, you know that the primary aim of Bush and his Republican supporters is to secure the flow of Kuwaiti oil revenue into the United States banking systems which is essential to finance the deficit. This will be a capitalist and racist war. We must stop it. I hope you have the courage to join in the fight and not just run off to Mexico."

Nathan did not respond for a long time, and the longer he waited, the more Judy anticipated his words. "All right, Judy. I hear you. I am not saying no, but before I make up my mind, I need to talk to Doctor Brown in Columbus. You promised to take me there."

"Yes. You are right, and I am going to take you to Columbus. But what exactly are we going to do there?"

"We are going to the New Unity in Christ Church Village. I have the address; it's just off Interstate 70. Before all this mess, I watched Dr. Brown on television, and I know he preaches there every Sunday. I want to attend service and schedule a meeting with Dr. Brown. As I said, I am hoping he will allow me to work at the Church's mission in Mexico."

"You really think Dr. Brown is going to get involved with someone the FBI is looking for? Nathan, Dr. Brown won't even return my telephone calls. You are being awfully naive." Nathan had been thinking of that and shied from the thought.

"Well, he is not just a T.V. evangelist. I have read his books. I believe him to be truly a man of Christ. Jesus and the Disciples were fugitives from the law, and I have a strong feeling about Doctor Brown. I am thinking we drive late and get a motel off Interstate 70 just outside Columbus."

Judy stared outside the café window as the words sank in. She then reached for her purse, took out her business card, wrote something on the back, and handed it to Nathan.

"Look Nathan, I know you are going to Sonoyta. But, if anything happens to you, just call me, or call William Kunstler at the number on the back. You must hire a good lawyer, and I will help you."

"Judy, I do not expect to be arrested, but if that happens, I do not have money to hire an attorney. I think the Marines will provide me with a lawyer."

Nathan put the card in his wallet as the waitress brought the food and filled their coffee cups.

◌◈◌

At 2:30 a.m., Nathan spotted a motel just off Interstate 70 in Kingdom City, Missouri, less than an hour from the New Unity in Christ Church Village. Although very late at night, the *Vacancy* sign remained lit, and an open Walmart sat across the street. As Judy pulled under the canopy, Nathan noticed the night clerk asleep in his chair. The sound of opening the door, and a polite "excuse me," added up to enough to wake the clerk.

"Do you have a room for two adults?"

The clerk made a big show of checking his roster instead of turning around and looking at the keys hanging on the hooks behind him. Eventually, he looked up and said, "Yes, Sir. I can do that."

"How much?"

"Forty dollars per night—double beds with breakfast buffet in the morning."

Nathan removed his wallet and started to pull out the cash. The clerk quickly stated, "Forty-seven dollars with tax."

Nathan returned to the car, and Judy drove around to the rear. They walked up the exterior concrete stairs and found the room, which seemed large but rundown. At least the carpet and bedspread looked clean.

"I need to run over to Walmart and buy some fresh clothes. You want to shower first, or go with?" Nathan announced.

"I'll shower."

"Need anything from Walmart"

"Nope."

Despite the late hour and rainy weather, Walmart had a surprisingly large number of customers. Nathan guessed tonight might be Saturday night after payday, and the sporting goods aisles were jammed with shopping carts filled with hunting gear. Nathan also guessed that the Missouri deer season opened that weekend. He moved on to the men's clothing section, hastily selected, and tried on a pair of off-brand jeans, a white shirt, a gray blazer off the sale rack, and a five-dollar tie.

"Will there be anything else?" As just one of the hundreds of customers to be checked out that day, the young woman did not take any notice of Nathan, and he remained confident his anonymity had been maintained. He paid with cash and hustled back across the street to the motel. When Nathan got back to the motel, Judy stood at the bathroom sink drying her wet hair. She turned her head, smiled, and looked back at the mirror.

"Be out in a second."

Nathan sat on the bed across from the bathroom door to unlace his boots and stole glances at Judy. A few years older than Nathan, her face remained oval and smooth, and balanced perfectly on a long, smooth stalk of a neck. Her skin seemed a brown velvet stretched across fine bones with large and wide lips. Tiny, mocha freckles sprinkled across her nose, she was classy, and as elegant as a movie star. When Judy finally came out of the bathroom, she wore only a towel. Again, Nathan noticed her smooth skin and black luminescent hair.

Nathan took a long shower, letting the hot water run off his head for ten minutes before soaping up. He finished in the shower, dried off, and shaved. Physically, he felt tired, but mentally awaken from being clean for the first time in months. When he exited the bathroom, Judy lay stretched out on the bed still wearing only the towel, her back propped up by two pillows and the television on with the sound turned down. Her skin still glowed from her bath, and Nathan could smell her shampoo. Her body looked incredibly shapely, and inviting, with her lean legs braced up. Nathan approached the bed and slowly pulled Judy's towel open. Judy just watched him, then her eyebrows rose, she smiled, slid down the bed, and spread her legs.

They kissed a long and passionate kiss. Judy always seemed different than the younger women Nathan had enjoyed, much different than his ex-wife, Stacy. Judy maintained control, making sure that she experienced her own pleasure. In minutes, they both lay exhausted, and Nathan instantly fell asleep.

In a couple of hours, Nathan opened his eyes. The motel heater was quiet, yet he felt hot, suffocated. He could not sleep. He had become accustomed to the cave, the cold air, and the sound of the trees and animals moving outside. Here it felt still, too comfortable.

Chapter 21

Nathan woke up and ran to the bathroom. Inside, he looked in the mirror and worried that his hair had grown long in the woods. He tried to do something with it, but no matter what he did, it looked like he had an Afro. He even considered going back to Walmart to purchase clippers or scissors but decided he did not have the time.

At 6:30 a.m. he and Judy stepped out the door of the motel. Judy yawned and rubbed her eyes. They then headed west on I-70. Seven miles before the exit they could see a magnificent bell tower which rose 200 feet and supported a golden cross.

Shortly after the exit, Nathan could see a long row of cars being directed by road guards with flags. Judy moved to the slow line.

Inside the tall brick fence that surrounded the New Unity in Christ Church Village Nathan could see a place like some grand French palace seen in history books, surrounded by fields, lakes, and forests. Every square foot of the place was exquisitely landscaped. The same type of brick used for the fence had been used to construct dozens of expensive-looking buildings that served as libraries, classrooms, and dormitories. The display of wealth shocked Nathan.

Judy followed the lead cars to a parking space in front of the Church. For a moment they sat in the Mustang and stared at the imposing chapel structure. As they exited the car, Nathan put on the cheap tie from Walmart. A line of people marched up the elaborate stairs. But Nathan did not see any young people or Blacks. When he and Judy arrived at the top of the stairs, a security guard stuck out his arm in front of Nathan.

"Would you two please move over here?"

Nathan and Judy followed the guard down the hallway to the side. He spoke in a firm voice.

"I am sorry, I can't admit you to the services." With a stunned look on his face, Nathan looked at Judy, and then at his clothes.

"Why not?"

"Televised services. We maintain a strict dress code for our viewers."

"I am a member of the Mt. Carmel, Illinois Church and I have driven a long way. I purchased these clothes just to attend the services."

"The rules are no boots and no jeans. You need to leave."

Nathan remembered seeing others in the line wearing jeans but said nothing. He paused, raised his eyes to look around the Church, and looked down.

"Come on Judy. I guess I made another mistake."

At the Mustang, Nathan waited for Judy to find her keys and loosened his tie. A Ford Ranger pickup marked "Security" pulled to the side, and a guard walked over to Judy. He had thick shoulders, a large chest, and a beer belly.

"Young lady, I need to see your driver's license."

Nathan recognized Judy's angry eyes. "We are leaving."

"I know you are leaving. That's why I am here. I said show me your driver's license."

"I am not going to show you anything. Leave us alone." Judy said simply.

The security guard reached for Judy's wrist, but her reflexes were fast, and he grabbed nothing but air.

"Stop! Didn't you hear? Leave her alone!" Nathan growled.

The guard turned towards Nathan who now stood on Judy's side of the Mustang, only a couple of feet away. The two men glared at each other, neither backing down. With a cold, ugly look in his eyes, the guard reached for his revolver. Nathan instantly threw a long-left hook. It caught the guard as designed, hard on the ear, and the guard's head snapped sideways, by which time Nathan was already throwing a right-hand uppercut under the guard's chin. The guard stayed on his feet for a few seconds, wobbling around like a drunk man. His face registered a look that fell somewhere between shock and rage. Soon, his facial features melted and blurred, his mouth sagged, and his whole face seemed instantly swollen. There were tears and snot. He then folded in half and went down onto the pavement—out cold. For several moments Nathan stared at the guard's still form, not quite believing what he had done. He could see the guard was still breathing.

"Nice and easy Judy. Get in and drive us out of here."

ೞ

Judy drove the Mustang carefully across Missouri and back to Illinois. Nathan said little. He fought his emotions and kept replaying what had happened in his mind. *The New Unity in Christ Church congregation in Mt Carmel were true Christians. Kind, humble, always trying to help their fellow man. How could the New Unity in Christ Village be so different?*

In Chester, Illinois, they stopped again for dinner at Flossie's Café. "What are you going to do, Nathan?"

Nathan felt an obligation to explain his thinking, but sensed that it could not be explained, and attempting to do so would serve no useful purpose. He finally spoke. "Judy, I don't want to disappoint you. Please. I need to go back to the Marines, take my punishment, and get back home to take care of my grandmother. I am sorry, but I am finished with the church and the anti-war movement."

Judy looked stunned. She started to speak, then became quiet. Tears formed in her eyes.

"All right, Nathan. Let's not argue. But I am going to raise some money so that you can hire a lawyer. You will need one."

After they had eaten, Nathan handed Judy 20 dollars. "If you could take care of this, I need to make some phone calls to my family."

Thinking of his grandmother made Nathan's throat ache, but if he dwelled on memories now, the heartache could be immobilizing. He dialed the pay phone and did not suspect that the call was being recorded by the FBI.

"Grandma, it is Nathan. Are you all right?"

"Oh, Nathan! I am so glad to hear from you. Are you doing OK?"

"Yes. I am fine. But Grandma, you didn't answer. Is Jeremiah taking care of you?"

"Of course he is. Everything is fine. I just miss having you here. It's lonely."

"I have decided to turn myself in."

"That's wonderful. I know it's the right thing."

"I don't know where they will send me for my court-martial but it likely will be Camp Lejeune or somewhere far from Illinois. At some point, I am sure they will let me call you. I will probably be in prison for a while."

"I know. You're strong, Nathan. Just don't let them change you. I will see you when you get out. I love you and will miss you, but I will be fine. Stop worrying about me."

"OK, Grandma. Remember, no matter what my sentence is, they usually pardon deserters a year or so after the war ends. I should be back home in a few years at most."

"I will see you then, Grandson, and I will pray for you every day."

"Love you, Grandma."

"Love you, Nathan."

Next, Nathan pulled out the card Marshal Collins had given him the night he carried her out of the woods. He dialed the number.

"Marshal Collins, this is Sergeant Nathan Jones. I want to turn myself in tomorrow. I will be at the Courthouse in Benton at nine o'clock."

"That is wonderful, Nathan. I will be there waiting for you. Come straight to my office. Room 220."

"All right then. Marshal, I will talk to you tomorrow morning."

"Nathan, be very careful tonight. You are a high-profile fugitive, and bad things can happen when people are being arrested."

Judy drove the car southeast, through Murphysboro, and into the winding, hilly roads of Southern Illinois. It started as just another dark and moonless night, but soon the rain poured down like the night before, heavily, steadily, and relentlessly. The only sounds inside the car were the swish of the tires on the wet pavement and the cadence of the windshield wipers. It made driving more difficult for Judy, and the miles passed in silence as the finality of Nathan's decision sank in.

"Nathan, are you going to call a lawyer?"

"Not until after I turn myself into Marshal Collins."

Judy started to object but did not get a chance. She rounded a curve and had to brake hard. A road flare burned at the side of the road. And beyond, a pickup truck pulling a horse trailer that had gone off the road into a ditch. Another pickup, a sturdy ton crew-cab blocked the road with a chain hooked to the front bumper of the pickup in the ditch. There were already three pickups and four men.

One man sat dazed on the shoulder, with his elbows on his knees and his head down, probably the driver of the truck with the horse trailer in the ditch. He wore a camouflage cowboy hat. Nathan figured he was drunk—just another trail-riding story in Southern Illinois. Too many beers on the trail, a dark winding road, and a corner taken too fast. Thank God, the cowboy had apparently left his horse somewhere else.

"No big deal, Judy. Take it easy. If a cop shows up, we just wait for directions and drive on. If asked, tell the truth, you are a professor at Wabash Valley College and headed home. I am just a friend. We should be out of here in ten minutes."

Soon, Nathan could see the flashing lights and heard the sirens of two police cars. An Illinois Highway Patrolman parked on the shoulder behind Judy, and a Jackson County Deputy Sheriff parked on the road. The Mustang was blocked in. The police vehicle lights continued to flash. Neither seemed to notice Judy's car, and they did not interfere with the rescuers' efforts to pull the pickup out of the ditch. Instead, both went straight to the drunken cowboy, who with great effort managed to stand up.

As Judy and Nathan watched, the cowboy pulled out his wallet and handed the patrolman something, probably his driver's license. By then the rescuers had both vehicles parked on the opposite side of the road.

"When they move that horse trailer, let's slowly ease out of here on the right side," Nathan suggested.

When the pickup and horse trailer were out of the way, Judy started to move further to the right, but the Deputy noticed the car for the first time and motioned for Judy to stay still. Another police car came from the opposite direction. Nathan and Judy watched as the cops handcuffed the cowboy and placed him in the back of the

Deputy's car. The Illinois Highway Patrolman moved over to Judy's window which she rolled down.

"Driver's licenses please."

Judy looked at Nathan who said nothing.

"I don't understand officer, why do you need my driver's license? I've done nothing wrong." Judy said defensively.

"You are a potential witness. I need your contact information." The officer sounded annoyed. "Sir, I need to see your driver's license also."

Nathan slowly pulled out his wallet and looked at his driver's license and military identification card, trying to decide which one to hand to the highway patrolman. He passed his driver's license to Judy, and she handed it to the patrolman.

The patrolman took the licenses back to his vehicle and Nathan could see him talking on his radio. Then the Deputy motioned for the Highway Patrolman. The two walked to the Patrolman's car. Nathan saw the Patrolmen start to return and motioning another deputy to the Mustang. All of them drew their pistols. Nathan slowly raised his hands over his head. He expected, at best, to be beaten, and, at worst, to be murdered.

"Step out of the car!"

Nathan tried to remain calm and collected. He felt almost grateful that he had been caught. No more running. At least he could start paying the price. He spoke in a mild voice, just loud enough to be heard.

"Officer, do you want me to put my hands down to open the door?"

The patrolman opened the door. "Keep your hands up and slowly step out of the car."

Nathan complied.

"Hands on top of the car. Feet spread."

The patrolman frisked Nathan. With one movement he jerked Nathan's hands behind his back and roughly applied the handcuffs.

"You are under arrest for desertion."

Part 2

Article 85 – Desertion with Intent to Avoid Hazardous Duty

> (1) Any member of the armed forces who without authority goes or remains absent from his unit, organization, or place of duty with intent to remain away therefrom permanently;
>
> (2) quits his unit, organization, or place of duty with intent to avoid hazardous duty or to shirk important service; or
>
> (3) without being regularly separated from one of the armed forces enlists or accepts an appointment in the same or another one of the armed forces without fully disclosing the fact that he has not been regularly separated, or enters any foreign armed service except when authorized by the United States;

is guilty of desertion.

Chapter 22

"Have you seen this article in the *Times* magazine?"

Michael Beck looked up from his desk and saw his senior partner, Sidney Johnson, entering the office. Still military in his posture, Sid appeared to be full of energy this morning, and his bald head, broad shoulders, and thick arms seemed out of place in the expensive gray suit. He tossed the magazine in front of Mike.

"No," Mike answered as he focused upon a photograph spread across the front page.

"The fighting hasn't even started, and we have anti-war demonstrations!"

Mike scanned the article underneath the photograph and hurried to respond to Sidney Johnson but delayed too long.

"I remember reading the newspapers when this shit happened, but I didn't realize one of those yahoos is a Marine! A Sergeant of Marines participating in a peace rally! Can you believe this shit, Mike?

Sid paused for Mike to respond, but again, when Mike did not immediately answer, Sid continued his tirade. "A Marine refusing to report for duty!" Sid roared with anger.

"Well, yesterday they finally caught the bastard! By God, I hope they shoot that coward!"

Mike understood Sid's outrage. Sidney Johnson retired a proud Marine Corps Officer. Mike responded with the only thing he could think of saying. "I am sure he will be convicted and will spend a long time in Leavenworth."

"Mike, while my Marine brothers and I were fighting in Vietnam, a bunch of yellow-bellied rich boys were back here partying. Their daddies paid their golf-course buddy doctors to come up with phony medical excuses, usually flat feet. Damn it! These religious conscientious objector claims are pure bullshit—just pathetically convenient. If a son-of-a-bitch doesn't want to fight for this country, he should not live here. He damn sure should not join the Marine Corps. The only reason we are here is that brave men have been willing to fight and die for their country. Freedom isn't free, you have to pay for it."

Sid sat down in one of the chairs across from Mike and stared out the window at the Chicago skyline. He sometimes did this for five or ten minutes, then left without saying a word. Mike continued to prepare for his trial. This morning Sid spoke again.

"Mike, I am afraid our Country is going down the shitter. Today, young men think that money and technology will protect us. It won't. The only thing that will save America is men with the will to fight and win. Men willing to make the ultimate sacrifice. That's how we won World War II…hell, the German's had better equipment and technology.

"These reservist cowards are the worst. What is the point of joining the Marines if you are not going to fight? The Marine Reserve should mean more than free college tuition and an occasional weekend drill." Sid now spoke in a low monotone, like he was speaking to himself.

"How did this no-good son-of-a-bitch make it through boot camp? These cowardly mother-fuckers are nothing more than sunshine patriots! Opportunists… manipulators. They reap the benefits of the military, but when something is required of them, they fail to report with their fellow Marines and leave them empty handed to carry on the fight without them. Good Marines are going to die because this no-good cocksucker is not there to do his job. They should take him out and shoot him in front of a firing squad. By God, I would go back on active duty for that…"

Before Mike could say anything further, Sidney stood up and his big presence seemed even bigger. In an instant, he stormed out of the office.

Michael Beck looked every inch the successful trial lawyer someone would expect to see on television. Tall, physically fit, good-looking, with sharp features, alert eyes, and a sense of competency. But Mike did more than just look the part. An exceptionally gifted lawyer, he worked long hours at his job.

Before Sid's interruption, Mike had not given any thought towards deserters or the potential war. Ten years earlier he had joined the Marines, but for one purpose—to acquire the courtroom skills to become a successful civil litigator. The Marine Corps provided what it promised, four years of intensive trial experience, but Mike hated everything else about the Corps. Unlike his boss Sidney Johnson, Mike seldom mentioned his service in the Marines, and he did not own any of the Marine paraphernalia, such as the caps, T-shirts, and bumper stickers. As a member of the Individual Ready Reserve, he might be called up if Russia invaded North America, but otherwise, Mike wanted nothing further to do with the Marine Corps.

"I added the new exhibits to the exhibit book." Mike heard a voice and looked up as his secretary entered the office.

"You're in early today," Mike said as he flipped through the binders.

"I thought you would need the exhibit book for closing."

"I do. This is very helpful. Thank you, Brenda." Brenda smiled triumphantly and hurried out of the office.

At 6:55 a.m., Mike walked down to a small conference room on the 30th floor. The walls were all glass and provided a magnificent view of downtown Chicago. Mike found Sidney Johnson and an outside attorney, Darius Hancock, near the end of the table reviewing a stack of documents. Sidney had hired Darius to represent Mike on an ethics complaint filed by one of the firm's clients, the Larsen Corporation. Darius looked up, slid over one of the documents and started to speak.

"The Committee on Rules of Professional Conduct issued their opinion and adopted Rule 1.8(J) from the American Bar Association Model Rules. Illinois now follows the *per se* ban on sexual relations with clients. It does not matter if the sex is between two consenting adults, or that the client is not harmed. Samantha Gardner is general counsel for the corporation and is considered the client. Her husband's private detective has photographs of the two of you having sex. We have no defense and are going to have to make a deal." Darius let his words sink in carefully and continued.

"Fortunately, Bar Counsel is willing to enter a confidential settlement. The file will be sealed, and no judge, lawyer, or anybody else will know whether you were censored. There will be a private reprimand and a six-month suspension prohibiting you from practicing law in Illinois. But again, no one will know why you are not practicing."

Mike paused to think. "What about civil litigation? Can the Larson Corporation sue the firm?"

"Mike, you won the Larsen Corporation's case—a spectacular result. There are no damages. This is just a failed marriage and an angry husband."

Mike stared at Darius but said nothing for a long time.

"Darius, that will not work for me. I have very demanding clients. They are not going to accept me being gone for six months. They will fire me and hire someone else."

Mike and Darius looked at Sidney for an answer.

"Son, looks like you made yourself a shit sandwich, so you are just going to have to eat it one bite at a time." Sid smiled as he spoke, as if the whole thing were nothing but a joke.

"You are the finest young lawyer I have ever seen—smart, shrewd, articulate, and possessed of the guts to take risks with juries. You have worked 365 days a year, and you have made more money for this firm each year than anyone else, including myself. The firm owes you six months' vacation. You will get your regular draw."

"I don't know, Sid. My salary is not the issue."

Sid looked annoyed, and he now spoke in a louder voice. "Look, Mike, about ten years ago one of our partners got into a fee dispute with a client. He had worked here for fifteen years, made the firm lots of money. Unfortunately, the Illinois Bar Association sided with the client and issued a public reprimand. The cutthroat bastards who are my partners in this firm kicked the poor son-of-a-bitch out! They voted unanimously that no lawyer with an ethics violation can be a member of this firm. As Senior Partner and Manager, I am not going to risk losing you. I do not care how many clients we lose; we have plenty more wanting to hire you when you get back. Take this deal!" Sid paused and stared Mike in the eyes.

"Take a big bite of shit and swallow it, then get the hell out of Illinois for the six months. We will think up some cover story to explain your absence."

When Mike started to speak, his secretary interrupted by a knock on the door. "Mr. Beck, I am sorry, but Mr. Lombard is holding. He insisted that I let you know that his client has a settlement offer, and he would like to discuss it before the trial resumes this morning."

"Brenda, tell Lombard I will call him back in five minutes. All right, Darius, I will take the settlement. Can you wrap it up today?"

"Absolutely. I already have the settlement agreement for your signature."

Darius walked around the table and placed the agreement in front of Mike Beck. Mike signed the document, without reading, and stood.

"Sid, can you sit in on this telephone conference with Hitch Lombard?"

When Mike, Sid, and the two associates on the case were assembled in Sidney Johnson's office, Mike hit the speaker button on the phone.

"Good morning, Hitch, I have you on speaker with Sid, Rick, and Claire. What can I do for you?"

"Good morning, Mike, Sid, Claire and Rick." Mike knew instantly by the sound of Hitch's voice that the offer would be a good one. Mike believed that many of Hitch Lombard's jury trial techniques were outdated, but Mike remained amazed by Hitch's intelligence and dynamic personality. Hitch could be anything at any time, a nerdy detail lawyer, a bully, or a charmer. This morning Mike recognized the voice of the charmer.

"Did you get any sleep, Mike?'

"I got enough."

"Yes, I am sure you did, and you are ready to go this morning. Mike, however this thing turns out, I want to tell you that you did a hell of job on this case. Never seen anyone do better! Mike, how long will it take you to get in touch with your client?"

"Richard is usually easy to reach."

"Good. I am faxing over an offer of settlement at two million dollars. There will be mutual releases, dismissal with prejudice, and the amount confidential. I will tell you that the insurance carriers wanted to offer a million and a half, but I told them I would not do it. At this point, there is no time to negotiate. I made them give me the absolute highest amount, and I am sending it over as a take it or leave it offer. Seriously, Mike, I even have typed in a choice of an acceptance, or rejection, for you to sign and return. Please tell Richard this is his last chance, and that I will not consider a counteroffer. The deadline for a written response is seven-thirty this morning, but if you can't reach your client let me know, and I may be able to extend the time. Unless you have any questions, I will send the fax now."

"Fine. Send it over, Hitch, and I will get you a response." Mike carefully hung up the phone. "What do you think, Sid?"

"Lombard knows what he is doing. He figures that the jury is going to go against him, but there are too many unsettled legal issues on this one for us to turn down two million. No question we must accept the offer."

"Any other comments?" Mike looked at Claire and Rick. They were both thinking that if the case settled, they would not have to work 140 hours a week on the appeal. Before they could say anything, Mike's secretary knocked on the door and delivered copies of Lombard's facsimile.

"Unless anyone sees a problem with the terms, I will call Richard and recommend he accept the offer." No one answered and Mike dialed the number for his client.

❧❧

At eleven o'clock, Mike Beck and Richard Heinz returned to the large conference room at Johnson, Howell, Muller, & Brophy. Judge Patterson had approved the settlement and dismissed the jury. Mike carried a cashier's check for two million dollars. While they were in court, Sid Johnson with the help of four secretaries, and the firm's bookkeeper produced an accounting of all costs expended by the firm in the Heinz case and a calculation of the firm's share of the settlement. The manager of the First Illinois Bank was also present and ready to sign two cashier checks, one to Heinz for $1,324,408.98, and one to Johnson, Howell, Muller, & Brophy for $666,591.02. By noon, the funds had been run through the firm's trust account, the client had signed the acknowledgements and receipts, and the case ended. Sid and Mike sat alone in the conference room.

Sid handed Mike a new set of documents and a check for $100,000.

"While you were in court, I drafted an addendum to your partnership agreement. What I said in front of Darius is the truth. You have been the heavy lifter in this firm, and over the last six years you have tried eight cases a year. The firm average is only three a year. After six years you are expected to slow down. Here is what I have decided. I am offering you a full partnership with a sign-on bonus of a hundred thousand dollars. I've written the partnership agreement so it does not start for six months. Just sign the agreement and come back in six months as a full partner."

Mike grinned. "Thanks Sid. Seems like I am being rewarded for screwing up with Samantha Gardner."

"No, Mike you are getting a second chance. That's all. If there is another bar complaint you will be gone. You know that." Sid spoke without anger.

"What about Brenda? Are you going to pay her when I am gone for six months?"

"Of course; your secretary can work for me."

Mike pulled out his pen, signed the partnership agreement, and stuck the check in his pocket. "I guess I will see you in six months."

"Great, call me Monday with your cover story. And don't forget that you can't practice law in Illinois, period. Get out of town for six months."

Chapter 23

An icy wind whipped down Michigan Avenue, rattling awnings, scattering paper scraps, and raking Mike Beck's cheeks raw. He cursed himself for not wearing a heavier coat, turned up the collar on his jacket, and ducked his head to avoid the chill. Since he had driven all the way downtown, Mike toyed with the idea of stopping by the office and asking Sidney to lunch. Maybe he could avoid leaving Chicago. Mike realized that idea would not work and decided to walk the five blocks to O'Malley's Irish Bar for lunch by himself.

The wind increased, and by the time Mike could see O'Malley's he felt desperately cold. Mike pushed open the huge wooden doors and stepped inside. A blast of warm air greeted him. When the door shut the place seemed as dark as a movie theater and smelled of stale beer and tobacco. At first, the bar appeared empty, but when his eyes adjusted, Mike could see a bartender at the far end of the building washing glasses. He took a booth across from the bar and watched the bartender walk over carrying a dish towel.

"What can I get for you?"

"A Guinness, a shot of Jameson, and a menu."

"Sorry, the kitchen doesn't open until eleven."

"In that case, make it a double Jameson." The bartender smiled and headed back to the bar. While the bartender delivered the beer and whiskey, Mike opened his briefcase and took out a legal pad. He needed to figure out something to do, and somewhere to go, for six months. Staring at the legal pad depressed him. He realized he had no family, few friends, no interest in sports or traveling, no hobbies, and no desire to do anything but work. At 11:00 a.m. the bartender brought Mike's third round and a menu.

"I will have Irish stew and switch to Pabst beer. No more Jameson's."

The waitress scribbled on the pad and headed towards the kitchen. Mike's cell phone rang. The call was from an old friend, Steve Way.

"Hello."

"Hey, Mike; it's Steve. I just got your voice mail. What are you up to?"

"Not much. Just sitting in an Irish bar getting drunk."

"On a Monday morning?"

"Yep. I am on a six-month leave of absence from the firm."

"Holy Shit! You get caught in bed with a secretary?"

"Something like that…you know me…but my boss thinks all will be well if I am gone for the next six months."

"Wow. Can't wait to hear the details. You are always falling into shit and coming out smelling like a rose."

"How you doing, Wrong Way?'

"I am on active duty."

"Active duty?"

"Mike, remember I stayed active in the reserves? One weekend a month at Camp Lejeune and two weeks in the summer. Hell, I've even been promoted to major. You never thought you would hear that—Major Steve Way. Anyway, the Marine Corps called up everyone for Desert Shield. I am at Marine Corps Air Station, Yuma, Arizona, prosecuting deserters."

Mike sat stunned at the news. "Yuma, Arizona? I've never been there…but the heat in the summer?"

"I don't know about the summers yet, but winter here is awesome. On top of that, it is only a two-and-a-half-hour drive to San Diego. Don't tell Becky, but I've been there every weekend." Both laughed.

"Hey, Mike—the Marine Corps is desperate to find more reserve lawyers to help process these deserters. If you aren't working, why don't you sign up? We can have a blast out here."

"Steve, you know I hated the fucking Marine Corps. Not interested."

"No, you just hated the first part, being a Marine, the physical training, officer candidate school, and military stuff. You did great as a Marine lawyer. My boss is an old reservist and not into military shit at all. This would be a piece of cake for you—easy cases, working only forty hours a week. Besides, you got something better to do?"

Silence.

"Write down this phone number and call my boss, Lieutenant Colonel Bumbaugh. I will tell him about your trial work, and that I am recommending you. No offense, but right now he will take anybody."

⋯⋯

"Sid, I have my cover story!" Mike could not hide the excitement in his voice.

"I am listening."

"You know those Marine deserters we were talking about last week…that sergeant in the photograph. The Marine Corps needs lawyers right now. I spoke to a Lieutenant Colonel at Marine Corps Air Station Yuma, Arizona and I am going on active duty for six months to be a trial counsel and prosecute deserters."

"Hell, yes!" Sidney yelled into the phone, his excitement and joy obvious.

"No shit, Mike? You are going to be prosecuting that fucking coward in the photograph?"

"Well, of course, I don't know if I will be assigned that case, but I will be prosecuting deserters."

"Mike, I am so fucking proud of you. How in the hell did you pull this off?"

"Just started making phone calls and got to the right officer in charge. Every Marine deserter that is caught is sent to Yuma."

"I will be goddamned! I didn't even know there was a Marine base in Arizona."

"Sid, I didn't either."

"God bless your patriotism, Mike. As always you make me proud to know you." Sid's voice sounded emotional. "Mike this is the perfect cover story for your little problem with the Bar Association. The firm partners are going to love it! You know, I can hear them now— the firm is giving our best lawyer a sabbatical to serve his country in a time of need. It will be great public relations and a way to get continuances for hearings and depositions. I'll get a letter out to all your clients today. Who is going to object to a patriotic lawyer volunteering for active duty? Don't worry about losing any clients or about the partners asking questions."

"You know, Sid, I was not really a great Marine like you were, but I won't have to go through the training, just be in court prosecuting deserters. I know I can handle that." Mike Beck spoke hesitantly.

"Listen, Mike. Once we tell everyone that you volunteered for the Marines, there is no turning back. You can't quit in the middle of your six months."

"I understand. I won't quit."

"Mike, can I give you some advice as an old Marine?"

"Sure."

"Stay off the skyline. Get a place off-base. Just go to your office in the morning, do the work, and go back off-base. If you want to party, party off-base.

"Most importantly, Mike, I want you to promise me two things: First, you will not be chasing enlisted Women Marines. Believe me, the Marine Corps takes that shit seriously. And second, for God's sake, do not have an affair with another officer's wife. That is a cardinal sin—way worse than fucking a client." Sid seemed to pause for effect.

"If you cannot keep your dick in your pants for the next six months, the Marines will hang your ass. I am talking general court-martial, dismissal, maybe even prison. I will have to fire you."

"All right, Sid. I got it. I am not crazy. I won't even look at a woman on base."

Chapter 24

As Warren Leavy stepped into the office of his long-time partner, Ogden Loring, and closed the door, a jet passed over the run-down Laurel Street, San Diego office building, its thunder shaking every pane of glass. Warren and Ogden attended Stanford Law School together in the early sixties and graduated at the top of their class. At the time, many lawyers spent a year doing some kind of public-interest law before working at big firms for rich corporations. However, soon after Warren and Ogden started their year of legal aid, it became evident that they were a different breed. Neither cared about profits. Both were consumed by social injustice. They soon crossed paths and formed their own firm in 1967, Loring & Leavy, and since that time they had taken on every known social issue, including civil rights, age and sex discrimination, unfair housing, and police misconduct.

"What did you want to see me about?" Warren asked wearily after a long day at work.

Warren noticed that—as always—several cheap ashtrays littered Ogden's beat up desk, and smoke filled the room. Ogden smiled and shoved a stack of legal pads to the side of the desk. Meanwhile, Warren walked to the small window on the opposite wall and struggled to open it.

Like so many civil-rights lawyers, Ogden Loring was a real character. Today, he wore a blue denim shirt, faded blue jeans, and running shoes. He tied his long gray hair in a ponytail, and his black-framed reading glasses were perched on the end of his nose. He waited to speak until after Warren had returned to the chair in front of his desk.

"Hey, Warren; have you seen this month's *Time* Magazine?"

Ogden dug through a stack of papers, pulled out the issue of *Time*, and slid it in front of Warren. Warren quickly glanced at the cover.

"No. I hadn't seen this…"

"Well, I think there is going to be significant opposition to President Bush's plan to invade Iraq," Ogden said with authority in his voice. As he spoke, he pulled a small silver pipe and a baggie out of the bottom drawer.

"We are already getting our share of desertions cases. Do you think that's going to increase?"

Ogden ignored Warren's question. "Warren, have you heard of the National Peace Coalition?"

"Nope. But like I said, we are getting our fair share of cases, and I don't think I have the energy left to do the anti-war thing. The Vietnam War was my generation. Let the younger guys deal with Iraq."

"No! No! Warren, I am not talking about marches and rallies. The National Peace Coalition paid us good fees for defending conscientious objectors during Vietnam. Back then we didn't know how to charge. Hell, we didn't even have a billing system. When the power company shut off the lights, I called NPC and they sent us money." Ogden paused while he filled the tiny pipe and lit the end with a Bic lighter. He did not offer the pipe to Warren.

"All right, Og. I don't have a problem if you want to work with NPC."

"I am thinking of doing more than a few cases. The National Peace Coalition was organized during the Civil War and has opposed every American war since."

As Ogden spoke, Warren looked toward the window. He hated wearing clothes that smelt of marijuana but knew there was no point in objecting again. He also knew that most law firms blow up over the issue of money. He did not want to lose Ogden Loring as a partner.

"Can you guess how many members the NPC has had since the Civil War?"

"No idea," Warren answered.

"I don't know either, but it must be in the hundreds of thousands. Any idea of how many of those members died in the last one hundred years leaving money to the NPC?"

"No idea, but I am starting to get the picture."

"I am tired, Warren. I am tired of this shithole for an office. Tired of commuting two hours. Tired of driving a ten-year-old car. And tired of never having anything but bills to pay."

"Of course, Og. I don't blame you for being tired. We've paid our dues and we have fought the good fight. But I don't know if I am comfortable getting too close to one organization. You know me, Og; I only get motivated when it's a person that I am helping."

"But it's time for us to realize some decent money," Ogden pleaded.

"That is exactly the point; I'm not in it for the money. Not now, and never have been."

"Well, I know that thousands of people have left their estates to the NPC and the NPC has hundreds of millions of dollars. Hell, the interest on that money is more than we bill in a year. Bush is violating the Constitution, and there's nothing wrong in helping these kids that are refusing to report for duty with the military. And there is nothing wrong with us making a decent living."

"OK, OK, Ogden. I am not saying I am opposed to this. We're not going to turn down any person that needs help."

"That's cool, but Warren, I know the director at NPC, Roslyn Baker. Also, according to the article in *Time*, the Marines are sending all desertion cases to the air base in Yuma, Arizona. Hell, that's our backyard! It's less than a three-hour drive. There is no way east coast or San Francisco firms are going to want to travel to Yuma. Warren, I am sure we can get lots of clients in Yuma, and if we can get some clients, I am sure that I can get NPC to pay the attorney fees—good fees. You got a problem with any of that?"

"No problem, Og. Go for it."

Chapter 25

Roslyn Baker parked her green Jaguar and sundered inside the bar of Mitch's Seafood Restaurant. Tall, her silver hair done in a way to maximize both its fullness and attractiveness, she flashed startlingly blue eyes, and when she entered the bar, she turned heads. Although in her 50s, she worked out every day and remained fit and shapely. Today she wore a dark blue dress that flattered her hips and showed a glimpse of cleavage. Her makeup was perfect. As she moved across the room, she displayed a most provocative body and walking in those heels pushed it all sky-high. It was maddening for the middle-aged men sitting at the bar.

Mitch's Restaurant was a landmark in San Diego and justly enjoyed the reputation of serving some of the finest seafood in the area. Roslyn Baker had been a loyal customer since attending the University of San Diego in the sixties. She looked up and down the bar for the man she expected to meet but did not find him. She heard a familiar voice.

"Just in the neighborhood?" the proprietor Ryan Truitt asked, the wide gap between his front teeth on display through his smile.

"How are you, Mr. Truitt?"

"I am as worthless as an old politician, but I am still alive."

"I can see that your disposition hasn't improved," Roslyn answered playfully, her eyes sparkling, and her full lips glistening with lipstick. "You still serve those rotten oysters?"

"We threw some out this morning, but I can dig them out of the garbage. Just follow me. The rest of your party has already arrived. I recognized Ogden, and I hope you left-wing radicals aren't planning a riot in my little restaurant."

"Oh no, Ryan; we have bigger plans than that. We're thinking about a love-in for people over fifty. Are you interested?"

Ryan grunted and started towards a door at the end of the barroom opening on a flight of stairs. At the top of the stairs was a narrow hallway. Ryan led Roslyn to a private room. As they entered, the two men sitting at the table stood.

"How are you, Roslyn?" Ogden Loring asked with a smile and continued talking without giving Roslyn a chance to answer. "I hope you don't mind that I brought along my partner, Warren Leavy." Each of the men stood near their seats at the table.

"Please sit down, gentlemen."

"Roslyn, I don't think that you have met Warren," Ogden said, gesturing. Roslyn smiled at Warren. He looked younger than Ogden in his pin-striped, double-breasted blue suit.

"We met years ago, but I doubt that Warren remembers. It was at a peace rally in New York."

There was a knock at the door, and a waiter appeared with a beat-up tray holding two dozen oysters.

"Roslyn, if it is all right, I will get straight to the point. Loring and Leavy is now representing several military members who are opposed to the conflict in Kuwait, and we have been asked to represent many more. These service men and women have been arrested and charged with desertion. We have a great many Marine clients, all being held at the Marine Air Base in Yuma. From what we are learning, the Marine Corps is a dehumanizing institution that encourages conduct that in any other context would be regarded as criminal. These young men have deserted to preserve their humanity. Warren and I want to help, but many of the service members have no money, and we can't take on something this big without some financial support."

Ogden looked over at Warren to see if he had anything to say. "Do you see anything that the National Peace Coalition can do to help?"

"Well, of course, NPC will help the servicemen with counsel. And Ogden, you know I have the utmost admiration for your work. But I must tell you that the Board of Directors has already asked me to start funding soldiers represented by William Kunstler. I have a meeting scheduled with him in New York this Thursday."

"Look, Roslyn, Bill Kunstler has been my hero for the past thirty years. He is the reason that I became a civil rights lawyer. His defense of the Chicago Seven, his work for the American Indian Movement, Attica—just historical and fundamental changes in our society. But

William Kunstler lives and practices on the East Coast. There will be a lot of Army and Navy court-martial cases at the East Coast bases. Warren and I want to focus on the Marine Corps cases at Yuma."

"All right, Ogden. I am listening."

"We will put our background and experience in this area up against anyone's any day. You know the work we did during Vietnam. We have already handled a score of desertion cases and know what we are doing. Besides, Bill Kunstler can easily raise all the money he needs from rich donors on the East Coast—NPC should be helping the little guys like me and Warren."

"Wow, Ogden. You are passionate about this, aren't you?

"You are damn right, Roslyn. Bush wants to start a war for American profits and cheap oil. Bush is just looking for a way out of the huge deficit he created. It is wrong. Warren and I have done the research. We have a plan. Warren, tell her what you came up with."

"It is sometimes called the Nuremberg Defense. The Gulf War is illegal. Therefore, an order to participate in the war is also illegal, and under international law, specifically, the law established by the International Military Tribunal at Nuremberg, a soldier has a duty to disobey an unlawful order." Warren spoke slowly, with absolute confidence, and paused to let Roslyn digest the concept.

"Now, Roslyn, given the conservative judges on the East Coast, this would be an uphill battle, but we think there is good chance to win here in California with the Ninth Circuit judges. We want to show that the Gulf War violates the Constitution." Warren paused, looked Roslyn in the eyes, and continued.

"Article I, Section 8 of the Constitution gives Congress the sole power to declare war. As you know, Congress has not declared war against Iraq. The executive branch, President Bush, should not be able to use military force without Congressional action, and until Congress acts, an order to participate is illegal."

Warren paused again and Ogden started talking. "Think about it, Roslyn. Our defense will be to show that the War is unconstitutional. We will show Bush's connections with the big oil corporations, and that the purpose of the War is to salvage their investments in Kuwait. We'll show Bush's ties to the defense contractors that are making billions off the War. We will try and subpoena the President, and if that doesn't work, we'll subpoena the oil corporations and defense contractors. Can you imagine the media attention this will generate?"

While she listened, Roslyn flashed a beautiful smile. "Listen, guys, this is very exciting. We have a chance to stop this war before our young men and women die! I am sure that my directors will provide you all the funding you need."

Chapter 26

In the middle of the night, Captain Michael Beck, Marine Corps Reserve, wearing civilian clothes, parked the rental car and headed for the entryway to the Headquarters Building, Marine Corps Air Station, Yuma, Arizona. As he passed the parking space labeled *Commanding Officer,* he felt a nervous sickness in his stomach, like being eye-bawled by his drill instructor at officer's candidate school. He looked around, half expecting a senior officer to come out and yell at him for some military infraction that he was not aware of, like wearing wrinkled clothes, or reporting for duty at two o'clock in the morning. Of course, no one was there but as he ascended the steps, he did his best to move with military bearing. When he pulled on the entry door, he found it locked. A small sign posted to the right of the door instructed: "Ring buzzer for Officer of the Day."

Five minutes later, a skinny old Marine appeared inside wearing shower thongs and a towel wrapped around his waist secured at the top with a canvas belt. His arms, neck, and face were deeply tanned and wrinkled, but the rest of his body was pale white. As he got closer, Beck could see a wide scar running from the base of his neck to the bottom of his armpit. Smaller scars were visible on his left leg and right ankle. The old Marine put his finger in front of his lips to signal Beck to be quiet, carefully unlocked the door, and led him down the hall.

Inside, the Headquarters Building had the standard highly polished black-and-white vinyl tiles and framed posters depicting Marine Corps historical events. Desktops were clean, file cabinets locked, and papers stowed away. The windows sparkled and doorknobs and fire hose fittings were recently polished. Overall, the place seemed immaculately clean and smelled like Windex and Brasso polish. As Beck followed the Marine the soles of his civilian sneakers squeaked on the vinyl tiles. The old Marine turned into an office with an *Officer of the Day* red and gold sign over the door and sat behind the desk, bare-chested with an almost toothless grin. Captain Beck awkwardly dug through his briefcase, located his orders, and passed them across the desk.

Scanning Beck's orders, the old Marine spoke in a deep raspy voice: "The Officer of the Day is trying to get some shut-eye, so we best be quiet. Welcome aboard, Sir. I am the Assistant Officer of the Day, Gunnery Sergeant Files."

The Gunny then slid the Officer of the Day logbook to his left and pulled a government-issued black ink pen out of the center drawer. The Gunny squinted at the orders for a long time. He grinned again, leaned across the desk, and whispered. "I will need to see your modifications, Captain."

"I don't have any, Gunny."

Gunny Files read the orders a second time, turned, and looked up at the wall calendar behind the desk, then stared back at the orders. He stopped grinning.

"Something is screwed up, Captain. According to these orders, you were supposed to have reported two days ago." Captain Beck swallowed and tried to look Gunny Files in the eye when he answered.

"I know, Gunny. I am reporting late. What do I have to do?" It sounded ludicrous even to his own ears.

Gunny Files stood up, started out of the office, and motioned for Beck to follow him up the stairwell to an office on the second deck. He closed the door and gazed at the ceiling for a minute before he spoke.

"Jesus Christ, Captain! Unauthorized absence is a serious offense in the Marine Corps! This is going to be a lot more than an ass chewing. You're likely to get yourself court-martialed over this. At least, it will ruin your career."

The Gunny paused and tried to compose himself. "Did you call someone at your unit to let them know you would be late in reporting?"

Beck stumbled over to one of the metal chairs in front of the desk and sat down. He tried to speak, but his voice seemed gone, so he just shook his head from side to side. He realized that at best this would end his career as a lawyer in Chicago, and at worst, he might go to military prison. The Gunny sat next to him and stared at the ceiling again. After a long time, the Gunny walked to the other side of the desk and removed a phone book from the right-side drawer. He found the number and called someone on the phone.

"Gunner, this is Gunnery Sergeant Files. I have the Assistant Officer of the Day duty, and we have a situation here regarding a Captain, Michael Beck." A pause followed and the Gunny looked at Beck's orders again.

"Well, Sir, Captain Beck is reporting two days late. I don't know what to do here."

Another pause. Gunny Files hung up the phone. "Gunner Carson says to stay in the office with the door shut until he gets here. If anyone comes around, act like you're working on something important. Don't say nothing except that you are waiting for Gunner Carson, the Provost Marshal."

In a few minutes, Gunny Files returned carrying two cups of coffee and dressed in his Charlie uniform: green wool pants, khaki shirt, and black dress shoes. He wore enough cheap cologne for a platoon.

"I am going to wait downstairs for the Gunner. If I were you, Captain, I would drink that coffee, and work on your story."

Beck stared out the office window at the Headquarters parking lot and saw a motorcycle pull in and park next to the entrance. He recognized the motorcycle as a 1991 Harley Davidson Softail Custom, the same bike he considered buying in Chicago before leaving for Yuma. The rider dismounted, lit a cigarette, and blew smoke at the sky. When he finished the cigarette, he carefully spread the remaining ashes and tobacco, then put the filter inside his jacket pocket in the manner required at boot camp. Soon, Beck heard footsteps coming up the stairwell and down the hallway, and when the office door opened, he stood at attention. He heard a deep voice give the command.

"Take it easy, Captain. I am Chief Warrant Officer Charlie Carson, the Provost Marshal."

The first thing that hit Captain Beck when Gunner Carson entered the room was his ferocious appearance: short, bald, muscular, and mean. He wore a sleeveless T-shirt that exposed a mass of tattoos, blue jeans, and motorcycle boots. He sat down with the same smooth economy of movement he had parked his Harley. Colorless eyes fixed a disconcerting stare on Beck, then Carson extended his hand. Beck shook hands and sat back in the chair, stared straight ahead, and tried to control the nervous tremor in his right leg.

Carson picked up Beck's orders package and service record book off the desk, leaned back in the swivel chair, put his boots on the desk corner, and started reading. Beck continued to study his appearance. He had the face of a hardened man, a man who had fought many fights. Beck smelled the alcohol on his breath.

"All right, Captain; let's hear it." Carson folded his arms and assumed a listening posture. Beck relaxed a bit. He expected Carson to first advise him of his Article 31 Right to remain silent, and since this was not mentioned, maybe Gunner Carson would help him get out of this mess.

"My flight on Friday morning got canceled, so I waited in a cocktail lounge at O'Hare Airport. I sat in the back of the lounge waiting for my flight when a lady came in and sat up front. She was followed by a large man who appeared to be drunk. He started giving her a hard time. I couldn't hear what he said, but I could tell that the woman asked him to leave her alone. I didn't do anything. I guess I was thinking that one of the men closer to her would help, but they did not.

"The next thing I saw was the drunk shove the lady's shoulder and walk out. She started to cry. I never felt like a bigger coward in my life. I just kept thinking, *what if my mother saw me sit here while a woman got assaulted by a drunk?* I told myself that I would never let that happen again. That's when the drunk came back."

Carson's face remained expressionless, but Gunny Files' eyes were bright, and he started grinning ear to ear. "I walked up and tried to talk to him, but he took a swing at me. The only way I can explain what I did next is to tell you that he was one big son-of-a-bitch. He must have been six-foot-three and three hundred pounds. No way could I hurt this guy with my fists, so I hit him in the face with a chair. He didn't expect it, went flying out the front of the bar, fell backward, and hit his head on the floor. The woman got up and ran out the door. Most of the people in the bar did the same thing. The drunk just lay knocked out on the floor in the middle of the terminal. I heard the bartender calling for the police. When airport security arrived, they told me to just stay seated at my table. The Chicago police arrived, put me in handcuffs, and arrested me. I tried to explain what happened, but they were not interested in listening, just in getting me out of the airport."

"What about the bartender? Didn't he confirm your story with the police?" Carson asked.

"I'm not sure what he told them. They locked me in a vacant room before they even asked him anything. I sat in there for a couple of hours, and they brought in a black man who looked like he had too much to drink. An hour later, two cops showed up, put us in their car and drove us downtown to the Cook County Jail. They did not allow phone calls, and I sat in a holding cell on Saturday and Sunday. I got lucky on Monday."

Gunner Carson raised his hand for Captain Beck to stop talking and looked at Gunny Files. He ran his hands over his smooth skull.

"Gunny, will you bring the logbook up here?'

Files headed out the door, and Beck continued. "They bussed us to the courthouse and sat us inside one of the court rooms. After a while the district attorney called my name and asked me if I was traveling to report for duty. I showed him my identification card and explained what happened, and when they called my case, the district attorney asked the judge to dismiss the charges. I caught a cab and got on the next flight."

"That all sounds pretty good, Captain, but why didn't you check in with your unit when you got back to the airport?"

"I don't know. I was already a day late, and I thought it would be better to just wait and explain the situation in person."

Files handed the logbook to Carson, who placed it on the desk, flipped through the pages, and studied the entries made over the last two days. He then handed the logbook to Beck.

"All right. Captain Beck. You tear out the last five pages, then copy everything back using the same handwriting. Add this statement at

2300 two days ago: "Captain Michael J. Beck reported for duty with the Law Center."

Carson took a note pad from the desk and started signing the name "W. V. Findlay" while staring at the logbook. After practicing the signature several times, he took Captain Beck's orders, filled out the endorsement showing that Beck had reported two days earlier, and signed "W. V. Findlay."

"I will take your orders over to the Gunny Lopez at the Law Center in the morning, and tell her I had them, and forgot to turn them in. I've forged the officer of the day's signature on your orders, and with the phony logbook entry, only the three of us should ever know what happened."

Gunner Carson starred seriously at Gunnery Sergeant Files.

"Are you on board with all of this Gunny?"

"Hell yes, Sir. I am glad the captain kicked that son-of-a-bitch's ass. That was the right thing to do."

"This will be our little secret. And I do mean a close hold. We could all get into some serious trouble, probably a court-martial. Do not ever mention this night to anyone for any reason. Check?"

Both Captain Beck and Gunny Files answered, "Check, Sir."

Afterward, Beck drove his car slowly to the Bachelor's Officer Quarters to check in, being careful to stay within the 20 miles-per-hour speed limit.

There is no way this is going to work. What will the Marines do to me? Sid said if I get sent back to Chicago, all hell is going to break loose.

Chapter 27

The next day, expecting the worse, Captain Michael Beck would not be disappointed.

In Chicago, Mike Beck felt completely self-confident as a lawyer, always in charge, and recognized as one of the best trial lawyers in the firm. But at MCAS, Yuma, he woke feeling out of his element. He tried to convince himself he would be fine but that old feeling of trying to stay off the skyline, not look stupid, not get your ass chewed, had returned. *This is nuts, being back in uniform. My God, I have already screwed up by reporting two days late. If Gunner Carson hadn't saved my ass, I would be facing a court-martial, headed back to Chicago, and losing my job at the firm.*

These things dominated Beck's thoughts as he dragged open the heavy doors, entered the Fourth Marine Division (Rear) Headquarters Building, and walked down the hallway.

Captain Beck's heels tapped loudly on the polished floor as he turned inside the doorway marked *Lieutenant Colonel Bumbaugh, Staff Judge Advocate*. The reception area looked as spotless and organized as the rest of the Headquarters Building. A well-dressed and attractive middle-aged woman sat behind a tidy desk and smiled professionally when he walked inside. He could see through the open doorway to a heavy-set, gray-haired man reading from a folder spread out on a mountain of paper covering the desk.

"Good morning. I am Captain Beck, and I have a ten o'clock appointment with Lieutenant Colonel Bumbaugh."

The secretary glanced at her calendar. "Oh Yes. Lieutenant Colonel Bumbaugh is expecting you."

The secretary stood up, walked inside Bumbaugh's office, and closed the door. In a moment she returned with a smile. "Please have a seat, Captain. The Staff Judge Advocate will see you shortly."

Beck sat in the leather chair across from the secretary's desk and watched her carefully insert a clean sheet of typing paper and four carbon sheets into the manual typewriter. She typed slowly, but with perfect posture as if she were a ballet dancer. Beck prepared for the worse by carefully rehearsing in his mind his best arguments for why he should be assigned to prosecute deserters. *Should I mention that my boss, Sidney Johnson, is a retired Marine Colonel? Should I bad-mouth deserters the way Sid did?*

Thirty minutes later the secretary finished typing and carried the sheet of paper to Bumbaugh's office. When she returned, she instructed Beck that he could enter the Staff Judge Advocate's office. With his stomach in his throat, Beck entered the open door.

The office seemed large and impressive, with a small conference area, leather furniture, and oak bookcases. LtCol. Bumbaugh sat behind a huge wooden desk framed by the United States and Marine Corps flags. He looked old, and seriously overweight for a Marine, wore horn-rimmed spectacles, and his hair looked a little too long to meet regulation. On his desk sat a large ornately carved wooden nameplate with a lieutenant colonel's rank insignia over red felt on one side and a silver Marine Corps officer's emblem on the other. A painting of Revolutionary War Marines shooting from the masts of a sailing ship hung directly behind him.

Captain Beck stood at attention but did not salute. Like naval officers, Marines do not salute unless under arms or "covered" with a uniform cap. He mentally debated whether he should remain quiet or yell "Captain Beck reporting as ordered!" Before he could decide, Bumbaugh looked up with a confused expression.

"Have a seat, Captain. What can I do for you?"

"Sir. I am Captain Beck. I am the reservist from Chicago. We spoke on the phone a couple of weeks ago. I received my orders from Headquarters, and I am reporting for duty."

Bumbaugh turned in his swivel chair and continued to look at Beck with a blank expression. For a couple of minutes he sorted through the foot-high stack of papers on the credenza. He slumped back in his chair as if overwhelmed by the pressure of his office.

"Here it is. Ah…let me see here, Captain Beck. Here you are."

LtCol. Bumbaugh seemed pleased that he could find the name and smiled for the first time. Captain Beck decided that being the Staff Judge Advocate had to be a dull job.

"Active duty 1980 to 1984. Been in the IRR since. No reserve duty and no military continuing legal education?"

"That is correct, Sir."

The Lieutenant Colonel rubbed his chin, stared for a moment outside the window, and then returned to reading the papers he had retrieved from the credenza.

"Recommended by Major Way. Number one in your class at Naval Justice School. Usual four-year tour at Camp Lejeune, defense counsel, and trial counsel. What is your preference, Captain? Do you want to be assigned to prosecution, defense, or legal assistance?"

"Sir, as we discussed over the phone, my very strong preference is to be assigned as trial counsel to prosecute deserters. In fact, the managing partner of my firm is a retired Marine Colonel, and he granted me a sabbatical with the understanding that I would be prosecuting deserters. In his view, those cowards voluntarily joined the Marines, accepted the benefits, but now refuse to report for duty when they are needed. To preserve discipline, it is important that all the deserters receive severe sentences. In fact, it was my understanding from our telephone conversation that I was being mobilized specifically to be a trial counsel. Most importantly, I am qualified to be a prosecutor. I have over ten years of jury trial experience, and that is the reason I volunteered for active duty."

Bumbaugh continued staring out the window for a moment then turned and looked at Beck with that blank stare, as if not sure about something.

"Well, your timing is not good. Yesterday, I met with the Chief Trial Counsel, Major Hendrix, and assigned all the reservists she thinks she needs for the prosecution. Sorry, no more boat spaces, Captain." Bumbaugh grinned as if that were somehow funny.

"But my Legal Assistance Officer is desperate for help with all the wills and powers of attorneys needed for the deploying Marines. Seems to me, being a civilian attorney, you have the experience to handle that assignment. Captain Beck, I am assigning you to legal assistance."

Bumbaugh stood up and extended his right hand. Beck, too stunned, too scared, and too angry to speak, limply shook hands.

"Good luck to you, Captain. Let me know if I can ever do anything else for you."

ℭ୫ଌ

As he drove toward the Legal Assistance Office, Captain Beck tried to understand what had happened and how things had gone so wrong so fast—reporting two days late, and now this hated assignment to legal assistance. *Damn Beck! How could you fuck up your life this bad? First, sex with your client's general counsel, and she was not even good looking. A bar complaint. Now you have put yourself back in the Marine Corps. The next six months are going to suck, nothing is more boring than preparing wills and powers of attorney.*

Beck soon reached the office located inside a Quonset hut which he recognized as the type of barracks shown on the television show "Gomer Pyle." The Quonset hut used by the Legal Assistance Office had been bomb-proofed by the construction of a five-foot block wall around each side with a three-foot interval filled with sand. Thankfully, Captain Beck soon learned that the sand provided good insulation from the desert heat.

Tall and skinny, the Officer in Charge of the Legal Assistance Center, Major Lucas Herdy, looked frail and comically homely. He wore the black-rimmed glasses issued at boot camp with thick lenses that made his eyes look small like in the World War II propaganda depictions of the Japanese. His inept appearance shocked Beck, and later he learned that most of the officers at Yuma referred to Major Herdy as Major "Nerdy."

Nevertheless, in the months ahead, Captain Beck found Major Herdy personable and pleasant. He liked to share his encyclopedic knowledge of the Marine Corps' glorious history. He obeyed all the rules, kept his uniform pristine, and exhibited a naïve enthusiasm for running the legal assistance office.

"Welcome Aboard, Captain!" Major Herdy moved around the desk and extended his hand. "I am happy to have you here. I really need your help."

Next, Major Herdy retreated behind his desk, opened the upper right-hand drawer, and took from it a large ashtray with a box of matches in its center. He placed the ashtray on the right side of his desk, then went back into the drawer, and came out with a package of unfiltered Camel cigarettes. He lit the cigarette with one of the wooden matches and enjoyed a long drag. The smoke settled into a fog not far from their heads.

"Smoke?"

"No, thank you."

After a tour of the office and introductions, Major Herdy enthusiastically reviewed the office's most recent monthly report, detailing the services provided.

"You can see, Captain, we are in a legal assistance crisis!" Herdy's loud voice made it sound like the two Marines were under attack.

"Last month we had one-hundred-sixty office visits, eighty-nine telephone calls, seventy-seven wills, sixty powers of attorney, fourteen divorce consultations, and nine landlord-tenant disputes." Major Herdy took another drag on his Camel and let the smoke trail out his nostrils.

"With all the reservists being mobilized, I just don't know how we are going to meet the demand for wills and powers of attorney!" Herdy took one more long drag on his smoke and then crushed it out in the ashtray.

"Could we extend the office working hours?" Captain Beck asked the obvious question.

"Since we have a civilian employee, we can't do that. We must come up with a way to produce more wills and powers of attorney in the same amount of time."

Major Herdy went on to explain to Captain Beck that because Beck was not admitted to the Arizona Bar, he could not appear in court, could not file court pleadings, could not prepare legal documents, and could not give advice on Arizona law. Basically, Captain

Beck could do less legal work than anyone of his secretaries back in Chicago.

Captain Beck's office was too small to swing a cat in it, just enough room for the metal desk, two client chairs, filing cabinet, and bookshelf. While settling into his office Beck noticed a pimpled-faced private standing in the doorway. The private placed an intake form and business card on Beck's desk. "Sir, we have a last-minute walk-in that Major Herdy said you could handle. A pilot reporting in from Naval Air Station, Meridian, Mississippi says his lease got canceled. He wants to know if there is anything, he can do about it."

Captain Beck nodded at the private as if his statement confirmed something, then glanced at the nearly blank intake form that only stated, "I got screwed by my landlord." The attached business card included a photograph of a McDonald-Douglas AV-8B Harrier Jet with the name "Lieutenant Colonel Wayne Turner, U.S.M.C." in the center. Underneath the name, the card said, "THE MAN MOSCOW FEARS MOST."

Beck quickly walked to the reception area to meet Turner. A blond-haired and darkly tanned Marine pilot rushed toward him with a big grin and his hand extended. He wore a grey-green flight suit with the pockets and leg vents unzipped. *Lieutenant Colonel Wayne Turner* was printed in gold letters on a brown leather rectangle over a slanted zipper-closed pocket. He smelled of body odor, hydraulic fluid, and jet fuel.

"Thanks for seeing me, Captain, I am in a hurt-locker." Turner turned to his right. "This is my wife, Nicole."

The voluptuous woman smiled as their eyes met, and Beck attempted to return her smile without looking excited and motioned for the new clients to follow him down the hallway. At the doorway, he paused to let them enter first. Nicole Turner passed close, replacing Turner's stench with the smell of perfume. When she eased herself into one of the chairs, she casually opened the top button of her cotton dress and fanned the newly exposed skin.

Turner explained his landlord problem in excessive detail, and Capt. Beck concentrated on keeping his eyes off his gorgeous wife.

Beck remained determined to honor his promise to his senior partner and not even look at a woman on base.

Chapter 28

"Good morning. I am Lieutenant Bob Ward, the Battalion Communications Officer, and I will be giving this morning's brief on the Rules of Engagement for Operations in Southwest Asia."

A company of Marines endured the wet-dog smell of the large tent used as a classroom at Camp Gray. The camp sat on a ridge south of Jubayl, Saudi Arabia. Earthen berms, constructed by the Seabees, surrounded the camp, and reams of barbed wire and rolls of concertina reached down the hill on all sides. Inside the compound, a dozen 155mm artillery pieces had been emplaced on the right side of the road inside circular parapets. A cluster of 81mm mortar pits were located on the left side, and in the center, stood a sand-bagged command operations bunker. For the Marines training here, the camp seemed nothing more than a depressing environment of tents, Port-A-Johns, and diesel generators.

Lieutenant Colonel Evert Easterday sat in the back row of the tent trying to stay awake listening to Ward give the lecture that Easterday had heard numerous times.

When a group of Marines entered the tent, a wave of dirt blew underneath the tent flap and settled like snow over Easterday's uniform. At 0800 the temperature had reached 115 degrees, and the walk from his billeting tent to the classroom soaked Easterday's uniform with sweat and covered his boots in fine white dust. Ward started with a review of the basic concepts of the rules of engagement.

"Self Defense. Service members have the inherent authority and obligation to use all necessary means and to take all appropriate action in self-defense of themselves and their units. What this means: Use necessary and proportional force in self-defense when threatened or attacked."

Ward continued the lecture he had given many times. "Positive identification is required prior to engagement. PID is a reasonable certainty that the object of attack is a legitimate military target. This means you must comply with the Law of Armed Conflict concerning discrimination of targets. PID is a determination based on reasonable military judgment."

"Proportional force. Force employed must be proportional. You may use necessary force, including deadly force to protect yourself, unit, or coalition forces."

No matter how hard he tried, Easterday could not concentrate on the lecture. He had arrived the previous day with the Fourth Tank Battalion and felt like he had cobwebs in his brain. The Battalion had ridden buses from Marine Corps Base Twentynine Palms, California to Norton Air Force Base, then boarded a direct flight on a Boeing 747 to Riyadh, Saudi Arabia. But this morning, as the Battalion's Commanding Officer, he was deeply worried.

Until two months ago, Fourth Tank Battalion fielded 58 worn-out M60 Patton Main Battle Tanks, initially produced in 1960, and mounting the 105mm rifled main gun. Over the years, the active-duty Marines received the upgraded M60A1/A3 tanks with better armor protection, shock absorbers, and a stabilization system for the main gun. But as a reserve unit, Fourth Tanks never received the new tanks and for many years had not been considered "combat ready."

No one at Fourth Tanks ever expected to be called up for active duty. But in September the unthinkable happened. The Battalion received mobilization orders and the word that they would transition to the new M1A1 Abrams Main Battle Tank.

At their U.S. training base, Marine Corps Base Twentynine Palms, the M1A1 Abrams tank proved to be a tanker's dream. The M1A1 was heavily armed with a 120mm smoothbore cannon. It used a powerful gas turbine engine, was protected by sophisticated composite armor, and included separate ammunition storage for crew safety.

Most importantly for Easterday, the radios in the M1A1 Abrams worked. But Easterday constantly worried about the radios in the old Amphibious Tractors, commonly called "Amtracs," which were used to transport the battle staff. The radios were working now, but there had been problems back at Twentynine Palms.

The Tank Battalion's Two Command Groups consisted of the Commanding Officer/Executive Officer, Air Officers, Fire Direction

Officers, Intelligence Officers, Operations Officers, and their support staff of radio operators. Each Command Group traveled in one of the AAVC-7A1 Amtracs, and the officers depended upon the radios mounted in the Amtracs to communicate with the tanks and other units. If the Amtrac radios went down, the Battalion lost everything: close air support, artillery, and command and control of the M1A1 Abrams tanks.

As a Marine officer, LtCol. Easterday would do whatever was humanly possible to reduce the Marine losses by the only means that has ever looked like it worked—training and more training. He needed to train his Marines how to fix the Amtrac radios, but the Battalion's capable Communications Chief, Sergeant Nathan Jones, failed to report for mobilization. Sergeant Jones was still UA.

The other Marines in Fourth Tanks had done their best, but without Sergeant Nathan Jones's help, Easterday worried about the potential disaster for his unit and the loss of many Marine lives.

Chapter 29

On November 10, 1775, the Second Continental Congress passed a resolution that two battalions of Marines be raised for service as landing forces with the fleet. While the Continental sailors were busy manning the ships, the Marines had no work, except to keep their uniforms immaculate, perfecting their marksmanship, practicing close-order drill, and maintaining excellent physical condition. Today, the Marine Corps' size, and mission, have grown, but the old skills and Naval traditions continue.

One tradition is "Request Mast." If a Sailor or Marine had a grievance not addressed by his immediate superior, he could take the matter to the captain of the ship. All hands were brought on deck before the mainsail mast. The Sailor or Marine would march forward at attention, and when told to speak, stated the grievance. The captain then addressed the grievance as he deemed appropriate.

At precisely 0900, Colonel Cahill heard three loud knocks on his door. He responded, and Chief Warrant Officer Charlie Carson marched to a point exactly centered and three feet in front of Col. Cahill's desk. "Gunner Carson reporting for Request Mast."

"At ease, Gunner. Have a seat." Carson sat at one of the chairs in front of Cahill's desk.

"I have read your request mast. What else should I know about this?"

Gunner Carson spoke slowly and evenly with a great deal of emotion in his voice. "Sir, I have called my monitor. There is a need in Saudi Arabia for officers to command companies to guard our forward operating bases and run convoys. As a Chief Warrant Officer, I am an expert in these matters. True, I am a little senior for a combat assignment, but I am still in excellent physical condition, and I know I could do the job better than some inexperienced officer coming out of the Basic School. I have never requested mast and never insisted on anything from the Corps during my entire career. But I am a combat Marine, and this is my last chance to serve in combat. Respectfully, I do not want to be in the rear, I want to be up front in the fight. I feel like Saudi Arabia is the place I must end my career."

Cahill paused and looked out the office window. He remembered his own request for transfer and his mistreatment by General Reynolds. He handed Gunner Carson a four-page document.

"Gunner, here is a copy of my favorable endorsement of your request for transfer. I researched your career and believe that you deserve this assignment. Indeed, in preparing the endorsement I was amazed at your exemplary service record. I received the Medal of Honor for things I did on a single day. Your heroism in Vietnam extended over months and years. America and the Marine Corps owe you a great debt.

"The rest of your career is something I envy. You excelled at every assignment, every billet—marksmanship instructor, weapons expert, recruiter, drill instructor, security-force member, and military policeman.

"You finished at the top of your class in every school, and I have never seen a Marine with the outstanding fitness reports you earned over the years.

"Because of your record, in addition to my favorable endorsement, I called the Chief of Staff at Fourth Division and asked that he do anything he can to facilitate your transfer. Having said all of that, you should know that the odds of Headquarters approving your transfer are slim. Personally, I submitted my own request for transfer to a combat unit, and it was denied by Headquarters, probably because of my seniority. The only good news I have for you is that two-thirds of the Marine Corps is now in Saudi Arabia. Maybe at some point, they will need old dogs like us."

The two men sat staring at one another. "Thank you, Sir. That's all I can ask for from my Commanding Officer. If Headquarters will not let me go, then I promise you that I will do my very best here. May I be dismissed?"

"Gunner Carson, as one old veteran to another, are you doing all right these days?"

"I think so, Sir."

"Since I arrived here, I have heard rumors—motorcycle riding with enlisted, hanging out in biker bars, and excessive drinking at the Officers' Club. I have not seen any evidence of these things, and I am not going to act on scuttlebutt.

"But nobody knows better than me that past accomplishments can only carry a Marine so far. There is a point in time when the paper pushers at Headquarters prefer that an old Marine just retire. The Marine Corps will not ignore misconduct even from highly decorated Chief Warrant Officers. If you are losing it, and I am not saying that you are, better to ask for help or take your retirement than to see your outstanding career end in disgrace."

Cahill paused to gauge Carson's reaction and noticed that there was no anger or disagreement in Carson's demeanor.

"Again, I only offer these suggestions. There are motorcycle clubs at Pendleton and Lejeune with enlisted, senior staff non-commissioned officers, and even a few commissioned officers as members. They ride but also raise money for charity, have poker runs and get their picture in the base paper. No one complains about the officer's participation. Maybe you should start a club here, get some mufflers for your Harley and stop riding on base.

"The Marine Corps position on alcohol has changed. I would not have more than one drink at the O'Club. Do not go to the same bar every night in town. And, of course, if you get a DUI your career is over with. So be very careful when and where you drink."

"Again, Gunner, if the drinking is getting out of control, we can get you some help."

"Aye, aye, Sir. Thank you for the sound advice, and I assure you it will be followed."

Chapter 30

After numerous phone calls and jurisdictional debates, NCIS Agent Norval Palmer got assigned as the "chaser" and given the task of transporting Sergeant Nathan Jones from Southern Illinois to Marine Corps Air Station, Yuma, Arizona.

He booked two coach tickets on America West Airlines from St. Louis to Yuma, one way for Nathan and a round trip for himself. After arriving in St. Louis, he drove to the Jackson County Jail in Murphysboro, Illinois.

The deputy in charge of the small jail seemed to have lots of time to spare. He poured two cups of coffee and chatted up Palmer—asking why Jones deserted from the Marines. He also insisted on telling Palmer a long story about his enlisting in the Marine Corps 20 years earlier, going through boot camp at San Diego, and being sent home because of a hole in his eardrum.

"What's this guy got—pre-traumatic stress disorder—he's afraid to fight?" The deputy busted out laughing at his own joke.

"I don't think he's a coward. His religious beliefs changed after joining the Marines. I don't approve of his participation in the peace rally, but he may be a legitimate conscientious objector." Palmer responded.

After enduring the deputy for half an hour, Palmer used the excuse that he needed to leave to catch his flight, and the Deputy brought Nathan out. Jones looked exhausted, depressed, and traumatized. His hair had been cut short, and he still wore the Walmart suit with his black Marine boots. Agent Palmer did not bother with handcuffs.

The drive back to Lambert International Airport took two-and-a-half hours. Palmer shared some of the nice things people had to say about Nathan during his interviews. Norval figured it would be a long time before Nathan could obtain a drink, and after boarding the plane, let him order three airline bottles of Woodford Reserve

Whisky. He also gave him a pen and paper to write a letter to his grandmother which he promised to mail on their arrival in Yuma.

After landing in Yuma, Norval drove Nathan—still wearing the Walmart suit—to the brig. Once locked inside his cell, Sergeant Nathan Jones felt defeated. He could not stop agonizing over what he had done, and the decisions he had made in Southern Illinois.

He thought about Dr. Brown and the New Unity in Christ Church. The congregation looked like clones: healthy, good-looking, well-dressed, and all white. He recalled the way they looked at him and Judy, with the look that black men often see: fear that can quickly turn into hate. Jesus welcomed the masses, the poor, the sick. Dr. Brown only wanted rich white people to donate money. The Mexico orphanage was just a sales gimmick to raise money, and Dr. Brown nothing but a false profit.

Nathan remembered his home, his grandmother, and his brother. He also thought a lot about Judy Novotney and the motel room. For some reason, he did not expect to see Judy Novotney again. A beautiful woman, a good Christian, and honestly opposed to war, but not the kind of woman to sit around waiting for Nathan to get out of federal prison.

Nathan sat on the side of his bed. Sleep would elude him, he knew, but he had to try nonetheless.

God has placed me in this prison to teach me a lesson.

Chapter 31

Lieutenant Colonel Bumbaugh, Major Steve Way, Major Lucas Herdy, and Major Cindy Hendrix sat at the conference table inside the Staff Judge Advocate's office for their weekly staff meeting.

"Respectfully, Lieutenant Colonel Bumbaugh, this is not right! You said it was my choice to move to defense or stay in prosecution. I agreed to become your Chief Defense Counsel only because you said you were going to beef up the defense with additional reserve lawyers. I have not seen one new lawyer." Major Hendrix turned, stared at Major Way, and continued.

"While Major Way averages ten cases per attorney, my defense counsel handle over thirty cases per attorney. I need more lawyers!"

Hendrix glared across the conference table at both Way and her boss, LtCol. Bumbaugh. Bumbaugh nervously looked over to Way to answer and Way tried to speak calmly. "Cindy, we have Marine Corps Headquarters looking over our shoulders. Since most of your clients are now hiring civilian counsel, General Reynolds does not think they should even have a military lawyer. We know that's bunk, but we get push back every time we divert a lawyer to defense."

"Look, Steve, you know that some defendants have civilian counsel, but some do not. You know General Reynolds is wrong, and you can't justify this because a lot of Marines are now represented by the San Diego attorneys. Also, short-staffing the defense shop is pushing more Marines to civilian counsel. Think about it, if you were facing a court-martial, and knew that your military defense counsel was handling thirty cases, wouldn't you want civilian counsel? That is why they are all signing up with Loring and Leavy."

"Cindy, we can find more reserve lawyers for the defense, but it's going to take some time."

Major Hendrix paused before answering, seeming to choose her words with great care.

"Look, Major Way, most states follow the rule that assigning a public defender more than twenty cases is *per se* ineffective assistance of counsel. I honestly believe that thirty clients per defense counsel is an obvious issue for appeal. To avoid having this issue raised on appeal, you need to assign more lawyers to the defense right now."

Bumbaugh hated conflict and just looked at Maj. Way who this time said nothing.

"Major Way, can you send one of your prosecutors over to defense?" Bumbaugh asked.

"Yes, Sir. I could spare Lieutenant Dean." Major Way answered, his voice cracking.

Major Hendrix angrily shouted. "Lieutenant Dean! Lieutenant Dean! Oh, come on Way, he is a nice guy and all, but he's hopeless in the courtroom. He's ineffective assistance of counsel waiting to happen!"

The four attorneys just sat and stared at each other, and Major Hendrix looked angry. Finally, she spoke. "Look, as a civilian, Lieutenant Dean is a probate lawyer, and he is the perfect choice to assist Major Herdy with wills. Send Dean to legal assistance, and give me Captain Beck."

Again, the four judge advocates paused to think. Bumbaugh spoke first. "I seem to remember that Captain Beck wants to be in the courtroom. What do you think, Lucas?"

"Sir, I just completed training Beck on all our legal assistance forms. It will take me another two weeks to train Lieutenant Dean. I need Beck, at least until I can get Dean up to speed."

Bumbaugh looked out the window again, as if he could ignore the problem. Steve Way dreaded the prospect of litigating against Mike Beck, but out of friendship with Mike, he did not want to block Mike's return to the courtroom.

Way made a proposal. "Sir, I have a solution. I will immediately send Lieutenant Dean to legal assistance. Major Herdy, until you get Dean trained, you keep Captain Beck in the mornings. Cindy, you can have Beck in the afternoons. As soon as Dean gets up to speed in a couple of weeks, Cindy gets Beck full time. Does that work, Cindy?"

"I guess it will have to work for now. But I am going to need Captain Beck full time as soon as possible, and additional reserve defense counsel as soon as we can mobilize them."

"Good. That's resolved."

Lieutenant Colonel Bumbaugh said nothing, stood and hurried out of the conference room.

Chapter 32

After a routine morning at the legal assistance office, Capt. Beck sat at his desk proofreading the wills prepared for the Marines he had seen yesterday. Suddenly, Gunner Carson barged into his office and yelled in a voice just off the drill field.

"Let's go, Beck! I am taking you to lunch. My treat."

As the two rushed out the back door of the legal assistance office, Beck saw a new Corvette parked to the side of the building. Painted gleaming red, it promised a fast ride. Carson went around to the driver's side and carefully crawled into the cramped quarters of the driver's seat. Beck stood in awe as Carson's wide soldiers, thick chest, and massive arms squeezed inside the Corvette.

Captain Beck hurried to the passenger's side and climbed inside. Carson raced the engine, shoved the gear shift in first, and gave Beck a wicked smile before pulling out of the legal assistance parking lot. He then drove down the flight line and through the enlisted housing area, cut across the dispensary parking lot, pulled into the back lot of the Officer's Club, and parked at the gate next to the swimming pool. He passed through the gate before Beck could get out of the car.

Inside the Officer's Club, Carson walked straight past the dining room into the bar room where a dozen pilots stood at the bar drinking beer and another dozen sat at the tables eating lunch. Carson proceeded to the back and sat at a table almost out of sight next to the kitchen. Shortly, an oriental waitress appeared with a tumbler filled with ice and a clear liquid that Beck guessed was gin or vodka.

"What'll you have to drink, Beck?"

"I'll just have water." Beck feebly replied.

"Captain, every officer is allowed one drink at lunch. Sure, you won't have one with me?"

"OK, I will have a Coors Light."

The waitress soon returned from the bar and Carson waived his hand over his drink motioning that today he would not have another.

"So, Captain Beck, I got good news for you. You are headed out of legal assistance and back into the courtroom."

"Sir, I really appreciate what you did for me the night I reported late. I know that you are risking your career to protect me."

The comment irritated Carson. "Look, Beck, I told you to never mention that night!" Carson's voice chilled into an ultimatum. "You need to understand something. The Staff Judge Advocate is Colonel Bumbaugh. Everyone calls him 'bum-scoop' because he gets everything wrong. He is obviously senile and wakes up in a new world every day. I am the acting Provost Marshal, and I take care of anything legal at Fourth Division. You told me you wanted to be in the courtroom, so I took care of it."

"I haven't heard about this," Beck responded with visible puzzlement, paused, and continued. "I don't know if I can leave Major Heady without help."

Gunner Carson's already sour face twisted into a frown, his anger growing rapidly. "Look, Captain, I don't have time for this pussy-ass shit. You let Major Nerdy worry about himself. Maybe instead of spending two days a week on his statistical reports, Nerdy should start helping some Marines with their legal problems. Besides, I had to call in a lot of favors to get you out of legal assistance. That's what you said you wanted. Remember?"

"I appreciate everything you have done for me," Beck answered apologetically.

Carson gulped down the rest of his drink. When he looked back at Beck, he had a weird grin on his face. His anger had gone as suddenly as it had arrived.

"Look, Mike, Major Hendrix will take care of you. She's a good officer. You do whatever Cindy says. Listen and learn."

"OK. That sounds good." Beck agreed.

"What do you want for lunch? I am buying."

Chapter 33

At 1430, Major Cindy Hendrix returned to her office from the weekly docket meeting, juggled a hot cup of coffee with one hand, and opened the office door with the other. She took a seat behind her desk and reviewed her calendar: "1500 Captain Michael Beck, Reservist, Check-In."

She was pleased that Bumbaugh decided to immediately send Beck over to the defense, even for half a day, but wondered why Bumbaugh activated a Chicago lawyer who had not worn the uniform in seven years. She knew that a Marine who failed to participate in the reserve for six years was supposed to be kicked out. Beck's Officer Qualification Record or OQR reported that Beck had done nothing since his release from active duty, no reserve time, no continuing education courses, no retirement points, absolutely nothing—for over seven years.

At 1445, Capt. Beck knocked on Maj. Hendrix's door in the manner of a civilian, not loud, and not the three knocks taught in boot camp, and ambled in without any pretense of reporting to a senior officer. Hendrix occupied a room that must have been a laboratory in the old hospital. It seemed as large as four normal offices, with ample windows, and the walls were covered in blue and white tile. A large bookshelf on the interior wall held law books. Four chairs surrounded a small conference table.

Over the past weeks, Beck had kept his promise to his law firm manager, Sidney Johnson, and did nothing but toil away at the legal assistance office. He lived in an off-base apartment, had never been to the O'Club, except the lunch with Gunner Carson, drove straight home after work and never looked at a Woman Marine. He even avoided his old friend, Maj. Steve Way. But the instant Beck saw Cindy Hendrix in her office, he could not control his thoughts. As she sauntered around the desk to extend her hand, his mind focused on her extraordinary beauty—tall, graceful, and perfect skin. She had a uniquely exotic look, with high cheekbones, and striking oval eyes.

Hendrix smiled and motioned Beck over to the chairs around the conference table. She started speaking before they were seated.

"Captain Beck, what was your active-duty experience?"

As Hendrix spoke, Beck slowly nodded his head, and stumbled to answer the question. "Trial and defense at Camp Lejeune. I tried several murder cases as individual military counsel."

"And after completing your contract, you got out, and did nothing in the Reserves?" Hendrix seemed to stiffen with the question.

"I was too busy with my civilian practice."

"Why now after all these years? Nothing, then active-duty orders? You know that with seven bad years, there is no way you can receive a retirement." Hendrix continued to stare at Beck expectantly.

"Not interested in retirement. This is the first time that I could leave my civilian practice. My firm's managing partner is a retired Marine Colonel, and he encouraged me to volunteer, offered me a sabbatical. Also, there is a lot of super-patriotism back in Chicago with judges and clients not objecting to me being gone."

"Are you going to have a problem defending deserters?"

"Of course not. As a civilian, I represent the highest paying client, and as a Marine, I do what I am told—prosecution or defense. Besides, I am a trial lawyer and bored to death in legal assistance."

"Did you do any criminal law as a civilian?"

"Yes. A lot. Mostly, security fraud cases. I have a ton of courtroom experience and a good handle on Federal criminal law, rules of evidence, and procedure."

"Maybe you have heard that a San Diego civil rights law firm, Loring and Leavy, has opened an office in Yuma. They are funded by the National Peace Coalition and provide representation at no cost to the defendants. Almost half of our Marines have signed up with these guys. I want someone who will not be intimidated by these civilian lawyers and make certain that every Marine knows what they are getting into hiring an activist lawyer. In other words, I don't want to see our Marines used for someone else's political agenda. Think you can handle that assignment?"

"Yes, Ma'am. No problem."

"Let's introduce you to the shop and get your office set up."

Maj. Hendrix then walked Capt. Beck around the defense offices and introduced him to the staff.

Chapter 34

A week after his return, Sergeant Nathan Jones sat in his jail cell reading his Bible. As the only Noncommissioned Officer Detainee, he occupied the third floor of the brig by himself. He wore his brand-new woodland camouflage battle dress with the sleeves rolled up and the black metal rank insignia on the collar. The uniform had been starched and pressed, and the black boots shined. He had the "high and tight" haircut given to him at the Jackson County Jail.

He heard the guard yell "Get ready, Jones!" and quickly stood at attention, waiting for the cell door to open. He then turned, placing his hands behind his back to be handcuffed. The military policeman, Gunnery Sergeant Tyler, placed the handcuffs on Jones so violently that it felt like a punch in the back, and Jones struggled not to cry out in pain. Then Tyler spun Jones around.

Tyler was six feet tall, skinny, and nervous. He acted like he must have been beaten up daily in high school and had become mean, very mean. Next, Gunny Tyler shoved Jones out of the cell, down the hallway, down the stairs, and outside into the Brig's parking lot. Sergeant Jones saw the white military police car and tried to keep on his feet as Tyler continued to manhandle him. At the car, Tyler opened the rear door and shoved Jones into the back seat. A wire mesh separated the rear seat from the driver's seat. Tyler drove without saying a word. After a half-hour, he turned the car into a parking lot where a sign stated *Provost Marshal.* He roughly pulled Sgt. Jones out of the car, took him inside, and stood him in front the Desk Sergeant's tall, massive counter. Using the same voice, Tyler announced: "Detainee Jones here to see Gunner Carson."

Soon another military policeman led Jones down a narrow hallway, opened a door, and roughly pushed Jones inside, yelling "Take a seat behind the conference table next to the wall."

The unlit room had one small window covered by blinds. Jones felt his way in the darkness to the opposite side of the small conference table and sat in the center chair. He sat there for half an hour. Suddenly, the door opened, then closed. Jones could barely see a short, stocky man with a cigarette in his mouth. A feeling of foreboding, unease, and apprehension came over Nathan Jones. The dark figure walked over to the conference table and slowly paced back and forth. Just the menacing way he moved, cocky, aggressive, further unnerved him.

"I am Gunner Carson, the Provost Marshal. I am a hard-dicked bitch, and I will double-possum fuck you every chance I get." The man spoke in a scratchy raspy voice straight off the drill field.

"As far as I am concerned, Fucknut, you are the worst sergeant in the history of the Marine Corps. You are here because you failed to report to your unit going to Saudi Arabia. I can't even imagine—an NCO abandoning his Marines to let them go die by themselves. Then you appeared at a peace rally!" Nathan could hear the anger building in Gunner Carson's voice.

"I am here to tell you, Chickenshit, Yuma is my base. You are nothing but a wort on my ass. There are other officers here, but I am the one in charge of the military police. I run the Brig. You got that, Scumbag?"

"Yes, Sir!" Nathan replied in the voice of a recruit.

"Now, Jones, things may get a little rough for you in the Brig. You may think about calling your syphilitic wife, your whore momma, Suzi Rottencrotch, or those fucking peace advocates. Hell, you may want to call your congressman or a civilian lawyer. But I am telling you right now, you yellow-belly son-of-a-bitch, that is not going to happen.

"You will not be allowed phone calls. Your mail will be censored. If you file a complaint, it will come to me, and me alone. I want you to memorize that, know it like you once knew your mother's nipples."

The thought of what he said seemed to calm Carson and he paused to think. "Got it, Jones?"

"Yes, Sir!" Nathan replied.

"Your lawyers may tell you that anything you say to them is confidential. But they will just be diddling your ass. I know everything that happens in the Brig."

In the dark, Jones thought he could see Carson wickedly glaring at him.

"Do we understand each other?"

"Yes, Sir!"

"The Commandant says that today there are four types of Marines. Marines that are in Saudi Arabia. Marines that want to go to Saudi Arabia. Marines that don't want to go but are going anyway. And those that refuse to go and are going to prison.

"In your case, Jones, you are going to prison. You are going to prison for a long, long time. You will receive a Dishonorable Discharge. You will very soon be out of my Marine Corps and at Fort Leavenworth. I goddamn promise you that, Fuckface."

"Yes, Sir!" Jones responded without giving Gunner Carson the chance to ask if he understood.

"I also want you to know that as far as I am concerned, you are not a conscientious objector, you're a worthless coward. You are just plain yellow. It makes me sick to even look at you. That is all I got to say to you, you worthless piece of shit."

"Yes, Sir!"

Gunner Carson stormed out of the room, and Sgt. Jones sat in the dark for another hour before Gunny Tyler came and returned him to the Brig.

Chapter 35

Colonel Cahill parked his car in the small lot and strode towards the Brig's entrance. He noticed that all the windows had been sealed with concrete blocks and crudely painted over. A red and gold sign over the steel entrance door read, *All Visitors Ring Bell.* After a five-minute delay, a lance corporal opened the door. The bored look on his face turned to terror when he saw the eagles on Cahill's collar.

"How may I be of service, Sir?"

"I am Colonel Cahill the Fourth Division Commanding Officer. I want to speak with the Officer in Charge."

The lance corporal held the entrance door open and gestured toward a conference table seen behind a large glass window. "Sir, would you care to wait in the visiting room while I report your visit to Gunnery Sergeant Tyler?"

Reading the Marine's name tag, Cahill responded, "That will work, Lance Corporal Kimmel."

Cahill walked inside the visiting room and left the door open. The adjustment on the chair he pulled from the conference table was broken so the back leaned almost to the floor. He walked around the table and found a chair that seemed useable. Looking through the window, he could see a counter across the room, a dozen dilapidated chairs against the walls, and the locked steel door that Kimmel had used. In a few minutes, an older looking Gunnery Sergeant entered.

"What can I do for you, Sir?"

"I just stopped by for an informal inspection of the Brig. A primary mission of Fourth Marine Division (Rear) is processing deserters. Pretrial confinement is an important part of that mission, and I will be paying close attention to your operation. Do you have any convicted prisoners?"

"Yes, Sir. Six. That is the court docket for last week. We hold them here until we can arrange transportation to the Camp Pendleton Confinement Facility, or if the sentence exceeds two years, to

Leavenworth, Kansas. Prisoners are always separated from pretrial detainees."

"How many pretrial detainees?"

"Sixty-one, but we are expecting more soon."

"What's this room used for?"

"Intended for lawyer and civilian visitations, and as a conference room, but it has been rarely used so far."

"Gunny, I want all these chairs replaced immediately. If you have other furniture that is unserviceable, replace it. Any problems call the G-4. I will have him roll in on the problem."

"Yes, Sir."

"I waited outside for five minutes after ringing the buzzer. You need a better system. Why do you need two locked doors?"

Gunny Tyler squinted his mouth and eyes in an almost comical fashion. "I don't know…that's the way it's been set up. Just increased security, I guess. Since we are out in the middle of the desert, surrounded by a twelve-foot chain link fence, I don't know that it is really needed. Maybe I could move one of my administrative people up here and leave the outside door open from eight to five."

"Any reason I shouldn't inspect the Brig right now?'

"No, Sir. Just follow me."

Two locked doors segregated each wing of the Brig. Gunny Tyler opened the first with a key, and once inside the small cubicle, he rang a buzzer. A guard from inside the second door loudly announced Gunny Tyler's arrival, "Visitor on deck! Stand at attention!"

Col. Cahill slowly walked down the corridor looking inside each cell, usually occupied by two detainees positioned near the doors. Most of the detainees looked a mess, standing at a kind of semi-attention, with stupid looks on their faces. Their uniforms were wrinkled, boots not shined, and most needed haircuts. The cells were not clean or neat. Cahill noticed that the racks were not properly made, wall locker doors were open, towels haphazardly hung, and magazines thrown around.

"Gunny, the next time I am here, I expect all detainees to have haircuts, pressed uniforms, and spit-shined boots. Check?"

"Check, Sir." The Gunnery Sergeant's embarrassment could be heard in his voice.

"Also, you get those cells cleaned up and squared away. I want them to look like a squad bay at Marine Corps Recruit Depot, San Diego. Got it?"

"Got it, Sir."

"What have you got on the third deck?"

"Colonel Cahill, on the third deck, 'Delta Wing,' we have only one Non-Commissioned Officer, Sergeant Nathan Jones."

"I have heard of Sergeant Jones. He was photographed at an anti-war rally in St. Louis. Let's go up and look."

On arrival at Sergeant Jones's cell, Cahill noticed the obvious contrast between Jones and the other detainees. Sergeant Jones's military bearing appeared exemplary, as if straight off the drill field. He stood at attention in exactly the proper manner, his uniform immaculate, cell spotless, and everything in perfect order. Cahill thought, *What a shame. He is totally squared away, but a fool or a coward. He left the Marines in his unit to fend for themselves. Then appeared at a peace rally. Disgraceful.*

Cahill fought to control his anger. "Sergeant Jones, stand at ease."

Jones smartly moved his hands behind his back and spread his feet slightly, straight out of the Marine Guide Book.

"How are you being treated?"

The words were neutral, but Jones could sense Cahill's contempt.

"The guards are very professional, Sir. No complaints."

Cahill glanced at Gunny Tyler with a look that conveyed doubt in something. Doubt that Sergeant Jones was being treated professionally, or doubt that he had no complaints, and certainly doubt that Sgt. Jones was telling him everything.

"The chow?"

"Sufficient in quantity and quality. In fact, excellent, Sir."

Col. Cahill abruptly turned and left. Jones snapped back to attention and watched the colonel walk down the hallway.

Chapter 36

"Sergeant Jones, you have visitors."

The guard spoke through the bars of Jones's cell. Like the other guards, over the last four weeks he had come to like, and respect, Sgt. Nathan Jones as a "Marine's Marine." Every morning Jones went through a rigorous exercise program: pushups, sit-ups, running in place. When he was not exercising, he was reading. He read stacks and stacks of books. Some of the guards even brought him day-old newspapers, or month-old magazines, which he read from cover to cover.

Jones frequently counseled the younger prisoners, patiently listening to their problems, and gently offering advice. He would pray with them and read the Bible. On his own initiative, Sgt. Jones organized work details to correct problems around the Brig. The work crews repaired the tables and chairs in the mess hall, painted the conference room, cleaned the filters for the furnace and air conditioners, and even fixed leaky faucets. Everyone at the Brig, guards, and prisoners alike, was more comfortable with Nathan Jones as a prisoner.

Jones stood, turned, and placed his hands behind his back.

"We can skip the cuffs; just head left to the end of the hallway."

When Jones approached the door at the end of the hallway, another guard staring through the window opened it from the other side. Jones followed him to another door which the guard unlocked and opened.

"Please enter and stand aside the door."

When Jones entered the conference room the guard locked the door behind him, and Jones stared at three men he had not seen before.

"Nathan, I am Ogden Loring, this is my partner, Warren Leavy, and this is Captain Beck, your detailed defense counsel. We got a call from Judy Novotney, Dean at Wabash Valley College in Mt. Carmel,

Illinois. She said you wanted to hire us but had no funds. We are here to let you know that the National Peace Coalition has agreed to pay our fees, and we are here to volunteer our attorney services at no cost to you. You may also be represented by Captain Beck at no cost to you. Please have a seat."

Sgt. Jones quickly sized up the three men. Ogden Loring looked to be somewhere past 60 years of age, and his friendly, intelligent eyes were weathered and tired. He wore a scraggly gray mustache, and his long hair was tied in a ponytail. The top button of his shirt was free, and his tie loosened.

Warren Leavy appeared to be the same age but had the opposite look—tall, thin, and regal looking, even with his long silver hair. He carried himself with dignity, back upright, and eyes that looked straight at everyone. He had an unmistakable sophistication.

Capt. Beck was Hollywood handsome, almost too handsome to be taken seriously. With his dark hair, square jaw, a face chiseled from stone, and dark gray eyes, he sparkled with self-confidence, and a compelling aura, and obviously stood well with the female half of the species. His hair appeared to be just barely within Marine Corps regulation and known by barbers as a "five."

Beck proceeded, calmly looking Sergeant Jones in the eye. "Sergeant Jones, I was detailed to represent you by your Commanding Officer. You also have the right to be represented by a military counsel of your own selection referred to as individual military counsel, or IMC, provided that the counsel you request is reasonably available. Even if you choose to have civilian counsel, your military lawyer will continue on the case."

"Can I change my mind in the future?"

"Of course. Sergeant Jones, you will always make the decisions, including a decision to terminate civilian counsel or replace your military lawyer. In fact, you don't need a reason as long as your termination doesn't delay the proceedings."

"At this point, I don't see how it could hurt anything to have all three of you represent me. Do I need to sign something?" Ogden put the retainer agreement in front of Nathan, and he signed it before anyone could say anything further.

"Can you get me out of the Brig?" Sergeant Jones asked in a shaky voice filled with emotion.

"Of course; we will do everything possible."

"I understand that I will have to serve time in Leavenworth, but the most important thing for me is being released from this Brig as soon as possible. Who can do that?"

The lawyers stared at one another for a moment. Capt. Beck could see the fear in Jones's eyes. Then Ogden spoke, "Like everything, we will all work together on getting you released from pretrial confinement. All three of us. Is there something going on in the Brig?"

Nathan hesitated, then answered, "No problem. It's just that there are no windows, and it drives me crazy."

Beck spoke. "There is a procedure to have your pretrial confinement reviewed. You are entitled to a hearing before a pretrial confinement officer. That hearing should happen very soon. I will also schedule a hearing on your application for conscientious objector status."

Warren Leavy took his chance to speak. "Nathan, Ogden and I have already done the research, and we have a plan to get you out of jail. We will file a writ of *habeas corpus* in the Federal Court in San Diego. A writ of *habeas corpus* requires the Marine Corps to appear in front of a federal judge and prove the legality of your confinement. Our writ will be based upon the Nuremberg Defense. The Gulf War is illegal, and therefore, an order to participate in the war is also illegal, and under international law, specifically, the law established by the International Military Tribunal at Nuremberg, a soldier has a duty to disobey an unlawful order."

"OK. I want you to file the writ…"

Ogden flashed Nathan a big smile. "Is there anything we can get you, need anything?"

"No, Sir."

"All right! We will get to work on the Pretrial Confinement Hearing, the Application for Conscientious Objector Status, and the Writ of Habeas Corpus. See you soon."

Chapter 37

Ogden Loring and Capt. Beck motioned Sgt. Jones to take a seat across from a frail-looking major who sat at the end of the table reviewing what Jones quickly recognized as his application for conscientious objector status.

"Good morning, Sergeant Jones. I am Major John Thompson. I like to conduct these hearings informally. I am a reservist on active duty and assigned as the legal officer for Headquarters and Service Battalion, Fourth Marine Division (Rear). I have been appointed as the Investigating Officer in your case to make a recommendation on whether your Application for Conscientious Objector Status should be granted. First, do you understand that regardless of what action is now taken on your Application for Conscientious Objector status, you remain subject to court-martial for failing to report for mobilization?"

"Yes, Sir. I understand."

"I have reviewed your Service Record Book and read your application and attached documents. I have also read the Letter of Opinion of the Chaplain and the Psychiatric Evaluation. You have a right to counsel at your own expense. Do you desire an attorney at this hearing?"

Ogden Loring spoke with his commanding voice. "Major Thompson, my name is Ogden Loring with the law firm of Loring and Leavy. I am licensed to practice law in the State of California. I will be representing Sergeant Jones at no cost to the government. Also, seated next to me is Captain Beck a military attorney certified under Article 27, who will represent Sergeant Jones as co-counsel."

"Very well. Sergeant Jones, you have a right to a verbatim transcript of this hearing at your own expense. Do you desire a verbatim transcript?"

Again, Ogden spoke. "Sergeant Jones requests a transcript of this hearing. I have already made arrangements with the court reporter to obtain the transcript at no cost to the government."

"You have a right to question me as to any potential bias, or prejudice. Do you want to ask me any questions?"

Ogden answered, "No, Sir."

"You have a right to present additional evidence in support of your application, including additional documents, or witnesses. Do you have additional information to submit?"

Ogden answered, "No, Sir."

"Very well, Sergeant Jones. I have some questions to ask. Why did you file the application for conscientious objector status?" The Investigating Officer studied Sergeant Jones's eyes, hoping to read them and be able to determine if he was telling the truth.

"Because I have a sincere commitment to the Marine Corps, but also to God."

The pronouncement seemed unexpected and dramatic. The Investigating Officer lifted his eyebrows, but not his eyes, as he concentrated on writing everything down on his legal pad. The Investigating Officer spent the next hour asking questions about Jones's general background, education, civilian employment, military service, and church affiliations—again, making extensive notes.

"How have your beliefs evolved?"

"My Grandma raised me a Methodist. My father died in Vietnam, and I was taught that my father died for a noble and honorable cause serving his country. During bootcamp I felt closer to God than I ever did before. Some of the Marines made fun of me, but I prayed constantly and attended the Protestant services. I felt being a Marine had to be the right thing for me. When I returned home from active duty, I began once again to attend the Methodist Church, but I began to doubt the doctrine of the Methodist Church during a sermon on baptism. The minister said that if a baby died even a second before baptism, he would be damned to hell. This could not be my idea of a Loving God.

"I began having long talks with one of my college professors, Judy Novotney. She is a devout Christian, and she influenced me a great deal in my changing beliefs. She loaned me many books on Christianity and interpretations of the Scriptures. Some of the books tended to stress a pacifist, non-violent view of Christianity.

"We began to attend the New Unity in Christ Church. I read a book by the church's founder, Doctor Robert Brown. The New Unity in Christ Church was supposed to be a missionary church with missions in Sonora, Mexico. I am no longer a member of the Church and don't believe Doctor Brown is a true Christian, but at the time, the Church and Doctor Brown's teachings against participation in a war influenced my thinking.

"I also read books that were not Christian oriented. I read *Born on the Fourth of July* by Ron Kovic. It impressed me. At one time, Mr. Kovic had been a gung-ho Marine. Although his views are not the same as mine, I felt a strong sense of comradery with him.

"I thought a lot about my father's death in Vietnam. He died for a cause that he had been told was honorable but which the American people later abandoned. His death became meaningless. He died for absolutely nothing. We never even saw each other. That is wrong.

"I began to change my religious beliefs. I became more of a pacifist, more of an environmentalist, and more concerned about my society, not only because my faith changed, but because I changed. I do not want it to seem as if I changed overnight. My support of the Marine Corps continued for some time. But the more I read, the more I studied, and the more I thought about religion and my inner beliefs, the more I realized I was a different person from the one I was when I enlisted. I saw that Christ taught us to love one another, and I now believe that to kill another man is to deprive him of the ability to learn about the Lord and to enter Heaven. I truly feel that I could never take a human life, except perhaps in the most extreme situation to defend another from death.

"Two years ago, I spoke to my commanding officer, Lieutenant Colonel Easterday, about my conscientious objector status. I told him that I wanted to apply to obtain non-combatant status. Lieutenant Colonel Easterday said that my unit, the Fourth Tank Battalion, had never been activated, and would never be mobilized, unless Russia invaded North America. Our M-60 tanks were obsolete, and the logistic costs of transporting the Battalion to another country were prohibitively high. Lieutenant Colonel Easterday convinced me not to try for non-combatant status. He said it would never be granted and would cause me, and the Battalion, a lot of trouble. Since I only had ten months left on my enlistment contract, he convinced me to just wait and not re-enlist.

"When President Bush called up the reserves, I suffered terrible duress about whether to try and keep my oath to the Marine Corps or do what I felt was required of me as a Christian."

Sergeant Jones went quiet, and the Investigating Officer continued taking notes. Finally, the Investigating Officer resumed his questions. "Do you know what a conscientious objector is?"

"I know how the Marine Corps defines a conscientious objector."

"How is that?"

"A Marine that has a sincere and deeply held objection to the participation in war in any form founded upon religious belief."

"It sounds like you have studied the issue."

"As I said, I have read everything I could find. Prayed about it. Thought about it."

"Do you personally agree with the definition?"

"No. I do not but acknowledge that it is not my decision. The definition doesn't seem to fit a request for re-assignment to non-combatant service. I believe that war is always bad. But it also seems that conscientious objector status is very restricted.

"I understand that some Christians believe that Jesus has forbidden any form of participation in military service—whether combatant or non-combatant, and whether in defense or offense. That is probably the teachings of the New Unity in Christ Church. For me, that position can be taken to a logical and spiritual extreme. I believe that Jesus's teaching that we love our neighbor compels a Christian to defend his loved ones when unjustly attacked. For example, in the event of an invasion of our Country and an attack upon my family and friends, I would defend them. Also, participation in a war in a non-combatant manner would not violate my religious beliefs.

"Some believe a Christian may participate only in a just war. But the definition of conscientious objector seems to follow the "blank check" model. By joining the military, a person grants complete approval to whatever actions the government chooses to pursue. In my mind, the just-war theory amounts to granting an allegiance to Caesar which, for a Christian, rightly belongs only to Christ.

"I am somewhere in between. If our Country becomes involved in war, I believe the Bible instructs me to maintain a spirit of Christian love and goodwill, avoid hatred, and be obedient to all governmental laws that are not in conflict with Scriptural teachings. I believe that to follow my faith which commands me to model myself after Christ, I must seek assignment to noncombatant training and service and request conscientious objector status 1-A-0.

"My faith in God has given me the strength to come forward and profess my beliefs. My faith has also given unto me the confidence that I am just and correct in my stance as a conscientious objector."

"What is your position on the President sending troops to Southwest Asia?"

"I am concerned. I took an oath to defend and support the Constitution of the United States and only Congress has the power to declare war. The President has no legal authority, none whatsoever, to commit American troops to war in the Persian Gulf, or anywhere else, without congressional authorization.

"Do you think a war with Iraq will be a just war?"

"There is greater merit in preventing war by peaceful negotiation, and conciliation, than by vindicating rights by bloodshed. War must be the last resort. The President has not allowed enough time for economic sanctions to work or exhausted attempts at negotiating peace."

"Are you a member of any anti-war organization?"

"I never joined any anti-war organization as a member, but I did appear at a peace rally sponsored by the National Campaign for Peace."

"Tell me about that."

"I reside close to St Louis. I and several soldiers were asked to attend. I didn't say anything, but my photograph was taken, and it appeared in several newspapers."

"That sounds political, not religious."

"There were religious leaders at the rally who spoke about Scripture, and I was thinking that a Christian should do what they can to prevent war. I am sure that Jesus teaches us that oil is not worth lives."

"Sergeant Jones, is there anything else you want to say?"

"What I have said here today is sincere and the truth. I think I can better serve the Marine Corps in a noncombatant status."

"All right. I am going to ask you all to return to your duty stations while I review my notes and deliberate on what I have heard this morning. I will contact you when I have reached a decision."

Ogden, Beck, and Jones waited at the defense shop until 1400 when they received a call from Maj. Thompson. Then, they returned to the hearing room.

"Sergeant Jones, I have made my decision. I have been the Investigating Officer on many conscientious objector cases. I am impressed here by several things. You are obviously well-informed on this issue and have given this matter a great deal of thought. I find your testimony to be completely truthful. I understand how your father's unnecessary death in Vietnam weighs on your mind today. Your commanding officer gave you the wrong advice, and he should have processed your application.

"You said you are not sure you agree with the Marine Corps' definition of conscientious objector. Frankly, I am not sure I agree with it. You are somewhere in between.

"Unfortunately, this is the definition required by Congress, and it is my duty to apply the law given to us by Congress. Because you are a sincere and honest person, you have admitted that you are not opposed to participation in war in any form. Instead, you would fight to defend your friends and family if the United States were attacked. I am sorry, but I have no choice but to recommend the denial of your application.

"Of course, I only make a recommendation, and I will state my reasons clearly. I will be careful to make a record so that my decision can be reviewed. Your Commanding Officer has the final say on the matter."

Chapter 38

Over the next week, Ogden Loring and Warren Leavy researched the law on illegal orders and on Thursday night stayed up finishing a masterful 50-page brief. At 7:30 a.m. Ogden left the office to personally file the brief with the United States District Court for the Southern District of California. He wanted the case assigned to District Court Judge George Moorman, probably the most liberal judge in the Ninth Circuit. Ogden had won a dismissal of DUI charges against the clerk in charge of assigning cases at the District Court and knew the clerk would tip him off when Judge Moorman was next in the rotation. After returning to the office, Ogden felt utterly exhausted when his phone rang.

"Hello."

"Hey Og. It's Jim Collins. Got a second?"

"No problem, Doc."

"Are you coming out to the marina this afternoon?" Collins asked uncertainly.

"I haven't decided. I have a few things to do today, but I thought I might get out later this afternoon depending on the weather."

"Well, listen Og, you should try and make it as soon as you can. Sun is out, and the weather is incredible. Man, it's a great day to be on the water."

"You taking your boat out?" Ogden asked.

"Yeah. Probably, around two o'clock, and I have room for you and Warren."

"I am sure we can make it by then," Ogden answered with his voice trailing.

"Say, Og."

"Yeah?"

"I don't mean to rush you, but like I said it is going to be a beautiful day on the water. Any chance you could come a little earlier and bring something for me?"

Ogden paused to think. He wanted to accommodate his long-time customer Doctor Collins, a renowned San Diego cardiologist.

"What do you want? One or two?"

"Two will do fine, if you can spare that much."

"All right, Doc. I will come over to your boat, say around 1:30."

"Og, I really appreciate it. I will have the boat ready to sail. See you then—and bring Warren."

Ogden Loring's house appeared empty when he arrived from the downtown office an hour later. He opened the garage, found his wife's car gone, and smiled. He put a pot of coffee on and walked to the converted basement that now served as his home office. The walls were covered with dozens of photographs of his boat and of parties at the marina. Most included bikini-clad women holding cans of beer. For the past few years, Ogden spent every weekend, and all his free time, on his boat without the company of his wife. Most of the owners at the marina were wealthy—doctors, lawyers, and successful businessmen—and could afford larger boats. But Ogden's old Cris Craft, probably the smallest boat at the Harbor Island Marina, remained his pride and joy.

The combination on the Canyon gun safe required complete concentration and usually two or three attempts, but today it opened on Ogden's first try. He searched inside until he found the large Zip-Loc baggie. He pulled out the scales and a box of smaller baggies and started weighing out the marijuana. Ogden did not see himself as a drug dealer. At first, he bought for a few friends and sold at his cost. He never made a dime. However, more and more friends asked Ogden to get them something. When he started purchasing larger quantities, he received big discounts. He always told himself that he did not charge anything, he just kept the discount. The rule at the marina made it work: "What happens on the dock stays on the dock."

Since most of the now-wealthy boat owners went to college in the 60s, they preferred grass to booze, and these people trusted Ogden. They figured that as a lawyer he had too much to lose and would be extremely careful. He became their regular source. As a result, Ogden now spent a lot of his time buying, packaging, and delivering marijuana to his longtime customers. Almost every few days he had to stop by some office building to make a sale.

When the grants and fundraisers supporting public-interest law dried up, Ogden survived by selling marijuana. He could make as much as $3,000 over a weekend at the marina and usually cleared $6,000 a month. There were times when without this money he could not pay his mortgage and household expenses.

This morning, Ogden carefully weighed out six baggies. Each one a little short but he knew that his customers would never complain. He realized he could probably sell more, but he knew that would increase his risk. If he got busted with six baggies, he would be charged with dealing but could deal down to a misdemeanor. The California Bar Association would put him on probation and require him to complete a substance-abuse course. With more than six baggies, the district attorney would not deal for less than a class-six felony, and that would result in suspension of his bar license.

Ogden triple wrapped the six baggies, slipped them into his duffle bag, and returned to the kitchen table where he smoked his pipe and drank coffee. He then called his partner, Warren Leavy, who remained at the office working.

"Hey, Warren; what are you doing?"

"Just finishing up a memorandum on that Smith case. Getting ready to go home, sit on the balcony, and dream of ways I can inflict pain and suffering on the Wicked Witch of the West."

"Did you talk to her this morning?"

"I am not sure 'talking' is an accurate description of my phone call, but yeah, we yelled at each other."

"Is she going to let the kids come out for the summer?"

"Nope. She's conveniently signed them up for swimming lessons. She is also taking them to Hawaii with her latest and greatest boyfriend."

"I am sorry, Warren. I know you were hoping to spend time with them."

"Yeah, life's a bitch when you make the mistake of marrying one."

"My brain's fried from finishing that Jones memorandum. Let's go drink a bottle of McCallan on the boat," Ogden suggested.

"That sounds perfect. I am also beat," Warren shot back.

"OK. I will pick you up in two hours." Ogden's voice revealed his sudden good mood.

Warren Leavy hurried home but took a moment to sit on his balcony to watch the joggers on Cedar Street. Warren shared the small condominium in the heart of downtown San Diego with a Los Angeles attorney who flew in for meetings three or four times a month. Warren felt lucky to live in the impressive 15-story building that provided spectacular views of the Bay.

As a young man, woman never gave Warren Leavy a second look. At that time his long black hair, dark eyes, and odd taste in clothes gave him a sort of greasy-slick-ethnic look. Now with the divorce, and being in his mid-50s, things had changed. Warren watched his diet, worked out, and stayed in shape. He found a great hair stylist and became a lot more conservative in his clothing choices. He was not exactly movie star material, but young female professionals seemed attracted to his confident looks.

Just then, Warren saw the old car pull up to the condominium and rushed down the stairs to meet Ogden.

"So, how is Sharon?" Warren asked as he opened the door to Ogden's car.

"Grab me a beer out of the cooler," Ogden responded, ignoring the question.

Warren reached in the back seat and dug through the ice in the cooler to pull out two Miller Lites. When he looked for the cup holders, he noticed Ogden's porcelain pipe shaped like a cigarette in the ashtray.

"Jesus, Og. Can't you at least keep that shit out of sight? You know the San Diego cops aren't stupid. They know what a marijuana pipe looks like. All they need is probable cause to search your car, and we are both screwed."

In the 20 years they had known each other, Warren voiced this complaint over 1,000 times. As usual, Ogden simply shoved the pipe in the glove box without speaking. As Ogden pulled away from the curb, Warren popped the top on the nearly frozen beer and smiled.

"What's happening at the Marina?"

"Doctor Collins called. He says there's a pretty good crowd. He is taking his boat out at two o'clock, and we are invited."

"Still a little cold for the bikinis, isn't it?" Warren asked.

"Yeah. But there are always a few slip skanks on the dock willing to brave the cold. Just try and stay away from the married ones this time."

Warren laughed heartedly.

"Is Sharon still working at the library?"

"Yeah. She works half days. It's weird, Warren. I mean you knew her. I always thought we would be friends for life, but it was the change of life that got her. She's not been the same since."

"She's just pissed off at you for something, which I am sure she has a good reason to be. She will get over it," Warren replied with an inconsequential waive of his hand.

"I wish you were right, Warren, but that is not the way it is now. A couple of months ago she stopped talking to me. Things haven't been the same."

"Well at least she keeps quiet. You should have lived with the Wicked Witch. She picked a fight every day. Yelling, screaming, throwing shit at me. Man, it became a nightmare. It's a wonder I didn't kill her."

"I don't know, Warren. Believe me, Sharon's silent treatment is just as bad. I like to watch the news and have a piece of toast in the morning with my coffee. All Sharon does is sit at the table reading some novel. Now and then, if she is interested in the news story, she puts that little book marker in the book, places it on the table, and stares at the television. Then she picks it up and starts reading again. She does this without ever looking at me or saying a word. It's enough to drive you nuts."

"You must hang in there for the girls." Warren said sharply.

"I know. I just can't believe that everything in life seems to turn to shit."

Chapter 39

On Monday morning at 4:30 a.m., Warren Leavy pulled his 1985 BMW out of his condominium parking garage and headed east towards the I-5 ramp. The dark night and fog made it nearly impossible to see, but he could make out the headlights of traffic in the opposite lane already streaming into downtown San Diego. At the intersection with I-8, Warren turned east and headed towards Yuma, Arizona.

At the conclusion of an hour-long telephone conference the night before, the three lawyers had agreed that Capt. Beck should speak at the upcoming pretrial confinement hearing. Nevertheless, Warren wanted to be present in case he could offer any assistance to Beck. He also wanted to assure Sgt. Jones that the firm of Loring & Leavy would actively represent him in all aspects of his case. The firm would not take the NPC's money and then let the military lawyer do the work.

Warren arrived at the Main Gate at Marine Corps Air Station, Yuma, Arizona at exactly 8:00 am, then drove to the legal assistance office to meet Capt. Beck. Sgt. Jones would be escorted to the hearing room by the military police.

At 0900, the Magistrate, Colonel Butcher, walked into the MAG-10 conference room. Slim, sharp-featured, and lithely muscular, Col. Butcher served as the Executive Officer for Marine Air Group 10. His black hair and mustache were long, like Beck's, and just barely within regulation. His demeanor was calm, relaxed, and friendly. His uniform carried five rows of ribbons and the gold Naval Aviator Wings.

"Please be seated."

Capt. Beck, Warren Leavy, and Sgt. Jones took seats across the conference table.

"Sergeant Jones, my name is Colonel Butcher, and I have been appointed as the magistrate in your case to determine whether you should be held in pretrial confinement. I am not a lawyer, and I like to conduct these hearings informally."

Pausing to look at Capt. Beck's name tag, Col. Butcher continued. "I see you are represented by military counsel, Captain Beck. Do you have other military counsel or a civilian attorney?"

Beck responded. "Sergeant Jones is also represented in this matter by civilian counsel, Loring and Leavy, San Diego, California. Mr. Warren Leavy is seated on my left."

"Welcome to Yuma, Mr. Leavy." Col. Butcher smiled warmly as he spoke.

"Thank you, Sir. I am present to assist if I can, but Captain Jones will do all the speaking this morning."

"That's fine," Col. Butcher answered, then looked at Sgt. Jones.

"Sergeant Jones, you are entitled to make a statement or remain silent. If you remain silent, that will not be held against you. You may also present anything you think is relevant to the issue of whether you should continue to be held in pretrial confinement. It doesn't have to be admissible evidence in a court-martial."

Beck responded. "Sir, Sergeant Jones will exercise his right to remain silent but has several matters to present."

Capt. Beck slid the three-ring binder across the desk. The binder had been prepared with the assistance of Maj. Hendrix. It included Jones's Service Record Book, all his award citations, sworn affidavits from Emma Lee Jones, Dean Judy Novotney, and an expertly written section entitled "Applicable Law." Capt. Beck paused to allow Butcher time to read the binder. After 30 minutes, Butcher closed the binder and Beck spoke.

"I have arranged for telephonic testimony from a United States Marshal from Illinois who is standing by her phone. With your permission, Colonel Butcher, I would like to use the conference room telephone to call her, put her on speaker, and record her testimony."

Butcher looked surprised and stopped to think before answering.

"That will be fine, Captain. Just make sure that after the hearing you turn in a long-distance telephone chit to the S-1 down the hall. I don't want to have to figure out later who made a long-distance call to Illinois on the conference room phone."

Capt. Beck quickly repositioned the telephone, set up his recorder, and dialed the number.

"Hello."

"Hello. This is Captain Beck. Is this Marshal Collins?"

"Yes. This is Marshal Shelia Collins."

"Marshal, I have you on speaker, and this is a pretrial confinement hearing for Sergeant Nathan Jones before a military magistrate, Colonel Butcher, being held at Marine Corps Air Station, Yuma, Arizona. I want to make sure you understand this is sworn testimony in a legal proceeding."

"I understand that, Captain, and I swear under oath that all of my testimony will be the truth to the best of my knowledge and belief."

"How long have you been a United States Marshal?"

"Twenty-seven years."

"What is your present assignment?"

"United States District Court, Southern District of Illinois, Benton, Illinois."

"Do you know Nathan Jones?"

"Yes. He saved my life."

Again, Capt. Jones noticed the shock on Col. Butcher's face.

"Tell us how that happened."

"The Chief Marshal for Illinois ordered me to assist NCIS Agent Palmer from Yuma to locate Nathan Jones. Nathan was suspected of desertion from the Marine Corps. I interviewed several witnesses and developed a theory that Nathan might be hiding out in the Shawnee National Forrest. It is very rugged country. One day, I went out in the woods looking for Nathan or his hideout. I slipped and had a dangerous fall, breaking my ribs and leg, and losing my cell phone. I think I would have frozen to death, but Nathan heard my screams for help, found me, and carried me back to my vehicle on his back."

"In your witness interviews, did you determine Nathan's reputation in that area?"

"Nathan has the reputation of being a good, law-abiding, and deeply religious man."

"After the day Nathan carried you out of the woods, did you ever talk to him again?"

"The day in the woods, I gave Nathan my card and told him if he wanted to turn himself in, or if he needed anything, to call me. Two days later, Nathan called me. He stated he wanted to turn himself in, and we arranged to meet the next morning at my office in Benton, Illinois. Unfortunately, Nathan got arrested by the Illinois Highway Patrol on his way to my office."

"Did you believe Sergeant Jones when he told you he would surrender to authorities?"

"Yes. Absolutely. I believed him. I have also read a transcript of a wiretap on Nathan's mother's phone. Immediately prior to calling me, Nathan called his mother, Emma Lee Jones, and told her that he intended to turn himself over to authorities the next day."

"Do you have any additional information on whether if released from pretrial confinement Sergeant Jones would be a danger to himself, danger to others, or a flight risk?"

"There has never been any reason to think Nathan could be a danger to himself or a danger to others. As I said, he is a good, law-abiding citizen. During his telephone conversations with his mother, and myself, Nathan stated that he wanted to return to the Marines and 'face the music.' He did not want to continue running or hiding. I do not know much about the military, but I know what kind of a man Nathan is. There is no chance of Nathan leaving the Marines again. There is zero chance of him breaking the law."

"Thank you; those are all the questions I have. Colonel Butcher, do you have questions for Marshal Collins?"

Colonel Butcher shook his head no.

"Marshal Collins, we are going to hang up now." Beck hung up the phone, stopped the recorder, and again addressed Butcher.

"Sir. The only thing else we must present is a brief argument."

"Go ahead, Captain."

"The Magistrate can verify everything I say from Sergeant Jones's service record book. You can see that he has an outstanding military record of achievement. Six years' service with no office hours, no counseling entries, excellent performance of duty, and no misconduct of any kind. Five-by-five, professional marks, and conduct marks. Three times meritoriously promoted. Top grades in all service schools and correspondence courses. Navy Achievement Medal. Good Conduct Medal. Select Marine Corps Reserve Medal. Sea

Service Deployment Ribbon. Meritorious Unit Citation. Organized Marine Corps Reserve Medal. Armed Forces Reserve Medal.

The testimony of Marshal Collins proves that at the time of his arrest, Sergeant Jones was on his way to voluntarily return to his unit. Specifically, he was traveling to the District Court in Benton Illinois to turn himself in to Marshal Collins.

"It is well established that as a matter of law when a Marine voluntarily returns to military authority, there is no legal basis for pre-trial confinement. That concludes my argument."

Col. Butcher paused, then addressed Sgt. Jones.

"Sergeant Jones, I congratulate you on an outstanding service record. Your lawyers have presented a powerful case. I have always made my ruling as part of the hearing. But this is an unusual case. Captain Beck, is there any problem if I re-read the materials and chew on this overnight? I will decide tomorrow."

"Absolutely not. In fact, that would be Sergeant Jones's request."

"Very well. This hearing is adjourned. I will enter a written order tomorrow."

Chapter 40

"Grab your cover, Beck. How about buying me lunch this time?"

Gunner Carson stood in the doorway grinning from ear to ear, the smoke from his cigarette hanging in the air. Without hesitation, Beck followed Carson down the hallway and through the front door. Outside, Beck saw that Carson drove a jacked-up blue and white Chevrolet Blazer with huge off-road tires, and not the red Corvette. Beck ran to the passenger's side and struggled to climb inside. At the Officer's Club, Carson went straight to his usual table.

"Beck, I hear you did a hell of a job on Sergeant Jones's pretrial confinement hearing...calling the marshal and all. But I don't get it. Why waste your time on a yellow-bellied piece of shit like Jones? Besides, Colonel Butcher ain't never let anyone out of jail and never will."

Carson laughed. Beck started to explain, thought about it, and just shrugged his shoulders.

"Yeah. I know. Maybe just showing off for those San Diego attorneys—make a good first impression? Or maybe trying to impress the boss, Major Hendrix."

As they walked into the O Club bar, a few pilots in dirty flight suits sat drinking beer. Carson motioned to the waitress.

"Listen, Captain Beck, I need a favor."

"Sure," Capt. Beck replied, looking puzzled.

"We got a Marine in the Yellow Barracks yesterday. Name's Lance Corporal Jim Sanders. His sister was beaten up by her husband, really bad deal. She's been in the hospital back in your hometown, Chicago. Sanders' unit fucked up and wouldn't give him leave, so he went UA to go back and take care of his sister. I guess he beat up his brother-in-law pretty bad. Kind of like you in the airport... huh, Beck?" Carson grinned and laughed while the waitress delivered the second vodka.

"Well, Sanders voluntarily came back in two weeks ago but has been charged with unauthorized absence. Beck, this kid doesn't deserve a court-martial. Should be office hours, bust to PFC, and back to duty. I want you to handle his case and get the court-martial dismissed."

"Does he have detailed counsel?" Beck asked the question in a professional voice.

"If he does, his lawyer hasn't taken the time to speak to Sanders. Anyway, I know Sanders is entitled to individual military counsel, and I told him to request you."

Capt. Beck pondered the problem, then spoke. "Major Hendrix must assign me as counsel for Sanders. I don't know how she feels about this kind of situation." Beck's voice became shaky, and it seemed hard for him to speak.

"Look, Beck, don't blow smoke up my ass. There is no way they can deny Sanders' request for you as individual military counsel. You don't even have that many cases. Anyway, Cindy Hendrix owes me a favor so I will talk to her. You just make sure Sanders is back with his unit this week. Got it?"

"I will do everything I can."

Carson and Beck ordered lunch, and the waitress brought another vodka and a beer.

◌◌

The next morning at 0830, Maj. Hendrix telephoned Beck at the legal assistance office and told him he was detailed as LCpl. Jim Sanders' defense counsel. At 1150, GySgt. Tyler appeared at the legal assistance office with Sanders, and Beck interviewed Sanders over the lunch hour. Beck then called the Chief Trial Counsel, Maj. Steve Way. After reviewing all the facts with Way, Beck asked that the court-martial be dismissed, and the case referred to office hours. Maj. Way responded, "That will never happen."

At 1500, Maj. Way called Beck. "I don't get it, Mike. Why is Gunner Carson involved in the Sanders' case?"

"I don't know. He just likes the kid for some reason."

"Did you tell him to talk to Bumbaugh?"

"Of course not. Steve, you know I wouldn't try and go around you."

"I just got off the phone with Bumbaugh. Sanders' court-martial has been dismissed. He is scheduled for office hours in front of the H&HS Battalion Commanding Officer tomorrow morning at 1000."

"Wow."

"Get this. Bumbaugh says you are to meet with Sanders tonight to advise him of his legal rights and explain what is happening. Sanders will be accompanied at the office hours by Gunner Carson, and you will not appear. Lance Corporal Sanders will be reduced one rank and receive no other punishment. So, how the fuck did this just happen?"

"No idea, Steve. I guess Carson does have some juice around here."

Chapter 41

Over the last 12 hours, Warren Leavy had read, copied, and annotated every case cited in both Loring & Leavy's brief and the government's brief. At 12:30 a.m. he walked into his partner Ogden Loring's office and laid photocopies of the 25 cases cited by the government on Ogden's desk. The copies were given to Ogden for review and his preparation for tomorrow's hearing. By this time, both lawyers were very tired and ready to go home. An hour later, Warren returned to Ogden's office and could see that Ogden had finished reviewing the cases. Warren sat in one of the chairs across from Ogden's desk.

"What do you think our chances are, Og?" Warren asked, as if he hadn't previously considered the issue.

"Better than fifty-fifty with Judge Moorman. Less than fifty-fifty with the Ninth Circuit on appeal. Zero with the Supreme Court. The language of the Constitution is clear, but I doubt that the federal judges will have the balls to declare President Bush's actions illegal, except maybe Judge Moorman."

"Yeah, Og, that's exactly the way I see it."

Ogden rubbed his eyes, then stretched his arms. "You know Warren, a lot of things in life do not turn out. I have been a shit father and a worse husband. Too much booze, too much grass, too much partying. But I can always think about all the good things we have done as lawyers. In my heart, I feel we have been on the right side of history. Fought the good fight. Yeah...I feel guilty that I've pushed Roslyn Baker and the National Peace Coalition for big fees, but we need the money just to survive. We are still doing the right thing here, and I am going to do my absolute best to get Nathan Jones back to his home in Illinois."

"I am with you Ogden. We must make enough to pay our overhead and support our families...It's late and we better get some rest for the hearing tomorrow."

⚘

As Capt. Beck pulled into the driveway, Maj. Hendrix's front door opened, and she emerged carrying a briefcase. Capt. Beck fought to ignore her beauty, but when she climbed inside the Range Rover, she smiled at Capt. Beck with beautiful eyes and ivory teeth. Even in her uniform, she wore deep red lipstick and an intoxicating perfume. An exciting feeling coursed through Beck's brain, but he told himself again to control it. He backed out and swore he would not look at Cindy's legs during the entire trip.

The drive took three hours. After crossing the Colorado River on the "Ocean to Ocean Bridge," Capt. Beck drove 50 miles through the mountains of sand called "The Dunes," then across the green El Centro Valley, over the mountains, and down towards the Pacific to downtown San Diego. The federal courthouse was a dull-as-dirt, ugly, dark brown, four-story building located near the Gas Lamp District of San Diego. It seemed amazing to Beck how many homeless people were on the streets surrounding the courthouse. One older black man held up a sign that read *VETERAN, HOMELESS, PLEASE HELP*. As Capt. Beck and Maj. Hendrix walked by, he grinned from ear to ear.

"Whoo...Eee. Semper Fi, Sister!"

The old man then snapped to attention and saluted Maj. Hendrix in remarkably correct form. Maj. Hendrix glanced at the man, returned a little grin, and continued to walk towards the entrance. At nine o'clock, one hour before the scheduled hearing, Maj. Hendrix and Capt. Beck seated themselves in Judge Moorman's courtroom.

The importance of the matter was emphasized by Col. Butcher's denial of Sgt. Jones's request for release from pretrial confinement two days before.

Over 20 lawyers sat in Judge Moorman's courtroom intensely studying their notes in last minute preparation for their scheduled hearings. Ogden Loring arrived at 9:45 a.m., sat next to Capt. Beck and handed him a copy of the docket. Beck saw that ten cases were scheduled for 10:00 a.m., and that Sgt. Jones's was last on the list. Ogden Loring looked different from the lawyer who visited Marines in Yuma wearing jeans and a T-shirt. This morning, he wore a tailored three-piece wool suit, a crisp white shirt, and a red power tie. His beard was meticulously groomed, and his ponytail appeared entirely appropriate. Ogden projected confidence. It was a look befitting a famous civil-rights attorney in America, and just by Ogden's appearance, Capt. Beck instantly knew Ogden Loring was a competent trial lawyer.

"We're probably going to be sitting here awhile. Here is your copy of Warren's brief and the government's response."

Capt. Beck passed the government's brief to Maj. Hendrix and started reading the Loring & Leavy brief. Warren Leavy had done an excellent job. Thoroughly researched, and expertly written, it looked like a brief produced by one of the large insurance defense firms in Chicago.

The Honorable George Moorman had been drafted during Vietnam and served his tour as a clerk typist at Fort Lenard Wood, Missouri. Appointed by Lyndon Johnson as a U.S. District Court Judge for the Southern District of California, he had presided over most of the important civil rights cases for the past 24 years. As a federal judge he received less compensation than Mike Beck did as a civilian lawyer in Chicago. Still, Judge Moorman professionally endured the drudgery of hearing many routine matters and seldom bothered to write an opinion of more than one page. Like his law clerk, though, he became intrigued by the facts and law of Sgt. Jones's case and was eager to assume jurisdiction.

The bailiff's voice boomed out, and everyone in the courtroom stood as Judge Moorman entered from a door behind the bench. Mike Beck had appeared in front of hundreds of judges, but Judge Moorman seemed the image of a judge, white hair, intelligent face, black reading glasses, and black robe. He sat behind the elevated bench, which emphasized the power of the court and required lawyers to elevate their heads up 20 degrees. Mike considered the many lives that had been changed in this one courtroom by this one judge.

"Be seated," Judge Moorman said. He sorted through papers on his desk and glanced up over his glasses. Finally, he said, "*United States of America versus William Campbell*, appearances please." Judge Moorman proceeded to efficiently dispose of the first nine cases, took a 15-minute recess, and returned to the bench. Sgt.

Jones's case was called. Ogden motioned for Capt. Beck to sit with him at counsel's table. An Assistant U.S. Attorney, and a Judge Advocate Colonel from Headquarters, represented the Government.

Without using notes, Ogden Loring laid out Sgt. Jones's argument that the mobilization order constituted an illegal order under both domestic and international law, and Sgt. Jones had a duty to disobey the order. His voice was rich and moved high and low with the dramatic flair of a fine actor.

"Article I, Section 8 of the United States Constitution gives Congress the power to declare war. Under the 1973 War Powers Act, Congress by concurrent resolution may authorize military action or require the President to cease military operations. In this case, Congress has not passed a joint resolution authorizing President Bush to invoke military action against Iraq, nor has Congress appropriated funds, or otherwise endorsed, acquiesced in, or approved war against Iraq. The Nuremberg trials at the end of World War Two established the precedent that soldiers can be punished for participation in a war of aggression, and following a superior's order is not a justification for violating international law. Under Article VI of the Constitution all treaties, including the U.N. Charter, are part of the 'supreme law of the land.' The U.N. Charter is aimed at minimizing the use of military force. There are only two instances that permit the use of military force against another state: self-defense or when approved by the Security Council. Aggression must be met with the least possible counterforce. U.N. Resolution 678 authorizing the allies to use all necessary means was not an approval of an attack on Iraq by the United States, but instead, requires a prior showing of failure of economic sanctions and attempts to negotiate peace."

Victor Brown, an assistant U.S. Attorney for the Southern District of California, argued the Government's case. This case would be the most important yet in his brief career as a federal prosecutor. During Ogden's argument, Brown appeared nervous, passing files back and forth with the Colonel from Headquarters. The underlying theme of his written brief boiled down to the assertion that Sgt. Jones's petition amounted to nothing more than harassment of the Government. Now he stood and read shakily from his notes.

"Under military law, the only defense for failing to follow an order is that the accused knew the order to be unlawful or a person of ordinary sense and understanding would have known the order to be unlawful. Absent a formal resolution from Congress explicitly declaring a particular military action unauthorized, military action is presumptively valid, as are the orders for Marines to participate therein. Fifty-four members of Congress already filed for an injunction in District Court for the District of Columbia to prevent President Bush from starting military action against Iraq. The court dismissed the case because Congress as a whole had not taken action to oppose the President's plan. Sgt. Jones's case is controlled by this holding entered in *Dellums v Bush*. In the absence of a formal resolution passed by a majority of Congress, the legality, or illegality, of the President's actions is a non-justiciable question."

Mr. Brown returned to counsel's table and Judge Moorman paused to think. "Counsel, thank you for your arguments and excellent briefs. This case presents a fascinating issue for the court and a break from the court's mundane cases. I will start with a question for Government Counsel. As I read Sergeant Jones's mobilization orders, he was not ordered to go to Iraq, or directly participate in military action against Iraq. As a reservist, he was simply ordered to active duty with his entire unit. Where is Sergeant Jones's unit today?"

The Colonel looked embarrassed. "Your honor, I cannot answer that question. Maybe Captain Beck knows."

Judge Moorman eyed Capt. Beck over his reading glasses. A wry smile crossed his face. "Captain Beck?"

"Yes, Your Honor. I spoke by telephone to members of Sergeant Jones's unit yesterday, and most of his unit is in transit to Camp Gray, Jubayl, Saudi Arabia. Some members have arrived in Saudi Arabia, and others remain at Marine Corps Base, Twentynine Palms, California"

Judge Moorman continued. "I do not believe this case presents a justiciable question currently. Not for the reasons argued by the Government. It is not my holding that there is a presumption of legality, or that Congress must pass a resolution prohibiting military action.

"This Country has been blessed with presidents that obey the rule of law. However, our founders had in mind the possibility that someday the public might elect an unscrupulous rogue or a wanna-be-dictator. If in this hypothetical, the wanna-be-dictator, without any Congressional approval, or disapproval, ordered military action against a peaceful and innocent nation, here I am imagining the type of actions taken by Hitler or Stalin, I believe our military men and women would be justified in disobeying such an order. That is my understanding of the Nuremberg principle.

"Of course, in this case, as of today, Congress has not acted either way. But neither has the President. So far, the President has merely ordered mobilization and the necessary training and preparations to attack Iraq if Hussein does not withdraw his troops from Kuwait. There still could be a peaceful settlement. Before the President orders military action, Congress could declare war. The U.N. General Assembly could expressly authorize military action.

Mr. Loring, I find many of your arguments to be sound and my holding should not be interpreted as adverse precedent. But before ruling, the Court must see what happens regarding these matters. The Court will not issue a writ of *habeas corpus* at this time but reserves jurisdiction to do so in the future depending upon the actions of Congress and the President."

♋

After the hearing, Beck and Hendrix drove down the hill to the waterfront for lunch at Cindy's favorite San Diego restaurant, Anthony's Fish Grotto. A long line of tourists extended onto the street, but a table for two remained open in the bar. Mike had dated beautiful women in Chicago, but as he and Cindy headed for their table, he noticed men discretely glancing at Cindy. It seemed that every man in the place stopped eating and gawked at her as she walked by. For some reason, this sent an electric shock through his system. *Jesus, Beck. She is off-limits. Stop thinking like this.*

"I recommend the seafood salad and one glass of the house wine," Cindy announced without looking at the menu.

"As a big shot Chicago lawyer, what did you think of the hearing?"

"I was very impressed. At first, I didn't think much of Ogden, but he did an excellent job on this motion. Impressive."

"Do you think Judge Moorman will issue a writ if President Bush orders military action?"

"He will if Congress does not pass a resolution first. What do you think?"

Maj. Hendrix's eyes sharpened. "I agree."

When the wine arrived, Cindy looked Mike in the eyes in a way he had not seen before. They sat sipping the wine and enjoying the spectacular view of the bay.

"Is there a girl back home, Captain?"

"No. My partners say I am in love with the law. I pretty much work all the time."

Cindy laughed, stared out the window, and studied the cruise ship slowly moving down the channel. Their food came a few minutes later. Mike tasted the seafood salad and his eyes widened. "Wow. I never thought I could be impressed by a salad, but that's damn good."

Cindy started to say something, then took a quick sip of her wine instead.

"I understand you are married to a Marine Corps pilot?" Mike asked, his tone almost too innocent. Astonished, Cindy took a long time to respond. She looked down at her wine glass. Turning back to Mike a moment later, she looked a little misty-eyed.

"Eight years."

"Children?"

It was suddenly quiet, and Mike watched Cindy clench her jaw muscles. "No."

"Maybe you are also in love with the law?"

Cindy laughed a slow laugh that for some reason seemed sad to Mike.

"Mike, if you are only in love with the law, you are really without love." She continued to laugh with a tiny rueful smile that tugged at Mike's heart. He didn't know how to respond, so he just kept quiet.

Chapter 42

At 1900 on Monday night, Charlie Carson left the PMO Office and drove to his off-base residence. He intended on watching the football game. Carson's house sat at the end of the street on the border of the Barry M. Goldwater Bombing Range. The original owner had been a big game hunter and added a reloading shed and a 100-yard rifle range on the back three acres, complete with earthen safety berms.

On arriving home, Carson showered and walked to his kitchen. He opened the refrigerator, stared inside, and then closed the door. He did the same at the freezer. After pausing to think, he filled a water glass with Smirnoff vodka. At this point every evening he used to tell himself he had to stop drinking, but he no longer bothered. He knew he would never stop—he couldn't stop.

Charlie Carson went to the living room and sat on his couch in front of the television. He tuned into the Monday night football game. He sloshed his vodka around in his glass and studied it at length. He took a sip, grimaced as if it tasted awful, and returned to the kitchen for ice.

He tried to watch the game, but his mind raced with thoughts about the new Commanding Officer and what he might do if he found out about all the recent shit Carson had been doing. Charlie Carson knew he was on thin ice—too much motorcycle riding, socializing with enlisted, too many nights in biker bars, fist fights, hookers, and way too much booze. *The old Commanding Officer was an idiot. But Colonel Cahill is super smart, and I will not underestimate a Medal of Honor winner. I cannot just kiss his ass. Somehow, he knows that I am losing it. I better get my shit together fast or put in for retirement.*

Staring at the television, guilt feelings abruptly overwhelmed Carson. His mind filled with so many blinding images that he felt like he would vomit. He relived being inside of the sewer tunnel, squatting down, and listening to the Vietcong heading his way. He saw PFC

Kenneth Jones' body, smelled his insides, and felt the blood stick to his body. Terrifying sensations pounded him from all corners.

Carson tried to pry his mind out of the tunnel, but he felt the weight of murdering Kenneth Jones and of his other atrocities. He remembered the overseas sins of generations of Marines. He replayed the shots taken too quickly. He saw dead Marines and dead civilians. He remembered the gang rapes in the Vietnamese jungles. His generation had turned thousands of young girls to prostitution.

Sometimes, Carson could push away, or at least diminish, these memories with vodka. But tonight, he seemed unable to do so. He guzzled the booze, glass after glass, but still could no longer control his mind. He slowly rose from the couch, stood on shaky legs, and rushed to the bathroom where he threw up. His stomach cleared, but his mind did not. He returned to the couch and tried to watch the game.

Soon those thoughts from that most terrible place returned to his mind. The world went dark inside the sewer tunnel. He was running and shooting at anything he saw. He felt the bullet ripping through his guts.

In complete panic, Charlie Carson jumped off the couch and ran outside through his back door. He told himself to settle down, just drink more vodka, and stay home, but the other voices in his mind were screaming, louder and louder. The darkness rose with him again and again.

He ran to the shed that he used to reload ammunition, opened one of the gun safes, and took out his well-used Colt M1911 .45 ACP, the one he brought back from Vietnam. For a moment, Carson just held the pistol with the muzzle in his mouth and thought about shooting himself. Somehow, he had to stop the pain. But his finger refused to pull the trigger.

He gave up and started admiring the pistol's rugged beauty. He picked up a cleaning cloth and slowly wiped down the metal. *How in the fuck could Headquarters replace this with that Italian piece of shit?*

He loaded six 8-round magazines, walked out to his backyard range, and put on his hearing protectors. He assumed his old-school shooting stance and started shooting at the metal targets. He rapidly fired off all six magazines of .45-caliber ammunition without missing, and breathed deeply, catching the scent of the gun smoke.

After shooting the Colt, Carson felt much better. The gun smoke, noise, and recoil eased his nerves. It felt like the lucky days when he had survived in the tunnels, the days he had killed many Vietcong without making a mistake. He returned to the shed, reloaded the six magazines, and started shooting again. Shooting his Colt, everything closed to a tight space again, a space in which he could survive.

⚭

After emptying all magazines a second time, Carson returned to the reloading shed, disassembled the Colt, cleaned his weapon, and returned it to the gun safe. Again, the smell of the bore cleaner and the ritual of breaking down and cleaning the pistol soothed his nerves.

He then drove his Harley Davidson motorcycle to the Mineola Tree Trailer Park, located directly behind the American Legion and just off the Air Base. The trailers sat close together with barely room to park a vehicle, and the owner rented the old trailers at the cheapest prices in town. Carson drove to Space H-33, Herlinda Hernandez's trailer.

Before Carson could drop the kickstand, Herlinda came outside with a big smile, wearing a T-shirt, no bra, and cutoff jeans. The smile told him that she had her fix of heroin for the day. Carson could never believe a heroin addict could be so good-looking—beautiful skin, raven hair, dark eyes, and voluptuous lips—a classic Mexican beauty.

"Que Paso, Amigo."

"Open for business?"

"Of course. I have a special military discount this evening."

Since Carson had been there many times, they did not discuss price. He flopped down on the dilapidated old couch, kicked off his boots, and completed undressing. By the time he made it to the tiny bedroom, Herlinda lay naked on her back with her legs spread in a V towards the ceiling. Again, Carson marveled at how she could do that, and they were finished in minutes.

When high, Herlinda could eat like a horse, so Carson agreed to take her to Alonso's Grocery. In the rear of the store, a middle-aged Hispanic lady washed pans but stopped to take their order. She heated two tortillas over the gas burner and dished out large servings of machaca from a simmering pot. Meanwhile, Carson pulled a 40-ounce Bud Light out of the cooler and sat at one of the metal Mexican beer tables. Herlinda brought over the burritos and wolfed hers down.

"You going to eat that?"

Without speaking Carson slid his plate over to Herlinda and watched her devour a second burrito.

From Alonso's Grocery, they rode the Harley over the bridge to the Riverside Tavern, a rough biker bar in Winterhaven, California that averaged a shooting or stabbing every month. Inside, they found an empty high-top table. Carson chain smoked cigarettes and drank shots of vodka while Herlinda sipped on beers.

Every time a large or mean-looking biker walked by, Carson challenged them to an arm-wrestling contest for 20 bucks. They all declined. By now, everyone at the Riverside Tavern knew that when Carson drank vodka he got mean, when he got mean he wanted to arm-wrestle, and when he arm-wrestled, he liked to fist fight.

Nobody wanted a fistfight with Carson tonight. After an hour, Carson gave up, and they drove the bike back to Herlinda's. Then, although he knew better, Carson rode to the Brig.

Chapter 43

At 2330, the lights on the third deck of the Brig suddenly came on, waking Sgt. Jones in his cell. Next, he heard loud footsteps coming down the hallway.

"Get your ass up, Yellow-Belly!" Nathan recognized the voice of Gunner Carson.

In seconds, Carson appeared in front of Jones's cell. He wore civilian clothes—cowboy boots, blue jeans, and a leather vest. He looked drunk, angry, and mean. Sgt. Jones quickly climbed out of his rack and stood at attention in his skivvies. The fear seized him as he rose.

"Did they tell you that you lost your civilian case?"

"No, Sir."

"Did they tell you that Colonel Butcher ain't letting you out of my Brig?"

"No, Sir."

"Well, it seems like your lawyers are losing everything, Jones. Conscientious objector application denied! Pretrial release denied! *Habeas corpus* denied!" Carson laughed.

"I already told you, Jones—I own your ass. You ain't getting out of this Brig unless I say so." Carson slurred his words and seem to lose his train of thought.

"I will tell you something else, Scumbag. Being squared away and working hard in my Brig doesn't mean jack-shit compared to what you did when you abandoned your unit. I bet the Marines at Fourth Tanks are sweating their asses off in Saudi Arabia, trying to get ready to fight. And you ain't there to help, are you?"

"No, Sir." It seemed crazy, but Carson's words caused an ocean of guilt to wash over Nathan. *Carson is right, I am a scumbag.*

Carson stopped talking and grabbed one of the cell bars to keep from falling. "You yellow-belly, chickenshit, son-of-a-bitch. You are just sitting here on your ass." Carson trembled with hatred. "You syphilitic twerp…I promise you there will be nobody from my Brig testifying for you at your sentencing hearing. If that's what you are thinking, forget it. Tell your lawyers not even to ask for a witness from the Brig. If they ask, it will be me testifying, and I will tell the truth—you are a low life, miserable, cowardly bastard. Got that, Jones?"

"Yes, Sir!"

"But I have some good news for you—I ain't going to hang you tonight. That can wait. Good night, motherfucker."

Chapter 44

With its neon sign, 1950s architecture, and red brick exterior, Jack and Rosie's Steakhouse reminded Mike Beck of his favorite taverns in Chicago. Stepping out of the Yuma evening sunlight and inside the door, the place seemed dark, like entering a movie theater for an afternoon matinee. As Mike's eyes adjusted, he could make out a nearly empty bar to his left and a packed dining room to his right. Mike always felt strange eating alone, like a loser with no friends, so he hurried inside the bar. He planned on having a drink, scoping out the place, and deciding whether to stay for dinner.

As soon as Mike entered the bar, he saw Cindy Hendrix sitting alone in a secluded corner. Mike had thought about meeting Cindy off base so often that tonight seemed a memory. Her hair, which she normally wore in a bun at work, hung down past her shoulders. She wore lipstick that contrasted starkly with her brown skin. Her civilian clothes revealed her body in a way her uniform did not. Mike could now see that her breasts were large and firm, and they pushed out against her bra through the thin cotton T-shirt so that her nipples could be seen as faint gray dots. To Mike, Cindy looked like a movie star, only with more class and intelligence.

For some reason, a flood of embarrassment washed over Mike, and he started to turn and leave the bar. It was too late. Mike and Cindy's eyes met, and she flashed him a dazzling smile. Her teeth were white and translucent, the same as fine-bone china. Mike's heart missed a beat, and it took a moment before he caught his breath. He had no choice but to walk over and say hello. Mike pushed past his embarrassment and wandered through the empty tables, continuing to enjoy Cindy's beautiful smile.

As soon as Mike arrived at her table, Cindy jumped from her chair and gave him a hug. He was surprised by her sudden show of friendship, though by no means disappointed. Mike hugged her back, putting his arms around her, and appreciating her thin waist. He enjoyed the soft pressure of her breasts against his chest and the smell of her perfume.

After the hug, Cindy picked up her empty glass and moved toward the bar, and Mike watched her body as she walked away. "Can I buy you a drink, Captain?"

"Yes, Ma'am. Jack and Coke, please."

While Cindy waited for the bartender to make her Manhattan and Mike's Jack and Coke, he tried to control his excitement.

"Did you put your name in for a table?" Cindy asked as she sat the drinks down.

"No. I really hadn't planned on dinner. Just stopped for a drink."

"But you must try Jack and Rosie's steaks! They are the best! Why don't you join me?"

"I would love to join you." Mike offered Cindy his best smile.

"Are you still enjoying being a Marine Corps' defense counsel?"

"Absolutely! I think I would die if I got sent back to legal assistance full time."

"Captain, I am doing my best to get you out of legal assistance permanently, but Lucas won't budge. He breaks out his statistics showing that even in half a day, you are doing more wills and powers of attorney than he and Dean put together."

Mike went to the bar for more drinks. This time it was Cindy who admired how Mike filled out his jeans. *My goodness; he is so handsome and charming.*

As soon as Mike returned with the drinks, a middle-aged waitress appeared, and escorted Mike and Cindy to a table inside a dining room filled with snowbirds and farmers. She seated them on the far wall. Both ordered ribeye steaks which came with soup and salad. Mike wondered about the quality because of the low price but ordered a bottle of Cabernet Sauvignon.

"Ma'am, is your husband still on deployment?"

"Yes, he is. Four months turned into a six-month carrier cruse."

"It must be tough on both of you."

"At this point, it seems normal. Joe's been on about a dozen deployments since we were married."

"Ma'am. Major Herdy told me that you were the first black woman Judge Advocate in the history of the Marine Corps."

"God! Captain, that makes me sound so old."

"No. It's very impressive. Would it be appropriate for me to ask, how did you end up in the Marine Corps?"

"You want to hear my life story?"

"I would love to."

"OK. Where should I start? My father is a physician and the head of cardiology at Northwestern University Hospital in Chicago. I am sure you have been to Park Ridge."

"Of course, I know Northwestern and Park Ridge. I love Park Ridge's older homes and beautiful tree-lined streets."

"That is where I grew up. I was a complete tomboy and followed my three older brothers around, playing baseball, and doing the things boys did for fun. My brothers were academic geniuses, straight As in high school and college, and easily admitted to medical school. But I hated school. Can you believe that I almost did not graduate from high school because of my poor grades?

"My father did everything he could to get me into Northwestern, but they would not even consider me. The University of Illinois rejected me. I finally got into Southern Illinois University. At that time SIU would accept anyone." Cindy grinned and laughed.

"I still hated classwork, but I was a good athlete. I had no difficulty getting on every sports team at SIU. I played college golf, soccer, softball, and basketball. I had a full scholarship and was elected the team captain on every team. If I had been a man, I would have been a celebrity, but at that time women in college sports remained unknown and underappreciated."

"Wow! That is amazing. Four sports. Never heard of anyone being able to do that." Mike was sincerely impressed. The waitress brought out the soup, and Mike poured the wine. Cindy paused the story, but for some reason, she felt comfortable talking to Mike like this, even though he was a junior officer.

"I love hearing your background, Will you continue?" Mike asked after a few minutes.

"Sure. At graduation, I knew I wasn't ready to go to work, and my father insisted that I pursue a postgraduate degree. He offered to pay all expenses at any school I chose. Unfortunately, I couldn't get into a post-graduate program. All the universities rejected me, even SIU."

Cindy finished her wine, and Mike refilled both glasses.

"After being rejected at a dozen universities, a friend told me about John Marshall Law School. I am sure the lawyers at your big firm look down on John Marshall graduates, but I wasn't worried about that at the time."

"That's not true, Ma'am. Many of Chicago's top trial lawyers are graduates of John Marshall. Believe me, I've been up against a few of them. Damn tough litigators, usually better than the Ivory League crowd."

"Well, anyway, at the time it was just a private law school offering night classes taught by practicing attorneys. And as they say, you don't go to John Marshall if you plan on practicing in New York or Los Angeles. You go to John Marshall, if, and only if, you want to practice law in Chicago. Of course, at the time my biggest concern was whether I would be able to pass the Illinois bar exam after graduating. I knew the high failure rate." Cindy paused again to sip her wine.

"During my second year at John Marshall, I attended a friend's wedding, and for some reason found myself having eye contact with a middle-aged black man. He turned out to be a Cook County Superior Court Judge, a Marine Judge Advocate, an active Reservist, and graduate of both SIU and John Marshal. He knew about my athletic accomplishments at SIU and immediately decided that I should pursue a career as a judge advocate in the Marines.

He gave me the number of an Officer Selection Officer in St. Louis. When I called the OSO Officer, he got excited. He said the Marines needed diversification, and he wanted to recruit a black woman lawyer. Honestly, he flat told me that the Marines did not care about where I attended law school, my grade point average, or where I passed the bar. If I joined the Marines, I could take the Indiana exam with its high pass rate.

"Also, the judge called me every week, offering encouragement and advice. He said he met a lot of underprivileged young black girls in the Marines who served as clerk typists in the law centers. He wanted me to set an example by becoming the first black women judge advocate in Marine Corps history. He helped me practice for the Marine physical fitness test. I always got a high score. So, when I showed up for Officer's Candidate School, no one could beat me. Always a perfect score on the PFT. The same thing at the Basic Infantry School.

"I taught myself how to study. I came to really enjoy reading the law. Also, my senior officers were great teachers. So, have I bored you to death?"

"Not at all, Ma'am. You have had an incredible career."

Chapter 45

The thought entered Col. Cahill's mind seemingly of its own accord. *The nail that sticks up is hammered down.*

He gazed at the stack of papers on the coffee table as if each were an order for his relief of command. Over the last two days, he had read every word and could remember the details contained in every document: Sgt. Jones's service record book, awards, medals, conscientious objector package, the transcripts of the hearings, affidavits, legal briefs, even the Naval Justice School books. *Sergeant Jones's service seems exemplary, a fucking water-walker. He got religion and submitted a conscientious-objector package months before the Gulf Conflict. His commanding officer, either through ignorance or laziness, sat on the package. Of course, there can be no doubt that Jones intended to voluntarily return to the military. The phone call telling his grandmother he was turning himself in was recorded in the wiretap and his telephone call to Marshal Collins. If it were any other case it would be easy. By law, a Marine who voluntarily returns should not be held in pretrial confinement. But if I release Jones, General Reynolds will go fucking ballistic.*

Cahill then laughed out loud and startled himself at the volume of his voice. But the thought of releasing Jones also produced a pang of guilt. *General Lenard should not have to deal with General Reynold's shit while preparing his Marines for war in Iraq. Sergeant Jones is either a religious fanatic or a coward. I won't let his case interfere with combat preparation.*

Earl Cahill got to his feet and walked to the kitchen. He filled his glass with ice and only a touch of the Jack Daniels sitting on the counter. *During my entire career Marines have respected me as a medal of honor winner. Should I throw that away, get relieved of my command, and retire in disgrace? Maybe for once it is time to take the easy way out, let the military judge release Sergeant Jones. Jones made himself into a nail that must be hammered down.*

ೲ

Sergeant Nathan Jones and Capt. Beck marched into Col. Cahill's office. The guard assigned as "chaser" stayed outside. LtCol. Bumbaugh, Maj. Steve Way, and Ogden Loring sat at chairs pulled to the side of the desk. Sgt. Jones looked stone-faced and stopped in the middle of the room, looking through Col. Cahill.

"Sergeant Jones reporting as ordered."

"Gentlemen, we are here this morning for the purpose of entering a decision on Sergeant Jones's appeal of Colonel Butcher's order continuing Sergeant Jones in pretrial confinement."

Col. Cahill glanced down at a note pad on his desk and continued to speak.

"I have read the Appellant's Brief on Pretrial Confinement Hearing and all the attachments. Major Way, have you been able to contact Lieutenant Colonel Easterday?"

"No, Sir."

"Why not?"

"Sir, I believe Lieutenant Colonel Easterday is conducting a field exercise near Jubayl, Saudi Arabia. As soon as he returns to camp, Lieutenant Colonel Easterday will be instructed to call me using a satellite phone."

"So, on the issue of submitting his original conscientious objector package, the only evidence we have regarding Lieutenant Colonel Easterday's action is what Sergeant Jones says—that Lieutenant Colonel Easterday told Sergeant Jones that submitting the package would be a waste of time."

"Sir, the only evidence on that issue at this point is Sergeant Jones's testimony."

"A few additional questions for you, Major Way. How many of the Marines in the Brig awaiting trial for desertion voluntarily returned to their unit or voluntarily turned themselves over to civilian authorities?"

"Sir, I haven't researched the issue, but I would say none."

"And Major Way why do you say 'none' without any research?"

"The policy is that if a Marine returns to his unit, or surrenders to civil authorities, the Marine is not placed in pretrial confinement," Maj. Way answered in a respectful tone.

"And that is because the return demonstrates the Marine's intent to have the charges legally resolved and to stand trial," Col. Cahill said firmly, then asked another question.

"Marshal Collins testified that she had a wiretap on Sergeant Jones's grandmother's phone. Neither Emma nor Sergeant Jones knew about the wiretap. Yet, hours before his arrest at the traffic scene, Sergeant Jones called his grandmother and told her he would turn himself in the next day. Do I have that correct?"

"Yes, Sir."

"Sergeant Jones also telephoned Marshal Collins and made an appointment to turn himself in at her office in Benton, Illinois the next day. Correct?"

"Yes, Sir."

"On the way to Benton, Sergeant Jones and Judy Novotney were detained by the local police. The police asked for identification and Sergeant Jones popped up as wanted for desertion. The traffic cops arrested him. So, Sergeant Jones was literally arrested on the way to turn himself in?"

"That is all correct, Sir," Maj. Way agreed.

"It seems that I would be legally required to treat Sergeant Jones like the other voluntary returnees and release him from confinement."

Maj. Way struggled for an answer. Snapping back to his surroundings, he finally responded. "Yes, legally you should treat Sergeant Jones as a voluntary returnee and release him from pretrial confinement."

"Staff Judge Advocate, what do you recommend?"

Lieutenant Colonel Bumbaugh's already sour face twisted into a deeper frown. "It is a high-profile case, but I do not see grounds for continuing pretrial confinement. If you choose not to release Sergeant Jones, I believe a military judge will do that as soon as the case is put in front of the court-martial. Sir, my recommendation is that you release him."

Visibly in deep thought, Col. Cahill rubbed his cheeks, glanced out the window, and stared at the top of his desk for a long time.

"Before I make my decision, I have a few questions for Sergeant Jones."

Col. Cahill looked at Mr. Loring and Capt. Beck.

"Any objection?"

Capt. Beck did not hesitate. "No objection, Sir."

Col. Cahill removed a Bible from his desk drawer and placed it in front of Jones.

"Sergeant Jones, I have concluded that you are a deeply religious man and I have the option of releasing you from the Brig and restricting you to the barracks, chow hall, workplace, and place of worship. If I do that, are you willing to swear on this Bible that you will obey the restriction order and appear whenever your court-martial is scheduled?"

Sgt. Jones stared Col. Cahill in the eye, stepped forward to the desk, and placed his right hand on the Bible.

"I swear on this Holy Bible, and upon my faith in the Lord Jesus Christ, that I will fully obey any restriction order. I will not leave Marine Corps Air Station, Yuma, Arizona without permission, and I will appear at my court-martial when scheduled."

Sgt. Jones then stepped back and remained at attention.

Col. Cahill looked again at Maj. Way.

"Major Way, you prepare the restriction order and the order for release. I would like Sgt. Jones assigned to the Chaplain's office. See if that is agreeable with the Chaplain. If not, find some other section willing to take him. Dismissed!"

Sgt. Jones did an about-face, and he and Capt. Beck marched out of the office.

Chapter 46

Without explanation, the Chaplain refused to allow Sgt. Jones to work at the Chapel, and worse, Maj. Way could not convince any officer at the Air Station to accept Jones into their unit. The only option for Jones that Maj. Way could find appeared to be the "casualty platoon," where Marines awaiting court-martial, and not in pretrial confinement, were routinely assigned.

Troop handlers from the Provost Marshal's Office supervised the members of the casualty platoon, and the platoon was billeted in Barracks No. 8 located in the P-1-11 Area. One of the last of the World War II wood barracks at MCAS, Yuma, Barracks No. 8 consisted of a two-story structure shaped like an H with squad bays on each end and administrative offices in the middle. The building sat vacant for years but remained in habitable condition. After the casualty platoon moved in, the troop handlers painted the front doors bright yellow. It became known as "the Yellow Barracks."

At 2200 the night following Col. Cahill's decision to release Sgt. Jones, GySgt. Tyler from the Provost Marshal's Office picked up Jones at the Brig and transported him to Barracks No 8. Sgt. Jones spent the night in the squad bay on a bare mattress, without a pillow, or sheet.

At 0500 the Staff Non-Commission Officer in Charge of Barracks No. 8, Master Sergeant Reggie Miller, came through screaming. He was very short, and he seemed angry about it. He had an oversized head and a way of lowering it, constantly glaring from under his brow. Madness could be seen dancing behind his black eyes. Sgt. Jones soon learned that Miller could insult a subordinate with hundreds of spectacularly profane phrases.

"Drop your cocks and grab your socks. Fall out in five minutes."

The Marines quickly fell outside wearing their utility uniforms, including heavy boots, and stood at attention. MSgt. Miller walked up and down, ranting, and raving about sand inside the Yellow Barracks. Jones noticed Miller's drill instructor's voice and weird smile, the smile that said: "I am enjoying this, I am enjoying every second of fucking with you." Pacing back and forth, Miller looked very stiff, moving his entire body instead of just his head, and his very large hands were formed into fists and laid atop his thighs, as if expecting to use them at any moment.

"You dirty scumbags. You will not track sand into my barracks. Give me twenty-five pushups."

While the platoon members attempted to complete 25 pushups, Miller moved around having a fit, screaming, cursing, and kicking anyone he thought was not doing a proper pushup.

"Starting now. No boots in the barracks. Remove them at the door."

MSgt. Miller then turned the platoon over to his assistant, Cpl. Weaver, and went back inside the barracks. Tall, skinny, and in his early 20s, Weaver weighed maybe 150 pounds. Sporting a high-and-tight haircut, he had hard features and piercing eyes, but his voice was high and nasal. The raffish angle of his cover seemed to say that he was not afraid of anyone.

From the barracks, Cpl. Weaver marched the platoon at double-time to what looked like a run-down baseball field with a rusty backstop, dirt end-field, and poorly irrigated grass outfield. Under the cloudless Yuma sky, Cpl. Weaver put the Marines through the standard calisthenics: pushups, sit-ups, jumping jacks, and squat thrusts. The Marines, including Sgt. Jones, were soon winded and sweating.

Next, they ran in platoon formation outside the P-1-11 main gate, circled back along a power line, and ran down an unimproved road for three miles. The Marines sank two or three inches into the sand with each stride. Finally, they arrived at what looked like the largest sand hill in the desert. They were told to form a single line. Screaming and hollering, Cpl. Weaver ordered individual Marines to scale its summit and race down the far side and back. Again, and again, the Marines were ordered to run over the sand hill until many could no longer stand upright.

Sgt. Jones felt himself breathing deeply and rapidly, and his lungs were pounding. Sweat dripped down his face and into his eyes. His leg muscles burned intensely.

When one Marine collapsed, Cpl. Weaver started kicking his ribs. Sgt. Jones managed to run over and help the Marine get back on his feet. Weaver did not try and stop him. After an hour of this treatment, the platoon ran back to the barracks and stood at attention.

An hour later with the platoon still at attention, MSgt. Miller walked out and addressed the platoon.

"This is for the Marines that arrived yesterday. Welcome to the Yellow Barracks! I bet a few of you bastards think you are tough guys just playing a game and getting out of going to Iraq. But I know that you're not. You're just soft, and you are scared shitless. If you weren't, you wouldn't be here. You'd be with your fellow Marines, fighting. Well, you listen to me chickenshits!

"You thought you could call yourself a Marine and leave the fighting to your brothers? Thought you would have it nice and easy staying behind in the States fucking college chicks. Well, I promise you yellow-bellies that before you leave here you will wish to God you were in Saudi Arabia with your unit. I'm going to make Marines out of you again.

"I work for the Provost Marshal, Gunner Carson, and he owns this barracks. These are his rules. And nobody else on this base, or in the Marine Corps, gives a shit how we treat you. Any complaints are to be made only to me—no one else.

"In the mornings you will participate in physical fitness training and drill. Afternoons are for work details. You will pull fire watch every night. You will immediately, and unhesitantly, obey any order from a troop handler. Your rack shall be made unless you are sleeping in it. Your locker shall be always organized and spotless. The uniform of the day, every day, is utilities—no civilian clothes, no PT gear. Your uniform will be cleaned and pressed every night. There will be no talking among yourselves—ever—you will speak only to the troop handlers. When you are given a work detail, you will carry it out at the double-time.

"There will be no smoking at any time—ever. And there will be no cigarettes inside or near the barracks. If you were a smoker, you just quit. No phone calls. You may write one letter per week, and you will hand it into the troop handlers who will read it and censor anything you say."

After MSgt. Miller's speech, Cpl. Weaver drilled the platoon at the barracks parking lot for another hour, marching them forward and back, wheeling and turning. At 1100, they marched over to the dining facility, stood at attention outside, and finally moved through the chow line like recruits at boot camp. No talking. Eating as fast as possible, then standing at attention outside the chow hall.

It became clear to Sgt. Jones that Barracks No. 8 was much worse than the Brig. MSgt. Miller and Cpl. Weaver assumed they could insult him, humiliate him, and physically abuse him.

After lunch, Cpl. Weaver marched the platoon back to the barracks and dismissed the Marines. Some hurried to the head, and others tried to catch a catnap on their racks. In a few minutes, Cpl. Weaver came through the squad bay passing out bright yellow T-shirts.

"Put these on and fall out in five minutes to police the airfield."

Sgt. Jones, still sweating in his green T-shirt, had enough. He stood and calmly addressed Cpl. Weaver.

"Corporal Weaver, I need to speak with you in private."

"No talking yellow belly."

Sgt. Jones slowly stepped forward, very close to Cpl. Weaver, face to face, staring him in the eye. Cpl. Weaver noticed tension in Sgt. Jones's body, and his hands were starting to curl into fists.

"I tried to be professional and spare you embarrassment. But if you want to talk here, fine by me. I am a Sergeant of Marines. I earned these stripes. I have not been convicted of anything and I am presumed innocent. You will address me as 'Sergeant Jones.' As a Sergeant, I don't take orders from Corporals. You may relay messages to me from the Master Sergeant, but that is all. I will wear the uniform of the day, not a yellow T-shirt. If you ever disrespect me again, I will knock your teeth out. Now, I am going to go find Master Sergeant Miller. You carry on here."

Sgt. Jones calmly walked down the squad bay, down the ladder to the first deck. He saw a red and gold sign over the door, *Master Sergeant Miller, SNCOIC.* The door stood open, and Sgt. Jones pounded on its side three times so hard it shook the window on the opposite wall. He heard a bear of voice answer, the unmistakable voice of a drill instructor.

"Who is it?"

"Sergeant Jones."

"Come in."

Sgt. Jones marched to a position three feet in front of MSgt. Miller's desk and stood at attention. Miller bored a hole into him with his eyes.

"I just spoke to Corporal Weaver. We need to get a few things straight." Sgt. Jones repeated what he had told Cpl. Weaver.

MSgt. Miller jerked his head up and back. He looked like he had been slapped. He said nothing, but his jaw tensed, and his face reddened. Then he sat back, turned his head, and seemed to be contemplating something.

"Sergeant Jones, you look familiar. Have we served together?" Miller's voice had changed to one soft with understanding. The same voice he used to calm a wounded Marine.

"I don't think so, Master Sergeant."

"Where have you been stationed?"

"MCRD, Twentynine Palms."

"Wait a minute! I am sure I would remember you if you were in one of my platoons, but maybe you were in the same company when I was a drill instructor. When were you at MCRD?"

"June 1984"

"No. I wasn't there in 1984. Where else?'

"Just my reserve unit in St. Louis. My ATD was also at Twentynine Palms."

"What's your home of record?"

"Caryville, Illinois."

"Was your father a Marine?'

"Yes. He was killed in the Battle of Hue City, February 11, 1968."

MSgt. Miller stared at Jones for a long time.

"February 11, 1968, is the day I was shot in the back in Hue City. I was medevac'd out on a barge."

Both men stared at each other.

"I may have known your father. First name?"

"Kenneth."

"Yeah, sure. PFC Kenny Jones. He was a tunnel rat, like me. Damn it, Sergeant! You look just like your old man."

Both men continued to stare at each other with curious looks on their faces.

"I don't know what the fuck is going on with you now, or why you are here in my barracks, but if you are Jones's kid you can't be the coward they say you are." MSgt. Miller paused to think again and let his words sink in.

"Move your trash downstairs to the empty office on the left side of the entry. That'll be your living quarters. Tell Corporal Weaver that I said you were not to participate in PT, drill, or work details."

MSgt. Miller watched Sgt. Jones's reaction.

"What's your MOS?"

"My primary MOS is 0629 Radio Chief, and my secondary is 0931 Marksmanship Instructor."

MSgt. Miller formed an exaggerated expression of contemplation. After a moment, he stood, walked over to a file cabinet, and searched through some files. He pulled out some papers and handed them to Jones.

"Here's the twenty-man roster for mess hall cleanup. You are now in charge. Muster at 0030 and march to the chow hall. Corporal Snow's been running the detail, so find him, and tell him I assigned you to take over. He'll be your assistant, and he can give you the details. You will report with your Marines every night, seven days a week at 0130, to the NCOIC, Master Gunnery Sergeant Richards. Start tonight."

MSgt. Miller seemed very pleased with himself. He thought some more and continued.

"You will keep what we said here, strictly confidential. Is that a problem?"

"No. I agree, Master Sergeant; my father should be a secret between us."

"That's all, Sergeant Jones."

Chapter 47

The Dining Facility, like all chow halls aboard air stations, served four meals a day—breakfast, lunch, dinner, and midnight rations, or *midrats*. The midrats served the pilots and crews assigned to night operations. Sgt. Jones supervised the cleanup crew that started work every night after midrats. Sgt. Jones's assistant, Cpl. Snow, a reservist with a degree from the San Francisco College of Mortuary Science, worked as an embalmer. He said he had seen enough bodies and became radically opposed to war. Soft-spoken, and utterly lacking in military bearing, he nevertheless did a good job supervising the crew.

The members of the cleanup crew liked working at night when there were no active-duty Marines around to call them cowards, chickenshits, or yellow-bellies. The cleanup process required little more than scrubbing pans, washing dishes, and mopping floors. In fact, by this time, the crew smoothly functioned without much oversight from Sgt. Jones. For most of the night, he just sat in the SNCOIC's office drinking coffee and counseling crew members that drifted in from time to time. They wanted to talk about the court-martial process, types of punitive discharges, pretrial agreements, and military prison. They seemed to understand—and trust—Sgt. Jones's explanations more than their lawyers'.

At the end of the shift, Sgt. Jones and Cpl. Snow carefully inspected the mess hall while the crew waited outside. As usual, tonight the work passed inspection and they headed out the front door.

"Attention on deck!"

Cpl. Snow did his best to sound like a drill instructor, but his high-pitched voice startled the new members who had never heard it before. Quickly, the cleanup crew assumed the position of attention.

"Gentlemen. Outstanding job tonight. I spoke with Master Gunnery Sergeant Richards and he is impressed with our work. I did not bring it up, but if you keep up the good work, he may be willing to provide testimony or a witness statement at your court-martial. That could reduce your sentences.

"Corporal Snow. Return the men to the barracks."

Chapter 48

At 0545 Sunday morning, the air felt chilly as Nathan awoke, opened the back door, and gazed out across the Sonoran Desert. The sun remained below the Gila Mountains but had begun to light the eastern horizon. Nathan stepped back inside, made a cup of coffee, and returned to the beat-up metal chair sitting outside his door. He sipped his coffee and scanned the vast and wide landscape below.

At first, Nathan felt ambivalent about the desert, but now he loved it, and unreservedly in the morning when the rising sun painted the mountains with shaman colors. Sandwiched between two mountain ridges where the country broke up into washes, ridges, and dead-end gulches, the pistol range lay at the boundary of Marine Corps Air Station, Yuma, and the Barry M. Goldwater Bombing Range. There were paloverde, mesquite, and ironwood trees, and saguaro and ocotillo cactus along the wash, and sometimes brittlebush and creosote on the ridges. Nathan soon heard the "coo...coo, coo...coo" of a male Gamble quail and watched the covey follow the rooster across the wash. Nathan bowed his head and thanked God for releasing him from the Brig and sending him to the pistol range. He prayed for a long time.

Nathan knew that at first no officer at MCAS, Yuma wanted him. But after two weeks, the Non-Commissioned Officer in Charge of the Pistol Range entered the hospital, and the G-3 Officer, LtCol. Harris, frantically, desperately, needed a replacement. As it happened, Gunner Carson and Sgt. Jones were the only Marines at Yuma who had completed the Marksmanship Instructor Course. Of course, Gunner Carson was not available and by regulation, only Sgt. Jones held the qualifications to serve as NCOIC for the pistol range.

Located at the end of a gravel road, about 100 yards south of the armory, the pistol range could accommodate 15 shooters. It had a dirt parking lot and a concrete block building with an office, classroom, storage room for targets, an inside bathroom with shower, and a larger bathroom with only an exterior door. The office had a metal desk, chair, wall locker, and a rack.

Unfortunately, the building had fallen into terrible condition. The roof leaked, the ceiling tiles were discolored, and the linoleum on the floor curled up at the corners. The air conditioning barely worked. Nevertheless, LtCol. Harris directed Jones to move into the office for 24/7 security and so Jones would always be at work when needed. Nathan now lived alone in the office using it as a poor man's BEQ. He preferred the office over Barracks No. 8.

All Marines must annually qualify on the weapon issued to them under the Table of Organization and Equipment. Enlisted Marines qualify on the rifle, but officers and staff non-commissioned officers are issued pistols. The annual qualification scores are included in promotion packages and Marine officers and SNCOs believe, rightly or wrongly, that their pistol score can be the tipping point for promotion.

Immediately, after assignment to the pistol range, Sgt. Jones discovered that the Marine Corps had implemented a program to replace the Colt M1911A1 pistol with the Beretta M9 pistol. The Colts were collected and stored in the armory. Because officers and SNCOs could not be burdened with spending a week at the range, pistol qualification was a "one and done" day of shooting. Most officers and SNCOs hated the Beretta and found it difficult to qualify on it in one day.

It turned out that Sgt. Jones still had a knack for pistol instruction, and he successfully helped many officers and staff non-commission officers to transition from the Colt to the Beretta. The word quickly got out. Officers and staff non-commissioned officers specifically requested Sgt. Jones's help.

After praying and still sitting on the old metal chair, drinking his coffee, Nathan thought of his family in Southern Illinois and wondered why he did not plan to attend the base chapel this morning. After his divorce, Nathan moved in with his grandmother and never missed church, mainly because his grandmother would have never allowed it. In that part of the world, a person who missed church was talked about. But now, after his experience at the New Unity in Christ

Church, Nathan never attended church. He just could not do it any-more.

At 0640, Nathan decided to make the 20-minute walk to the P-1-11 Dining Facility for "brunch," which only meant that a Marine could have eggs cooked to order. After brunch, Nathan attempted to call Judy Novotney from the payphone in front of the seven-day store, but she did not answer. Next, Nathan dialed up his grandmother, Emma Jones. They talked about Nathan's brother Jeremiah, Nathan's court-martial, his nephews, nieces, and cousins, and about the weather in Southern Illinois. Jeremiah had scored a record buck during deer season. Virtus Smith had taken over Nathan's pulling unit. More than once, Nathan apologized to Emma for the hardship he caused everyone. He asked for her forgiveness which was freely given. Next, Nathan used his last bit of change to telephone Ogden Loring on Ogden's cell phone.

"Hey, Nathan; it's great to hear from you. Everything good in Yuma?"

"Yes, Mr. Loring."

"What's the weather like?"

"It cooled this morning, but yesterday it got up to eighty degrees."

"Wow. I am at the marina here in San Diego, and I am wearing a sweatshirt. Nathan, I have some good news and bad news."

Nathan did not answer.

"First the good news. Captain Beck and I got an acquittal this week. I believe the fact that we got an acquittal from a jury will make the government easier to deal with on your case. So, here is the bad news. There is a joint resolution pending in Congress to authorize President Bush to use military force in Iraq. My sources tell me that it is likely to pass. It has the support of all Republicans and many Democrats. If this resolution passes, we won't have much of an argument left that the war is illegal and not much chance with another writ of habeas corpus. Sorry, Nathan."

"I understand, Mr. Loring. There is nothing more you can do."

"Well, Nathan, anything else to discuss?"

"No, Sir."

"All right. Call me anytime."

Nathan hung up, purchased a Sunday paper, and headed back to the pistol range.

Soon, Nathan's thoughts overcame him. He looked around making sure no one was watching. He did not know, and could not make sense of, what he had done by failing to report for duty. He struggled to control his emotions and rushed back to his office. He was expecting Maj. Hendrix and Capt. Beck at 0830.

⚬⚬⚬

The previous year, Maj. Cindy Hendrix shot Marksman on the Colt, the lowest level of qualification. Like many women officers, she found the Colt's grip too wide for her hands and its recoil painful. She believed that if this year she failed to make Expert, the highest qualification category, she would have no chance for promotion to Lieutenant Colonel. Indeed, she used her own money to purchase a civilian version of the Beretta and delayed qualification at the pistol course so that she could practice.

At 0825, Capt. Beck's Range Rover slid to a dusty stop in the parking lot outside the pistol range building. Gravel crunched beneath the tires.

"Good morning, Ma'am. Good morning, Captain Beck."

"Good morning, Sergeant Jones."

Maj. Hendrix followed Capt. Beck down to the shooting range and felt guilty again. More and more, she found herself having unprofessional thoughts about Capt. Beck, and it seemed her reactions to him were distinctly feminine. She admitted to herself that she had started using more makeup and wearing her tightest fitting uniforms. But she had not started flirting and wasn't about to do so.

After they walked down to the pistol range, Sgt. Jones set up several targets. He then pulled out a set of soft earplugs and a set noise-damping headsets called Mickey Mouse protectors. "I want you to use both the earplugs and the Mickey Mouse protectors at the same time. It is important that you hear nothing."

Capt. Beck, using Maj. Hendrix's pistol, went first. Fifteen rounds at ten yards, 15 rounds at 15 yards, and ten rounds at 25 yards. He scored 320, just enough for an Expert rating.

Then, Maj. Hendrix stepped up to shoot the qualification course. She loaded a magazine, then adopted a wide stance. She aimed at the target, snapped the trigger, and saw the Baretta jerk up. But the pistol did not fire. Sgt. Jones motioned for her to remove her hearing protection and hand him the pistol.

"See, you are jerking the trigger and flinching. Try it again. This time concentrate on slowly squeezing the trigger."

Hendrix put the hearing protectors back in place, aimed at the target, and squeezed the trigger. The Berretta did not fire but the muzzle jumped up. She turned and looked at Sgt. Jones.

Sgt. Jones removed the magazine and showed her he had exchanged her magazine for an empty one.

"The involuntary response is common. You are afraid of the recoil, you think the pistol's going to jump, so you make it jump. Trust me. Shooting the 9-millimeter Baretta is not going to hurt." Jones took the Berretta, slammed the magazine into place, cocked the slide, and placed it in Hendrix's hands aimed toward the target.

"Don't worry, a lot of Marines do this. I want you to relax, take your time, and empty all eight rounds. Keep concentrating on squeezing the trigger."

Hendrix kept shooting but hit all over the target. At one point, Beck stood behind her, reached around, and helped her steady the pistol in an almost hug-like fashion. The gesture did not seem to help Hendrix's shooting. After an hour, Hendrix's scored under a 200, not even close enough to pass the course.

At 0930, they took a water break under the shade of the building eves. As was common practice with Marines at Yuma, they all removed their Woodland Camo blouses and sat cooling off wearing only their green t-shirts.

"I really suck at this!" Hendrix announced.

"Relax. We will get you on target," Jones answered.

When they walked back to the range, Jones stopped and turned to Hendrix. "Ma'am, can I have your glasses?"

"Sergeant. I can't see the bull's eye. It's a blur."

"Good. Don't focus on the target. Just aim center mass, as best you can see, and keep focusing on squeezing the trigger."

Maj. Hendrix repeated shooting the course. Her score improved to 350. More than enough to qualify as Expert. Afterward, they returned to the shade of Sgt. Jones's office for another water break.

"Sergeant Jones, can I ask you a personal question?"

"Sure, Ma'am."

"Do you see a contradiction between your being a conscientious objector and running the pistol range? It just surprises me that you are so good with weapons."

"Back in Southern Illinois, I grew up hunting. Mostly shotguns and rifles. Maybe I just don't want to go back to jail, but I prayed on it, and I think it's the right thing."

"Even if you said 'no' to the pistol range, I don't think you would go back to jail."

"I appreciate that, Ma'am. The rifle is an offensive weapon. But I see the Beretta as strictly a defensive weapon. I do not teach Marines to kill. I teach them to stay alive. As long as we send Marines anywhere to fight, the most important thing I can do is make sure they can protect themselves. My business here at the range is saving lives, not taking them. I train Marines to use the pistol only for defense of their own life. They must choose when, and if, they will use it. Also, I feel like what I do at the range is important. It makes me feel less guilty about abandoning the Marines at Fourth Tank Battalion."

Chapter 49

From the exterior appearance, the Wagon Wheel Bar could accurately be described as a dive, a windowless flat-roofed concrete block building surrounded by a dirt parking lot. However, the inside had a near-perfect Marine Corps motif with an ancient carved wooden bar, large mirror, high tables, jute box, and pool tables. The walls were covered with photographs of past commandants, wing commanders, and Medal of Honor winners, interspersed with an assortment of plaques, awards, and posters. A large painting of Chesty Puller hung on the back of the bar.

At 1800, Capt. Beck walked inside and joined the group of Marine lawyers, judges, and staff judge advocates assembled there for the monthly JAFL meeting. In keeping with the military preference for using acronyms JAFL stood for "Just Another Fucking Lawyer." Dues were assessed on an *ad hoc* basis depending on what might be needed to buy beer and pizza. The single officers used the meetings to get limbered up before trolling for women out in town, and the married officers used the meetings as an excuse to get out of the house.

When Mike Beck entered, he looked around for Cindy Hendrix. They had been working together all day. Not finding Cindy, Mike headed for the line at the bar. As he moved through the line, he spotted Cindy sitting at a tall table at the end of the pool room. Mike felt his heart leap, and once or twice, he found it impossible to take his eyes off her.

At about the same time, Cindy noticed Mike. She had always thought that Marines were the most handsome in uniform, but tonight, seeing Mike in his boots and jeans, excited Cindy. *Jesus, Hendrix. What is wrong with you? You are married and he works for you. Adultery with a direct subordinate is not bending the rules, it is shattering them to pieces.*

Mike made small talk with Judge Dickerson. They covered the usual topics—weather in Yuma, the Range Rover's cost and performance, and the judge's next trip home to San Diego. Although perfectly proper, talking with a judge had to be done with great care.

The JAFL meetings were probably enjoyed most by LtCol. Bumbaugh. Beck discovered that Bumbaugh had mastered the game of pool. He spent the evening smoking cigars and beating junior officers at endless games.

Throughout the evening, the noise from the meeting rose geometrically to a clamorous roar. At 2130, Maj. Way picked up a garbage can in the corner of the pool room, beat the sides loudly with an empty beer bottle, and shouted above the din.

"Listen up! Listen up!" The bar quieted and Maj. Way stepped forward. "JAFLs, we have no farewells this month, but I ask you to hail the arrival of our newest members." Steve Way proceeded to introduce all the new reserve lawyers. As they were introduced, each waived at the crowd like beauty contestants and loud whistling and foot-stomping arose in the bar.

"The next order of business is the monthly judicial award." Maj. Way announced.

"I give you the world's greatest statistician, our own Major Lucas Herdy."

Maj. Herdy came out of the crowd and positioned an exhibit board on a pool table. A set of bar graphs had been drawn on the board. "JAFLs, to recap and to explain the judicial award to our new captains, I have tracked each of the judge's sentences for the current month. I consider the amount of confinement awarded by the judge without consideration for the number of trials, limits under pretrial agreements, or convening authority action."

Herdy continued. "In third place for this month is Major David Lomax with a mere sixty-four months." The defense lawyers clapped hands and whistled approval, while the prosecutors hissed and jeered.

"Throw him off the bench!" A prosecutor yelled.

"In second place we have the esteemed Major Thomas Ackerman with seventy months." The crowd's reaction was the same only more subdued.

"First place goes to Colonel Dickenson at one-hundred-eighty months."

This time the prosecutors yelled and screamed their approval, and the defense lawyers booed.

"Will the winner step forward?" Maj. Way hollered above the noise of the crowd and Col. Dickenson stepped in front of the crowd.

"Ladies and Gentlemen, Devil Dogs, and Esteemed Colleagues, I give you the winner of the monthly judicial award, Col. Dickenson, with an incredible total of one-hundred-eighty months of confinement imposed upon those pour accused who had the misfortune of ending up in his courtroom."

This time all the lawyers cheered. Maj. Way handed Col. Dickenson a large gavel that looked to be made of cardboard. Soon the crowd returned to drinking. The judges left first, followed by most of the lieutenants and captains, who just wanted to get out of playing more pool with Bumbaugh.

As the crowd thinned, Beck moved over and sat next to Cindy at her table. She seemed trapped in a conversation with Maj. Herdy but smiled at Mike from time to time. In Mike's mind, she had undergone the same metamorphosis he saw at Jack and Rosie's. The no-nonsense officer at work seemed now a smoking hot woman who bore no stamp of the Marine Corps. Sitting at the table, Cindy's calf and knee rested against Mike's, and as time passed, she smiled more and more, slouching toward him.

After a while, Capt. Lisa Ellsworth joined Mike at Cindy's table. "Major Hendrix, we're going to Johnny's. You want to come with us tonight?'

"Since you are my ride, I guess I will have to," Cindy answered for the first time breaking off the conversation with Lucas Herdy.

"How about you Mike? Can you join us?" Lisa asked in her southern voice.

"What's Johnny's?"

"The best country-western bar in Yuma. The best band in Yuma, Saddle Tramp, is playing and they are great."

"OK. I will meet you all there."

Not much to look at, located in a run-down strip mall, Beck found Johnny's with some difficulty. Beck's disappointment ended when he opened the door. A bar extended the full length of the room, lights low. Stage at the end, and the dance floor appeared packed. Beck spotted a gorgeous bartender and headed her way. But heard Lisa's voice before he could get there.

"Hey, Mike. Over here." Cindy, Lisa, and Lieutenant Dean were sitting at a table near the stage.

"Hey Lisa, this is great! Thanks for inviting me."

Lisa smiled and lightly rubbed Mike's leg under the table.

"Anyone for a Jack and Coke?" Mike asked. Everyone's hand went up, and Mike hurried to the bar. As soon as Mike returned with the drinks, the band started playing a two-step.

"Come on Beck...I need a dance partner," Cindy declared playfully.

Mike felt he could not dance until he had downed a few drinks. He tried to beg off.

"Sorry. I don't know the twostep. Maybe later?"

"I'll teach you," Cindy replied smiling.

"Well, at least let me drink my Jack Daniels first."

Cindy tried to look disappointed but quickly got into a conversation with Lisa. Mike paid for the drinks, and to his surprise, Cindy motioned at the waitress and ordered a round of shots. By the time Mike had slammed the Jack and Coke, the shots arrived. No one else had finished their Jack and Coke, but Mike slammed his shot. When Cindy noticed the two empty glasses in front of Mike she yelled.

"Woo Hoo! Ready to dance?"

Mike could rock and roll but had a hard time with the country-western dances. Fortunately, after drinking the Jack Daniels, Mike felt his dancing skills improve greatly. Mike and Cindy were on the dance floor all night.

Cindy always skipped the slow songs for another drink at their table. But finally, Mike asked her to dance to one. She went into Mike's arms slowly, warily, and a sudden tingle momentarily weakened her composure. Soon they were body to body. Cindy was so turned on that she kept one eye on the table to see if Lisa or Dean were watching. Before the song finished, Cindy felt that she could not be close enough to Mike to satisfy her need to touch him. When they returned to the table, a shock of awareness hit Cindy, and she realized how far she had been willing to go.

"Lisa. Take me home. It's getting late, and we must get through the Main Gate."

"Don't you want to hit Reds?" Lisa asked.

"Sorry. Not tonight. But no problem, if you want to go to Reds, I can call a cab to take me home."

Mike spoke up. "Hey, I am ready to go. Why don't I drop you off at the Base on my way to my apartment? It's right on the way."

"No. Captain Beck, we have had too much to drink for you to be driving on base. I will call a cab." Everyone noticed Cindy's sudden change of mood.

"Ma'am, with all the dancing, I am really not intoxicated. No problem for me getting through the Main Gate."

Lisa spoke next. "Ma'am, if you don't want to ride with Captain Beck, I am ready to head back to the base." All at once, Cindy felt bad and realized that Lisa would not allow her to take a cab. She didn't want to ruin Lisa's night and decided she could control herself on the ride home with Mike. "No. No. Captain Ellsworth, I guess I can ride with Captain Beck. He is correct. I think the dancing wore off the alcohol."

Mike led Cindy through the parking lot to his brand-new Range Rover and hoped she would be impressed. If so, she said nothing. In fact, they said little during the ride back, except that as they approached the gate Cindy reminded Mike to have his ID out, flash it at the guard, and keep driving. There was no problem at the gate, and Mike followed Cindy's directions to her house. Mike pulled into the driveway and shut off the engine.

For a moment, they sat quietly. Abruptly, Cindy reached out and with one hand behind Mike's neck, pulled him towards her. She leaned over the center console and kissed him. When her lips found his, she felt a moment of tension in Mike, then he relaxed, his lips softening and warming beneath hers as he returned the kiss. Quickly, Cindy realized what she had done, she gasped and broke off the kiss. On the verge of panic, she bolted from the Range Rover and ran to her front door.

Inside the house, Cindy felt caught in a trap of her own making. She had not planned on working so closely with Mike or spending so much time alone with him in the office. She certainly had not planned on falling in love with him.

Chapter 50

At full throttle with the blown-out exhaust pipes, the roar of the Charlie Carson's tricked out Harley became deafening. By the time Carson reached the Colorado River Bridge, his speedometer clocked over 100 miles per hour. He slowed for the entrance ramp onto east I-8, then again pulled back on the throttle. When he shifted to fifth gear, the speedometer pegged at 125. Herlinda Hernandez locked her hands around Carson and hung on for dear life.

MSgt. Miller, Cpl. Weaver, Cpl. Cunningham, and Gunny Sergeant Tyler tried to keep up on their Harleys, but soon they were far behind. Carson reached a point so far ahead that he could not see them in his rearview mirror, pulled over on the side of the road, and waited five minutes for them to catch up.

From I-8 the bikers drove south through the Avenues, slowing and turning to avoid potholes. When they turned up the gravel lane leading to Carson's house, Cunningham lost it. His rear tire slid out, and his tricked-out Harley Electra Glide dropped on top of him. The bike weighed too much to move, and Cunningham could not reach the throttle. He lay in the road, his Harley on top of him with the engine running. Carson calmly executed a U-turn, parked his bike, walked over, and lifted the Harley off Cunningham. There appeared to be little damage, only paint scratches. Obviously shaken, Cunningham managed to make it up the hill to Carson's house and parked his motorcycle.

The night had turned cold, and Miller built a fire in the pit next to the reloading room. The group sat close to the fire. Carson drank straight vodka while the rest sipped beers. For a while, there was no conversation. Finally, Carson spoke.

"Corporal Cunningham, you are a big old boy. What are you, six four?

"Six foot six."

"What do you weigh?"

"Three-oh-five."

"You got some guns too. You work out?"

"Yes, Sir. Everyday."

"What do you bench?"

"Over four-twenty, Sir."

Carson took a drag on his Camel cigarette and then crushed it out in the ashtray set on the table next to his chair. He eyed the remnants with longing.

"Twenty bucks says I can beat you at arm wrestling."

Surprising everyone, MSgt. Miller spoke up, and not in a respectful tone. He recognized the mean look on Carson's face. "Come on, Gunner. Why you always gotta do this shit? How about leaving the kid alone tonight? He's huge and you won't have a fucking chance. It will just piss you off, and you will do something mean."

"Not going to hurt him. Just a friendly match of strength. Are you up for it, Cunningham? Anybody that can bench four-twenty can easily beat me at arm wrestling."

"That is what I am saying—so why bother?" Miller sounded like a father scolding his son.

Cunningham followed Carson and the two squared off at a table inside the reloading room. To no one's surprise, Cunningham easily pushed Carson's arm slowly down. Carson pulled out his wallet and placed a $20 on the table. He then produced a $100 and placed it on the table.

"I bet the hundred-dollar bill, against that twenty, that I can beat you at Indian fighting."

"What's Indian fighting?" Cunningham asked without thinking.

"You hit me as hard as you can. Then, if I can, I get to hit you. We keep going until someone calls it quits."

"Sir, I can't hit you."

Carson raised his arms up. "Look, you see any fucking rank insignia? Tonight, I have abandoned my rank. I can do that anytime I want. Perfectly acceptable and legal. You have a right to hit me as hard as you can."

Again, Miller stepped in. "Carson. Let's stop this shit and have a real contest. Let's go shoot some rounds at your range. I'll bet you a hundred dollars that with a Colt and a full eight-round magazine, I can outshoot you."

Carson ignored Miller. He had an evil look on his face.

"OK, Cunningham. I have seen you looking at Herlinda all night. If you can beat me at Indian fighting, you can fuck her right here in my bedroom, fuck her tonight. And, on top of that, I'll give you two hundred dollars."

Herlinda giggled. Carson slowly stood, walked over in front of Cunningham, and laid another hundred-dollar bill on the table.

"Now, I don't want to hear any chickenshit crap, Marine. Take your best shot at me or I am just going to kick your ass anyway."

Cunningham was shocked. He first glanced at his roommate Cpl. Weaver, who just shrugged his shoulders. Then, Cunningham looked at MSgt. Miller who nodded. "Go ahead, Cunningham. And don't be afraid of hurting the son-of-a-bitch. Give him your best punch. Carson, this boy is going to break your jaw, knock you into next week, and maybe kill you."

Carson stood staring Cunningham in the eyes. Cunningham drew back. Carson did not flinch. Cunningham delivered a crushing right upper hook to Carson's face, raising him up, and slamming him across the room into the wall. Carson lay there, knocked out cold.

Miller walked over, picked up the money off the table, and handed it to Cunningham. "Son. Get on that bike and get the hell out of here. Gunner Carson is even meaner than he is ugly, and if he wakes up, it ain't going to be pretty."

Cunningham again looked at Weaver who this time spoke: "I will see you back at the hooch. Call me if your bike breaks down."

Miller, Tyler, Weaver, and Herlinda got fresh beers and went back outside to the fire. Carson lay on the floor, unconscious, for 30 minutes. When he finally opened his eyes, he stood, shakily walked to the bar, poured himself another vodka, and walked outside to the fire.

"Where's Cunningham?"

"Had to leave," Miller answered.

"I guess he earned the money. Did he fuck Herlinda?"

Everyone laughed for a long time.

"Let's do some shooting." The group followed Carson back inside the reloading room. He took out four Colt pistols and a full case of .45 ACP. They walked to the range and shot for two hours. Then, out of ammunition, they returned to the fire.

"You know they got Colts at the armory waiting to be shipped off for scrap metal? The Marine Corps is only getting fifty bucks a piece." Carson spoke in a soft, sad voice.

"What a bunch of bull shit. I still can't believe Marines will no longer carry the Colt. Hell, the Colt has been in every battle since World War One. In Nam, I blew a gook clean in half. No doubt saved my life."

"We should do something." Miller responded.

"Miller, you know we have our Vietnam 3rd Platoon reunion next June. I say we liberate some of those Colts from the armory and pass them out at the reunion."

Chapter 51

"Ladies and gentlemen, thank you for an excellent briefing. I would like Lieutenant Colonel Harris, Sergeant Major Gill, and Lieutenant Colonel Bumbaugh, to hang around afterward." All the Marines snapped to attention and filed out of the conference room, except Harris, Gill, and Bumbaugh who were each trying to figure out what they had done wrong. The Sergeant Major guessed it would be about Sgt. Jones. Col. Cahill turned and looked at Harris.

"All right, Lieutenant Colonel Harris, I am aware that Sergeant Jones has made your life much easier and that every pilot, administrative officer, and hell, even the lawyers on this base are now shooting Expert at the pistol range, but how the hell can you justify nominating Jones for Non-Commissioned Officer of the Quarter when he deserted his unit and is pending a general court-martial?"

The Marines were quick to catch the anger in Col. Cahill's voice. Harris appeared calm, but the pressure made his voice crack when he tried to answer. "Sergeant Jones has done an incredible job at the pistol range. He has rebuilt all the targets, reorganized the supply room, and as you said, he is a hell of a marksmanship coach. I mean, Sir, it's true. With Sergeant Jones's help, I increased my score by seventy points. We now have a lot of Marines headed to Saudi Arabia that are better able to protect themselves."

Lieutenant Colonel Harris waved his hands exaggerating his points, paused, and continued. "But it is not just the pistol range. Sergeant Jones oversees the chow hall cleaning crew for three hours every night, works seven days a week. Most Marines would bitch and moan, but the OIC of the dining facility, Master Gunnery Sergeant Richards is on my ass wanting Jones recognized for doing an outstanding job. Richards probably has been in the Corps longer than any of us, and he says we have the cleanest chow hall he's ever seen… he's never seen someone do such a good job."

Col. Cahill slowly drew his gaze from Harris and turned to the Sergeant Major. They stared uncomfortably at one another. "Sergeant Major, you look normal today, but you must be out of your fucking mind! Are you shitting me! You let Sergeant Jones be nominated for NCOIC of the Quarter?"

The Sergeant Major looked like he had been slapped in the face, then started twitching in his chair, and talking in a whiney voice, faster, louder, and higher than normal.

"Colonel! I know! I know it sounds crazy! But I brought this up at the sergeant major's meeting in front of all the squadron sergeant majors, the Group Ten Sergeant Major, and the Base Sergeant Major. That is a couple of hundred years of experience right there. One hundred percent consensus! We feel a Marine is innocent until proven guilty. We know that if a Marine like Sergeant Jones failed to report, he had a damn good reason. Nobody thinks he will be convicted."

The conversation died again. Col. Cahill's expression conveyed nothing. Finally, he spoke. "Oh! Do not give me that innocent until proven guilty shit, I am the crazy son-of-a-bitch that let him out of jail in the first place."

Col. Cahill visibly shook his head in disgust then waited for the heat to drain from his face. He turned his head to look at LtCol. Bumbaugh. "What about you SJA? What's your excuse? Aren't you asking that young prosecutor to get a dishonorable discharge and two-years confinement? How is your prosecutor going to feel when you stab him in the back by naming Sergeant Jones the NCOIC of the Quarter?"

LtCol. Bumbaugh stayed calm and thought about his answer. Unable to meet Col. Cahill's eyes, he starred down, and began to speak. "My bust, Sir. You are correct, I am stabbing the prosecutor in the back. I guess I caved into the lobbying from other officers."

Everyone sat around the conference room table looking angry. Finally, Col. Cahill spoke again. "Here is my decision. Starting right now, no one is eligible for NCOIC of the Quarter unless they have been at this base, and on the job, for the entire quarter, all ninety days. Sergeant Jones has been out of jail for less than sixty days and he is not eligible. If for some reason, he's still here next quarter, you can put him back in."

Col. Cahill stood to walk out, followed by all the officers standing at attention.

Chapter 52

Major Hendrix avoided Capt. Beck at the office for the next three days. On Friday, she entered Capt. Beck's office and closed the door. "Captain Beck, I want to talk to you about what happened the other night."

Beck sat stunned, expecting a reprimand from his superior officer.

"But I don't want to talk about it here. Meet me at the Circle K, 32nd Street and Avenue A, tonight at 2200.'

⟨⟩

Mike arrived at the Circle K ten minutes early. When Cindy arrived, she got out, and walked over to his car. She wore her running clothes—shoes, shorts, and T-shirt. "Follow me to Sear's parking lot. Park, and get in with me." Cindy left Sears and headed towards the Colorado River through Old Yuma near the Ocean-to-Ocean Bridge and down a narrow dirt road that wound its way through salt cedar trees.

"Where are we going?"

"It's just a spot where Joe goes fishing. Sometimes, I come along." Cindy spoke in a voice just above a whisper. Cindy soon turned off to a place with a picnic table, barbeque grill, and veranda. She parked facing the river. Mike did not know such scenic spots existed in Yuma. For a while, the two just stared out at the moon's reflection on the river. Then Cindy started the speech she had carefully rehearsed.

"Captain Beck, I take full responsibility for what happened that night. I ordered most of the Jack Daniels. I asked you to dance. I can understand how you got the wrong idea. I am not going to hold it against you. I just ask you to remember that I am a married woman and to keep this in strict confidence."

Cindy spoke in a grave tone with absolute sincerity. She had thought, hoped, and prayed that her marriage to Joe would last a lifetime. She had sacrificed so much to get promoted and did not want to ruin her career with an affair. The last three days had been hell.

Mike did not know what to say. An unseen vacuum sucked all the air out of the car. He just silently sat in the passenger's seat and looked Cindy in the eyes. Her eyes moistened, then tears spilled over her eyelids and rolled down her cheeks. Cindy gazed at Mike in the oddest way, as if memorizing his face. Mike leaned over the console and held Cindy close. He only wanted to comfort her, to somehow console her, nothing more.

Cindy's mind told her arms to push Mike away. But her arms did not move. At first, Mike just embraced Cindy, but after a time he kissed her. He still touched no part of her body, except her lips. Yet somehow, Cindy felt herself becoming incredibly aroused. She felt excited in a way she had not in years. For a very long time, she lay back in her seat, just enjoying Mike's kiss. Mike made no effort to start anything else.

Then Cindy felt tired. Her life as a woman seemed so empty. Nothing but work and the Marine Corps. *Just this one time. No one will know. I want him, just this once.*

Cindy shoved Mike with both hands, throwing him back into the passenger seat. She climbed over the console, straddled Mike, and started passionately kissing him. The tremors that had shaken Cindy the night they danced spread outward now, from the very core of her being, like ripples in a pool. Colors whirled wildly behind her closed eyelids, and every nerve ending seemed sensitized almost beyond bearing. Only Mike's lips on hers smothered the cry of pleasure aching to escape. Her body arched into his compulsively, and her desire spiraled suddenly into a frantic necessity.

Finally, she opened her eyes, and with both hands, Cindy jerked her T-shirt and sports bra over her head and tossed them toward the driver's seat. Mike admired her breasts in the moonlight reflected off the river, then extended both hands to lift them.

"God, you're beautiful," Mike moaned softly, his eyes searching out the curves revealed in the dim light. Cindy felt neither embarrassed nor uncomfortable with the intensity of Mike's stare; instead, something deep inside of her burst forward and bloomed in a new awareness of her own womanhood. Something had been unleashed, and she felt overwhelmed by her body's response.

At that moment, she stopped being a Marine and became a woman, and that remained the totality of her being, nothing else mattered. All modesty was gone.

Chapter 53

At 0900, Col. Cahill, LtCol. Bumbaugh, and Maj. Way sat in Cahill's office waiting for the telephone to ring. Cahill had arrived at the Fourth Marine Division Headquarters at 0500 and he had started to feel good about leaving Washington, D.C. and having a command, even if nothing but the Rear Element for a reserve division at MCAS, Yuma, Arizona. He had stopped thinking about being promoted to general.

Cahill's mood changed after learning that Brigadier General Glover, Staff Judge Advocate to the Commandant, had scheduled a conference call with LtGen. Reynolds, the Deputy Assistant to the Commandant, and Colonel Bob Wills, II MEF Chief of Staff. There now seemed an almost palpable sense of dread hanging in the air. Col. Cahill suspected the conference had something to do with Cpl. Kellerman's case, and he expected an ass-chewing from Gen. Reynolds for granting too lenient a pretrial agreement.

Normally, Cahill could handle another reprimand from Gen. Reynolds. But it disturbed him that the language of the Manual for Courts-Martial seemed perfectly clear. As the convening authority, it remained his sole responsibility to determine what charges should be preferred, to set the terms of any pretrial agreement, to review and approve, or disapprove, all findings, and to implement any sentence. If Gen. Reynolds planned on bullying him for harsher sentences, Cahill knew that would be illegal and unethical. The lawyers called it "unlawful command influence." Although Cahill intensely wanted to avoid another dispute with Reynolds, the one thing he could be proud of about his years in the Corps was that he had always done the right thing. No matter what, Cahill would provide his Marines with all their rights under the law.

"Good morning, gentlemen." Gen. Glover spoke in a pleasant voice.

"Colonel Cahill, can you provide us with the most recent desertion numbers?"

Col. Cahill looked to LtCol. Bumbaugh, who in turn, pointed at Maj. Way. "Sir, this is Major Way, Chief Trial Counsel and Assistant Staff Judge Advocate for Fourth Division (Rear). As of yesterday, we have 450 Marines in desertion status. That compares to 1,387 Army soldiers, 454 Navy sailors, and 82 Air Force personnel. We have 128 Marines here at Yuma awaiting trial, with 46 in pretrial confinement."

"This is Colonel Wills. Are you going to be able to timely complete that many cases?" Col. Cahill nodded at Maj. Way to answer.

"This is Major Way again. The answer is 'Affirmative.' We have stood up the defense with eight lawyers and the prosecution with ten lawyers. There are additional reserve lawyers in the pipeline. We now have three military judges, all certified for general courts-martial, and a contract for civilian court reporters. The brig, courtrooms, and office facilities are adequate."

"This is General Reynolds. I hear that some of the deserters have hired civilian lawyers. What's the situation there?"

Col. Cahill pointed his finger at his chest indicating to Maj. Way that he would answer.

"Many of the defendants have hired a civil rights firm from San Diego, Loring and Leavy. Ogden Loring and Warren Leavy are experienced, skilled, and aggressive attorneys. They filed writs of *habeas corpus* in the federal district courts and challenged the lawfulness of the mobilization orders. So far, the federal judges have denied all their writs of *habeas corpus*. They are also raising any issue they can think of in the military courts. But, so far, the prosecution has been able to handle anything they raise."

"If the deserters have civilian counsel, why do you need military lawyers for defense?" Gen. Reynolds interjected again.

Surprisingly, Gen. Glover spoke in a loud and confident tone. "General Reynolds, the law says that a Marine may hire civilian counsel at no expense to the government and still retain their detailed military counsel."

"Have you had any proof problems or contests on the merits?" By this time everyone recognized Gen. Reynold's voice.

"This is Major Way again. Almost all cases are paper cases, meaning the prosecution can prove its case through entries in the Marine's service record book. So far, we have not had any case contested on the merits. At this point in time, there are six cases where the unit failed to document receipt of the mobilization orders or made incomplete unit diary entries. I have been working with II MEF's SJA at Camp Gray in Jubayl, Saudi Arabia. Basically, he is using his lawyers in SWA to round up witnesses to fill in the paper gaps. We hope to present the witnesses' testimony by telephone, either at trial or by deposition."

"Colonel Cahill, this is General Reynolds. Tell me about Corporal Kellerman's case."

"Corporal Kellerman's mother was diagnosed with terminal cancer in early August. He applied for a hardship discharge. Tried to get leave. His unit dropped the ball and did nothing. Corporal Kellerman failed to report and stayed home with his sick mother. When his mother passed, he turned himself in. I agreed to a pretrial agreement for a reduction to E-1 and thirty days of confinement. Although a light sentence, I believe it is entirely appropriate under the circumstances."

"Well, those are compelling facts, but I would like optics on these things before they happen. I need to know what is coming down the pipeline, so I can explain it to the Commandant."

LtCol. Bumbaugh finally said something. "I could send the pretrial agreements to General Glover immediately after they are approved by the judge."

"I would like to see them sooner than that." Gen. Reynolds interjected again.

Col. Cahill and LtCol. Bumbaugh stared at each other. Col. Cahill shook his head "no." And motioned to Maj. Way to answer.

"General Reynolds, this is Major Way again. It is our legal opinion that if we disclose the pretrial agreements before being approved by the military judge, we would be raising unlawful command influence issues. I know that the civilian lawyers will be looking to raise those kinds of issues."

"As Staff Judge Advocate to the Commandant, I agree." Gen. Glover interjected.

"Well, I consider anything less than two years' confinement and a dishonorable discharge to be extraordinary and something I want to know about in advance." LtGen. Reynolds challenged.

Col. Cahill could tell by the inflection of his voice that Gen. Reynolds was on the verge of getting angry. He tried to think of the best strategy. He needed to convince Gen. Reynolds that his best place would be shared responsibility. Reynolds was that sort of weak leader. He just needed to know that if things went bad, he could blame Col. Cahill, LtGen. Lenard, or some other officer. Col. Cahill spoke after a long pause.

"Colonel Wills, what's II MEF's guidance on this?" Col. Cahill's question subtlety told LtGen. Reynolds that he was no longer Cahill's boss; instead, Cahill would be taking orders from II MEF, LtGen. Lenard.

"Here is what I think, Gentlemen. We don't want anything that can be argued as unlawful command influence. I expect Colonel Cahill to exercise his own judgment and not disclose the pretrial agreement unless first approved by the military judge."

"This is General Glover again. I agree one hundred percent and that is all we need to discuss now. Have a good day ladies and gentlemen."

"Good day, gentlemen." LtGen. Reynold hung up the phone.

☙

A week after the Headquarters telephone conference, Col. Bob Wills, II MEF Chief of Staff telephoned Col. Cahill.

"Earl, I have some bad news."

"Lieutenant General Reynolds is really after you now. The guy's brilliant, first in his class at every service school he's attended, but I can't understand how the Marine Corps puts up with a son-of-a-bitch that is so mean and vindictive. After our conference last week, General Reynolds demanded a written opinion from the

Commandant's Staff Judge Advocate on whether you could disclose the terms of pretrial agreements before being approved by the military judge. General Glover stuck to his guns and gave Reynolds a memorandum which says higher command cannot review pretrial agreements until after approved by the military judge."

"Bob, every Marine should understand why that rule is necessary," Cahill replied.

"General Reynolds also demanded an investigation into your automobile accident in Alexandria. As you said, you were never charged with driving under the influence, but the police report says you refused to perform a field sobriety test and refused the breathalyzer. General Reynolds says that proves you were drunk. But again, General Glover was not intimidated and responded that the exercise of your right against self-incrimination can't be used as a basis for disciplinary action. Earl, I do not know what all this means, except, do not give Reynolds any basis for having you relieved of command."

The telephone went silent for a long time.

"Thanks again, Bob. I am not going to do anything stupid. All I can do is exercise my best judgment to act legally and in the best interest of the Marine Corps."

Chapter 54

At 1030, the door to the Legal Assistance Office opened, and Gunner Carson stormed inside, walked past the receptionist, headed down the hallway, and peered inside each office. Capt. Beck had spent an hour trying to explain to Florence Smith, the widow of MSgt. Earl Smith, deceased, why she did not have a viable defense against the traffic ticket.

"Captain, I don't understand why you won't help me. I had to stop to avoid hitting that puppy. Is there someone else that knows something about Arizona law?"

Capt. Beck took a deep breath to control his temper and started to answer Mrs. Smith when Gunner Carson opened the office door.

"Sorry to interrupt, Ma'am, but I need to speak with Captain Beck. It's urgent. Captain Beck, I will be in Major Herdy's office."

Beck repeated what he had said five times earlier and practically shoved Mrs. Smith out the door. He knocked on Major Herdy's door three times. Major Herdy yelled. "Come in!"

The cigarette smoke hung thick in the air. When Capt. Beck entered, both Gunner Carson and Maj. Herdy ignored him and continued with their conversation about a court-martial that ended the night before with a guilty verdict. Beck awkwardly stood at the rear of the office.

"Lucas, if you don't mind, I stopped by to take Captain Beck to an early lunch. Do you have time to join us?"

"No. I ate breakfast this morning, but you are welcome to take Captain Beck."

The red Corvette stood in the same spot on the side of the legal assistance building, and Carson peeled out of the parking lot and barreled down the flight line road to the Officer's Club. Inside the O Club, Carson went straight to the bar, walked past his usual table, and sat at one against the wall in the back corner. No one had arrived for lunch and the bar was empty.

The bartender quickly brought Carson a drink. Carson drank the glass dry and motioned to the bartender. Capt. Beck sensed that for some reason Carson was in a bad mood and avoided direct eye contact like they say to do with a bear for fear of inciting him. But Beck admitted to himself that he already felt terrified. A fine sweat chilled the back of his neck.

"All right, Beck; explain to me what Dixon's complaining about."

"Lance Corporal Dixon is asking for credit towards his sentence based on the conditions at Barracks No. Eight. If Dixon were in the Brig, he would receive a day-for-day credit reducing the amount of time he has to serve on any confinement awarded at his court-martial. If a Marine is released from the Brig but placed on restriction, the military judge decides how much, if any, credit should be given based on the conditions of his release."

Carson got a faraway look, and his mouth formed an ugly grin.

"Dixon was not on restriction."

"Dixon wasn't on restriction, but he has a long list of complaints about the way he was treated by Master Sergeant Miller. Excessive physical training, excessive drill, demeaning work details, unnecessary guard duty. He also says the doors at the barracks were painted yellow and he had to wear a yellow T-shirt. He was called a yellow-belly, chickenshit, and other derogatory names."

Beck's fear increased in the cold hollow emptiness of his stomach. All his confidence was gone, and it made him feel sick. Carson rubbed his bald head and stared out the club window. He looked at Beck and glared. Soon, his respiration accelerated, his jaws clenched, and the anger seemed to energize his mind and body. His face appeared contorted with disbelief and furry. He glanced around the bar to make sure it remained empty.

"I've talked to the Major Way! You are not going to bring up this bullshit. Dixon has got a deal for twenty-four months. Major Way will reduce that to twenty-two months. That's more credit than the military judge will give for this crap, but Major Way owes me a favor."

Beck watched Carson's face and saw the anger still growing. Beck's stomach clenched harder, and his heart pounded. He thought that Carson might just punch him sitting in the O Club.

"Gunner Carson, I am sorry, but I can't guarantee Dixon will agree. Dixon has civilian counsel." The fear strained Beck's voice, and that cold feeling had now settled in the pit of his stomach.

"You piece of shit! You are nothing but a fuckface, ghostpecker." Carson's face was contorted in rage. Suddenly, the table seemed small, and Carson stood face-to-face with Beck. He was extremely agitated, his arms flying about. He pointed at Beck and his hands shook with anger.

"I can't believe that idiot Bumbaugh brought you on active duty. You are no Marine! You do not even understand what Marines do. We take young men who have no guts, no discipline, no self-respect, no code of honor, and we make men out of them. Real men. These deserters were Marines once. They made it through boot camp. But one weekend a month in the Reserve is not enough. Somewhere they lost their self-respect, and that's why they let their fellow Marines down."

"Master Sergeant Miller pulled three tours in Vietnam. We served together. Hell, he saved my fucking life. He also did three tours on the drill field at San Diego. He made Senior Drill Instructor. He's changed the lives of hundreds of young men. All he is trying to do is help these malingerers become Marines again. Regain some pride. Some courage."

The two men sat and stared at each other. Beck's legs shook under the table, and he fought to control the tremors in his arms.

"Beck, Marines take care of one another. That's why I saved your pussy ass when you reported two days late. I should have known better. I should have let them report you as UA, ended your career, and got you out of the Marine Corps.

"I see now that you are just a civilian in uniform. A fucking lawyer hiding out in my Marine Corps from whatever shit you got going in Chicago. I know about your ethics complaint. I bet the husband of the client you fucked is still looking for your sorry ass.

"Now you listen to me, Beck. You listen very carefully. The worst thing a Marine can do is fuck a fellow Marine's wife when he is on deployment. That's the lowest of the low. You don't even put a Marine's wife in a position where people will talk. Officer wives are talking about Cindy Hendrix. I know you were out dancing with her. Your

Range Rover's been parked at the dispensary as late as 0200 for the last week. All you have to do is walk through the playground and in five minutes you're at Hendrix's house. I don't think Cindy would fuck a piece of shit like you, but I don't want the officer wives talking.

"Listen up, Beck. You are going to sell the Dixon deal and stay away from Cindy Hendrix. Because if you don't, you will answer for it. And I am not talking about the fact that the forged logbook is in your handwriting. I am not talking about calling Joe Hendrix on deployment so he can kick your pansy-ass when he gets home. I am talking about personally kicking your ass."

Capt. Beck fought the fear and could barely breathe. He could not speak. Carson guzzled down his vodka and slammed the glass on the table.

"Just get the fuck out of my sight, Beck. You can walk back to the legal assistance office."

Part 3

"We caught a few days ago a corporal who deserted and have just finished giving him two hundred lashes, and have had his head shaved, but we will never cure this evil, until we can shoot one or two of them."

1799 Major William Ward Burrows
Commandant
United States Marine Corps

Chapter 55

It was all carefully planned.

Miller, Weaver, and Tyler remained silent as Carson drove to the almost empty lot of the Mountain View Motel. The motel was small, maybe ten rooms, and the parking lot was not paved. The Marines wore black jeans, dark T-shirts, and military boots.

As he stepped out, Carson felt the old stabbing pain shoot through his knee. The doctors told him that with exercise the pain might one day go away. He had come to doubt that and had accepted the reality that his knee would hurt for the rest of his life, a life he was lucky to have after all the shit in Vietnam.

Carson could smell the heat radiating off the pavement, heard the swish, swish, swish of the yard sprinklers in the surrounding subdivision, and saw the headlights of trucks on the interstate highway. He watched as Miller retrieved a pack and a Colt .45 pistol with a home-made silencer from the rear of the Blazer and quickly started down the unlit street towards the edge of town and the open desert.

At the end of the street, Carson looked each way and entered a dry wash. He calculated the distance to Camp P-1-11, the former headquarters for the Second Light Anti-Aircraft Missile Battalion at five miles and deliberately set a slow pace in order to conserve energy for the run out. He walked cross-country through a wide gulch and soon felt the weight of the pistol in its snug holster on his right hip. A short time later, he sensed the sweat pooling in the small of his back. He did not follow any path but moved by dead reckoning directly towards Camp P-1-11. It felt like Vietnam again.

At first, he stepped on boulders and brushed up against the cactus, but soon he acquired his superhuman night vision, the gift that had saved his life so many times in the tunnels. Even with a moonless night, he could now see well enough to effortlessly navigate his way through the desert.

After 30 minutes, the group reached the boundary of the Barry M. Goldwater Bombing Range, marked only by a six-strand barbed-wire fence and no-trespassing signs, and paused to negotiate this minor obstacle. Carson quickly found a place to cross the fence and led the rest steadily toward the armory. He felt his body pumping out the adrenaline, and as he snaked along in the dark, he imagined the adrenaline bathing the gray matter in his brain. He realized he had not felt this way for a long time, and suddenly, he saw things clearly: the tobacco and booze were nothing more than a way to survive, day to day; nothing but a weak substitute for this feeling. He needed the danger, real danger, to survive. He needed to be back in combat. The revelation of this adrenaline addiction felt intense. His possible re-tirement and any plans he had made for a normal life were now deemed useless. He could not live without this feeling. He craved the excitement of battle and would always have to kill or be killed.

Carson reached the crest of the ridge one mile from the armory, halted, pulled out his binoculars, and glassed the compound lying in a prone position. Miller instinctively set up a small 360-degree de-fense while Carson studied the armory for 20 minutes. He had no fear of being seen at this distance. The armory lay about one mile from the chow hall, just west of the pistol range, and it appeared aban-doned without movement of any sort. He could not even spot the guards, who apparently remained inside the guard shack.

Carson's hand signal at the 12-foot chain-link fence surrounding the armory caused Weaver to move forward with the bolt cutters. He quickly cut a small opening at the bottom. Everyone pulled on their masks and passed through the fence. They formed a modified V for-mation, moving close to the buildings and dodging in and out of the shadows. At the motor transportation yard, they stopped, and Carson went forward to reconnoiter.

A flat-roofed concrete block building with two metal doors served as the armory. The front door had a four-inch port hole in the center and a metal half-door for checking weapons in and out. A large con-crete apron sat on one side of the building with wooden tables used by Marines to clean weapons. Two metal wall lockers held cleaning supplies. Another 12-foot chain link fence, this one topped with concertina wire, surrounded the building at a 50-yard interval. Floodlights lit each corner.

Carson looked at his watch. It was 0115, and they were on schedule. Again, he carefully scanned the armory with his binoculars. Again, he saw no guard. He reached up to roll down his mask to cover his face and watched as Miller, Weaver, and Tyler did the same.

At 0125 the front door opened, and a beam of light radiated out across the armory yard south towards Carson's position. Carson paused for a moment, head turned, and eyes fixed on the sentry, who had just exited the building. Carson ducked down for a second, then he rose and watched the guard who stopped, turned, and hunched over to light a cigarette. The guard carried his M-16 rifle at sling-arms and appeared to be looking at the ground as he meandered around. Behind the mask a smile appeared on Carson's face, thinking that the robbery would be too easy. When he confirmed that the guard stood on the other side of the building, Carson raised his right arm and signaled Miller.

Again, Weaver used the bolt cutters to quickly make a small opening at the bottom of the second chain link fence. This time Carson entered alone. He moved to the side of the building and headed after the guard. At the end of the building, he stopped and slowly peered around the corner waiting for the guard to make the next turn. When he did, Carson moved to the next corner, pulled out his knife, and stood in the dark watching the guard, and waiting to make his move. Carson grinned again behind the mask.

The guard dropped the cigarette, stepped on it with his right foot, and bent over to pick up the butt. Before he could recover, Carson had his hand over the guard's mouth and the knife pressed against his neck. Carson moved his mouth close to the guard's ear.

"If you want to live, you better do exactly what I tell you."

Carson paused, feeling the guard's legs shake, and the blood trickle down from the point where the knife was held against his neck.

"I am going to take you back, and you are going to say whatever it takes to get your buddy to open that door. If he doesn't open it, I will cut your head off."

Carson retraced his steps around the building. As he came into view, Miller, Weaver, and Tyler moved inside the second fence and took up positions in front, and behind him. The guard stared wide-eyed at the group with their masks.

At the door, Carson positioned the guard directly in front of the port hole. Miller stood on the side. Carson moved the knife down and stuck the point in the small of the guard's back. The guard flinched with pain, looked around at Miller, and listened to Carson whisper in his ear.

"This is it. If that door doesn't open, you are going to be dead in the next thirty seconds"

Carson moved close to the door and slid down. He motioned for the guard to call for the inside guard.

The guard pounded on the door three times with the bottom of his fist.

"Open up, Lynch. I need a smoke."

Carson heard the trembling in the guard's voice and expected that things would now go bad. If the inside guard hesitated, he would stab the outside guard in the spine.

The port hole slowly opened.

"Where are your cigarettes? I will hand them out to you."

It was the outside guard's anger that saved his life. Carson heard the annoyance in his voice.

"Just open the damned door, asshole. I'll get my own fucking cigarettes."

Carson heard the latch fall as he turned to face the door. As soon as the door moved, he charged inside, knocking the inside guard down, and holding his knife at the inside guard's throat. No one spoke.

Miller pulled the outside guard inside, and everyone went to work. Both guards were searched, disarmed, and tied to the bench under the half door. Their mouths, legs, and hands were taped, and empty sandbags were placed over their heads.

At the same time, Carson picked up the guard keys and checked the logbook. The guards had reported to the Officer of the Day an hour ago, and they had an hour and 45 minutes before the Officer of the Day would start investigating.

Miller moved to the pistol rack holding the 1911A1 Colts. Carson, Weaver, and Tyler moved by holding their packs open with both hands. As they passed, Miller placed five Colt .45 pistols in each of their packs—a total of 20. Miller left the envelope containing ten $100 bills on the side of the pistol rack.

As he moved towards the door, Weaver secretly grabbed a box of .45 Government-issued ball ammunition and slid it into his pack along with the Colts.

☙❧

"I am sorry, Sergeant Jones," Master Gunnery Sergeant Richards said as he handed Jones the large cup of coffee, then returned to his desk chair. They both paused to sip the bitter and strong chow hall coffee.

"I told Lieutenant Colonel Harris that I could get by without your help, and as far as I am concerned, you could spend all your time at the pistol range. But the Colonel said he wasn't going to risk pissing off the Commanding Officer by mentioning your name again."

"No problem, Master Guns. I am very thankful for the opportunity to work here and for the letter of appreciation."

"Working here and the pistol range… that's a heavy schedule. I want you to start taking off on Sunday nights. Corporal Snow can handle it."

"That would be great. But if it is all right with you, I will stop by at closing time to do the inspection with Corporal Snow, at least for a few weeks to see how he does."

"Sure. Whatever you want to do. I am going to finish some paperwork and get out of here. Any news on your court-martial?"

"My lawyers are doing everything they can, filing motions, but I don't have a trial date."

"Like I said, tell your lawyers I am willing to testify for you if they need me."

☙❧

At 0230, Sgt. Jones dismissed the cleanup crew and began the walk from the chow hall to the pistol range. The wind blew hard, and the night air hung heavy with the odor of desert dust. Nathan thought about his meeting with MGySgt. Richards. He liked him a lot. What a thankless job for 25 years, constantly cooking, cleaning, cooking, cleaning. Only complaints from Marines, never compliments.

As Nathan felt his way in the dark, he thought that he should start carrying a flashlight, maybe buy a headlamp at the exchange. No moon tonight and with the warmer weather, rattlesnakes would start coming out, particularly sidewinders. Marines were already seeing the sidewinders laying on the warm pavement in the afternoons. Nathan Jones stepped carefully, straining his eyes and ears to make sure he did not step on a snake.

After ten minutes, he turned off the blacktop and onto the gravel road that led to the pistol range. He mentally reviewed what he still needed to do to prepare for the morning shoot, coffee, targets, roster, and so on. While still looking on the gravel road for snakes, he occasionally glanced over at the armory fence. Halfway to the pistol range, he saw it. Someone had cut a hole in the armory fence. Nathan froze and stared up the hill towards the armory. He spotted four faint figures moving towards him. His heart pounded heavily, and it took a moment before he caught his breath. He felt frightened. He instantly dropped down behind a creosote bush.

From behind the bush, he could no longer see the four figures. He thought about running back to the chow hall or to the pistol range. He did not; he sensed they were too close, almost on top of him, and they might just shoot if they saw him.

He heard the first man grunt. Then he could hear his heavy breathing, something dropping to the ground, metal rattling, clothing tearing on the fence. In a few seconds, the man stood, and ran by the creosote bush, within a foot of Nathan. The man never looked. He never saw Nathan, just ran into the desert. He looked like a big man and wore an Alice Pack.

In seconds, another man—the same sounds. They were close to each other, bunched up and trying to get through the hole in the fence. The second man ran by without looking. Then the third. *Maybe they won't see me.*

Nathan intensely listened for the fourth man. He seemed to have trouble getting through the fence. Grunting, heavy breathing. Nathan heard what he thought was another Alice Pack drop twice. He could hear the fourth man struggling to get moving again and stared trying to see around the creosote bush. The fourth man stumbled and stopped just past the bush. He appeared very short. Nathan saw him standing, panting, looking west towards the pistol range. In a second, he would look back east and see Nathan. Instinctively, Nathan lunged at the man and in half a second had his head in a choke hold. The man struggled, trying to shake Nathan off.

When Carson looked back, he saw the struggle. Tyler and Weaver were looking also but did not move. Carson's mind returned to the tunnels. Everything depended upon a split-second decision. Nothing but kill or be killed. There seemed something pure about it, no gray areas, and no room for anything else.

Carson drew his Colt, aimed at Nathan Jones's head, and pulled the trigger.

Chapter 56

Agent Palmer felt more than a little annoyed as he sat in the conference room listening to Gunner Carson's briefing. Last night there had been an assault on the armory, but Agent Palmer had not been called. He did not even know about it until he arrived at his office at 0730. Carson continued the briefing:

"At 0400 the armory guards failed to call in to the officer of the day, Lieutenant McComb. At 0535 Lieutenant McComb attempted to telephone the armory guards and then alerted the military police sergeant on duty, Sgt. Woods, who dispatched a patrol unit to the armory.

"When the military police arrived at the armory, the guards would not respond so they used a bolt cutter to open the exterior fence gate. Inside, the military police found the door to the armory unlocked and the guards tied up and gagged. The guards reported that the perpetrators seized the exterior guard and forced him to have the interior guard open the door on the pretext of needing his cigarettes.

"Twenty of the old M1911 Colt .45 pistols were stolen. An envelope containing one thousand dollars was left, seemingly as some type of payment. The Colts were being stored pending shipment to Barstow, California. We recovered five of the Colts from a pack at the crime scene. Immediately after the robbery, the guards heard gunfire.

"One of the perpetrators was found dead just outside the armory fence. He has been identified as Staff Sergeant Reggie Miller, assigned as a troop handler to Barracks Number Eight. The autopsy is pending, but apparently, he was shot in the heart with a forty-five.

"A second perpetrator was unconscious at the same location and shot in the left lung. He has been identified as Sergeant Nathan Jones the NCOIC of the pistol range.

"It appears that the forty-five round passed through Jones's chest and hit Miller in the heart.

"Jones is in critical condition and not expected to survive. Obviously, he's not available for interview, but we have posted guards at the Yuma Regional Medical Center to alert us if his condition changes.

"Agent Palmer, I would like you to accompany Gunny Sergeant Tyler and myself to search the pistol range building."

"Where was Sergeant Jones living?" Agent Palmer asked, a hint of suspicion in his voice.

"He was living in the office at the pistol range." Carson responded.

"In that case, Jones would have an expectation of privacy, and you will need a search warrant. Or wait until he passes away."

Gunner Carson paused, looked at Palmer with annoyance, then continued.

"All right. I will get a verbal search warrant from Colonel Butcher, and the keys from Lieutenant Colonel Harris. You pick up Sergeant Fisher at the photo lab, and I will meet you at the range building in thirty minutes," Gunner Carson announced.

"What about the crime scene? We should start there."

"I have already secured the crime scene and examined the armory. I need your help to search Jones's office." Carson replied.

"What do you mean, you have the armory secured?"

"We posted military police to keep everyone away from the area. Nothing is going to be disturbed."

It seemed everyone considered the Chief Warrant Officer an exemplary Marine, but Palmer had his doubts about Carson. Palmer had heard things, nothing to act upon, but disturbing conduct. Heading towards a confrontation with Carson, Agent Palmer decided to delay the fight for later that morning.

"All right, Gunner. I will be there," Palmer replied. "But I cannot spend more than an hour at the pistol range."

∞

On the gravel road leading to the pistol range, Agent Palmer stopped his vehicle so that Sgt. Fisher could take photographs of the hole in the armory fence. This made them late, and Gunner Carson and

GySgt. Tyler were waiting in Carson's Blazer when they arrived. Carson used LtCol. Harris's master key to open the front door. He then entered, followed by Tyler and Palmer.

Inside, Carson and Tyler hurried towards Jones's office, while Palmer and Fisher moved towards the classroom. Agent Palmer abruptly stopped, turned, and followed Gunner Carson into the office. When Carson saw Palmer inside the office, he looked perturbed.

"Hey, Palmer; go get Sergeant Fisher. I want lots of photographs."

Instead of leaving the office, Palmer yelled, "Hey, Fisher—get in here!"

When Fisher arrived, Carson awkwardly started searching Jones's desk, while Tyler went through his wall locker. Palmer just watched.

"I thought you were in a hurry, Palmer. It's crowded here. Why don't you take Fisher and search the classroom?" Agent Palmer's suspicions were growing, but he could not think of a reason why that didn't make sense. He and Fisher proceeded to the classroom and started methodically searching the instructor's desk and storage lockers.

"Hey! I found something! Sergeant Fisher. Get over here."

Palmer recognized Carson's voice. He and Fisher hustled into Jones's office. When they arrived, Carson and Tyler were pointing at the top shelf of Jones's wall locker. "Start photographing, Fisher." Carson demanded.

Agent Palmer could see the Colt .45 pistol inside the locker. He looked Gunner Carson in the eyes. At that moment, Agent Palmer knew that Gunner Carson had robbed the armory. He would prove it, if it was the last thing he ever did.

Chapter 57

It took another hour to complete the photographs and for Agent Palmer to mark and secure an evidence bag for the pistol found in Jones's wall locker. He carefully preserved any fingerprints. He expected that Carson and Tyler had wiped the pistol clean, but he did not want anyone to claim that he had lost Jones's fingerprints. When Agent Palmer and Sgt. Fisher returned to Palmer's car, Palmer drove past the armory and exited the Air Base. He then drove to a residence in the Yuma foothills area, about six miles northeast of P-1-11 area, parked out front, and dialed a number on his mobile phone.

"Good morning, Alonso. This is Norval Palmer."

"Good morning, Norval. Glad you called. I hear the fish are biting at Martinez Lake."

"Can't fish today. Our armory was robbed last night. Do you think you could do me a big favor and look for tracks?

"Sounds fun. What time?"

"Right now. I am parked in front of your house."

"Give me a couple of minutes. I will be right out."

Alonso Rodriquez retired from the U.S. Border Patrol after 30 years' service, most of it in Yuma, Arizona and El Centro, California. Back then, the Border Patrol would drag miles of sandy desert roads with automobile tires. The agents then drove the roads looking for tracks, and when they spotted a set, the agents would follow the tracks across the desert until the illegal immigrants could be found and apprehended. Over the years, Alonso had tracked hundreds of men across the Sonoran Desert and prior to his retirement Alonso had the reputation of being the best tracker in the agency.

Agent Palmer parked his car near the hole in the fence, checked in with the military policemen securing the area, and let Alonso Rodriquez lead the way. Alonso slowly moved forward with his head down.

"Somebody lost a lot of blood here."

Palmer stared at the spot and recognized the intense, putrid smell of human blood. Fisher snapped three photographs, and Palmer made notes on his clip board. Alonso continued to carefully examine the area. Soon, he stopped and pointed to an almost imperceptible disturbance in the sand.

"Here's a brush-out. Someone tried to hide a track using a shirt or jacket."

Agent Palmer made another note on his clip board labeled *No. 4*, and Sgt. Fisher took a photograph.

"All right, Fisher; I will make a note for every photograph you take. Make sure you label them and don't get the numbers mixed up," Palmer said seriously.

Alonso quickly found more brush-outs, and they were photographed and labeled. He followed the brush-outs north for about 50 yards. Then he carefully walked around in a large circle and returned, stopped, and pointed first to the west.

"Norval. We have four tracks coming in from the north headed for the hole in the fence."

Alonso pointed to a spot to the east. "We have three tracks leaving, headed back north."

Alonso Rodriquez then followed the three tracks headed north. Agent Palmer and Sgt. Fisher frantically tried to keep up with the photographing process. From time to time, Alonso would point out where the men had stopped and taken off their packs. The trail led across the desert, over sand hills, and down washes. The three continued the tracking process for four hours and arrived at the dirt parking lot for the Mountain View Motel. It took another half an hour for Alonso to examine the area next to the parking lot. He motioned for Palmer and Fisher to come over and start photographing.

"Norval. Here is where they parked their Chevrolet Blazer."

"How do you know it was a Blazer?'

"I've tracked every vehicle made and driven across this desert. The Blazer's wheelbase is shorter and wider than any pickup. You better get out your tape measure and get your photographs, but I am telling you this was a lifted Blazer, seventeen-inch wheels with BF

Goodrich All-Terrain T/A's tires. I've seen a hundred of them. It's the favorite off-road vehicle in this area."

Palmer and Fisher carefully measured and photographed the tire tracks while Alonso Rodriquez continued to study the area. He then pointed out additional tracks.

"Here's where four men got out. Driver, front passenger, and two men in the back seat. They walked around, got their packs out of the back of the Blazer, then took off south. And here's where three returned. First, they dropped their packs in the back, then got inside the driver's seat, front passenger seat, and one in the rear."

After more measurements, notes, and photographs, the three followed the four tracks back to the hole in the armory fence. They crawled through the hole and followed tracks up to the armory building and back, making notations and photographing.

"Here we have four men approaching and four men leaving. The fourth man stopped at the hole in the fence."

"Alonso. There was another Marine found shot near the hole. Can you tell anything about where he came from?"

"I can tell the same person has been walking up and down this road a lot. That person did not go through the hole in the fence but crouched down by this creosote bush."

Chapter 58

"Gentlemen, raise your glasses for a toast to a great Marine!"

Gunner Carson looked at Cpl. Weaver and Gunny Sergeant Tyler. They were seated on the barstools inside Carson's reloading room. Three glasses, and a bottle of port wine, sat on the bar. Each smoked a cigar. Their mood was somber, their voices low.

Carson stared out the window into the darkness. He had eaten nothing all day and finished two bottles of vodka. He had been inebriated since 0500 that morning and now was so drunk he could not stand up. Still, his mind focused upon the death of his friend Reggie Miller. In Vietnam, he had seen friends shot and had even held them while they died. Many horrific scenes played through his mind every day. But there seemed nothing as horrifying as a friendly-fire casualty, the accidental death of a fellow Marine.

He considered the fact that at one time he and Miller had both been decent young men but ultimately were ruined by Vietnam and the Marine Corps. Both had spent years of their scanty salary on sex, drugs, and alcohol. Their marriages were disasters. Their children, parents, and siblings all hated them and wanted nothing more to do with them. They owned nothing, had no investments, and could only look forward to a meager monthly retirement check. Sadly, surviving all their combat engagements, and the corresponding ribbons and awards, were their crowning achievements in life.

Carson remembered the night in the Philippines that Miller often bragged about. They drank San Miguel beers, received sample blow jobs from half a dozen bar girls, and went home with three bar girls for 30 dollars. Over their careers, Miller, and Carson each caught a dozen cases of the clap. Still, knowing it was phony and stupid did not mean they regretted it—not one iota. The Corps became their family. The Marines always forgave their drunkenness, and debauchery, and encouraged their brutality.

Carson grabbed the edge of the bar with both hands and struggled to stand. He nearly fell, knocked over the barstool, and awkwardly leaned against the bar.

"Here's to Staff Sergeant Reggie Miller, a fearless Marine. Four times wounded."

Carson slurred his words but spoke in a loud voice, as if he were in a ballroom.

The three Marines raised their glasses, then drank them empty. Carson wobbled and could not stand. Weaver stood the barstool back on its feet and refilled their glasses. Carson leaned against the bar.

"Reggie Miller was one of the best drill instructors in the history of the Corps. I give you his favorite toast: "Here's to honor. Get on-her and stay on-her." The three emptied their glasses again.

"That fake mother-fucking preacher, Sergeant Jones, pulled Master Sergeant Miller in front him. Guess it's all right to kill another man to save your own life. Huh. Well, surely, he will rot in hell for this." Carson got his worst evil look on his face. Weaver and Tyler were scared, feeling the port, and trying to drink as fast as Carson.

"Sir, I just don't get Sergeant Jones. His father being killed in Vietnam and all?"

"What the fuck you talking about, Weaver?" Carson mumbled, seemingly in a daze.

"Well, when Jones was sent to the Yellow Barracks, Master Sergeant Miller told me 'Hands off,' because he had served in Vietnam with Jones's father. His father was a tunnel rat, just like you and Miller. Killed at Hue City the same day the Master Sergeant was wounded."

Carson sat silently, elbows on the bar with his head down, and breathing hard. After a few minutes, Carson struggled to stand again and faced Weaver. His face was red, neck muscles tensed, fists clenched.

"That's a fucking lie, Weaver. Pure bullshit."

Weaver tried to speak. "Yes, Sir. I got that wrong somehow."

"All right, Weaver. It's OK. Not your fault boys. I am the one that fucked up. I should have let Miller handle Jones. Never should have risked the shot. Seems like I am always fucking up those situations."

Weaver and Tyler were shocked to see the tears in Carson's eyes. Carson had never been this drunk before.

"Sir, if Jones lives, we got to make sure he pays for this." Carson could hear the emotion in Tyler's voice and when he looked noticed that tears were also welling up in Tyler's eyes.

The three sat in silence for a long time. No one said anything. They just waited for Carson and Tyler to compose themselves. Finally, Carson rubbed his eyes dry on his shirt sleeve.

"You are correct, Gunny. But I talked to the doctors today, and Jones is not supposed to live."

Weaver poured another round of port.

"But I will never again allow a dead Marine's life to become meaningless like we did after Vietnam. If Jones survives his wound, he must die, and we will kill him."

"Sir, what about Master Sergeant Miller's funeral?"

"1000 on Thursday at the base Chapel. Wear your dress blues."

"Do we keep the Colts?"

"I already got rid of them. Buried in the desert. No one's ever going to find them."

Charlie Carson paused and struggled to look Weaver and Tyler in their eyes.

"Gentlemen, we are all God-dammed criminals now. Fucking felons. If we get caught, we will spend the rest of our lives in Leavenworth. But I know about criminal investigations. They will never get enough evidence unless one of us gives it to them." The words were jumbled, and Carson stared at the floor, head bent down, as he spoke. He fought to force himself back into the moment.

"Get rid of everything you wore last night. I mean everything. Alice Pack...boots, socks, jeans, shirt and...mask...Burn it or bury it in the desert. And I mean tonight! Immediately!" Carson paused, seemingly exhausted after the long sentence.

"Never speak about last night to anyone." Carson's eyes stayed closed, and he breathed heavily.

"Don't say anything to your girlfriend, your best buddy, or anyone else. Don't even talk among yourselves." Carson stopped and appeared to have passed out.

Weaver filled the glasses and emptied the bottle of port. Weaver and Tyler just drank in silence. Then suddenly, Carson's head popped up. He looked around, wide eyed.

"I propose a blood oath." This time, Carson spoke clearly in a calm and steady voice.

"We have to swear to each other on Master Sergeant Miller's life that we will, if necessary, avenge his death by killing Jones." Again, Carson bowed his head and stared at the ground for a moment.

"That we will destroy all evidence. Get rid of everything we wore, boots, pants, shirts, masks… everything.

"That we cannot tell anyone what we did…Nobody…That includes other Marines, future wives, even our own lawyers…

"If things get hot, law enforcement is going to offer one of us a deal. But no one can take it. We all go to trial. Even if convicted, we keep our mouths shut…

"You both agree?"

"I do." Tyler spoke first.

"I do," Weaver added.

Carson struggled again to raise his glass. Weaver and Tyler followed.

"I swear this oath upon my life and upon my honor as a Marine. I will destroy all evidence and keep silent. If anyone of us breaks this oath, the other two shall execute the offender."

All three repeated, "I swear upon my life and my honor as a United States Marine." Then they drank the last of the port.

Chapter 59

"Colonel Cahill, I have a call from Lieutenant General Reynolds."

Col. Cahill braced himself, waited on the line, and tried to prepare for another ass chewing.

"Cahill, I know about the robbery of your armory. How did you fuck that up?"

"I didn't fuck anything up. Four men broke into the armory, tied up the guards, and stole twenty unserviceable M1911 Colt .45s. Six have been recovered. One of the robbers was found dead, just outside the gate, a staff sergeant, our infamous Sergeant Jones, was shot and found unconscious. He is in critical condition at the local hospital and not expected to survive. NCIS is conducting the investigation."

"That's all they took, unserviceable forty-fives?"

"Correct. They also left an envelope containing a thousand dollars. That's the salvage value the Marine Corps is getting paid, fifty dollars for each of the Colts. A very strange case at this point."

"And you let Sergeant Jones out of the brig?"

"That's correct."

"Why would you risk your career on some coward?"

"Jones was on his way to turn himself in when he got arrested."

"Big fucking deal!"

"I was advised by my Staff Judge Advocate that legally there were no grounds to continue Jones in pretrial confinement."

"Bull shit. It was within your discretion as the Commanding Officer to leave him in the Brig. Cahill, you are so full of shit. I told you if you fucked up, I was going to run you out of the Corps. Start packing because you will be relieved of command before the week is over."

"Is that all?"

"If Sergeant Jones survives, I want him back in the Brig, is that clear."

"Yes, General Reynolds. That is the plan. If Jones is released from the hospital, he will go back into pretrial confinement for his own protection."

⋙⋘

"John, I only have a minute." LtGen. Reynolds spoke slowly on the satellite phone. LtGen. Lenard listened as he sat at his desk inside the headquarters tent at Camp Gray, Jubayl, Saudi Arabia.

"It is my recommendation that Colonel Cahill should be immediately relieved of his command." Gen. Reynolds sounded as if he wanted to propose an obvious solution to a mundane problem. "I have concerns."

"What are your concerns?" LtGen. Lenard responded, also in a mundane voice.

"The robbery of the Yuma armory and the murder of a staff sergeant."

"I know about the robbery. It was on the blotter this morning. But I have not seen anything that would make Colonel Cahill responsible. I want to give NCIS time to investigate."

"Cahill released one of the perpetrators, Sergeant Jones, from pretrial confinement. He says he was legally required to release him. Any competent field grade officer knows that you lock them up and let the legal beagles sort it out."

"Well, I don't know, John. I served as the pretrial confinement magistrate at Camp Pendleton for three years. I know from experience those decisions are difficult and usually just a gut call. Some of the Marines I let out of the Brig committed additional crimes or fled from authorities but never the ones I expected. No officer is going to make the right decision in every case. Besides, Cahill was following his staff judge advocate's advice that there were no legal grounds to hold Jones in confinement."

"What about security at the armory? That was Colonel Cahill's responsibility."

"Of course, but it is not like Colonel Cahill ignored the issue. I am told he inspected the armory and the Provost Marshal, who is a highly trained Chief Warrant Officer and a specialist on security, insisted that security was more than adequate. Colonel Cahill relied upon the advice of his expert."

"Well, General Lenard, you have obviously made up your mind."

"No. I haven't made up my mind. I have some concerns about Cahill. I just want to get all the facts."

"I intend to discuss the matter with the Commandant," Gen. Reynolds threatened.

"Look, as soon as we have more facts, I look forward to discussing Cahill with the Commandant."

Chapter 60

After dropping off Sgt. Fisher at the photo lab, Agent Palmer drove to Barracks No. 8, parked his car, and walked inside. He stopped at the office located to the left of the entrance. A corporal sat at a desk reviewing some sort of paperwork.

"Are you Corporal Weaver?" Palmer asked while displaying his NCIS badge.

"Yes, Sir. How can I help you?" The corporal's expression went perfectly blank.

Palmer studied Weaver's face and asked, "Do you know what happened to Master Sergeant Miller?"

"Gunner Carson called." Weaver spoke absently and could not meet Palmer's eyes.

"What did he say?"

During his career, Agent Palmer had conducted many interrogations. He became a student of speech and expressions. He knew that he could distinguish truth from lies with amazing accuracy. It had been his 25-year vocation. He watched Weaver carefully.

"Sergeant Jones shot Master Sergeant Miller at the armory. He is dead."

Palmer sensed that Weaver was lying.

"I am investigating his death. I need you to open his office."

"I can't do that. I need to call Gunner Carson first."

"I am working with Gunner Carson. So just do it." Palmer's face twisted into a deep frown.

Cpl. Weaver did not call Carson, instead, he led Palmer to the Miller's office, opened the door, and followed Agent Palmer inside.

"This will take some time. You're welcome to stay, but I suggest I come get you when I am finished." Cpl. Weaver went back to his office.

Little suggested that anyone had ever occupied Miller's office—no civilian clothes, one coffee cup, and one photograph on the wall which Palmer recognized as Miller and Carson in Vietnam. The wall locker contained a pair of inspection boots and three sets of clean uniforms, still in the plastic wrappers. Palmer wrote down the sizes. The file cabinet had only the necessary papers to operate the barracks. The desk was practically empty: a couple of government black pens and a legal pad with handwritten notes. Palmer put the legal pad in his briefcase and searched Miller's trash can. He found a few message forms and put them in the briefcase. After searching Miller's office, Palmer walked inside Cpl. Weaver's office and closed the door. From the earlier conversation, and Weaver's reactions, Palmer had decided that Weaver had accompanied Carson and Miller when they robbed the armory.

"What happened to Master Sergeant Miller's motorcycle?"

"I…don't know." Weaver's eyes were wide and his voice shaky.

"It's not at his barracks. I know you rode with Miller, so tell me where else could it be?" Palmer gambled that Weaver had ridden with Miller, but this represented a tried-and-true interview technique for eliciting new information.

"I said, I don't know. Maybe at one of his girlfriends out in town."

"What's his girlfriend's name?'

"I don't know their names."

"Where do they live?"

"One of them lives in a trailer park, kind of behind the Stardust Motel."

"Besides Miller, who else do you ride with?"

"Different Marines."

"How many times have you ridden with Gunner Carson?"

"A couple of times."

"Where do you live?"

"Barracks 930, Room 230."

"Your roommate's name?"

"Corporal Cunningham."

"Where does he work?"

"Crash Crew."

"Where were you last night?"

"Uh… stayed here." Both Palmer and Weaver glanced at the rack in Weaver's office.

"All night?"

"Yeah…sure."

Weaver stared at Palmer with both anger and concern. Palmer evaluated the look and decided to roll the dice.

"Look, Son; I have got witnesses that will testify you were not here. You drove in on your Harley at about 0500."

"That's a fucking lie. Man, I was here. I was here all night!"

Agent Palmer pulled out his billfold then handed Weaver one of his cards.

"Corporal Weaver, you listen to me very carefully. You are about to make the most important decision of your life. I have been around a long time, and that means I've been around a lot of liars. Sometimes I think all I know are liars. And, Son, I can tell. You are lying to me right now. Nobody gets away with lying to me. I know you were with three other Marines when they assaulted the armory. You were there when Master Sergeant Miller was shot. You may have shot him. Pretty soon, I will have enough evidence to prove it. I will be back, and you are going to be charged with murder." The whole time Palmer was talking Weaver's eyes kept widening and his jaw kept falling.

"You know why? There's three of you still alive. The first one to talk will get a deal. But, if you ain't first, you are last. If you don't start killing each other, one of you will talk. If you ain't the first to cut a deal, you're going to prison for the rest of your life. Think about it. Call me before one of the others do."

Chapter 61

Colonel Earl Cahill removed his BOQ room key from the laces of his running shoes and inserted it in the door. Before stepping inside, he looked toward the flight line and noticed the clouds in the west. It looked like there might be a rare rain shower before morning.

Inside, he glanced at the phone and again concluded that he just did not have the energy to call his soon-to-be-ex-wife and daughter. Walking past the phone, he kicked off his running shoes and stepped on the scales inside the bathroom. He had lost ten pounds since arriving in Yuma—partly from running, and partly because Earl Cahill did not like to eat alone and had no one in Yuma to share dinner with.

After putting on his sweats, he retrieved a bucket of ice from the machine located on the first deck, tuned on cable news, and stretched out on the couch. Again, he stared at the phone. His mind tried to pry open the door to depression again, this being the point each day when he would down a couple or more glasses of Jack Daniels, crawl into bed, and pass out. After a half-hour, he reluctantly turned off the television and dialed Patricia's number in San Clemente, California.

"Hello, Patricia. It's me, Earl." As usual, at this point the telephone line went silent.

"Can I speak with Elizabeth?"

"No. She's still on campus… Earl, I heard you got shit-canned at Headquarters. Oh, my God! You are back on the Jack Daniels. Drinking in the bars every night. A DUI in Arlington! That's why you are in Yuma, Arizona! Isn't it?"

"Is that the officer wives' version?" Earl responded with anger in his voice.

"Earl…" Cahill could hear the choking in her voice. "Please. Get yourself back together. You left me, but I hope you're not intending on abandoning your daughter." Patricia's voice strengthened, and she cleared her throat. "She's a young lady and she needs a father."

Earl chose to ignore the statement, but now he could hear the anger building in his wife's voice.

"For Christ's sake Earl, it's only a five-hour drive from Yuma to San Clemente. You've been in Yuma for weeks, and you have made no effort to see Elizabeth." Again, silence, but this time Patricia waited for a response.

"I am the commanding officer of the Fourth Marine Division (Rear). If you have noticed there's a mobilization going on—the largest since World War Two. There are some problems here, and I've been working around the clock."

"Same old story, Earl! The fucking-ass Marine Corps first, family second. Just don't blame me when you lose your daughter forever."

"Pat, can you get a pen and take down my work number?" After a moment, Patricia said, "Go ahead, Earl."

"928-782-2002. Please ask Liz to call me tomorrow. I will make sure my secretary puts her through."

"Hold on, Earl. . ."

Neither said anything else for a long time. Finally, Patricia spoke and in a different voice. "I am sorry...I shouldn't have said those things...Why don't you come over for Thanksgiving? There's a Hilton ten minutes away. There are lots of places for you to meet with Liz."

"I am sorry Pat. I can't do it. I have the duty on Thanksgiving." The wave of emotion hit Patricia like a mortar blast, deep, painful, and ancient.

"Damn it, Earl! Are you still doing that stupid bullshit? I was in the Marine Corps with you for twenty-six years. No other senior officer takes the duty on Thanksgiving. Every young officer knows that they must pull duty on a holiday a few times in their career. But you, you bastard, you have to volunteer, and let the lieutenant go home...you ruined every holiday we ever had. So now it's going to be the same for your daughter?"

On the other end of the phone a swell of emotion also rose inside Earl Cahill. Of course, Patricia was right. He had no answer. He should have already called Liz. He should have planned on visiting her on Thanksgiving.

"Pat. I'm terribly sorry, but it's just too late to change the roster. I promise that I won't do it again. I swear, I will not. I will spend every holiday with Liz. I really don't want to lose her. Could I come over for Christmas?"

"OK. But I'm not telling Liz until you are one hundred percent sure you can make it."

"That's fair. I will lock it on and let you know."

Earl Cahill hung up the phone and poured himself another large glass of Jack Daniels.

Chapter 62

It appeared to be a small trailer, that much Cpl. David Cunningham knew, though he was not sure of much else. He lay on his stomach on an old narrow couch that smelled like cat piss. His oversized body hung over the sides, and his feet dangled past the end. A window air conditioner blasted over his head. The room seemed dark, but sunlight shot through the blinds in narrow streaks. He closed his eyes and that felt painful. Then he forced them open again, rolled onto his side, and tried to focus on this murky world. A smell much worse than cat piss permeated the room—like a dead animal only sweat, pungent. He searched his mind for any memory but soon gave up. He frequently woke up in strange places and experienced alcoholic blackouts. But he felt something bad, really bad, about that smell.

Cunningham finally woke. He saw that he wore civilian clothes and had a two-day beard. He smelled of stale beer. Slowly, he stood, turned, and stared at what was left of a woman. Her body lay on the floor next to him. During the night a large pool of blood had formed, spreading, and moving away from her neck. He could not tell for certain, but she looked like Gunner Carson's girlfriend, Herlinda Hernandez.

Suddenly, he heard a vehicle. He looked out the dirty window and saw Gunner Carson's jacked-up blue and white Chevrolet Blazer with the huge off-road tires turn into the street. He froze, trying to decide if he should run, talk to Gunner Carson, or just try and walk away like nothing had happened. He did what he always did, he opened the back door, and ran.

First, he ran a quarter of a mile south along the canal. The sun blazed across the hard-packed dirt of the canal bank, and it felt humid next to the irrigated citrus groves. His shirt hung wet with sweat before he reached the farm road that turned west towards the Main Gate at Marine Corps Air Station, Yuma, Arizona. He slowed to a walk at the Pass and I.D. Office and pulled out his military identification card as he approached the gate sentry. He sucked in his stomach, stood up straight, and tried to look respectful while waiting for the sentry to motion two vehicles through the gate. Finally, the sentry turned toward Cunningham and accepted his identification card.

The sentry started to take the identification card inside the guard shack, but at that moment a Range Rover with a blue officer's sticker approached. The sentry handed the card back to Cunningham, motioned for him to proceed through the gate, and smartly saluted the driver of the Range Rover. Cunningham entered the base and crossed Morgan Loop to the sidewalk surrounding the parade deck. From there he looked back and saw Carson's blue and white Blazer stop next to the sentry. Cunningham started running again. There was nowhere to run except across Morgan Loop, behind the Pass and I.D. Office, and then west along the back of the Military Police Station. Fortunately, on a holiday weekend Sunday morning there appeared to be no one else outside. Cunningham ran through the alleys, behind barracks buildings, and across parking lots all the way to Barracks 930.

He climbed the stairs to the second deck wondering if his roommate, Cpl. Weaver, would be in the room. He hoped not. Cpl. Weaver worked for Gunner Carson, and they rode motorcycles together. Carson was head of the military police and might be chasing him from the trailer. Cunningham entered his room and closed the door.

He sat on the rack, elbows on his knees, head in hands, watching his legs shaking and the sweat dripping onto the vinyl floor. He tried to think. Did they see me coming out of the trailer? For a short moment, he considered calling his Section Leader for help, GySgt. Files, but decided it was too late. He would have to keep running.

Cunningham walked out of the room, went to the first deck pay phone, and called a taxi. When he returned to the room, he quickly showered and shaved. He put his dirty clothes in a paper sack and threw his shaving kit and a change of clothes in his gym bag. He counted $73 in his wallet and reached under his roommate's mattress. He knew where Cpl. Weaver stashed his money. He pulled out an old Crown Royal bag and took $135. Next, he took a piece of paper out of the spiral binder on the nightstand and left a note in Cpl. Weaver's boot.

"I didn't do nothing, but I think I will be blamed for some serious trouble, and I need a loan. I owe you $135.00. I promise to mail the money to you as soon as I can. Semper Fi, David."

Cunningham waited inside the front door of Barracks 930 until the cab arrived, and as he climbed inside, he asked the driver to use the North Gate, and to take him to the bus station. Sitting in the back seat, he could hear the air conditioner blowing but felt only a trace of cold air and he started sweating again. Soon his wet back stuck to the seat cover. He first heard the siren after the taxi turned east on Hawkins Avenue, and after a second, he could see the flashing lights of the military police car. He closed his eyes and started praying. Without asking, the driver pulled the cab over to the side of the road and stopped. Cunningham never opened his eyes but just rocked his body back and forth and whispered to himself. *Oh, God. Please, God. God help me.*

"Are you all right, buddy?" the driver asked, looking in the rear-view mirror.

David Cunningham opened his eyes. He saw the police car had passed and was headed east towards the North Gate.

"I am all right. A little hung over. Just take me to the bus station."

Chapter 63

Agent Palmer focused all his time on solving the assault on the armory. However, after receiving telephone call from the Yuma County Sheriff, Luke Johnson, he sat in a conference room at the Yuma County Sheriff's Office listening to a homicide detective.

"Good morning, gentlemen. Thank you for attending this briefing. At 1132 yesterday morning Yuma dispatch received an anonymous call, a male voice, reporting a homicide at the Mineola Tree Trailer Park, 903 West 48th Street. Uniform officers arrived at 0752 and secured the crime scene. The officers discovered a female body inside the trailer at space G-6, lying face-up on the floor with her throat cut. The cause of death is listed as exsanguination. A very clean, deep cut. No evidence of a struggle.

"The victim appears to be a Hispanic female, age thirty, height five-foot-four, weight one hundred and forty pounds. The time of death is estimated at 0230. No driver's license or identification has been located, but the landlord says the victim's name is Herlinda Hernandez. The landlord reported the victim's employment as a housekeeper at the Holiday Inn, but the motel manager states that the she has no record of employing a person under that name. The victim was known in the department to be a prostitute, and she had an arrest record.

"No witnesses have been located. Residents interviewed at the park deny any knowledge regarding the victim or any occurrences last night. However, the park is a known trouble spot with frequent disturbances and arrests. The park is frequently used by drug dealers, biker gangs, and prostitutes."

The detective paused and looked at Agent Palmer. "At this time, we don't have any information connecting the crime with the base, except a ditch rider saw a white male with a Marine haircut running on the canal outside the trailer park back towards the base. Also, since yesterday was a payday, we are thinking that one of your

Marines may have been a customer. Agent Palmer, if you discover any lead, we would appreciate hearing from you."

Agent Palmer glanced around the room and asked a question. "Any description on the runner?"

The detective reviewed his notes. "Just that he appeared to be a very large man and over six feet tall."

"How about money?"

The detective reviewed his notes again. "No money was found inside the trailer." He continued. "It is probably another john wanting his money back. But listen, we appreciate you attending this briefing and be on the lookout for anything that might help."

⋈

After the briefing, Agent Palmer dove toward the Emergency Services Section, a unit he visited often. He considered the Marines assigned to Crash Crew as the worst of the worst, lacking military skills, constantly beating each other up, and reporting for duty drunk or stoned. So much gear had been reported stolen out of Crash Crew that Agent Palmer wondered how the unit could operate. He also knew the Crash Crew members were the biggest dope dealers on the air station.

Not surprisingly, the Base Commander located Crash Crew away from the squadrons in an old hanger on the unused side of the air station. The parking lot was full of old motorcycles, mostly Harley Davidsons. As he walked inside the station, Agent Palmer saw the half-bodies of mechanics poking out from the undercarriages of emergency vehicles like frogs smashed on the pavement. Another group of lethargic mechanics in grease-stained jump suits had their heads stuck inside the engine hoods. The station itself emitted the caustic odor of gasoline mixed with dust, dirty oil, and other chemical smells. Agent Palmer felt sad that such a place could exist on a Marine base—no spirit, no esprit de corps, and no spit and polish.

Palmer marched up the stairs along the catwalk in front of the glass-fronted offices and saw the open door of the Staff Non-Commissioned Officer in Charge, GySgt. Files. He thought it a shame that a Marine of File's caliber should be stuck in a unit as bad as Crash

Crew. Palmer had served with Files for years and knew that Files' old MOS of 2049, Telephone Technician, had been discontinued by the Marine Corps. Too old for retraining, Gunny Files was given the MOS of 7000, Basic Airfield Services, and shit-canned to Crash Crew. Gunny Files saw Palmer and spoke first.

"What's up, Deputy Dog? Are you over here to haul off another one of my Marines?"

The Gunny leaned back in his chair and took a sip of coffee from a white mug with a gold Marine Corps emblem and the name *Ernie Files* painted on one side with gunnery-sergeant chevrons painted on the other.

"Who are you calling a dog, you old bastard? I am just a pup compared to you," Agent Palmer answered.

"Neither one of us are pups. What can I do for you?"

Agent Palmer pulled the paper out of his pocket and pondered it while he spoke. "I'm checking up on a Corporal David Cunningham. He's on the adjutant's unauthorized absence list this morning."

"Man! Palmer, you must have really screwed up if they got you investigating unauthorized absences."

Palmer exhibited a rare smile.

"Just between us, Gunny, a hooker got stabbed yesterday, and a ditch rider saw a Marine running on the canal back towards base. The Sheriff and a bunch of other smart guys are checking out her trailer. While they are doing a lot of fancy police work, they asked me to check out a few things. To start, can you give me a description of Cunningham?"

"Easy. He's a fricking monster. I think he is six and a half feet tall and weighs over three hundred pounds. Early twenties, blond, a good-looking kid."

"Know any reason why he would go UA?"

Gunny Files walked out onto the catwalk and yelled down to the fire station floor where a group of Marines sweated to reinstall the engine on one of the rescue vehicles. "Sergeant Meyer! Get up here ASAP. I need to talk to you!"

After a minute, a skinny sergeant, wearing dirt-encrusted utility trousers, an oil-stained green T-shirt, and scuffed boots stood in the doorway panting. Agent Palmer noticed his long face, huge nose, and the nasty scar running across one eye. He walked with the innate casual confidence found in career NCOs.

"What do you know about Corporal Cunningham?"

"He's U.A. Gunny."

GySgt. Files looked disgusted and bellowed at the Sergeant. "I already know that! He's one of your crew chiefs! Have you checked his barracks room? Talked to his barracks buddies?"

The sergeant looked stunned. "Damn Gunny. Why are you busting my balls? You know Cunningham. This weekend was payday. He's most likely on another drunk. He'll report when he sobers up."

Gunny Files appeared to calm down. "Yeah, you are probably right, but this Naval Investigative Service Agent is looking for him, so go round up his crew, and his barracks buddies, and see if someone knows something. We will wait."

The sergeant ran back down the stairs. Agent Palmer considered leaving but took out his notepad.

"Sounds like Cunningham's a shit-bird."

"No, not at all. When he is here, he is the best mechanic I have—smart as hell, hardworking, respectful. Hell, he's been meritoriously promoted to sergeant twice. Just can't handle the booze. Once or twice a month he gets drunk. That's when he gets mean and stupid. Stays drunk for a day or two, sometimes longer. And that's when he gets busted back to corporal."

"Who does he hang out with?"

"Don't know for sure. Like most of these kids, he's a biker, rides a Harley. I know he hangs with his barracks mate...who I think is at PMO. This is crazy, but I think Cunningham even rides motorcycles with Gunner Carson sometimes."

"Do you know if he likes hookers?"

Gunny Files shrugged his shoulders before responding. "Don't they all?"

At that point, the sergeant returned with three Marines following behind.

"Gunny, Lance Corporal Tobias says that Cunningham never showed up anywhere after Saturday night."

Files looked at Palmer and then asked a question. "Did anyone check his barracks room this morning?"

The Marines all shook their heads. Files looked at Palmer who immediately responded. "What do you think, Gunny? Is it time for a health and welfare inspection of Cunningham's room?"

GySgt. Files and Agent Palmer drove over to Barracks 930 in Agent Palmers vehicle, parked in the rear, and headed to the Barrack's Sergeant's office to obtain the keys to Cunningham's room. Agent Palmer stopped before going inside the office.

"Look, Gunny, let's tell the Barracks Sergeant you are doing a health and safety inspection to make sure nothing has happened to Cunningham. Don't tell him anything else. If I already suspect Cunningham of having something to do with the murder, I would need to have probable cause and a search authorization. You follow me?"

Gunny Files nodded and the two walked inside. The Barrack's Sergeant pulled out his room roster. "There he is. Corporal David Cunningham, Room 230."

On hearing Cunningham's room number, Agent Palmer jerked out his notepad, and flipped through the pages to find his interrogation notes with Cpl. Weaver. Cpl. Weaver resided at Barracks 930, Room 230. As the middle-aged and slightly overweight men climbed the barracks' stairs to Room 230, the Yuma heat had the gunny's uniform soaked with perspiration. Agent Palmer also sweated in his civilian clothes. When they entered the room, Gunny Files asked, "Is there something in particular we are looking for?"

"Sure. Someone cut that woman's throat, so look for blood, torn clothing, or a knife. I am also interested in Cunningham's roommate, Corporal Weaver. So, let me know if you see anything unusual."

Agent Palmer and Gunny Files carefully searched the room. Both Cpl. Cunningham's rack, and Cpl. Weaver's rack, appeared made and everything seemed in order. After finding nothing visible in the room, Gunny Files walked back down to the first deck and told the Barracks Sergeant to get his bolt cutters and to cut the lock on both Cpl. Weaver's and Cpl. Cunningham's lockers.

With the locker doors open, Agent Palmer, without touching anything, carefully inventoried the contents. Palmer immediately recognized the box in Cpl. Weaver's locker as original issue government .45-caliber pistol rounds, the type of ammunition stolen from the armory. He carefully copied down the production numbers off the box then telephoned Sgt. Fisher to bring his camera to Barracks 930, Room 230.

While Palmer and Files were concentrating on the locker, the Barracks Sergeant noticed a pair of boots sitting next to the bed. They were scratched and dusty, unsatisfactory for wear.

"Damn, Gunny. You see those boots? What a mess."

Without thinking, Gunny Files turned and picked up one of the boots. A small piece of folded paper floated down to the floor. The Barracks Sergeant picked it up and read it out loud.

"I didn't do nothing, but I think I will be blamed for some serious trouble, and I need a loan. I owe you $135.00. I promise to mail the money to you as soon as I can. Semper Fi, David."

"Pull the mattresses off!" Agent Palmer ordered.'

Files and the Barracks Sergeant looked at Palmer like he was nuts but removed the mattresses anyway. A black ski mask fell out from under Cpl. Weaver's mattress.

Sgt. Fisher arrived with his camera. Agent Palmer and Fisher repeated the routine of making notes, numbering, and photographing the mask, the ammunition, and Cunningham's note.

Palmer then drove Gunny Files and the Barracks Sergeant to the Naval Investigative Service's office, typed out affidavits, and then drove to the Headquarters Building to obtain a search authorization from the Commanding Officer. He returned to the barracks room, and over the next four hours, Palmer completed a detailed search, supervised Fisher taking 65 photographs, and bagged all the evidence.

Chapter 64

Gunner Carson drove his Blazer towards the Pioneer Shopping Center to pick up Cpl. Weaver and GySgt. Tyler. Halfway there, he suddenly could not remember where he was going, pulled to the side of the road, rolled down the driver's-side window, and cut the engine and lights.

The old dark memories flooded back to him. He closed his eyes as the horrible images careened out of control just like the last time—they were in the tunnel, the Vietcong were running at him firing bullets, he fired back and the Vietcong dropped, but then they turned into PFC Kenneth Jones. His heart fluttered and his gut lurched. As always, the perspiration started to pool on his forehead, his skin grew clammy, and his armpits became soaked with sweat. He closed his eyes, put his hands over his ears, and rocked back and forth.

Finally, he managed to pull the bottle of vodka from under the seat and guzzled half of it down. *I am losing it. For sure, I am going fucking crazy.*

Slowly, ever so slowly, Charlie Carson gripped the steering wheel and that gave him some semblance of control over what seemed to be happening to him. His mind settled down. He lay back against the seat, head out the window, and felt exhausted without having moved at all. He finished the vodka. Finally, he could drive again and continued towards the shopping center.

At the shopping center lot, he parked, and watched as Weaver and Tyler walked over, and climbed inside. The worry on Weaver's face matched the fear in his voice that Carson heard in their phone call that afternoon.

"Where are your motorcycles?"

"Sir, like you said, we parked our Harley's across the street in front of Fat Albert's Bar," Weaver answered in a shaky voice.

"Good." Carson cut eyes with Tyler then back at Weaver. "Did you tell anyone you were meeting us tonight?"

"No, Sir! What's up?" Weaver quickly responded.

"We need to talk," Carson replied and in that moment his heart sank at the prospect of what he and Tyler had to do, even though he knew what the outcome would be if they didn't. There would be blood spilled tonight, but Carson reminded himself that he had seen Marine lives wasted for a hell of a lot less. This seemed the only way to stay out of jail for the rest of his life.

Carson drove out of the parking lot and said nothing else. He continued south on Foothills Boulevard, which became the desert trail called El Camio del Diablo or the Devil's Highway. He drove for an hour to a familiar camping site near Spook Canyon. Weaver and Tyler cleaned out the fire pit, filled it with firewood from the back of the Blazer, started the fire, and set up the metal chairs. Carson unloaded the cooler containing the beer and his vodka.

The three men sat staring into the fire. The sky was clear and bright, and the night seemed still. The evening air hung heavy with the odor of the creosote bushes. Occasionally, the wind rustled just a bit and cooler air from the west stirred at the Palo Verde trees, moving the leaves lazily. The three sat near the fire and watched the crescent moon illuminate the surrounding light gray granite mountains. Carson sat to the right of Weaver, and for a long time just drank vodka, and stared at the fire.

"What did you and Palmer talk about at the Barracks?"

"He searched Master Sergeant Miller's office. Then, like you said, he wanted me to talk. Said I was going to get charged with murder and should make a deal. He kept saying, 'if you're not first, you're last.' I did not say nothing."

"Why does Palmer think you were involved?"

"He didn't say. Just said he knew I was there during the armory robbery."

"What did you say to Corporal Cunningham about the armory?"

"Nothing, Sir."

"Cunningham went UA this weekend. You know anything about that?"

"No, Sir."

"Palmer used Cunningham's UA to conduct a health and safety inspection of you and Cunningham's barracks room this afternoon." Carson and Tyler stared at Weaver to see his reaction. Not surprisingly, Weaver suffered a sudden loss of composure. He appeared on the verge of jumping out of his chair and running.

"How could he do that?" Weaver's voice trembled.

"When a Marine fails to report for duty, the command has a right to inspect his barracks room to see if he is sick or dead. It's called a health and safety inspection."

"That's not fair."

"May not be fair, but it's legal."

"Palmer searched your barracks room this morning and found your fucking boots and mask."

Carson pulled his Colt out from behind his back. Tyler pulled out his Beretta. Their decision was unspoken. Weaver stood up.

"Palmer also found a box of government issued .45-caliber ammunition in your locker. Every box has a serial number. They have already matched it with the armory inventory list. Explain that."

Weaver breathed heavily. His eyes bulged and his legs were racked with tremors. He looked for a place to run. Then, he started to cry with tears streaming down his cheeks.

"I guess I will have to go to prison. But I will never say anything about you two. That's a promise."

"Yes, Weaver; you are fucked. Double-possum-fucked." Carson's voice was calm and sad.

"You could spend the rest of your life in prison. Not much of a life. But remember our blood oath. Weaver, you promised to get rid of your boots and mask. And, why in the hell would you steal a box of ammo from the armory? Don't I let you shoot as much of mine as you want?"

There was no anger in Carson's voice. He sounded sad, defeated.

"Stupid. I am so fucking stupid. I wanted some ammo. But I swear that I didn't tell Cunningham or Palmer anything." Weaver whispered, the tears continuing. He then stared at the pistols for a long time.

"My bust. I don't blame you guys. I took the oath and would do the same."

Weaver turned away, his back to Carson and Tyler. He just stood like that for a long time. Finally, he started walking away from the fire into the desert, slowly, very slowly.

Carson did not move but sat gazing into the fire. Finally, as Weaver moved to the edge of the light from the fire, Tyler stood and followed Weaver into the darkness.

The noise of the shot echoed across the desert.

Chapter 65

At 0745 the next morning, Capt. Beck heard a faint knock on his office door.

"Sir, we have a walk in." The pimple-faced private handed Capt. Beck an intake sheet. The name on the sheet was "Colonel Earl Cahill," and the matter described as "confidential."

"How long has the Colonel been waiting?"

"Just ten minutes."

Capt. Beck practically ran over the private as he sprinted down the hallway towards the reception area.

"Sir, I am very sorry to keep you waiting! Honestly, I was not informed that you were here. Please follow me."

Capt. Beck closed the door and hurried to sit at his desk. He noticed Col. Cahill inventorying the room and his uniform and hoped that nothing was wrong.

"Sir, Major Herdy is here, if you would like for him to sit in on the consultation."

"No. I asked to see you, Captain Beck. I know that you are a reserve civilian attorney from Chicago. First, I need to confirm that what we discuss is strictly confidential?"

"Yes, Sir; absolutely."

"I mean, I don't want anyone else to know about this appointment or what we discuss. Not even Major Herdy. Understood?"

"Yes, Sir."

Col. Cahill opened the green pilot's helmet bag he used as a briefcase and slid the property settlement agreement prepared by Patricia's California attorney over to Capt. Beck.

"Ever do any divorce work, Captain?"

"Yes, Sir. I have tried several divorce cases for my firms' clients. But I don't know anything about California law."

"I am in agreement with everything in the settlement agreement, but would like you to read it over, and let me know if you see anything unfair, or any minefields."

Capt. Beck carefully read the settlement agreement, cover to cover, while making notes on his legal pad.

"Sir, do you have any assets in addition to your military retirement?'

"Sadly, no. Some worn out furniture from my tour in the Philippines, a couple of cars that aren't paid for, and that's it. We don't even own a house. No money. No investments."

"Well, under the property settlement agreement you do not have to pay alimony and the child support worksheet attached to the settlement agreement seems straightforward. Did you confirm the accuracy of your base pay number?"

"Yes. Everything is accurate. I don't have an issue with the amount of child support. Anyway, my daughter is seventeen, and I understand the child support obligation ends when she turns eighteen."

"That's correct. Timing is important. Do you see you, or your wife, wanting to remarry in near future?"

"Not me. Frankly, I don't know for certain what my wife has been up to; she has been living in California. I don't think she has a boyfriend. After twenty-six years with me, she is more likely to have a girlfriend." Cahill smiled and laughed, a rare event.

"Well, as soon as a state court dissolves your marriage, you will no longer be entitled to military spousal benefits, and your pay and allowances will be reduced substantially. The flip side is that from the date the divorce is final, your wife will no longer be entitled to one-half of your retirement. In other words, if you don't retire for another five years after the divorce, the retired pay attributed to those years is yours, one hundred percent. The choice is to stay separated but married for a couple of years or immediately proceed with the divorce decree."

"Captain, are you saying that even if we aren't living together, I can continue to claim spousal benefits indefinitely?"

"That is the way it is administered. I guess the idea is that no couple knows for sure they will go through with a divorce until it happens. Of course, I would finalize the divorce before entering a relationship with another woman."

"Obviously, I would not commit adultery."

"Yes, Sir."

"All right, Captain. That is all I needed to know. I will share this with my wife, and see if she wants to finalize the divorce, or maybe wait awhile. With my daughter entering college next year, we are a little strapped for cash."

Col. Cahill reached across Beck's desk and grabbed the intake sheet. He put it and the property settlement agreement back inside the helmet bag and started for the door. He stopped and looked back at Capt. Beck.

"Captain, this is also confidential. I may have an issue with an officer. If an officer is relieved of command, is there an appeal process?"

"I could research the issue, but I do not believe there are any restrictions on the inherent right of a commanding officer to relieve a subordinate based on loss of confidence. Of course, if there is an adverse fitness report, that can be challenged like any other adverse entry. Do you want me to do the research?"

"No. Not now. I can always come back and see you."

Chapter 66

Sitting in the back row with Warren Leavy, Roslyn Baker watched the trial from beginning to end. Ogden Loring and Capt. Beck were a masterful team in the courtroom, meticulously prepared, and always two steps ahead of the prosecutor. Capt. Beck resonated charm and seemed to own the judge. Ogden's pleasantly deep voice held the jury from start to finish. Both were at home, comfortable and relaxed, and most important, thoroughly credible.

At noon, Roslyn Baker's green Jaguar slid to a stop in the gravel parking lot behind Alberto's. Located in the oldest, and poorest, residential neighborhood of Yuma, and constructed of corrugated metal with no windows, the building did not appear to be a restaurant open for business. As she stepped out, Roslyn glanced at the tiny tile-roofed houses that gave the area the feel of Mexico. Roslyn and Warren then entered through the ancient backdoor, found themselves in the middle of the kitchen, and continued towards another door. Roslyn grinned at Warren.

"Warren, the food smells heavenly! I just love places like this."

Inside the next door they were greeted by a handsome, middle-aged Hispanic gentlemen. Dressed in a white Guayabera shirt, black dress slacks, and dress cowboy boots, Alberto neatly parted his raven black hair in the center of his forehead and slicked it over. He had the same professional presence as a head waiter at one of Roslyn's five-star restaurants in San Diego.

"I am Alberto, welcome to my restaurant. Two for lunch?" He said with a practiced smile, as if seeing Roslyn became the highlight of his day.

"We are meeting some Marines," Warren replied.

"Please follow me. They are in the nacho room." Alberto tucked two menus under his arm.

Today, Roslyn looked her absolute best, trim, healthy, beautifully dressed, and simply a stunning middle-aged woman. As she moved with her royal grace, it became obvious to everyone that she did not live in Yuma. When they entered the small room, Warren did the introductions.

"Roslyn, this is Ogden's wife Sharon."

"Here to keep an eye on Ogden?" Roslyn asked playfully.

"I would not want to be here in the summer, but this time of year, Yuma is a lovely small town. Og and I have so much fun." Sharon grinned and looked at Ogden.

"Really? What are the highlights?"

"You are about to experience one. Yuma probably has the best Mexican food on the planet. Sonoran style."

"Roslyn, this is Major Cindy Hendrix. She is the chief defense counsel and has been very helpful to us." Warren continued the introductions, and Roslyn nodded at Maj. Hendrix.

"This is Captain Michael Beck."

"Oh, Captain. You were magnificent this morning! You did such a good job defending that young man."

Warren, Ogden, Sharon, Mike, and Cindy started to sit, but Roslyn strolled around the table examining the hundreds of picture frames haphazardly posted on the walls. Some held photographs, most included squadron insignia, and all recorded some pilot's record for eating nachos: "On June 12, 1987, Major Harry Metcalf, call sign "No Balls," consumed 310 nachos."

"What is the deal with these nachos? Super-hot?" Roslyn directed the question to everyone in the room.

Cindy answered, "Not that hot. Just a chip with cheese and a slice of jalapeno. They are pretty good. But somehow it just became a Marine tradition."

"Oh. I want to order some."

Roslyn sat next to Warren, they all ordered lunch, and Roslyn ordered a margarita. Sharon and Roslyn continued to talk about Yuma until the drinks came. Roslyn then looked slowly around the table.

"Ladies and Gentlemen. After hearing Captain Beck's arguments this morning, I cannot believe the Marines are being so hard on these young men."

Warren answered, "The Marine Corps is still reeling from the desertions during Vietnam. They want to make examples of our clients."

"Well! I think I am going to talk to Senator Wilson. This is ridiculous!" Roslyn said furiously.

"That is fine Roslyn, but do not mention any specific names. Believe me, the Marines are not past retaliation in these matters," Ogden interjected.

"Why are these wonderful young men pleading guilty?"

Capt. Beck, Maj. Hendrix, and Ogden Loring looked at each other in frustration, then Ogden answered. "There are a lot of reasons. A common one is that if they plead not guilty, and are acquitted, they are back in the Marine Corps. They do not want to be Marines anymore, and they fear the retaliation I mentioned. On the other hand, the standard plea agreement is a dishonorable discharge and two years' confinement. With credit for pretrial confinement, good conduct credit in Leavenworth, they can be back home in eighteen months."

"Ogden. If everyone is pleading guilty, what good are we doing?"

Capt. Beck admired Ogden's ability to remain calm and confident. It seemed like he was thrilled to hear the question.

"We must keep the pressure on the Marines, otherwise their pretrial offers will become more and more unfavorable. We thoroughly investigate every case, and we have some that we are going to contest."

Ogden's promise of vigorous defenses on all fronts was impressive, but his show of confidence was not altogether believable to Roslyn.

"Thanks for the summary, Ogden. What else can the National Peace Coalition do to help?"

"Roslyn, you've funded our defense. We have everything we need."

Chapter 67

Sgt. Nathan Jones tried to open his eyes, but they were far too heavy. The rest of his body was the same, his head swimming in a fog. In his mind, he had passed from earth to heaven where his grandmother was waiting with outstretched arms.

Suddenly, the voice beside him interrupted his dreaming, and Nathan found himself looking into the beautiful eyes of a young Hispanic woman. He recognized a profoundly peaceful feeling. He noticed an unfamiliar smell, clean, like bleach. He nodded off, then woke up again. *Did I oversleep? Did Curley cancel work? This isn't my bed.*

He looked at the lady again.

"Are you an angel?"

He heard the women laugh softly. Her eyes sparkled. Then he noticed her face mask and light blue uniform.

"Mr. Jones. Just relax. I am your recovery nurse. You had surgery this morning." She spoke soothingly.

Nathan carefully surveyed the machines, the bandages, the tubes in his arm, and heard something beeping. Slowly, he understood he was in a hospital. He tried to remember.

An hour later the beautiful nurse, with the help of another, rolled Nathan's bed out of the recovery room. At the exit door, they were met by a military policeman, who followed them up to the third floor, and waited outside Nathan's room.

The peaceful feeling returned, and soon, Nathan was asleep again.

Chapter 68

Over the previous hour, Mike Beck had accomplished nothing. He could only think about Cindy Hendrix. He felt sure that before she left the law center, she would stop by his office and invite him to her house.

"Hey, Mike; could you look over this motion?" Capt. Lisa Ellsworth asked as she entered Mike's office. She handed Mike a four-page document, sat in one of the client chairs, and plopped her feet on the edge of Mike's desk. After reading Lisa's motion to dismiss, Mike slid open the file drawer in his metal desk, flipped through the files, and pulled out a motion he had filed in a previous case.

"Here is what I filed on this issue. I have a couple more arguments you may want to use."

Lisa quickly read through Mike's motion and smiled at Mike.

"Thanks so much Mike. You headed straight home?"

"Yeah. Like you, I have a trial starting tomorrow."

"Maybe we could get a drink this weekend?

"Sounds great," Mike answered with fake sincerity.

After Lisa had left, Cindy Hendrix stuck her head in Mike's door.

"How sweet…helping cute little Captain Ellsworth? You are such a nice guy!" Cindy said shaking her head. Mike could not tell if Cindy was angry and just smiled.

"You want to come over in an hour?

"I will be there."

Capt. Beck left the law center 15 minutes after Cindy. His Range Rover remained parked at the office. He walked to the Officer's Club and drank one beer. He closely looked at his watch and left the Officer's Club 45 minutes after he had spoken to Cindy. Mike arrived at Cindy's house and didn't knock or ring the doorbell, because he knew the door would be open. Even after Carson's threats, he could not stay away from Cindy, even for one night. After closing and locking the door, he moved directly to the bedroom.

Cindy lay on the bed, her back propped up, wearing glasses, and reading a book. She smiled a seductive smile, and Mike bent over to kiss her. She touched his hair, kissed his lips, guided his hand to her heart, and pressed it there. Mike kissed her in return. Soon their mouths melded, and Mike's hands began to explore the soft contours of Cindy's body.

When they started making love Cindy sank her fingers in Mike's hair and clasped his head.

"Open your eyes, Mike. Look at me," she said in a soft, urgent voice.

"Look at my face."

Mike did as Cindy asked. When it was over, they held each other for a long time.

Chapter 69

At 0655 Col. Cahill walked from his office towards the conference room for the daily staff conference. He saw the adjutant standing near the doorway and heard her say, "Standby." She stepped inside the conference room and announced in a much louder voice, "Attention on deck!"

Col. Cahill entered the room, "At ease, ladies and gentlemen. Please take your seats."

Col. Cahill took a seat at the head of the table, paused, and made eye contact with each officer, then nodded towards the Chief of Staff, LtCol. Picket, who took charge of the meeting.

After each officer, including the G-1, G-2, G-3, and G-4, had given a short report, all eyes turned towards the Staff Judge Advocate, LtCol. Bumbaugh. Most of the officers already knew that Sgt. Jones had recovered.

"What have you got today, SJA?" LtCol. Picket asked in his friendly but professional matter. Bumbaugh turned his eyes towards Col. Cahill, nervously paused, and spoke in a shaky voice.

"Sir, I have some good news. Sergeant Jones's surgery was a success. He is doing well and expected to be released from the hospital next week."

"Has he provided any information on what happened at the armory?" The G-3, LtCol. Harris injected. Cahill, Picket, and Bumbaugh were taken aback by Harris's interruption, which was considered inappropriate, but Col. Cahill calmly nodded at Bumbaugh to answer.

"No. His attorneys have advised him not to make a statement."

"Well, that seems like bullshit, after all the breaks we gave him," Harris added angrily.

"I want Sergeant Jones transferred from the hospital directly to the Brig and confined there for his own protection," Col. Cahill said firmly.

"I am not sure we can do that, Sir, unless we refer additional charges," LtCol. Bumbaugh weakly replied.

"Then refer additional charges! Look, I do not care if Colonel Butcher lets him out, or if he is released by a military judge, but we are going to do everything we can to keep him locked up this time. Understood?" Col. Cahill's voice was laced with annoyance.

"Yes, Sir. Got it." Bumbaugh said with unusual force.

Chapter 70

Standing in front of the old jail, the Sheriff of Yuma County looked like he stepped out of a movie set for *Cool Hand Luke.* He wore a heavy mustache, mirrored sunglasses, and a cowboy outfit, complete with hat, boots, and an old-style revolver. Despite the colorful attire, Agent Palmer knew that Sheriff Luke Johnson represented a hard-working and competent law enforcement officer.

"How is it going, Palmer? We haven't seen you at the Yuma Area Law Enforcement meetings in six months."

Agent Palmer squirmed before answering. "Yeah, I am sorry, Luke. I don't seem to have the energy to get out anymore."

"We need your guys from the base to start attending. That's the whole point of the meetings. I want everyone to feel like they are on the same team."

Again, Agent Palmer felt uncomfortable.

"I agree one hundred percent. I am going to make sure I am there for the next meeting. This is Special Agent Steve Owen, Alcohol, Tobacco, and Firearms out of Phoenix."

"Glad to meet you, Sheriff."

"Glad to meet you. What can I do for you Gentlemen?"

Agent Palmer answered. "Two things. First, maybe one of your deputies could show me the Herlinda Hernandez evidence. And second, I would like to use your conference room for a very private meeting."

The Sheriff peered at Agent Palmer and Agent Owen.

"Of course, you're welcome to use the conference room. But, Hernandez, isn't that the hooker murder? I don't know that we have anything that would interest you on that case."

"At this point, I don't have evidence of a connection, but the day after the Hernandez murder, a Corporal Cunningham disappeared. A Marine matching his description was seen running from the Mineola Tree Trailer Park, the scene of the murder, towards the Base. I interrogated Cunningham's roommate, Corporal Weaver and now he is missing."

"That sounds like a connection to me. If we can help you follow up, just let me know."

"Thanks, Sheriff."

The Sheriff walked to the door, stepped inside the jail, and yelled down the hallway. "Hey, Deputy Aguilar. Do you have a minute?"

After 30 seconds, a young deputy hurried to the front office, and five minutes later they headed across the street to a featureless concrete block building used by Yuma County as an evidence locker. Inside, it looked like the deputies had packed up everything on every case in the history of Yuma County, including furniture, bedding, clothes, dishes, and an assortment of household items. Large items were tagged, but the smaller things were in sealed plastic bags. The building lacked ventilation, and after five minutes the deputy decided he could trust Agent Palmer and Agent Owen. He returned to his office, leaving Palmer and Owen to sift through the menagerie of items.

At 0950, Agent Palmer looked at his watch and headed back to the Jail to meet Capt. Beck who had arrived exactly on time.

"Captain Beck, this is Special Agent Owen, an Alcohol, Tobacco, and Firearms agent in Phoenix. Thanks for coming. I have some things to tell you and hope you can share some information with me." The three men shook hands and eyed each other like stray tom cats. They started walking down the hallway towards the conference room.

"Can we speak confidentially without you making a record?" Capt. Beck asked.

"That's the way we want it."

"I think you know that I represent Sergeant Nathan Jones."

"Yes, we know that." Agent Palmer answered. "I wish you would let me interview him."

"I cannot do that, and I cannot even tell you why. But I am here to share some information that I believe may assist you in your investigation."

The three entered the conference room and Palmer closed the door. Capt. Beck glanced around instinctively looking for cameras or microphones.

"First, please confirm that our conversation is not being recorded."

"Of course not, Captain. Relax. You can trust us to keep this meeting strictly confidential." Palmer and Owen looked Mike directly in the eyes. "If I sound a little paranoid, it is because my telling you this probably violates the attorney-client relationship, so I could theoretically be disbarred. Of course, I can never confirm any of this in court, or anywhere else, and I will deny saying anything. You will have to come up with the evidence to prove the facts, but this is what Sergeant Jones told me."

Both Agent Palmer and Agent Owen nodded their heads and pulled out their note pads. "Both of us fully understand." Agent Owen answered this time, and Beck started talking.

"Every night Sergeant Jones supervised the cleanup crew at the dining facility. Afterwards, he walked back to the pistol range building and slept in his office. He ran the daily pistol qualifications in the mornings. The night of the robbery Sergeant Jones was on his way back when he noticed a hole in the armory fence. He hid and saw four masked men crawl through the hole. He grabbed the last one, who turned out to be Master Sergeant Miller. One of the other masked men shot him."

Palmer and Owen just listened.

"Astonishingly, Sergeant Jones told me that the masked man who shot him is the Provost Marshal at MCAS, Yuma. His name is Major Charlie Carson."

Capt. Beck stopped and watched Agent Palmer's reaction. He did not seem at all surprised by the information.

"Jones says he recognized Gunner Carson because of his size and body shape. He is very short for a Marine. Also, Gunner Carson frequently used the pistol range, and he has a unique shooting stance, what Sergeant Jones called 'a perfect old school stance.' I guess Marines used to be taught to stand a specific way, perpendicular to the target, feet spread, elbow exactly one place. That is the way Gunner Carson shoots, but no one does that anymore."

Again, Beck tried to gauge the reaction of Palmer and Owen and they both seemed like they were already aware of the information.

"Sergeant Jones told me that the pistol found in his office at the pistol range was a plant."

Mike paused to organize his thoughts. "I personally have had substantial contact with Carson. He seems to be having some sort of mental breakdown. He served as a tunnel rat in Vietnam, highly decorated, wounded, prisoner of war, and went through a world of shit. He has an outstanding service record, but lately he's been losing it— some kind of post-traumatic stress syndrome. Sometimes, he acts like a psychopath. It's just unbelievable how much vodka he drinks every day.

"That's all the information I have, but I need to tell you that I think Gunner Carson may have murdered Master Sergeant Miller and Herlinda Hernandez."

The three men sat staring at one another for a long time. Then Agent Palmer spoke. "Thanks for sharing this information, Captain. We have evidence to confirm a lot of what you just told us. Yes, Gunner Carson has become extremely dangerous. He is the subject of an extensive investigation by the Bureau of Alcohol, Tobacco, and Firearms. I have interviewed Corporal Snow and the rest of the cleanup crew. I knew that Sergeant Jones was working at the chow hall on the night of the assault. There is no way he could have participated in robbing the armory. I believe his story. I know that Carson planted the Colt pistol in Jones's office…I was there. It was a stupid and desperate act. I just cannot say anything yet because the other military police would vouch for Carson. You know he has an outstanding record of service as a Marine.

"Like you, I believe Herlinda Hernandez knew something and Carson murdered her. Maybe Corporal Weaver is hiding, or maybe Carson found out that I was about to arrest him, and he is dead. If he is still alive and I can find him, I can nail Carson. In a few days, Sergeant Jones is going to be charged with Federal firearm violations, but we are doing that only because we need a reason to move him to Phoenix for his protection. Hopefully, it will happen this week.

"I don't want to scare you, but you are also in danger. If Carson thinks you have evidence against him, he may try and eliminate you." Agent Palmer looked at Agent Owen to see if he had forgotten anything, then continued.

"You need to say nothing about Carson to anyone. Stay away from him. Your office may be bugged, so be very careful. Remember, ATF and NCIS will be watching you and Carson. We will be there if needed."

Chapter 71

On the 20th day after his surgery, the second deck light at the Brig suddenly switched on and Sgt. Nathan Jones crawled out of his rack. He saw Gunner Carson and Gunny Sergeant Tyler standing outside his cell.

"Pack your trash, Jones; you are being turned over to civilian authorities for robbing the armory. The ATF agents will be at my office in an hour."

Jones quickly threw his Bible and extra clothes in an Alice pack and stepped out of his cell. As they exited the Brig, Jones noticed Gunner Carson's blue-and-white Blazer parked outside. Tyler shoved him inside, secured him to the passenger seat, then climbed into the rear seat from the driver's side.

As Gunner Carson drove away, Sgt. Jones stared at the Brig. He hoped to never return.

Sgt. Jones realized there would be trouble as soon as Gunner Carson turned north onto Avenue 5E instead of continuing west towards MCAS, Yuma. Sgt. Jones sat paralyzed and just watched the farmers and fruit pickers going past on their way to the morning harvest.

The Blazer turned east on Interstate 8 towards the small agricultural town of Wellton. Carson then turned south at Avenue 29E towards the Barry M. Goldwater Range and accessed the El Camino del Diablo, known as the Devil's Highway, which at that point consisted of an unimproved sand track. The back road seemed surprisingly smooth, and Carson sped along at 50 miles per hour to the Tinajas Altas, or High Tanks. They met no other vehicles and saw no one. When the El Camino del Diablo veered east, Carson turned right and took another two-track trail straight south towards the border with Mexico.

After a half-hour, metal signs warned of the approaching border, and Carson turned west up a wash, finally stopping under the shade of a large Palo Verde tree. When they exited the vehicle, Gunny Tyler unholstered his Berretta and pointed it at Jones. Carson removed Jones's cuffs and handed him a shovel out of the back of the Blazer.

"Start digging, Jones. Three feet wide, six feet long, and four feet deep."

Jones said nothing and removed his woodland camo blouse and started digging. The wash looked like sand, but soon there were rocks and then large boulders. Jones had to stop, set the shovel aside, and remove the boulders by hand. His mouth stayed dusty, and he felt streaks of sweat trickle down his back. As the clouds moved in and out, the humidity rose, and the morning sun beat down with surprising fury. In minutes, Jones began sweating profusely and made slow progress.

In another hour, Jones felt the temperature dropping, looked up, and saw the dark clouds appear over the Tineas Altas Mountains to the west. He continued digging while Carson and Tyler sat under the Palo Verde tree watching. They were not talking, just watching. Soon the wind started, small gusts at first, but quickly the Palo Verde and ironwood trees were swaying, and the dust was blowing in Nathan's face.

"Hurry up, Yellow Belly. I don't want to get wet," Carson said hoarsely looking up at the sky.

Digging at an even pace, Nathan kept thinking. *Carson and Tyler are too far to hit with the shovel. Throwing it would be useless. All those cowboy movies where the good guy throws sand in the face of the bad guy really cannot work.*

The dark clouds were hulking closer and closer, now lit up with lightning. Soon the lightning cracked closely followed by thunder again, and again—loud thunder. Then it started to rain, at first, just light drops speckling the dust and sand. Carson and Tyler moved inside the Blazer. Carson sat in the driver's seat with the door open and his Colt pistol pointed at Jones. Tyler did the same from the back seat with his Berretta. The wind increased in violence, and it became difficult to see in the dust. Finally, the clouds unloaded, and the rain poured down hard. Jones's clothes were instantly soaked.

The wind continued, and whipped the rain at his eyes, and into his mouth. He saw the Blazer doors close. Then Nathan saw the wall of water coming down the wash. He clawed his way out of the hole and up the opposite bank. Without looking back, he ran south across the open desert and towards the distant mountains. He ran as fast as he could, splashing across smaller washes, crashing into trees, and stumbling through cactus—never looking back. He kept running with all his strength towards the mountains to the south-east. After another 30 minutes he was almost at the foot of the mountains but completely exhausted.

At the base, he had to stop. He bent over to catch his breath, trying to continue walking, but only stumbling forward, barely able to remain upright. In an hour, the rain suddenly stopped. The dark clouds moved east, and the sky cleared. Then, Nathan saw the Blazer speeding directly towards him. Violently swerving through trees and bouncing through washes. Struggling for breath, he managed to move behind a formation of boulders at the foot of the mountains.

Carson drove the Blazer to the place where Jones vanished from sight, and he and Tyler bailed out. With pistols drawn, Carson went left, and Tyler went right. At this time, Jones hid behind the largest boulder. He stayed still until he saw Carson running his way. He then ran the opposite direction, and slammed directly into Tyler, knocking him down, and sending the Beretta tumbling across the rocks. Jones beat Tyler to the gun, then pulled Tyler up, standing behind him with the Berretta pointed at his head.

"Well, look at the yellow son-of-a-bitch still hiding behind another Marine."

Carson yelled the words standing 60 yards away with his Colt pointed at Jones and Tyler.

"Throw down your weapon and give me the keys to the Blazer, or I'll have to shoot Gunnery Sergeant Tyler." Nathan shouted back.

"No, you won't," Carson laughed.

"I read your candy-ass conscientious objector package, Jones. You said you could not kill another man. What a bunch of bullshit. You think you are some kind of born-again Christian, but you are just plain fucking yellow."

Nathan Jones stood silently watching Carson return his pistol to his holster.

"Come on, Yellow Belly; shove Tyler out of the way. You and me. An old-style western shoot out." Carson took one step towards Jones.

"Carson, you are stark-raving mad. Give me the keys. I'll never come back from Mexico. You and Tyler can say whatever you want about the armory," Nathan pleaded.

"No. Time to turn the other cheek, Jones." Gunner Carson again took a step towards Jones.

"Stop, Carson. I don't want to, but I will if I must." Jones yelled back.

"Shoot this motherfucker," Gunny Tyler yelled at Carson.

"You know, Jones, I shared the mud and blood of Vietnam with my black brother Marines. I heard your father was a tunnel rat. I did not know him but the Marine Corps is the only place you will ever be treated equally. And what did you do? You shit on your brothers to appear at a fucking peace rally. I hope those skanky college chicks fucked your brains out, but I can't let that pass. It's either you or me."

Carson took another step towards Nathan and drew his pistol out again.

"Carson, one more step and Gunny Tyler's dead."

"I can see you shaking, Jones."

Carson took another step, assumed his unique shooting stance, and aimed at Jones's head. Jones stepped back and carefully aimed at Carson, using Tyler's shoulder as a rest. The two men just stared at each other.

Blam!

Tyler bent over and grabbed his right ear. Carson's Colt went flying 20 feet over his head, and he started shaking his hand like it was on fire.

"Holy Shit, Yellow Belly! That was a hell-of-a shot! Just like Clint Eastwood. You shot my pistol out of my hands at fifty yards. That has got to be some kind of fucking record."

Jones stared at Carson for a long time then spoke in a shaky voice. "Nope. Carson, at this distance I did what any marksman instructor would tell you to do. I didn't shoot for your pistol, I shot center mass of target."

Carson started laughing, a crazy laugh. He laughed and laughed. Then, pulled out the Blazer keys and tossed them towards Jones. Nathan moved Tyler next to Carson then picked up the keys and Carson's pistol.

"Sorry, Gentlemen, but give me your wallets. I will need some money for Mexico."

Nathan removed the cash and returned the wallets.

"Regardless. I want you assholes to know that you don't need to worry about me. I am never coming back from Mexico. Start walking."

Carson and Tyler slowly started walking north, back towards Yuma. Sgt. Jones watched them disappear across the desert, then crawled inside the Blazer. He put the pistols and wallets in the console, started the Blazer, and drove slowly down the wash.

When Nathan reached a desert trail, he turned right and floored the Blazer. The passage of many vehicles had turned the hardened soil of the trail into loose sand, but the rain had compacted it. Nathan did not want to get stuck and kept the Blazer moving as fast as possible. The mountains were still off to the right, with the washes running down, and at intervals crossing the road. Every wash contained a deep rut that violently bounced the Blazer high into the air. The road constantly weaved back and forth, making it difficult to avoid the Palo Verde trees, Creosote bushes, and Ocotillo cactus. The Blazer heaved and lurched across potholes so deep that the vehicle's heavy frame was crashing down past its springs onto the axels. Several times Nathan missed a turn and had to slam on the brakes, then back up, and start again.

After an hour, Nathan saw a barbed-wire fence and a crude gate. Nathan slammed to a stop and ran to the gate. On one end, there were two loops of wire attached to a railroad tie. A smaller fence post was attached to the barbwire. Nathan struggled to push the top of the post close enough to the railroad tie to lift the top wire loop but lacked the strength to unfasten the gate. He pushed and pushed with all his might, and thought about giving up, and just driving the Blazer through the gate. Finally, the wire loop cleared the post and the gate opened.

The desert trail soon intersected a narrow black-top road and Nathan turned right towards dark mountains to the west. The road ran to the village of La Joyita—nothing but a Pemex Gas Station and a few dilapidated houses. Nathan then turned south along the west side of a lava field and could see impassable mounds of black basaltic rock. Finally, he came to the village of Toritos, again nothing but a Pemex Gas Station and a few tiny houses. He stopped at the road junction.

One arrow pointed right, *EL GULFO DE SANTA CLARA, 130 KILOMETERS.*

Another arrow on the sign pointed left, *SONOYTA, 325 KILOMETERS.*

Nathan thought about the photographs of the orphanage and the Christian missions in Sonoyta. He remembered regularly sending money to the New Unity in Christ Church to support those missions. For many years, Nathan Jones had dreamed about going to Sonoyta and helping poor orphaned Mexican children.

Nathan smiled at the memory of this dream. *I have finally made it. A left turn will take me to Sonoyta and the orphanage.*

Chapter 72

It took six hours for Carson and Tyler to walk back to the Circle K in Wellton and use the pay phone to call for help. The rain stopped and restarted four times, sometimes a steady drizzle, but other times a torrent of water, wind, thunder, and lightning. After the rain, the El Camino del Diablo seemed more like a riverbed than a road, and at places the water was three feet deep, forcing Carson and Tyler to abandon the road and struggle along the ridges of the Welton Hills and Copper Mountains.

While walking, Carson planned their story and rehearsed the details with Tyler. Carson had known Tyler for years but today was surprised by his intelligence. He was always asking Carson to clarify important details, and never changed the account of what happened. The essence of their testimony would be that they went to the Brig to escort Jones to the Provost Marshal's Office and to hand him over to the Federal authorities. There was no doubt that Agent Owen would have to admit that he drove to the Provost Marshal's Office that morning for the planned transfer. It would be reasonable for Gunner Carson to himself bring Sgt. Jones from the Brig to the Provost Marshal's Office.

Carson and Tyler would claim that immediately after leaving the Brig, Sgt. Jones grabbed Tyler's pistol. To avoid bloodshed, Carson handed over his Colt to Jones. Sgt. Jones then forced Gunner Carson to drive to the border, and at the border, Sgt. Jones took their money, pistols, and the Blazer. Sgt. Jones then headed south into Mexico.

Over the six-hour walkout, Carson and Tyler confirmed every detail—estimated times, seating locations, Jones's actions, and their responses. First, Gunny Sergeant Tyler practiced his answers with Gunner Carson doing the interrogation. Next, Tyler interrogated Carson.

"Tyler, this ain't the way I planned this thing to work out, but everything is going to be all right for us. Just stick to the story and say nothing else. If an ATF agent asks you a question we have not discussed, just say 'I don't know.' I believe Sergeant Jones—there is no reason that Jones would ever come back to the United States. And the Federal Government cannot do anything in Mexico. They will never catch Jones.

"Of course, Agent Palmer will investigate this thing forever. He will try and scare you like he did Weaver, but Palmer will never find any evidence against us. With this rain, no one will find the pistols or Weaver's body. So long as we stick to our story, and say nothing, we will be fine. You and I must distance ourselves. It does not mean I don't like you, just don't contact me, and don't talk to anybody."

Chapter 73

At 10:00 p.m., Col. Cahill locked his office and drove to the Bachelor Officer's Quarters. He was deeply worried. The feeling of impending doom had returned. Gunner Carson's story about Sgt. Jones seizing GySgt. Tyler's pistol and escaping to Mexico made no sense. Something very bad was going on, and sooner or later, it would end Cahill's career.

This time of the year, the BOQ looked like it was on its last legs surrounded by brown Bermuda Grass, dying Mexican fan palms, and huge old Ficus trees. He stepped out of his car, climbed the stairs, opened the lock, and entered his room. For reasons he had not figured out, Cahill's room held the designation of VIP Quarters, even though it consisted of nothing more than a three-story barracks constructed for temporary housing in World War II.

The old wood floor produced a loud noise when he walked across the room, then down the hallway to the ice machine. He filled his room's ice bucket, returned to the room, pulled the cellophane off one of the plastic cups in the bathroom, filled it with ice, and poured a shot of whisky. Sipping the Jack Daniels, Col. Cahill looked at the phone, but decided he just did not have the energy to call is daughter in San Clemente, California. He did not look forward to being relieved of command and having to explain that to his soon-to-be ex-wife.

Cahill pulled the shades back and looked out the window. It appeared almost dark, but he decided to change into his running gear, thinking that he would have just enough time for a run. As he left the room, he stopped to look in the mirror. He had lost 20 pounds since arriving in Yuma, his brown hair appeared grayer each day, and wrinkles were forming across his forehead. The good-looking Marine who had served as a model at Quantico, Virginia was aging too fast. His memories and burdens were heavy, but he still chose to keep them to himself. The horrors he had survived in Hue City, Vietnam would never be discussed, not by him anyway, but it seemed they were now taking a toll.

From the BOQ he ran down the hill towards the flight line. He was amazed at how fast it had cooled since the sun went down. He slowed his pace, letting his heartbeat even out, and just enjoyed himself. As he ran, he paid attention to his body trying to feel each muscle. The runner's high kicked in early—running purged the world's evils and delayed the shit storm he felt was soon coming, at least for a little while.

After three miles, Cahill passed a dilapidated obstacle course, the same type of course he ran 24 years ago in Quantico at the Basic School with telephone-pole hurdles, wooden walls, ropes, cargo ladders, and monkey bars. He remembered with fondness his skill at the course and even started to run it, but soon realized that some young Marine might be watching his now-pathetic performance. He ran back to the road and headed east towards the Main Gate.

After another two miles, he passed the Officers' Club. By now, Cahill realized that no single officer really wanted to go to Yuma. They only went there if they had to, maybe for advanced flight training, or a command billet, and from the number of cars parked in the BOQ lot, he guessed there might be nothing better to do in Yuma for a young officer than go to the O Club. He also guessed that a crowd of young pilots were inside drinking beer, playing pool, and eating the complimentary hors d'oeuvres of chicken wings, meat balls, and taquitos—standard O Club food.

Carefully avoiding the O Club, Cahill headed back up the hill to his BOQ room. By the time he returned, he was soaked with sweat, but did not bother with a shower. He immediately refilled the plastic glass with ice and Jack Daniels and decided that would be his dinner for tonight. As usual, Jack Daniels would also be his sleeping pill. *Cahill you have not done a damn thing for the Marine Corps since Hue City. Reynolds is right. It is time to stop playing the hero and get to work.*

He drank the glass slowly, enjoying the flavor of the whiskey. He started to screw the cap back on the bottle, but noticed that it was almost empty, and decided that he would finish this one last bottle.

Beginning tomorrow, he would completely stop drinking. Soon, he fell asleep in the chair. He woke an hour later, staggered to the bed, turned off the lamp on the nightstand, and lay back, staring up into the darkness. He spoke a word to himself out loud. The word seemed in his mind to sum up exactly how he felt about Reynolds and the entire situation.

BULLSHIT! I should be in Saudi Arabia. But I am a Marine, and Marines go where they are told to go.

Chapter 74

As he drove his Dodge Challenger through the main gate and toward the MCAS, Yuma, Officer's Club, Steve Way prayed that the four aspirin would kick in to stop the ache in his head. His drinking buddy, Mike Beck, sat silently in the passenger seat, eyes closed and occasionally rubbing his stomach and rolling down the window. Way's mouth tasted like a dirty penny, and whenever he closed his eyelids, it felt as if bits of sand grated across them. The two had spent the night in downtown San Diego at the Field Pub drinking Smethwick's beers, shots of Jameson, and worst of all, Irish Car Bombs. Steve Way slept with a girl from St. Louis attending a bachelorette party, and Mike Beck snoozed alone on the couch in the motel suite. Both were awakened and asked to leave at 8:00 a.m.

The morning seemed unusually hot for this time of the year, and the sun produced an intense mirage that made it difficult for Way to focus on the road. Even with the Challenger's air conditioner turned to a full blast, the Marines' backs were wet with sweat by the time they arrived at the O Club parking lot. Stepping outside the car, the smell of the hot engine, dirty asphalt, and over-irrigated Bermuda grass almost caused Way to throw up, but he managed to hurry inside the rear entrance of the Club.

Inside the O Club, a dozen Marine and Navy pilots wearing flight suits smelling of jet fuel sat at the bar or at tables, silently eating late breakfasts and drinking coffee or beer. Steve held two fingers up and mouthed "Coronas" at the Filipino bartender, then led Mike to two open seats at the bar directly beneath an air-conditioning vent. Before the bartender could bring the beers, Steve began talking and laughing with a group of pilots. The things that made Steve Way a great trial lawyer included his ability to communicate with people, all kinds of people, but it also made him a pain in the ass in a bar. Steve could not help but strike up meaningless conversations with everyone in the bar, male or female. Steve was also an alcoholic, but not a simple alcoholic concerned only with his own drunkenness; no, he was a fully functioning social alcoholic and believed it his duty to make sure everyone else in the bar also got drunk.

After church let out around 1030, Mike noticed the plump officer wives and kids crawling out of the cars in the parking lot and the families cutting through the pool toward the O Club dining room for Sunday brunch, a surprisingly good array of food for an amazingly low price. As usual aboard Marine bases, the Sunday brunch enjoyed the patronage of almost all families.

"What do you think, Mike? Ready to brave the brunch line?" Steve asked in a weak voice.

"Hell, no. I can't handle the rug-rats this morning. Let's eat here." Mike slowly moaned in reply.

After eating the chorizo, eggs, and tortillas, Steve and Mike continued to order beers and sat staring out the window toward the pool, contemplating how to spend the rest of the day.

On Friday, Maj. Hendrix had made it absolutely clear to Mike that she was off limits for the weekend—she had an officer wives' event Saturday, church on Sunday morning, and a pool party with one of Joe's friends on Sunday afternoon. Mike fought his depression and noticed that, as time went by, more pilots drifted in, sat at the bar rolling dice, or stared out the window drinking.

"Hey, Mike. What say we head by your hooch, pickup our trunks, pack some beers, and drive up to Parker?" Steve paused to look at his watch and continued. "We can be there by 1500 and get back early. There's a bar on the river called the Sundowner. It's next to a beach and usually has a decent band on Sunday afternoons. The last time I was up there, the place was packed with bikinis."

"I don't know, Steve," Mike whispered hoarsely. "I think I need some more rack time."

Steve dropped the subject, hoping that after a few more beers, the old Mike would start thinking about bikinis, and would want to make the drive to Parker. Soon, Mike noticed Steve staring through the bar window in the direction of the pool. He followed Steve's eyes and saw a couple of middle-aged officer wives wearing one-piece suits accompanied by packs of screaming kids. Then Mike saw what Steve focused upon. The suit for the closest woman looked two sizes too small. She bent over to help her child and her breasts pushed together and rose as one until Mike thought they would surely pop out.

"Damn it! Steve! You will still nail anything, won't you? I must get away from you. I'll get a court-martial." The strength in Mike's voice had returned.

Without any sign of embarrassment, Steve Way grinned and shrugged his shoulders. "Hey, they look pretty good to me. Did you get a look at those big ol' knockers? I say we get our suits on and catch some rays here. I can party with the mommas, and you can take a nap."

"No thanks, Wrong Way. I like Plan A better. Let's drive up to Parker. I cannot risk spending time with you on base."

Soon the conversation ended, and the two Marines just sat in silence sipping their cold Coronas and watching officer wives show up at the pool. Except, from time to time, just to annoy Mike, Steve would grin, nod toward an overweight mother, wink, and say, "That's a good ol' big one." Mike responded by frowning and shaking his head from side to side.

Suddenly, a flash of light from the door signaled the entrance of someone from the pool, and when Steve Way's eyes adjusted, he saw a voluptuous middle-aged woman wearing a tiny bathing suit strolling to the bar. As she neared the table, she stopped, smiled at Beck, and casually re-adjusted the towel wrapped around her waist exposing a shapely leg. She had mastered the aloof look of the wife of a senior officer. When the gorgeous female reached the bar, she eased herself on an empty bar stool, ordered a margarita, and lit up a cigarette.

Steve glanced over at Mike who recognized the woman as Nicole Turner, his first legal assistant client. A second streak of light pierced the bar and a bear-rumble of a voice familiar to Mike boomed.

"Well, I will be a son-of-a-bitch! What in the hell are you doing in the Club on Sunday morning?"

Mike stood, grinned, and watched LtCol. Wayne Turner, wearing his outdated swim trunks and beach shirt walk to their table. Turner slapped Mike on the back and spoke again in his commanding voice.

"I remember you, Captain Beck. But I figured a young stud like you would be in San Diego."

"We were, but my buddy has a big trial on Monday." Mike motioned toward Steve. "This is Major Steve Way. He's one of the trial counsels on base."

Maj. Way stuck out his hand, and the Marines shook. LtCol. Turner then moved to an open spot at the bar next to Nicole and motioned for Capt. Beck and Maj. Way to follow.

"I owe Captain Beck, big time. He saved my bacon on my rental. One telephone call scared the shit out of my landlord, and me and Nicole are all moved in. So, belly up to the bar, and I am buying you scoundrels a drink."

Beck and Way hurried to the bar, but to get a better view, Steve stopped two steps short, and stood on the side of LtCol. Turner, staring wide-eyed at Nicole, and taking in the full view of her almost naked body. She seemed not to be listening to Wayne's conversation with Mike and smiled warmly at Steve, occasionally taking a drag on her cigarette, and blowing the smoke with a seductive pucker. As conversation continued, Steve stood speechless, looking at Nicole's huge breasts.

"Hey, Mike, aren't you a reserve lawyer mobilized to prosecute those deserters? We need to shoot a couple of those yellow bastards!" LtCol. Turner spoke with surprising anger in his voice. Mike started to answer but was immediately interrupted by Turner.

"Goddamn it, Major Way! Stop gawking at my wife's tits." LtCol. Turner roared, peering down at Steve Way, hands on his hips like a drill instructor. Then his head went back, and he laughed. Maj. Way stood red-faced while the bar erupted in laughter. The bartender, waitress, and the Marines playing dice whooped and hollered. Nicole laughed so hard that she nearly slipped off the bar stool. Finally, Maj. Way answered LtCol. Turner, unconsciously standing at attention.

"I apologize if it appeared as though I was looking at the lady. I assure you. I was not staring at her bosom. I was merely lost in thoughts about tomorrow's trial."

Next, Maj. Way stepped close to the bar on the opposite side of Nicole. "Ma'am. Please accept my humble apologies for any embarrassment I may have caused you."

A ship's bell clanged, and an explosive cheer went through the room as all the patrons headed for the bar to order their free round of drinks. Maj. Way looked at his feet and saw the red dot painted on the floor that reserved that portion of the bar for the waitresses.

"Son-of-a-bitch!" Steve exclaimed. "This just ain't my day."

For another five minutes, everyone in the bar yelled in an obstreperous rally around the bar. Most held drinks in both hands. After serving everyone, the bartender shuffled over to Steve with a cash register tape. "The total's forty-six bucks. Should I add something for you?"

"Yeah, give me another Corona," Steve mumbled sadly. LtCol. Turner guided Maj. Way and Capt. Beck to a safe place at the bar.

Chapter 75

Nathan Jones opened his eyes and realized that he lay on a dirty blanket on the sandy beach of El Gulfo de Santa Clara, Sonora, Mexico.

Occasionally swatting at the fly buzzing his ear, he raised his head and saw a long, wide stretch of aquamarine water shimmering in the sun. He marveled at the intense color, the bluest he had ever seen. The Sea of Cortez appeared vast and utterly stunning. Streaks of the rising sun leaked through the crevasses of the jagged mountains to the east, and the waves beat rhythmically against the shore. The gulls, pelicans, and other sea birds sang a rising chorale of chirps and squawks, and the fragrant and chilly sea breeze felt refreshing.

After sitting for a moment, Nathan slowly stood up and spotted Carson's Blazer stuck in the sand. He vaguely remembered spinning the big tires. Further away, he noticed a large ramshackle building with a sign out front that said *Jose's Cantina*. The building had a veranda facing the sea, open windows on all sides, and a few palm leaf cabanas. A small gathering of men sat on the veranda eating burritos and sipping coffee.

Nathan left his boots off and walked barefoot to the cantina still wearing his woodland camo pants and green Marine Corps T-shirt. Curious but non-threatening looks appeared on the faces of the men at the cantina as Nathan climbed the stairs and proceeded inside. Nathan immediately smelled bacon cooking and saw three plump middle-aged Hispanic women folding burritos. An older man sat at the counter taking money and making change out of a cigar box. He looked obese, with puffy, unhealthy skin, and had an almost perfect waxed mustache. Huge black sideburns ran down below his ears. As soon as he saw Nathan he smiled, broad and infectious, like a game-show host, then spoke in a voice as coarse and unfiltered as the cigarette sticking out the side of his huge mouth.

"*Buenos Dias, Señor.* I am Jose. Welcome to my cantina."

Nathan smiled at his first chance to use Spanish since Wabash Valley College. "*Buenos Dias, Señor.*"

"How about some breakfast, *Amigo*?"

"*Si. Si. Uno bacon y egg burrito and taza de cafe, por favor*"

"*Uno peso.*" Jose replied and glanced out the window toward the stuck Blazer.

"It looks like you got stuck, *Amigo*?"

Nathan looked at the Blazer and answered. "*Si*, I guess I drove too far in the dark."

"*No, hay problema*. I will help you later. But tell me *Señor*, why you drove here in the dark."

"I wanted to get down early for the weekend," Nathan answered in a shaky voice.

Jose looked intrigued. "Do you come from Yuma? This time of year, is too hot for the Gringos. There won't be anyone here, even on the weekend."

Nathan tried to think fast. "No, I live in San Diego. I don't like crowds, and I heard about this place. I am glad to have the beach to myself."

The look on Jose's face told Nathan he was not buying the story, but Jose just grinned and handed Nathan a cup of hot coffee. Nathan strolled onto the veranda to enjoy the view and cool breeze as he ate the burrito. He watched the men amble down to a line of wooden boats pulled up on the beach, and once there, they moved quickly to organize their nets, bait, and other fishing gear. In a short time, an old Army truck roared down from the village of El Gulfo de Santa Clara. The body of the truck had been raised four feet above the wheels, and the fishermen used it to drag their boats out into the water. Once in the water, they yanked the starter ropes on the outboard engines, and one by one, headed out to sea.

After the fishermen left and Nathan finished his breakfast, Jose came out carrying a Mexican license plate, two spray cans of white paint, an old pair of pliers, a screwdriver, two pairs of gaudy swimming trunks, and two T-shirts that said, "Jose's Cantina." He sat the pile of goods at Nathan's table.

"Twenty dollars, *Señor*, and a shade for one month. A good place to sleep and much cooler in the day." Jose pointed at an old rickety carport structure on the side of the cantina. "*Policia* will not bother you at Jose's."

Nathan Jones got the message, and 20 dollars seemed fair. He pulled out a 20 and handed it to Jose. Jose yelled something at the men on the veranda, and Nathan, Jose and the men pushed the Blazer out of the sand hole and into the carport. Jose and Nathan each took a can of paint and sprayed over the blue areas to make the Blazer all white. They changed the license plate and walked back to the veranda.

The rest of the morning, Nathan and Jose sat on the veranda drinking coffee and gazing across the sea at the Baja Mountains. After lunch, Nathan started drinking ice-cold Coronas. At dark, he crawled inside the Blazer, curled up in the dirty blanket, and passed out.

ଔଷ୬

It had been two weeks, and the sun beat down on the sandy beach where Nathan lifted his head. The sky was gray now. It was almost dawn, and as usual, the sea birds swooped and settled and chirped with gratitude. He could not recall how he got to this spot. Gradually, he understood that last night he had passed out on the sand before he could climb inside the white Blazer. He drank too much tequila at Jose's.

He gripped the Blazer's fender, and tried to climb up, but he did not have the strength. Finally, he managed to crawl up the side, pull himself up, and lean his body on the side of the vehicle. Next, he eased around, lowered the tailgate, and sat staring at the sea and the mountains. He rubbed the sleep from his eyes. Then he saw the sky bright and stark blue. The Sea of Cortez, iridescent and beautiful. *God, how I love this place. If I could just stop feeling guilty.*

Soon his stomach heaved up as it did almost every morning. At least this morning he made it 20 feet before throwing up, and the vomit could be easily buried by kicking sand with his foot. He recovered with the pleasure of fatigue and the relief he sometimes got after vomiting. He tried to remember exactly what happened last night. He remembered the Coronas and tequila and talking to Edricka. Her eyes. So electric. Dark. So beautiful. But that was it. No other memory of anything.

The Blazer seemed comfortable enough at night. But even with the car port shade he rented from Jose, it felt too hot during the day. In the early morning, Nathan would stare at the beach sitting in an old lawn chair thinking pleasant things. As strange as it was, lounging on the beach felt as normal as anything had since the day he failed to report for duty back in Southern Illinois.

At Yuma, Nathan thought about his family and Judy Novotney every day, but since arriving in El Gulfo, they never entered his mind. Also, at El Gulfo Nathan never thought about the Bible, religion, or the orphanage in Sonoyta. He had pushed those thoughts away. He never prayed, not once. His only thoughts seemed to be his next meal, and most importantly, his next drink of tequila.

Every day, when it got too hot, he moved to the shade of Jose's veranda and drank ice-cold beer, visiting with Jose and trying to improve his Spanish. As the day continued, Nathan would order tequila, usually a bottle. Occasionally, Nathan wandered into El Gulfo de Santa Clara to buy the pink and green pastries sold at the *panaderia* or to replenish his supply of soap, shaving cream, or toothpaste. He also purchased Mexican Newspapers to follow the events in Saudi Arabia. It looked like fighting might start any day, and Nathan sometimes worried about the Marines in Fourth Tank Battalion.

El Gulfo de Santa Clara had long been a fishing village and appeared deserted during most of the day with the only activity occurring at dusk when the fisherman returned to unload their catch from the small wooden boats into refrigerated trucks for transport to San Luis. The summer heat coaxed out the smell of dead fish, and Nathan was unable to get used to that odor. From time to time, Nathan shopped for clothes and now owned a complete Mexican wardrobe—several gaudier shorts and shirts designed for fat men for the days, and pointed-toed cowboy boots, straight-legged jeans and long-sleeve western shirts for night wear. Nathan also bought a white straw cowboy hat that he wore day and night. Overall, living in El Gulfo felt peaceful and relaxing, and Nathan tried to forget the trouble he left a few miles north of the border. Maybe someday he would go back to see his grandma, Jeremiah, and Judy, but right now he would just hide out and drink.

Thinking of the breakfast of bacon, potato, and egg burritos he would soon enjoy, Nathan grabbed his sunglasses and looked up at Jose's Cantina. The restaurant remained empty, and he realized that the heat had woken him early. It would be another half an hour before the place opened. He pulled on a T-shirt, slipped on a pair of sandals, and walked down to the water's edge. The tide stood far out, as if overnight the heat had evaporated the water in the Sea of Cortez. As he moved along the sand, the sun beat down relentlessly, heat radiated up through the rubber soles of the cheap sandals, and he thought about hiking all the way to the water's edge but figured it was not worth it and decided to sit in the shade until Jose's opened. As he turned back Nathan spotted a young man standing on the side of the Blazer. The boy removed his straw hat and spoke in English and Spanish.

"*Buenos Dias, Señor.*"

Nathan found it difficult to guess the boy's age. He looked like he could be 12 or 20. His skin seemed very dark with a wrinkled face and small black blotches that Nathan had seen on the older fishermen. His bony hands were scarred, and he was missing several front teeth.

"*Buenos Dias,*" Nathan replied.

"May we talk for a moment, *Señor?*" The boy said respectfully.

"Sure," Nathan answered. "What can I do for you?"

"I am Carlos Pantoja, and my family owns a good boat. I see you every day just sitting by your truck or at the cantina. With the north current, today is a good day for the fish, but my father, he is too sick to fish. Will you work for me today, *Señor?*"

"I am sorry, but I don't know anything about boats or fishing," Nathan explained.

"No problem, *Señor.* I can teach you," The boy said thoughtfully. "I will pay you one peso. If we catch fish, I can pay you today. I think it is better than just sitting here."

Nathan chuckled, and for a moment the two stood side by side staring silently toward the sea. "Yes, I guess I could help you today," Nathan said almost to himself. "My name is Nathan...Nathan Smith."

"*Gracias, Señor* Nathan Smith. We go now to the boat." The boy answered, his eyes gleaming.

Nathan reached in the cab of the Blazer, and grabbed his suntan lotion, and half empty bottle of tequila.

"No. No." Carlos challenged. "You must also take your pants, and a shirt, *Señor.*" Carlos pinched the long sleeves of his old shirt and patted the legs of his faded pants. "The sun is very hot on the water."

Nathan opened the Blazer door, grabbed his jeans, shirt, and cowboy hat, and put the hat on his head and everything else inside a plastic garbage bag. Carlos smiled and headed toward one of the boats nearest the water. As they neared the shoreline Nathan saw the jacked-up Army truck dragging boats into the water and expected that the truck would soon hook on to Carlos's boat.

Carlos climbed inside and motioned for Nathan to pass up a pile of gear stacked near the bow. Nathan handed Carlos two plastic milk containers filled with water, a dozen old coffee cans with fish line wrapped around them, a roll of wet newspaper, another coffee can with hooks and sinkers, a wooden box with rusty pliers, hammer, screwdriver and other tools, a five-gallon gas can, a plastic container with outboard motor oil, and an assortment of smaller items. Carlos carefully placed each item in its spot, climbed out of the boat, leaned against it, and stared at the rising shoreline. Ten minutes passed, and Nathan noticed the old Army truck headed back to El Gulfo.

"When do we get pulled in? Nathan asked.

"I have no money to pay for a tow." The boy answered and motioned at two other boats still sitting near the water.

"We must wait for the tide. Do not worry, it will not be long."

Nathan rested against Carlos's boat waiting for the water to rise and enjoying the clean early smell of the ocean blowing in from the sea. As predicted by Carlos, within a half an hour the shoreline had reached the boats, and Carlos gestured for Nathan to follow him to the one furthest away. Four fishermen from two other boats followed.

It was easy for the eight men to shove the four remaining boats into the water.

Carlos lowered the propeller into the water, squeezed the rubber ball on the gasoline tank, pulled the choke on, and carefully adjusted the throttle. He then tugged the starter rope in a fluid but forceful motion. The engine fired, sputtered blue smoke, and died. Carlos re-adjusted the throttle and jerked the starter rope again. This time the engine continued to sputter until he slowly pushed in the carburetor choke and cranked up the throttle. The engine rumbled to full power, and Carlos pointed the bow toward the open sea.

The sun had risen but the wind and the spray from the boat moving across the water gave Nathan a chill. He moved to the center seat and crossed his arms. He considered putting on his long-sleeved shirt but decided to wait. Soon the water turned from brown to a dark iridescent blue, and the coast appeared as only a long white line with gray-brown hills behind it.

At first Nathan saw nothing, just the water and the mountains across the Sea of Cortez, but in an hour, he caught sight of rock projecting above the waves. He realized that the boy had somehow steered directly for it. When the boat crested a swell, he could see the other boats, low on the water spread out around the rock island. Nathan heard the engine sputter, and the deceleration threw him out of his seat onto the worn wood of the bow. He crawled up and watched the boy calmly go to work.

First, Carlos ran his hand along the rubber fuel line to the point where it connected to the gasoline can. Next, he took the pliers and carefully tightened the hose connection. He used a screwdriver to disassemble the fuel filter, then placed his lips around the end and blew vigorously. He smiled at the lump of rust that landed on the side of his pants. After reassembling the engine, Carlos went through the starting procedure. The engine sprang to life, and the boat resumed the voyage toward the island. As they approached the island, Carlos throttled down the engine and slowly circled the other fisherman looking to see if they had caught anything. From what Nathan could tell, it had not been a good day. Finally, Carlos eased in between two boats on the west side of the island and started putting his baits out.

"OK, *Señor*. Now I show you how to fish," The boy said grinning. "Give me a line."

Nathan passed one of the coffee cans bundled in fishing line and watched as he opened the wet newspaper wrapped around a couple dozen shad minnows. Next, the boy unspooled the hook and attached the bait. Each bait fish was hooked in the center of the back just under the spine then carefully lowered into the water. The boy reeled off 50 meters of line and looped each line onto a small limber stick so that any pull on the bait would make the stick dip. After 30 minutes, Nathan and Carlos had a half-dozen lines out. With the boat dead in the water, the sun soon burned the back of Nathan's neck, and he felt the sweat start to trickle down his back. Carlos stared disapprovingly as Nathan started to rub suntan lotion on his bare arms and legs.

"No. *Señor*. The fish can smell. Please do not use. Put on your shirt and pants."

Nathan thought the boy was nuts but did not want to have any trouble and replaced his shorts and T-shirt with the jeans and cowboy shirt. Nathan watched all morning, but the sticks never moved. None of the other fisherman caught anything. Shortly after noon the boats started to leave the rock island. Carlos stayed. The last boat left at around 2:00 p.m., and Carlos adjusted the depth of the baits. He raised one to 20 meters, two were lowered one to 60 meters and one lowered to 70 meters. The rest were left at 30 meters. Carlos placed the rope lashings of the oars onto the hole pins and started to row. He rowed slow and steady to keep the lines straight and at the proper depth. He first headed west toward the Baja and then turned north keeping about 50 yards off the island's rocky shoreline. In two hours, he had circled the island, and stopped at the starting point.

"The current is right, but the fish no bite today, *Señor* Nathan. Pull in the bait. We go home."

Carlos went silent and tried to focus on the task at hand, which was a big one. He and Nathan painstakingly hauled in each bait line, taking care not to tangle the line as they wrapped the coffee cans, gently removing each bait fish from its hook, and returning the bait to the roll of newspapers. By 4:30 p.m. they were ready to return to El

Gulfo and Carlos commenced the starting procedure. When the boy pulled on the starter rope the engine did not start. It did not even sputter. Carlos raised the propeller out of the water, stripped naked, and eased himself off the stern of the boat. He meticulously examined the propeller, the water intake, and the exhaust port. He then pulled himself back inside the boat. Next, Carlos removed the cap from the gasoline tank and stuck one of the sticks inside to check the fuel level. He ran his hand along the fuel line and tightened the hose connection. He removed the fuel filter, placed his lips around the end and blew it out like before. This time, nothing came out. Using the crescent wrench, the boy removed the spark plug. He scraped off the carbon on the end of the plug and re-inserted it in the engine.

After checking the reassembled engine, Carlos went through the starting procedure again. He squeezed the rubber ball on the gasoline tank, turned the choke on, and adjusted the throttle. He yanked the starter rope. Again, the engine gave no sign of combustion. For the next hour Carlos and Nathan took turns heaving on the starter rope. Between pulls Carlos re-adjusted the choke and the throttle. While Carlos concentrated on the engine, Nathan noticed the wind increasing and the temperature dropping. Shortly, the boat bobbed roughly in the water and dark clouds moved in from the south. White caps could be seen in the distance. After ten minutes, it started to rain.

Carlos frequently glanced up apprehensively towards the wall of blue-black clouds rolling in from the north. He knew from experience that there was no weather phenomenon more beautiful or deadly than a northern storm on the Sea of Cortez. Finally, Carlos gave up on the engine and hauled the propeller out of the water. He stood on the center bench and gazed across the Sea of Cortez. "It is too rough to cross, *Señor* Nathan. We must stay here tonight. But we must get to the leeward side."

Nathan could hear the panic in Carlos's voice. Carlos returned the rope lashings on the oars back to the hole pins and signaled for Nathan to sit next to him. The two started rowing, hopelessly trying to beat the rain. Nathan felt unnerved. He desperately wanted to help but found it difficult to keep up with Carlos. Nathan rowed as fast and as hard as he could, but no matter how hard he tried the boat kept rotating toward him, forcing Carlos to stop to let Nathan catch up. Everything about the storm intensified in minutes. The rain poured down. The wind roared. The waves crashed onto the side of the boat. Nathan could see the fear in Carlos's eyes, when the boat rounded the west end of the island, and rapidly accelerated.

"We're caught in the storm tide!" Carlos shouted above the wind and the rain.

"We must get out of this."

Nathan stopped trying to row in time with Carlos. Instead, he ignored Carlos' strokes and just pulled on the oar with all his strength. He watched helplessly as the boat sped past the island toward the open sea.

"Keep rowing, Nathan. We will come around."

After passing the island, Nathan and Carlos fought to keep an easterly course, but the strong wind constantly pushed the bow to the north. Nathan rowed for his life, but the island slipped further and further away. After 20 minutes, they were 1,000 yards from the island. They rowed for another hour. Eventually, the boat moved east and out of the storm tide. Then, Carlos steered south toward the leeward side of the island. The closer they advanced to the island the faster their progress. As they inched toward the shore, Nathan saw that Carlos had navigated the boat into a cramped cove with a tiny beach. Nathan's arms ached, and his lungs burned but he kept rowing. As the boat slid into the gravel of the beach Carlos jumped over the bow and tied the bowline to a chain wrapped around a large rock. Nathan assumed that the chain had been left by fishermen for this purpose.

"Bring one of the oars, *Señor* Nathan," Carlos yelled back.

Nathan ran for the rock with the oar and saw that Carlos had rigged two rings in the rope. Carlos stuck the length of the oar in a ring and the end in another. Each time Nathan levered the oar, the boat moved a few inches up the beach, and Carlos took up the slack. After an hour they had the boat out of the water and safe from the storm. The rain continued to pour, blown almost horizontal by the fierce wind. Nathan struggled to climb aboard the boat to retrieve the garbage bag with his clothes and tequila. He put his T-shirt and shorts over his cowboy shirt and jeans and made the garbage bag into a sort of poncho by tearing a hole for his head in the center. He followed Carlos to the rock overhang. The two sat side-by-side, shivering, and watching the rain.

Chapter 76

At 1615 Capt. Beck left the Law Center and drove to the Headquarters Building, parked, and marched up the stairs toward the main entrance. Today, the old hospital building looked so ugly Beck could not believe the Government paid an architect to design the nondescript structure wrapped in dull brick. As he entered the hallway, he recalled the night he reported late and the meeting with Gunner Carson. The fear returned to where his confidence usually resided. *What will I fuck up today?*

As he walked down the hallway, he remembered the clean smell, the stately appearance of the interior, and the click of his heels hitting the highly polished floor. He thought about going in the head to reblouse and check his uniform, but he did not have time. He proceeded past the Staff Judge Advocate's office, then stepped inside the command office where a LCpl. jumped to a position of attention and spoke. "Good afternoon, Sir. May I help you?"

"Good afternoon, Lance Corporal. I am Captain Beck reporting for duty as the officer of the day."

Before the Lance Corporal could answer, a gravelly voice bellowed from the adjoining office of the Commanding Officer. "Come in here, Captain!"

Entering the office, Capt. Beck found the Commanding Officer, Col. Cahill, opening and closing credenza drawers and throwing items into the pilot's helmet bag which Cahill used as a briefcase. He turned toward Beck and placed a hardback green notebook, a holstered .45-caliber pistol, and a red armband on the desk.

"Shit, Captain Beck. This is a holiday weekend, and we got this unusually hot weather. How many times have you pulled the duty?"

Capt. Beck awkwardly continued to stand at attention and answered.

"Sir, it's my first time."

Col. Cahill frowned, and he yelled towards the door. "Lance Corporal Clay, get me the Adjutant. Get her in here right now!"

After a minute, the Lance Corporal stuck his head inside the office. "Colonel, the Adjutant has secured for the day."

Cahill pulled off his glasses, closed his eyes, and rubbed his temples. "Captain Beck, the Adjutant fucked up assigning you this holiday weekend. With the warm weather, it may be a busy weekend—fist fights at the enlisted club, arrests out in the town, domestic disputes, car wrecks…hell, maybe even boating accidents up at Martinez Lake. The Adjutant should have exercised some judgment to assign the duty to an officer with experience. But they all probably bitched, moaned, and complained, and lacking the intestinal fortitude to stand up to the whiners, the Adjutant selected one of the most junior officers on station, that being you, thinking that you would not complain. You think you can handle it?"

Capt. Beck, happy that he had not fucked up anything so far, confidently answered, "No problem, Sir."

"An audacious answer, Captain." Col. Cahill looked doubtful. "Has anyone briefed you on the OD's responsibilities?"

"I have not been formally briefed, but I talked to several of the judge advocates, and they told me what I needed to do. Major Way said I could call him anytime tonight for help."

Col. Cahill wrote something on a message slip and handed it to Capt. Beck.

"Here is my duty cell number. I am visiting my daughter in California, but I always have my duty phone. If there is anything that you and Major Way cannot handle, don't hesitate to call me. Just read the logbook and do the same things that ODs do every day. Write down the same entries in the logbook. Whatever happens, don't get sucked into the middle of a fist fight, just call the MPs and stay out of the way. Good luck."

Col. Cahill started out the door, then stopped and turned towards Beck. "Captain, I see you are wearing only two ribbons. That is a little short for a Captain, isn't it?"

"Sir, when I was released from active duty, I only had the National Defense Service Ribbon. When I reported here, Major Way sent me over to see the G-1 and he determined that I should also wear the Armed Forces Reserve Medal. But unfortunately, that is it."

"How many years of active duty?"

"Four, with Second Division at Camp Lejeune."

"Well, if you are here, you must have stayed in the reserves."

"Yes, Sir. But I did not participate in the active reserves, only the Individual Ready Reserve."

"How many years?"

"Seven."

"I thought you were kicked out after six years of no participation."

"I asked for a year's extension, and the Marine Corps gave it to me."

"Captain, I take pride in knowing the criteria for every medal a Marine can wear. The Armed Forces Reserve Medal is awarded for four years in the IRR, so you are entitled to at least that one. Also, there is probably a unit citation for Second Division during the time you were on active duty, those sometimes do not come down until years later. I want you to go back and see the G-1 again and tell him I sent you over and that I want him to find you some more medals! Next time I see you make sure you are wearing every medal to which you are entitled."

"Yes, Sir!"

"I mean it, Captain Beck; I don't mind you calling me if there's any kind of trouble."

"Yes, Sir."

⋘⋙

"Fuck me!" Earl Cahill yelled at himself and slowed his car to a stop. He starred at the San Diego traffic and the mile long line of cars trying to merge onto I-5 from I-8. He pulled out his duty phone, and dialed is wife's number in San Clemente.

"Hello?"

"Patricia, this is Earl. I am stuck in traffic in San Diego. It will be after midnight before I get to the BOQ at MCAS, El Toro. Please tell Liz that I will see her tomorrow."

"That is terrible. Liz was so excited to see you tonight and she has softball practice tomorrow."

"I am sorry." Earl said trying not to show his anger at the situation.

"Well, by now Liz understands California traffic. Call me in the morning and we can go from there."

૭૪૪૭

"Oh, what a lovely view. This must be the most elegant officer's club in the Marine Corps." Patricia spoke quietly and gazed at the Marine Corps Air Station, El Toro golf course.

"Yes, Patricia...the flyboys know how to live. Way better than the O Club at Camp Pendleton."

"Earl, you didn't have to take me to lunch."

"I thought it would give us a chance to talk."

"Yes, Earl, we need to talk. Did you review the property settlement agreement?"

"Yes. No problem with the terms, but I want to talk about the divorce schedule. I have had a lot of time to sit in my BOQ room in Yuma and just think. We always assumed I would retire as a general, at least a one star, and end up with a good retirement. I realize now that I just took it for granted. I enjoyed great assignments and had a lot of fun. I was spoiled. I passed up headquarter assignments, finished in the bottom half of my class at Command and Staff College, and stayed with the infantry too long."

For the first time Patricia started to speak, then changed her mind. The two sat in silence for a long time.

"When they finally sent me to Headquarters, I didn't try to get along. I thought I was a 'Real Marine,' better than those paper pushers."

Patricia heard the emotion in Earl's voice and when he paused saw it in his eyes.

"At some point in every Marine's career, they have a commanding officer they cannot please. If it is early in your career, you can overcome a bad fitness report, but for me it just happened. My old boss at Headquarters, General Reynolds, hates me. He's trying to have me relieved of my command at Yuma. If I could get an assignment in Saudi Arabia, I might have a chance for promotion to general. But I must face the facts—that is not going to happen.

"I'm stuck in Yuma. At best, I won't make general, and in two years the Marine Corps will force me to retire. At worst, I will be relieved of command. So maybe the best thing is for us to just stay married for a while and draw my dependent's rate BAQ."

"I don't know, Earl. Send me the numbers and if it makes sense, we can do that. I certainly do not plan on remarrying. . . Hey, if it is legal and means more money for Elizabeth, I guess we can just stay married for a while."

"OK. I will talk to my G-1, get the numbers, and get back."

Chapter 77

"*Señor* Nathan, wake up." Carlos called tapping Nathan's foot. Nathan opened his eyes and saw only darkness. Nathan sensed that the rain had stopped, and the wind had died down, but Nathan felt wet, miserable, and cold.

"We might as well catch some fish," Carlos said cheerfully.

"The fish always bite after a storm. With no moon, thay can't see the bait fish and wake up hungry."

"How do we get back to El Gulfo?" Nathan mumbled his first thought.

"Most of the fishermen in El Gulfo will fish to the South, but one may come here after Mass or someone from San Philippi may come. If no one comes, we can row back in six hours."

Nathan stood, removed the garbage bag poncho, T-shirt and shorts, and attempted to see what Carlos was doing in the dark. First, Carlos used a coffee can to bail out the boat. Next, Carlos moved the bowline to a rock near the water and rigged the loops for the oar. Nathan repeated the lever action with Carlos taking up slack and watched as the boat eased sideways next to the water. Using both oars, Carlos and Nathan pried the boat into the water.

With the sun breaking over the distant hills, Carlos took the oars, sat on the center bench, and started to row. As the sun rose higher, the sea appeared perfectly still, like a saucer of olive oil on an undisturbed table, and the boat slid across the water, the oars making little radar like ripples that radiated out and quickly died. After 200 yards, Carlos stopped and secured the oars.

Nathan gathered the coffee cans lying in the bottom and handed them to Carlos one at a time. Carlos unwrapped what was left of the wet newspaper and reattached the shad minnows to the hooks. He handed Nathan the first baited line.

"Let out forty meters."

Nathan pulled off the line, measured the meters by an outstretched arm, and watched the bait slowly sink. After counting off 28 meters, Nathan noticed the line moving in the water. He pulled on the line and immediately felt resistance.

"Carlos, I think we hooked a fish."

Carlos carefully took the line. "*Si, Señor.* We have a fish," Carlos said, grinning. "It feels like Tortuava, a very good fish."

Carlos continued to steadily pull in the line. When the fish surfaced near the boat, he effortlessly placed his hand in the gills and pulled the three-foot-long fish inside the boat.

"Tortuava!" Carlos yelled with a gleam in his eye.

"Good money, Nathan."

Carlos and Nathan each started lowering bait lines in the water. Before the lines reached 30 meters, they both hooked fish, and pulled them up. As the fish surfaced, Carlos hauled them into the boat by the gills.

After catching another eight fish, Carlos cut the bait fish into two pieces before baiting the hooks. This did not bother the Tortuava. Next, Carlos cut the bait fish into four pieces, and they still caught fish, only slower. When they ran out of bait fish, Carlos tried using various parts of the Tortuava in the boat, but they got no bites.

At 11:00 a.m. they pulled in the lines and headed across the Sea of Cortez toward El Gulfo, Carlos and Nathan sitting side by side rowing in perfect unison. Even with 30 fish in the bottom of the boat, the boat moved easily through the dead calm water. Exactly as predicted by Carlos, they landed in El Gulfo at 5:00 p.m. next to the refrigerated trucks parked out on the beach.

Nathan watched Carlos argue price with the fish merchant and then they started cleaning the fish and carrying them to the truck. A flock of birds fought over the entrails tossed into the water. When they finished the cleaning and hauling, the fish merchant handed Carlos a wad of bills. Carlos rowed the boat south along the shoreline to the place where the Nathan had parked the Blazer next to Jose's Cantina and dropped off Nathan.

"Here is two pesos for two days of work Señor Nathan. And here is ten pesos, your bite of the profits. I am sorry I cannot share more, but my family needs money badly."

"Thanks, Carlos. That is enough money to last me a month," Nathan replied, counting the 12 pesos. "Just let me know when you need help again."

Nathan headed straight for Jose's Cantina for beer, tacos, and tequila, and spent the rest of the evening sleeping in the Blazer.

Chapter 78

Mike Beck sat in his desk chair watching Cindy Hendrix put on her uniform. He marveled at her dressing speed. In just a few seconds she pulled on her trousers and laced up her boots. She stood, flipped her head forward, and rolled her hair into a tight knot.

"I will see you tomorrow at 0800 for the scheduling conference," she said.

Mike wanted to say something charming but found he could only mutter. "Sure."

Cindy starred into Mike's eyes for a moment, and whispered, "I love you, Mike Beck."

She then rushed out of the office. He listened to her boot steps echo down the hall, the door opening and closing, and then her steps as she descended the stairs. Next, he heard her punch the bar on the heavy steel door leading to the parking lot, and seconds later the door slammed shut. He walked to the window and followed her movement to her car. When she drove off, he sat down again, still breathing hard and sweating. For a while, he replayed in his mind what had just happened. Then he dressed, grabbed a legal pad, and started outlining his cross-examination for trial tomorrow. Three hours later, Capt. Beck hit the bar on the steel door and headed for his Range Rover at the end of the parking lot. He was almost to Range Rover when two dark figures stepped out from behind the trash dumpster.

"Working late, Captain?"

Beck froze. He thought he recognized the voice as Gunner Carson. Both men wore old style combat boots, black pants, and dark-green sweatshirts. Black ski masks were pulled over their faces, and they pointed their pistols at Beck's chest. Beck looked around for Agent Palmer, but he wasn't there.

"You drive, Beck."

Carson sat directly behind Beck. He slid down to the floorboards when Beck exited the Main Gate. Beck passed through a dark neighborhood, then drove up a dirt lane to a house on the edge of the desert. Carson took off his mask and led Beck to an outbuilding with a liquor bar, two gun safes, tables, and shelves. The second man removed his mask and Beck could tell he was a Marine because of the short haircut. The two men then tied Beck to a metal chair with duct tape.

"Hey, Beck. You think Texas barbeque is the best in the world?" Gunner Carson asked with a menacing smile.

"I don't know. I am not really an expert on barbeque," Beck answered, almost to himself.

"Some people have a knack for certain things. You know what the Vietnamese have a knack for?" Carson asked cordially.

"Noodles?" Capt. Beck responded with visible puzzlement.

"Naw, that's what civilians think. But what they are really good at is torture. They know how to inflict pain. It is a fucking science for them. Americans...we just start beating on people. Doesn't get worse, it is just the same pain, over and over. Easy to take it."

Carson carefully formed his right fist with the middle knuckle extended. He then approached the chair, squatted slightly, and threw a jabbing punch at the junction of Beck's rib cage. Carson's face had the air of a child viewing his first circus. Beck screamed. It was a long, loud scream. A guttural sound.

Beck twisted in the chair. His face contorted and his eyes watered. This pain felt different, something new. It came from deep inside. Like getting kicked in the balls, only worse. In addition, there was a sharp, knife-like pain that blended, then continued. Beck stared at Carson. Tyler looked on with a horrified expression.

"It hurts really bad, doesn't it, Beck?" Carson asked, still using his cordial voice.

"Jesus, Carson it hurts worse than anything," Beck pleaded.

"That is what I thought the first time the gooks did that to me. But here is the astounding thing. I just punched a nerve to your kidney. Some people call it a kidney punch. The more you hit that nerve, the more it swells and the worse it hurts."

Carson stared at the wall, remembering another time, another place. He looked down, drew out a cigarette from the pack sitting on the bar and lit it. He glanced at the smoke for a long moment, and then put it out in the ashtray.

"That one was for Cindy Hendrix. I told you if you didn't stay away from her, I would hurt you really bad. The second punch ain't going to be the same pain. It's different. Worse. Every time I punch that nerve it is going to hurt, worse and worse. You don't believe that do you Beck?"

Beck did not answer. He had the expression of a hunted animal looking for a way out. Carson started forming his fist again, approached the chair, and did the semi-squat.

"No! No! Please Carson don't do it. I'm sorry."

Beck started violently shaking from side to side, finally making the chair turn over. Anything to avoid another hit. Carson helped Tyler stand the chair back up, and while Tyler held the chair, Carson threw another punch at Beck's ribs.

"Oh…! Ahaa …! Oh, my God!"

The contorted look on Beck's face returned. Tears rolled down his cheeks. His head bent down, and he sobbed. Carson stepped back and calmly observed Beck. Then grinned widely.

"What do you think Beck? Isn't it amazing? Hurts twice as bad, doesn't it?"

"Fucking ten times worse, you bastard!" Beck shouted, took a breath, and continued. "Oh, my God, Carson you have to stop. Please, there's got to be something I can do to stop you."

Again, Carson seemed to be in another place. He wasn't listening to Beck. "I don't know about ten times. You really think it hurts ten times as bad? Maybe?"

Carson's voice remained calm. The old memory stayed, and he kept staring at the wall. Then he started forming the fist and moved to the chair. Beck's eyes went wild, and he started fighting the chair. "Carson! Carson we are in Yuma. You are not in Vietnam. Please. Just fucking shoot me in the head."

Beck's words jolted Carson. He froze. He then looked over at Tyler with a confused look. Tyler nodded. After a while, Carson walked over to Beck again.

"Oh, yes, Beck. I know. I know. We are in Yuma. What did you and Palmer talk about?" Carson asked, slowly returning to his surroundings.

"Palmer's never been in my office."

Carson grinned insanely. He slowly went through the ritual again and punched Beck. This time Beck completely lost it. Screaming. Screaming. Screaming. No longer just cries of pain, but hysterical terror—death screams. It scared the shit out of Tyler.

Beck continued screaming for 30 minutes, then collapsed in the chair, bent over and trembling in pain.

While Beck screamed, Carson walked over behind the liquor bar, reached down, and pulled out two tumblers. He filled them with vodka, and returned to where Tyler stood, shaking, tears in his eyes. He handed one to Tyler and raised his as if making a toast.

"Don't worry, Tyler; he'll be able to talk in another half an hour."

Carson slammed down his drink, then returned to the bar, and filled his glass again with vodka. He sat on one of the stools calmly, this time slowly sipping the vodka. When he finished the vodka, he approached Beck, and lifted his head. Again, from the look on Carson's face his mind had returned to Vietnam.

"Isn't it amazing, Beck? Just fucking amazing! I know you didn't believe me. You did not think it could hurt worse each time. POWs who claim they got to love the pain are liars. You can learn to take it, tolerate it, beat it, but you never love it. You just learn to survive it. Now you want to tell me what you and Palmer talked about?"

"I swear I will tell you everything. The truth. Anything. Please. Please. Kill me, just shoot me in the head, but please God don't hit me like that again."

The tears returned, and Beck cried. He sobbed so hard he had trouble breathing. He had come apart emotionally and physically. His whole body shook violently. His skin had turned pasty, and he had pissed his pants. He sprayed spittle when he spoke. Beck seemed unaware of the massive amount of snot that ran down from his nose.

"Good. Maybe I won't have to hit you again."

Beck stopped crying and looked at Tyler, then Carson. "I met Palmer and an ATF agent at the Yuma County Jail about three weeks ago. Palmer thought it was you, Miller, Weaver, and Weaver's room-mate, Corporal Cunningham, who robbed the armory. Palmer thought you were an arms' dealer. Sold the Colts into Mexico."

Carson laughed a horse laugh.

"I told Palmer what Jones told me—that you shot Miller and Jones. Jones recognized you as the shooter because of your unique shooting stance. Palmer also thinks you killed Corporal Weaver and Herlinda Hernandez to cover up the robbery."

Carson walked back to the bar and poured himself another vodka. He sat on a stool with his back to Tyler and Beck. Just sipping the vodka. After 20 minutes, he returned to Beck.

"Poor fucking Weaver. The kid turned out to be a total fuck up. Hey, Tyler, tell Beck—the dumb son-of-a-bitch Weaver had to die. I did not enjoy it."

Beck continued to look pleadingly at Palmer. Just from Beck's appearance it seemed obvious that he had given up.

"Maybe. I should not have talked to Palmer, but I was worried you might kill me. Also, you won't believe this, but I'm honestly in love with Cindy. I don't want to hurt her husband, but I have to see her. We're getting married."

"Yes, she is a beautiful woman. It would be hard to stop seeing her." Carson seemed to understand but then stopped and just gazed into his vodka.

Beck looked terrified. At first, he looked like he was thinking, but then he just looked exhausted. "I am going to tell you the truth Carson. You can kill me, but please just don't hit me again. I told Palmer you robbed the armory. And that you murdered Miller and Herlinda. I do not blame you for killing me, but do not hit me again."

For the first time Carson looked angry. Fuming. Emotional. He ran over, and punched Beck in the face, not in the kidney.

"I never hurt Herlinda. People called her a whore because she sold her body for money. But she was a good person. Just hooked on that Mexican heroin. I tell you Beck, I never hurt her. Someone else did that shit, and if I find out who did it, I will kill them."

Carson returned to the bar, filled another glass with vodka, and stood at the bar drinking. Carson seemed stricken with grief, unable to do anything but drink and think.

"I say it is all fucking Headquarters' fault. After everything I did for the Corps, three tours in Vietnam, clearing those God damn tunnels, shot three times, captured…Hell, Beck, I gave my life to the Corps. The only thing I ever asked was to go to Saudi. One miserly request in twenty-seven years. I would have been great guarding bases, running convoys. But no, the son-of-a-bitches kept me here. Robbing the armory was just to show the bastards. You can't fuck with Carson and not feel pain. Then it all went to shit.

"Master Sergeant Miller. Great Marine. Loved him. That was a fucking accident. Corporal Weaver. That poor stupid kid. This thing was just over his head. I am sorry, Beck. I shouldn't have called you a piece of shit that time. I don't think I could have taken all those punches I gave you tonight. You are a Marine—a real man."

Carson stopped talking. He still had a sad look on his face. He looked at Beck, then Tyler, then looked away. Tears formed in his eyes.

"What do you think, Tyler?"

"Kill him. We have too. We have done so much already, and we can end this tonight. For good. Get it over with." Tyler was not emotional and stared hard at Beck.

Carson shook his head and said "No." He staggered towards the bar stool, stumbling, almost falling, but grabbing the top of the bar to break the fall, then he filled another glass with vodka and sat on the stool sipping it.

"Sorry, Tyler. I can't do it."

Tyler walked to the center of the room. He pulled out his Beretta, then pulled the pistol slide back to make sure a round was chambered. He assumed a shooting stance, flipped off the safety, and pointed the pistol at Beck's head. Beck stared Tyler in the eyes and somehow felt at peace. No more pain. Tyler hesitated, dropped the pistol towards the floor. Then raised it.

The next thing Beck saw was Tyler's chest explode. Blood, bones, and guts spattered Beck's face, but he continued to lock eyes with

Tyler. He saw the shock in Tyler's face, then his face went peaceful, and he fell to the floor.

Behind Tyler, Beck saw Carson rising from the barstool with his Colt in his hand. Beck heard another explosion and Carson went down.

It was over.

Chapter 79

Nathan and Stacy parked Nathan's old pickup and stumbled towards the front door of the mobile home. They had spent the evening at Mark's Tavern, drinking, playing pool, and dancing. They were both shit-faced. At the doorway stairs, Stacy stopped, turned, and passionately kissed Nathan. Nathan pulled away from the kiss, so that he could see her face. Inside, they kissed again, then Nathan followed Stacy down the narrow hallway to the tiny bedroom where Stacy sat on the bed. They had been married for two months and the heat between them increased every day. Stacy looked Nathan in the eyes, pulled at his belt, and slid his jeans all the way down to the top of his boots. Soon they were naked in the bed, making love. All the time Nathan intensely stared at Stacy's beautiful breasts, watching them sway, back and forth, with his movements. Her breasts filled both his hands, springy, soft as velvet. Her responsive nipples rose when he touched them. She moaned comfortably when he rolled the nipples with his tongue.

"*Señor* Nathan! *Señor* Nathan!"

Nathan slowly stirred from his dream and recognized Carlos's voice. It was almost dark. Nathan could barely see Carlos and his three cousins in the old four-wheel drive Ford pickup.

"Come to our party! Bring your Blazer and stay the night."

It took Nathan some time to fully wake up and to move to the cab of the Blazer. When he turned the key, the battery was dead. Carlos's cousins roared into action faster than a pit crew at the Daytona 500. They had the hood up and the battery cables attached in no time. With the engine running, Nathan followed the Ford down the beach.

Carlos's cousins drove very fast, and close to the sea, occasionally hitting pools and sending up large geysers of water. Every few miles they stopped and drove slowly across deep trenches filled with water returning to the sea as the tide receded.

Nathan made it through two of the ditches but became stuck in the third. Again, the pit crew stormed into action, attaching a tow strap, and pulling the Blazer through the rough spot in minutes. They continued this way about 30 miles down the beach and arrived at a small collection of shacks and dilapidated travel trailers parked on an outcrop of rocks. The cousins towed the Blazer up a sandy road to a parking spot on the northern edge of the little village. Nathan turned off the engine and stared towards a fire in the dark. Carlos led him to the fire in the center of the village.

When Nathan looked around, he saw an old man cleaning buckets full of fish, sharks, and other sea creatures that Nathan did not recognize. The old man cut the edible meat in to pieces and handed them to a woman who dropped the pieces, first into a batter, and then into hot oil that filled a large disc from a farm implement resting on top a stack of bricks in the middle of the fire. On the other side of the fire Nathan saw two women patting out tortillas and baking them on top a 55-gallon drum with a wood fire smoldering inside.

Carlos returned with a gallon plastic milk container and a bowl of salt and limes. He handed the milk container to Nathan. "Sonora bacanora! Made by my Uncle Alonso. It is the best!" Nathan carefully took a sip. Agave-based pure alcohol that tasted like Southern Illinois moonshine.

"At home, that's what we call the good stuff. Thank you, Carlos."

For the rest of the night, Nathan and Carlos sat in old lawn chairs, drinking shots of bacanora, and eating the fried fish. The bacanora relaxed them, they poked fun at each other, and laughed a lot. At midnight Nathan stumbled over to the Blazer and managed to crawl in the bed.

The Marine Corps, the New Unity in Christ Church, and Southern Illinois all seemed far away.

Chapter 80

Blinding pain filled Mike Beck's body. He opened his eyes and saw nothing but a dark, blurred image of a room. He could barely make out the outline of a door. He tried to move. Eventually he twisted his body into a more natural position and managed to raise his head. His head throbbed, his eyes went blind, and he felt as if he were about to throw up. Shutting his eyes, he lay completely still. Only now did the memory of what happened return. Soon Mike went back to sleep.

Three hours later, Cindy Hendrix quietly opened the door and peaked inside Mike Beck's hospital room. She glanced at the heart-rate monitor which kept a steady beat. At the sight of Mike hooked up to tubes and IVs, she nearly broke down in tears. After a moment, Mike opened his eyes and saw her. He fumbled to find the control for the hospital bed but could not and quickly gave up. Both of Mike's arms were taped down with the IVs so Cindy just touched his fingers. He started to say something but was not able to find his voice. Cindy saw a chair just outside the curtain, moved it next to the bed, and sat down. She found the control for the hospital bed and slowly raised it to a sitting position. She held Mike's limp hand in hers.

"Are you OK?"

"Yeah, I am fine." Speaking seemed to exhaust Mike. He just looked at Cindy like he always did, and she saw the desire in his eyes. They had been sleeping together for the last two months.

"I talked to Agent Palmer. It must have been so terrible," Cindy whispered. Mike remained silent.

"They're sending me to Balboa in San Diego for dialysis."

"I will miss you, but I am sure they have the right specialist at Balboa."

Mike nodded. Cindy held Mike's finger with both hands.

"God, this whole thing is so unreal." The tears rolled down Cindy's face, and Mike could feel her hands trembling. The two looked into each other's eyes in silence. Mike fell back asleep.

Chapter 81

From his second-story hospital room at Balboa Naval Hospital, Mike Beck turned to the window and saw a flicker of light. He wondered if it was dusk or dawn. It seemed like he had been lying in the bed for weeks, and he could not sleep without the constant nightmares. He studied the sky and guessed the time as 8:00 a.m.

The knock at the door came so gently, he wondered if he had imagined it. His response sounded more like a question than an answer.

"Come in."

Cindy Hendrix eased her head in and greeted him with a voice so soft it bordered on a whisper. Mike saw that she wore her dress uniform and guessed she was not in San Diego just to see him.

"Good morning, Mike. Feeling better?" Cindy stood three feet from the bed. No kiss. No touch.

"I am fine; just sick of this hospital room."

"Everyone wishes you the best. Any word on when you will be released?" Cindy's cheery words did not match her worried eyes.

"My kidneys are slowly improving, but they won't say when I can get out of here. My doctor says he doesn't think I can return to work for weeks, and he's probably going to put me on convalescent leave. I am thinking I will just hang around Yuma."

Mike noticed Cindy's tears. "So, what are you doing in your Alpha uniform in San Diego?" Mike could tell something was up.

"Joe's deployment has ended. His squadron is flying into Miramar at 1030. I am meeting him and driving him back to Yuma."

A sea of emotion washed over Mike. He was angry. Sad. Confused. He sat stunned, unable to think or talk. Cindy looked out the window and sobbed. Then, she closed the door and turned back to Mike.

"Mike, I can't see you anymore." A long silence followed.

"Cindy, please. I have to see you. We will just have to be super, super careful. That's all."

Cindy fumbled for the right words. She'd rehearsed them a million times, but now she wasn't sure how to respond.

"No, Mike. That will not work. I've thought about it. I love you, but I am not divorcing Joe, and I am not sneaking around. My sixth sense tells me that some people already suspect we are having an affair. Sooner or later, we will get caught."

By this time Cindy appeared to be losing it. Her body trembled. Tears streamed down her face. She gasped for breath.

"Mike, I've always known there was something missing in my relationship with Joe. We just don't have the passion. But Joe is a good man. He is fearlessly committed to me and our marriage. I can always count on him." Cindy paused and stared out the window. "You know that I love you, but you are scared to death of commitment. Even if you tried, you couldn't handle marriage, or even living together. I could never count on you."

Cindy went silent, and the tears returned. Suddenly, she slid over to the bed and kissed Mike for a very long time. When she stopped, she smiled, and walked out the door. Mike yelled at the door.

"Cindy! Cindy!"

A nurse rushed in. "Are you all right?"

"Yeah. I was just trying to call back my last visitor."

"You want me to try and catch her?"

"No. That's all right."

Mike lay in the hospital bed thinking of Cindy.

The next day, Mike telephoned the Yuma law center. At first the receptionist put the call through but came back saying that Maj. Hendrix had a court appearance but would return the call. Cindy never called back. Mike called three more times and finally decided he could not risk more calls to the receptionist.

Day after day, all Mike did was think about Cindy. He even considered telephoning her house but knew that he could never do that.

As he turned things over in his mind, he tried to blame Cindy for the breakup, some instance when she had been unreasonable. Eventually, he gave up, and reflected upon his own actions. Cindy was right and he would never make a decent husband.

He felt utterly miserable.

Chapter 82

The young corpsman was helping Mike from the bathroom back to his bed when the door opened. Warren Leavy, wearing a sharp looking suit, and carrying a stack of magazines and newspapers, stepped inside.

"Here are some things to keep your mind occupied. How yeah doing?"

"Actually, I am recovering remarkably fast."

"I hope so, for your sake and mine. Ogden's moved into the Stardust Motel in Yuma, leaving me to deal with everything in San Diego."

"Anything happening?"

"One reason I brought the newspapers is that yesterday Congress adopted a joint resolution authorizing the President to use military force to evict Iraq from Kuwait. The House vote was 250 to 183, not even close. The resolution almost failed in the Senate—the vote was 52 to 47. Anyway, the resolution kills our illegal-order argument, and I don't see a basis for refiling any of our *habeas corpus* petitions."

"Too bad."

"Og has doubled down on demanding pretrial confinement credit for the Marines that were in Barracks Number Eight, and with all the shit that happened, the command doesn't want to argue about it. The Chief Trial Counsel, Major Way, is agreeing to a day-for-day credit. Colonel Cahill shut down Barracks Number Eight and is assigning Marines awaiting courts-martial to various units around the base. Everyone is a lot happier."

"Any word on Sergeant Jones?

"Agent Palmer believes that Carson and Tyler murdered Sergeant Jones and buried his body somewhere in the desert. Palmer has located a couple camp sites where Carson and his buddies used to party. The Marines are sending out crews to search those areas, but it is hard to find a grave in the desert, particularly after a couple of heavy rains."

"Well, I hope nothing happened to Sergeant Jones, I really liked that guy."

"Mike, I agree. But even if Jones is all right, Palmer does not see him ever getting caught, or coming back to Yuma. We are sure Jones learned his lesson the last time he went on the lam. That's a case we can scratch off our work list."

⋘⋙

On Mike's fifth week at Balboa, Roslyn Baker stopped by with a flower arrangement and box of Garibaldi chocolates. When she entered the room, Mike ran his eyes over her long healthy frame, her elegant clothes, her perfectly coiffed hair, and her blemish-free complexion. Roslyn sashayed to the bed and gave Mike a gentle hug and peck on the cheek.

"Mike, I am so sorry this happened to you."

"I'm going to be all right."

"Those Marines are just animals."

"Yes, Roslyn. Some of them got mentally messed up and never recovered from Vietnam."

"What's going to happen with your cases?"

"Mr. Loring can handle them. Ogden's a hell of a lawyer and has worked very hard. His clients, the judges, and even the prosecutors respect him a great deal."

"So, you won't be going back to Yuma?"

"Not certain. There is a possibility that I will get a medical discharge and just head straight back to Chicago."

"Listen, Young Man. If you can get out of here for an evening, I would love to take you to dinner. You call me if you need anything."

Chapter 83

Carson's old blue-and-white Blazer, now all white, had sat at the same spot in the little fishing settlement since the night of Carlos's party. It served as Nathan's beach house. Today was Sunday, no fishing, so Nathan did not wake until noon. Last night, Nathan dreamed about Stacy again, and drank too much—the bacanora was cheap, and he just could not seem to go to sleep without half a jug.

Today felt so hot that the beach smelled like sand burning in a dirty oven. It quickly made Nathan sick to his stomach, and he rolled off the mattress, fell out, and stumbled a few steps before falling to his knees and vomiting. He cussed when the sand burned his hands.

He opened the cab, unlocked the suitcase, and counted his money. One peso a day was not much, and he realized he would have to budget himself, less food and bacanora. He pulled out his last milk carton of bacanora, took a swig, and rinsed his mouth. He then sat on the edge of the tailgate looking across the blue waters of the Sea of Cortez. A flight of brown pelicans lumbered along the waterline scanning for targets, and one by one, dropped out of the sky with uncanny resemblance to the dive-bombers at Midway. Nathan started the mental debate he had every Sunday morning.

Are grandma and Jeremiah in church? Does Stacy have a boyfriend, or married? Is Gunner Carson still running the Brig? Are the Federales or the Marine Corps looking for me in Mexico?

He then noticed his friend Carlos running down the beach. "What's happening, Carlos?"

"Nathan, my friend, I need a favor. My cousin is getting married. There will be music, food, dancing, and tequila—good tequila. We must go as soon as possible. I will pay you to take me."

Nathan continued staring at the sea, took a big swig of bacanora, handed it to Carlos, and answered the question.

"I am sorry, *amigo*, but you know I must be careful of the police. I am safe here, but not anywhere else. You take my Blazer."

"Nathan, you know that I can't drive. I've no license."

"Well, go find your cousins, or José, or someone else to drive you in my Blazer."

"My cousins left last night. There is no one here to drive me, but you, Nathan. Please."

"Sorry. It is just too dangerous."

"Please, Nathan. It's no problem. My Aunt lives in Nochebuena, this side of Nogales. It is in the middle of nowhere and there are no police.

"Come on! I know all the back roads. We can get Corona and ice for the trip, and I will give you ten pesos and buy you five gallons of bacanora when we get back. Enough to last you a month."

⋯

At the village of Toritos, a half hour from El Gulfo, Nathan turned the Blazer east into the Mexican Sonoran Desert and took the unimproved dirt road south of the Pinacate Lava Field. Nathan and Carlos had already drunk all the Corona, six each, and they were inebriated.

An hour later, they decided to change the route and headed north towards La Joyita where Carlos promised to buy more beer. In La Joyita they filled the Blazer at a Pemex gas station and bought a case of Corona and more ice in the grocery store. They then headed east on Route 2.

The highway followed the border just inside Mexico. As they drove along drinking beer, Nathan spotted the barbwire gate, and two track road he had used to escape Gunner Carson two months ago. The fear was still there, and the ominous dread settled again in his stomach. Nathan stopped drinking beer, drove carefully, and kept an eye out for the Mexican police. When the Blazer topped a hill, Nathan saw an overturned SUV in the wash on the south side of the road. He slowed, pulled off the road, and jumped out of the Blazer. Carlos protested.

"No, Nathan. We cannot stop. Someone else will be along soon. The police will arrest you."

Carlos's heart raced so fast he could hear it thumping against his chest. He looked around in panic for the police to arrive any second and arrest Nathan. Nathan ignored Carlos and ran to the SUV. Before he got there, he saw a Hispanic woman sitting in the wash, holding a baby, crying and rocking back and forth. The baby also cried loudly, and the women appeared in distress. Further ahead, an overweight man knelt over a young, unconscious boy.

As Nathan passed the woman, she screamed at him in Spanish. "It was my fault. I fell asleep!"

Nathan got down on his knees beside the man and carefully examined the young boy. He could smell the alcohol on the man's breath. The boy was breathing but had a weak pulse. He had a deep gash and knot on his head.

Nathan spoke in Spanish. "Your son's been knocked out. A bad concussion. His brain will swell, and he will die if we don't get him to a hospital."

Nathan looked at Carlos who was also in tears. "Where's the nearest hospital?"

"San Luis. But the only way to get there is to go back to El Gulfo, then north through the farms to San Luis. Probably four or maybe five hours."

"All right. I know a way through the desert to the hospital in Yuma. We can make it there in maybe two hours."

Carlos' eyes went as wide saucers. "No, Nathan. The hospital will call the police and you will go back to prison."

"I don't care, Carlos. This is the right thing to do. We might run into the Border Patrol, and they can call in a helicopter."

The mother joined the group. From the tremor in her voice, Nathan could tell she was terribly frightened. Carlos, the father, and the mother had a long conversation in Spanish. At one point, the father and mother were yelling at each other. Finally, Nathan yelled at everyone.

"We are wasting time arguing. I am going to go to Yuma."

Nathan carried the boy to the Blazer and laid him on the mattress in the back. Carlos sat next to him. Nathan had that bad feeling in the pit of his stomach again.

"Come on son; stay with me now." Nathan spoke in English.

The mother and father just starred. The mother then crawled in the passenger seat and held the baby, while the father sat on the mattress in the back looking at his son.

The drive to Yuma seemed to take forever. Nathan jammed his foot on the gas, bringing the Blazer to over 90 miles an hour on Route 2 and drove back to the gate in the border fence. He did not stop but drove right through the barbed-wire gate. He then raced north across the desert towards Wellton.

The Blazer bounced and swayed, violently throwing the father and Carlos back and forth and side to side. Fortunately, the injured boy laying on the mattress in the back did not seem to move. Soon, Nathan passed the road leading to the grave he had dug for himself and contemplated whether he could just drop the family off at the hospital, get back across the border, and return to El Gulfo.

For an hour, Nathan clenched the steering wheel and drove as fast as he could on the Camino del Diablo, dodging rocks, bumps, and potholes. Outside Wellton, he turned west onto Interstate 8 and floored the Blazer, honking the horn, and flashing his lights all the way. A half mile outside the Yuma city limits, a Yuma County Deputy pulled the Blazer over, but when he saw the injured boy in the back, and heard Nathan's explanation, the Deputy escorted them to the hospital. Siren blaring and lights flashing the squad car and Blazer sped across town to the hospital.

Carlos looked like he would start crying.

"I am sorry, my friend. I have sent you to prison."

At the hospital, Carlos ran inside, and two nurses came out with a stretcher. The three-hour trip had taken less than an hour and a half. And, as they eased the boy out of the Blazer, he suddenly opened his eyes, and strained to find his mother. When the boy saw his mother, he smiled at Nathan.

The young Deputy waited in the lobby as the nurse led Nathan out of the emergency room and to the waiting area. The Deputy came over and asked Nathan to step outside. They stood in the shade of the emergency room entrance.

"My name is Nathan Jones. I am a Sergeant in the United States Marine Corps. There is a warrant for my arrest."

Chapter 84

Mike reached for the remote and turned off the television when he saw Ogden Loring entering his hospital room.

"Big news, Mike." Ogden smiled from ear to ear.

"Sergeant Jones is alive. Surrendered himself to authorities yesterday at Yuma Regional Medical Center."

Mike tried to wake up and responded, "What's his story?"

"As we all suspected, Gunner Carson with Gunny Sergeant Tyler drove Sergeant Jones out in the desert and tried to kill him. Somehow Jones escaped, stole Carson's Blazer, and drove to one of the beach towns on the Sea of Cortez. He's been living there, but on Wednesday he came across an automobile accident in Mexico with an injured boy. To save time, Jones cut across the border and drove the boy to Yuma Regional Medical Center. He is back in pretrial confinement.

"The Government will not file new charges, but Major Way wants the original desertion charge resolved. He offered a super-favorable pretrial agreement: Bad Conduct Discharge and six months confinement. Best offer yet, but Sergeant Jones refuses to discuss any pretrial agreement with me. He seems really depressed and tells me he just wants to go to trial. The one thing that is helping me is that Jones refuses to agree to substitute military counsel. He says he will wait for you to come back to Yuma.

"Mike, I really need your help to convince Sergeant Jones to take this deal. The only leverage I have is that the Government does not want to substitute counsel over Jones's objection. It is crazy—we have no defense, and if we do not take this deal, Jones will end up with a three- or four-year sentence. Can you call Sergeant Jones and talk some sense into him?"

Chapter 85

Capt. Beck pulled the double doors open and led Ogden Loring and Sgt. Jones up the center aisle to the defense table at the front of Courtroom Number One. He glanced back at the first row of seats and for a moment found himself staring into the eyes of Maj. Cindy Hendrix. She quickly looked down at her legal pad. The door on the right side opened, Col. William V. Dickenson entered, and took his seat on the bench.

"This general court-martial is called to order at Marine Corps Air Station, Yuma, Arizona in the case of *United States versus Sergeant Nathan D. Jones, United States Marine Corps.* Trial counsel, please state the jurisdictional data for the court-martial followed by your qualifications."

Maj. Steve Way stood and addressed the Military Judge.

"This court-martial is convened by Colonel Earl L. Cahill, Commanding Officer, Fourth Division (Rear) by General Court-Martial Convening Order 1-66, dated 27 November 1990. There are no modifications or corrections to the convening order. The general nature of the charge in this case is a violation of Article 85, Desertion with Intent to Avoid Hazardous Duty. The charge was preferred by Gunnery Sergeant J. M. Fields, United States Marine Corps, and forwarded with recommendations as to disposition by LtCol. R. J. Harris, United States Marine Corps.

"The Article 32 hearing officer was Major R. M. Meeks, United States Marine Corps Reserve. The charges have been properly referred to this court-martial for trial by Colonel Earl L. Cahill, the convening authority, and have not been referred to any other court. The charges were served on the accused on 13 October 1990, and the five-day waiting period expired. The accused and the following persons detailed to this court-martial are present:

"Colonel William V. Dickenson, United States Marine Corps Reserve, as MILITARY JUDGE;

"Major Steve Way, United States Marine Corps Reserve, as TRIAL COUNSEL;

"Captain Michael J. Beck, United States Marine Corps Reserve, as DETAILED DEFENSE COUNSEL;

"Mr. Ogden Loring, Loring and Leavy, 997 West Laurel Street, San Diego, California, as CIVILIAN COUNSEL;

"And CORPORAL HATHAWAY has been detailed as the court reporter for this court-martial and has been previously sworn. All members of the prosecution are qualified, and certified under Article 27 (b), and sworn under Article 42 (a) of the Uniform Code of Military Justice. No member of the prosecution has acted in any manner that might tend to disqualify them in this court-martial."

"Are you Sergeant Nathan D. Jones, the accused in this case?

Sgt. Jones, Capt. Beck, and Ogden Loring stood.

"Yes, Sir"

"All right. Thank you. You can go ahead and be seated and then remain seated unless I ask you to stand up."

"Yes, Sir."

"Captain Beck, is your client properly attired with all awards and decorations to which he is entitled?"

"Yes, Sir. Sergeant Jones is attired in the 'Service C' uniform. He is entitled to wear the Navy Achievement Medal (with Gold Star in lieu of second award), the Good Conduct Medal, the Select Marine Corps Reserve Medal, the National Defense Service Medal, the Sea Service Deployment Ribbon, a Meritorious Unit Citation, the Organized Marine Corps Reserve Medal, and the Armed Forces Reserve Medal."

"Sergeant Jones, you have the right to be represented in this court-martial by Captain Beck, your detailed defense counsel. You also have the right to be represented by a military counsel of your own selection if found to be available. Your military counsel is provided to you free of charge. In addition to your right to military counsel, you have the right to be represented by civilian counsel at no expense to the United States. Civilian counsel may represent you alone or along with your military counsel.

"Do you understand your rights to military counsel?"

"Yes, Your Honor."

"By whom to you wish to be represented?"

"By Captain Beck and Mr. Loring."

"Do you wish to be represented by any other attorney, either military or civilian?"

"No, Your Honor."

"Captain Beck, please put your qualifications on the record."

"My name is Captain Michael J. Beck. I have been detailed to this case by Major Cindy Hendrix, the Chief Defense Counsel, MCAS, Yuma, Arizona. I am qualified and certified under Article 27 (b) and sworn under Article 42 (a) and have not acted in any manner which would disqualify me in this case."

"All right. Sergeant Jones, you have the right to be tried by a court-martial composed of a panel of members including, if you request, at least one-third enlisted persons on the panel. The members would determine if you are guilty or not guilty. And if you are found guilty, then the members would also determine your sentence. You also have the right to request trial by military judge alone. If that request is approved, the military judge will decide whether you're guilty or not guilty. And if you're convicted of the offense, then the military judge would determine your sentence. Do you wish to be tried by a court composed of members, a court composed of members with enlisted representation, or by military judge?"

Capt. Jones stood and addressed the Military Judge. "Sergeant Jones desires to be tried by military judge alone."

"Very well, the request is granted. Does the defense desire that the charge and specification be read?"

"No, Sir."

"The reading may be omitted."

"Will the Accused and defense counsel please rise. Sergeant Jones, how do you plead?"

"Not guilty to the charge and specification."

"Opening Statements?"

Maj. Way rose. "Government waives opening statement."

Capt. Beck rose. "Defense waives opening statement."

"Major Way, call your first witness."

"Your Honor, the Government calls Lieutenant Colonel Evert Easterday who will testify telephonically from Camp Gray near Jubayl, Saudi Arabia." The bailiff checked the speaker phones sitting on the bench, prosecution table, and defense table. The court reporter moved closer to the bench to better hear the telephone.

"State you name, rank and duty station."

"Lieutenant Colonel Evert Easterday, Fourth Tank Battalion, at Camp Gray near Jubayl, Saudi Arabia."

"Lieutenant Colonel, did you just take an oath to tell the truth?"

"Yes."

"And do you understand that even though we are conducting this trial telephonically, it is the same as if you were testifying in person and present at the court-martial?"

"Yes."

"Do you understand that the people present here, and listening, are myself, Major Way, as the Trial Counsel, Colonel Dickenson, the Military Judge, the accused Sergeant Jones, his attorneys Captain Beck and Ogden Loring, and the court reporter, and that your testimony is being recorded so it may be considered by the judge in the case of *United States versus Sergeant Nathan Jones*?"

"Yes."

"Do you know Sergeant Jones?"

"Yes. Sergeant Jones was a member of the Fourth Amtrac Battalion detachment for the Fourth Tank Battalion. I was his commanding officer."

"Is that a reserve unit?'

"Yes. We had several detachments. Sergeant Jones lived in southern Illinois and was attached to the St. Louis, Missouri unit."

"When you were Sergeant Jones's commanding officer did your unit receive mobilization orders?"

"Yes. We were one of the first units ordered to active duty in September 1990. We were ordered to turn in our M-60 tanks and to receive Abram M1A1 tanks from the Army at Marine Corps Base Twentynine Palms. We had to familiarize ourselves with the new tanks."

"Were there written mobilization orders?"

"Yes. There were written orders. We were all ordered to report at the St. Louis Reserve Center at 0800 on September 22, 1990."

"Did Sergeant Jones receive a copy of those orders?"

"Yes. I personally gave everyone in the unit a copy of the orders."

"I want to make sure we have a clear answer. Did you personally hand Sergeant Jones a copy of the written mobilization order?"

"Yes, I did."

"The orders that you personally handed to Sergeant Jones, did those orders require him to report to the St. Louis Reserve Center at 0800 on September 22, 1990?"

"Yes, they did."

"Is there a reason why there was no record made in Sergeant Jones's service record book of his receipt of the mobilization orders?"

"It should have been in there. If it is not, then somebody screwed up."

"Did the orders say that your unit would be going to Saudi Arabia, or what we call the Persian Gulf?"

"No. The orders were to report for active duty at Twentynine Palms California. They did not say anything about Saudi Arabia or the Persian Gulf."

"Did you tell Sergeant Jones that after transitioning to the new M1A1 tanks the unit would go to the Persian Gulf?"

"No. Everyone in the unit expected to go to the Persian Gulf, but I don't recall a specific conversation with Sergeant Jones."

"Why did everyone in the unit expect to go to the Persian Gulf?"

"News reports. The only reason to transition to M1A1 tanks was to go fight in the Persian Gulf."

"Did Sergeant Jones report to the St. Louis Reserve Center at 0800 on September 22, 1990?"

"No. He did not."

"How do you know that?"

"I was there at that time and date, and Sergeant Jones was not there."

"Again. Is there any reason that you know of why the unit diary does not show Sergeant Jones in an unauthorized absence status as of September 22, 1990?"

"There was a point in time when everyone in the unit assumed that some emergency had delayed Sergeant Jones and that he would soon show up. My guess is that the unit diary clerk took it upon himself to not make an entry, then forgot about it."

Capt. Beck stood, "Objection. Speculation. No foundation."

"Objection sustained."

"Did Sergeant Jones have any authority to absent himself from your unit on September 22, 1990?"

"No. He was supposed to be there with everyone else."

"Did you talk to Sergeant Jones after he failed to report on September 22, 1990?"

"No. I got a message that he called me. I was working twenty hours a day and trying to get one thousand things done. I regret that I never returned his call. As a Marine Officer, I should have worked twenty-one hours and done one-thousand-one things. I should have made the time to call Sergeant Jones. Maybe, if I had talked with him, things would have been different."

"All right. Lieutenant Colonel Easterday, those are all the questions I have. Sergeant Jones's attorney, Captain Beck, will now ask you some questions."

"How would you characterize the performance of duty of Sergeant Jones during the time he served under you?"

"You can use any accolade you want. He was the best Marine in the unit."

"Is there anything, in particular, he excelled at?"

"Everything. Appearance, physical fitness, marksmanship, technical knowledge, attention to detail, leadership, you name it, he was the best."

"What was Sergeant Jones's reputation for truth and veracity?"

"If Sergeant Jones came in my office and said aliens had landed on the parade deck, I would believe him without even walking outside to look."

"I appreciate that, Lieutenant Colonel Easterday, but that is an opinion. The question was Sergeant Jones's reputation. In other words, how did the other Marines in the unit feel about Sergeant Jones's truth and veracity?"

"The same. He had...I guess I should say a perfect reputation. Sergeant Jones was incapable of lying."

"Did Sergeant Jones ever tell you he was a conscientious objector?'

"Yes. I think it was at the December drill in 1989. Sergeant Jones told me he was considering submitting a conscientious-objector package to be assigned to noncombatant duties. He had not made up his mind. I told him he had the right to submit a conscientious-objector package, but from what I knew it would never be granted, and if it was, he would be discharged. I did not think the Marine Corps would assign a sergeant to noncombatant duties.

"Also, I told him the Marine Corps Reserve had not been called up for combat since the Korean War. That our M-60 tanks were obsolete, and I had seen studies saying that the logistical cost of shipping our tanks anywhere would exceed their value. I thought there was a zero chance that he would ever be asked to participate in combat with the M-60 tanks unless Russia invaded North America. I suggested that Sergeant Jones avoid everyone the hassle and get out when his re-enlistment contract came up."

"What did Sergeant Jones say?"

"He asked me if I could check it out. Which I did. It took some time, but I spoke to the Staff Judge Advocate at Fourth Marine Division. He went through the Marine Corps order and sent me a copy. It took until our annual training in July at Twentynine Palms. By that time, Sergeant Jones only had ten months left on his contract, again, at that time everyone thought there was a zero chance that Fourth Tank Battalion would ever be assigned to combat."

"Is it fair to say you discouraged Sergeant Jones from submitting a conscientious objector application?"

"I told him he could submit one if he wanted, but it is fair to say that I discouraged him from doing so."

"Thank you, Lieutenant Colonel Easterday. That is all the questions I have."

"Would it be all right if I ask Sergeant Jones a question regarding our radios?"

"Lieutenant Colonel Easterday, stand by. This is the Military Judge speaking.

"Any objection by the Government to Lieutenant Colonel Easterday asking the accused a question about the unit's radios?

"No, Sir."

"Defense?"

"No, Sir."

"All right, Lieutenant Colonel Easterday, go ahead with your question to Sergeant Jones."

"Good afternoon, Sergeant Jones…or whatever time it is there."

"Good afternoon, Lieutenant Colonel Easterday."

"Sergeant Jones, our communications for Tanks and Tracks have been down for several days. We are making no progress. Everyone is having problems with the PRC-105 UFHs. We have been replacing the encryption override switches. But we have used all our spares, and we cannot get replacements. I have read the manuals backward and forward. I am at a loss. Do you have any ideas?"

"You can wire around the encryption override switches."

"The manual says no. And we tried yesterday. Blew up the radio."

"I did it a couple of years ago at Twentynine Palms and it worked. You must shut everything down, and I mean everything. The terminal points must be field soldered and insulated. Again, there has to be a complete radio and intercom shut down before start up, otherwise you can get damage from a voltage surge. I know this will work because I have done it several times."

"Sergeant Jones, if you say it works, I know it will."

"It will work, Sir."

"One last thing. I apologize if I let you down. If things change for you, everyone would welcome you back in the unit. Obviously, we really need your help."

"Lieutenant Colonel Easterday, this is the Military Judge again. You can hang up, but do not discuss your testimony with anyone except the lawyers in this case. Understood?"

"Yes, Your Honor. I am hanging up."

Capt. Beck rose and addressed Col. Dickenson. "Your Honor. The Defense requests a fifteen-minute recess."

"Granted. The court will reconvene at 1045."

Capt. Beck, Ogden Loring, and Sgt. Jones walked down the hall to the defense conference room. When the door closed, Sgt. Jones addressed Capt. Beck.

"Captain Beck, do I still have the right to request mast to Colonel Cahill? I need to talk to him."

"You still have the right, but what do you want to say?"

"I want to apologize for breaking my oath to him and ask him to send me to my unit in Saudi Arabia."

Capt. Beck looked at Ogden.

"You know, Colonel Cahill could withdraw the charges, send Sergeant Jones to Iraq, and then decide whether to refile. Colonel Cahill could refile anytime within the five-year statute of limitations."

"Is there a chance he would do that?" Ogden asked.

"I think there is a chance, at least. Let's see if Colonel Cahill is available and if Colonel Dickenson will grant us a continuance."

Chapter 86

At exactly 0900, Sgt. Jones and Capt. Beck marched into Col. Cahill's office. Again, LtCol. Bumbaugh and Maj. Way sat at the conference table. Ogden Loring sat next to them. Sgt. Jones stopped in front of Col. Cahill's desk, stood at attention, and looked through Col. Cahill.

"Sergeant Jones reporting as ordered."

"Sergeant Jones, stand at ease. You have exercised your right to request mast to your commanding officer. Speak."

"Sir. I request to withdraw my application for conscientious objector status and be immediately transferred to my unit in Saudi Arabia, Fourth Tanks. I understand that you may decide to continue with my court-martial when I return, but my unit needs my expertise."

"I have read your conscientious-objector package. Pretty persuasive. Are you certain that you want to withdraw it?"

"Yes, Sir. I know now that I am not a conscientious objector. When Gunner Carson had me in the desert, I wanted to kill him. I tried to kill him. The last time I was in your office I swore on your Bible that I would return for my court-martial. When I was in Mexico, I did not intend to ever come back here. I am not a good Christian, but I am a good Marine. Marines go where they are ordered to go and they fight who they are told to fight. Marines fight to win. Sir, I know that I am the only Marine who can keep Fourth Tank Battalion's radios working. If I do that, I believe I can save at least some of my fellow Marine's lives. That's what I want to do, regardless of what happens to me when I return."

Col. Cahill looked at LtCol. Bumbaugh.

"Can I do that?"

"Yes, Sir, you can do that. As the convening authority you may withdraw the desertion charge and re-refer it any time before the statute of limitations runs in five years. You do not need a reason to refile."

Col. Cahill looked out the window in deep thought.

"Sergeant Jones, you, Captain Beck, and Mr. Loring step outside for a moment. I want to discuss something in private with Lieutenant Colonel Bumbaugh and Major Way."

Sgt. Jones, Capt. Beck, and Ogden Loring stepped outside Cahill's office.

"Lieutenant Colonel Bumbaugh, I want to do this thing Sergeant Jones suggested. But I want to make the same offer to all the Marines pending courts-martial for desertion. Can I do that?"

"As the convening authority, it is within your discretion to make the same offer to all the Marines pending a court-martial for desertion."

"Can I be relieved of duty for doing this?"

"Arguably, any action to influence the disposition of a pending a court-martial is unlawful command influence. However, you may be relieved of duty for any reason that causes your commanding officer to lose confidence in your performance. So, I must answer in the affirmative. This could result in your relief of command."

"Officer to officer, if I am not relieved of command, do you think it will ruin my chances for promotion?"

"Yes. As far as I know, it has never been done. You will be seen as an outlaw, and I would expect a negative backlash on your career. Enough to end it."

"Will it get you or Major Way in trouble?"

"No. This conversation is protected by the attorney-client privilege. Besides, everyone will assume that I advised you against it, and you ignored our advice." For the first time, Cahill saw a smile on Bumbaugh's face.

They sat in silence for a long time.

"Well. It is the right thing to do. I am granting Sergeant Jones's request. I am also going to make the same offer to every Marine pending a court-martial for desertion. Talk to the squadrons and see if we can get a C-130 as soon as possible. I want the Marines in Saudi Arabia before General Reynolds can do anything.

"To be clear, I will withdraw charges against any Marine who shows up at flight operations and gets on that plane for Saudi Arabia.

If they serve honorably, I will not refile the charges. Write something up and get it to all Marines pending desertion charges.

"Call Sergeant Jones and ask him to spend the day spreading the word to the Marines in the Brig and wherever we are now billeting the deserters. Counsel them. Help them make the right decision."

"Anything else, Colonel Cahill?" LtCol. Bumbaugh asked with surprising military bearing.

"No. This is the first day in a long time that I am proud to be a Colonel of the Marines. Let us hope it turns out well for everyone."

Chapter 87

At 0630 the next morning, Col. Cahill called his wife. "Hello, Patricia."

"Hey there."

"Sorry to call so early, but I wanted to catch Liz before she left for school. Is she up?"

"No. I think her first class is not until this afternoon."

"Would it be convenient if I come over again this weekend?"

The long pregnant pause made Cahill think that Patricia might have hung up on him. Then finally, "Of course. I will let her know to expect you…Hey, Earl. You sound different. Did something happen?"

"I did a good thing for the Marine Corps yesterday. The first thing I've done right in a long time. But I am pretty sure that Headquarters is not going to like it. I won't be promoted to general, hell, I could get relieved of my command."

"In our years together, your priorities were always the Marine Corps' priorities, but your career was never one of them."

"You are right, Patricia. I guess I sort of forgot that the last few years. Pat, I spoke to a legal assistance attorney. The property settlement agreement is fine. If we get a divorce, you will receive half of my retirement, you will own it and can do anything you want. Remarry, whatever."

Earl paused, then continued. "Child support legally ends when Liz reaches eighteen, but of course I will pay for her college. And, if you stay in California, there is no tuition at the state schools for active-duty military or retirees."

Earl gathered his thoughts. "Like we thought, the financial problem with divorce is that we lose the spousal increase for my Basic Allowances for Subsistence and Housing, and that is a lot of money every month. The legal assistance attorney said it is perfectly legal for us to continue like we are, living apart but married, and receive the spousal rate for BAS and BAH. Of course, I can't be with any other women because that's still adultery and a military offense."

Again, another long pause. "I don't plan on seeing other women, so it's all right by me if we just stay married. Whatever you want to do."

"You are right. I think we should stay married." Patricia spoke softly with great emotion. "Maybe we should consider giving our marriage another chance," Patricia said in the soft voice.

Earl had not intended the conversation to go this way and tried to process Patricia's words. "I would like that." He replied.

"Earl, I think it is stupid for you to spend all that money on a hotel when I have an extra bedroom. Why don't you stay here and give the six hundred dollars to Liz? She could really use a little extra cash. I promise not to cause any problems."

"All right. We can give it a shot for Liz. But do you think it might send a false message, you know...get her hopes up?"

"No. Liz is a very practical young lady. She understands wasting money and how difficult it is today for married couples."

"OK. Patricia, I will see you guys Friday evening."

♥

At 0645, Col. Cahill grabbed his cover and started out the door. As he passed his secretary's desk the phone rang. Instinctively, he picked up the receiver anticipating some glitch with the aircraft.

"Colonel Cahill speaking."

"Cahill, this is General Reynolds. Have you lost your fucking mind? I just found out about your deferral plan. Stop it." His voice was loud and even more urgent than usual.

"It's too late."

"It is not too late! I know the departure time on the aircraft. I want that flight cancelled and those fucking deserters held in Yuma. They are going to stand courts-martial." Reynolds paused to let his words sink in. "End this goat rope before it goes any further. That is a direct order."

"Respectfully, General Reynolds that's an illegal order and will not be obeyed."

"Cahill are you fucking drunk already this morning?"

"I have not had a drink in thirty days. Maybe that is why I know I don't have to obey that order. You are not my commanding officer. I am the commanding officer of the Marines getting on that plane, and it is my decision to withdraw the charges, and my decision alone. You can't do a damn thing about that, General Reynolds!"

The phone went silent. "Cahill, it will take a lot of my time and effort, but I will lobby the Commandant, I will have you relieved of command, and the new commanding officer will have General Lenard send every one of those chickenshit deserters back to Yuma for courts-martial. This little trick is just a waste of jet fuel."

"No, you will not do that. You are going to leave the Marines alone and give them a second chance."

"What did you just say to me?" Reynolds was now yelling into the phone.

"I said, you won't do a damn thing. I am well aware that what you just said to me, and your threatened actions constitute unlawful command influence. You fuck with me anymore, Reynolds, and I am going straight to the civilian attorneys! Every court-martial we have completed will be set aside. And you will get the blame for that, not me. That ought to ruin your fucking paper pushing career along with mine."

The phone went silent for a long time. "All right. All right, Cahill. Let's settle down here…" The phone went silent again. "Fine, Cahill. As a superior officer, I am just here to help you. If you want to end your career for a bunch of deserters, that is up to you. Sooner or later, those scumbags will all fuck up and get sent back anyway."

"I am hanging up General Reynolds. I have a group of Marines to send off to war."

"Don't say I didn't warn you of the consequences, Cahill…" LtGen. Reynolds screamed into the phone as Cahill hung up.

❧

What would be worse for a commanding officer—holding up a plane or getting a speeding ticket?

Earl Cahill decided holding up a plane would be worse and drove 30 miles over the speed limit to get to the flight terminal. At the terminal, he saw Sgt. Jones and a group of Marines standing next to a C-141 Starlifter. He also recognized Ogden Loring, LtCol. Bumbaugh, Maj. Way, and Capt. Beck. He drove onto the flight line, jumped out, and walked towards the Marines. He heard Sgt. Jones call the formation to attention and Jones gave a salute worthy of the parade ground at Paris Island.

"At ease, Gentlemen. I know that you all have spoken with defense counsel and signed acknowledgments. I congratulate you on your decision to choose deferment. No one expects you to be perfect. Obey orders, do your best, and come home to your family with the pride and self-respect of a Marine. Good luck and God Bless."

The grumble of the aircraft engines reached the ears of the Marines waiting on the runway. Sgt. Jones called the formation to attention, then marched the Marines to the plane ramp. They were quickly on board and headed to Saudi Arabia.

Chapter 88

The Commandant of the Marine Corps pushed the Fourth Tank Battalion JAG-Manual Report of Investigation to the middle of his desk and waited for the flash of anger to subside.

The investigation noted that while the Army had successfully transitioned to satellite radios, Marine amphibious tractors still used line of sight technology. Marines were forced to expose themselves on ridgelines to communicate. Worse, the Marines in Saudi Arabia faced a consistent—and unsolved—problem with the encryption devices on the Amtracs. The investigating officer concluded that at any time only about half of the amtrac radios remained operational.

The Commandant marched down the hallway to the Deputy Assistant Commandant's office, LtGen. John Reynolds entered without knocking and threw the JAG-Manuel Report on his desk.

"General Reynolds, have you seen this JAG-Manuel Report? Why aren't you on top of this problem?"

Without looking at the JAG-Manuel Report, Reynolds yelled back. "Commandant, I am glad you are here! We have a critical problem in Yuma! Colonel Cahill has decided to defer desertion charges on Marines that voluntarily report for combat duty in Iraq. He is sending them to Camp Gray, Saudi Arabia, and promised that if they perform well, he will not refile the charges. One of the Marines is the infamous Sgt. Nathan Jones who appeared at that peace rally in St. Louis. Cahill's already put them on a C-141 and the plane has taken off from MCAS, Yuma. We must stop this!"

The Commandant paused to think. Then he looked at Reynolds, his face contorted with disbelief and fury. Reynolds thought the anger was at Cahill.

"Son-of-a-bitch, General Reynolds! I am sick and tired of hearing about Cahill. He does not even work for you anymore!

"I want you to get off your ass, stop worrying about Cahill, and start doing your fucking job here at Headquarters! You should have already solved this radio problem with our Amtracs in Saudi Arabia!

"Now, we are going to settle this shit once-and-for-all. I will be in my office. I want an immediate conference call with General Lenard and Col. Cahill.

"While you are setting up the conference call, you read the Fourth Tanks JAG-Manuel Report, and tell me how in the fuck you are going to fix this problem with our Amtracs."

The Commandant stormed out of the office and Reynolds sat in his chair stunned at the ass-chewing he had received.

ଔଊ

"Gentlemen, this is the Commandant. Doug, how is everything in Camp Gray?"

"Mainly, its hot," LtGen. Douglas Lenard answered, pleasantly.

"Doug, I am sorry to set this call up on short notice, but I wanted all of us to talk to Col. Cahill about the Marines he is sending your way. Earl, tell us what is going on."

"Aye, Aye, Commandant. Yesterday we started the trial for the infamous Sergeant Nathan Jones. The prosecutor set up a conference call with the Commanding Officer of Fourth Tanks to prove the charges. The Commanding Officer wanted to talk to Jones about fixing the unit's radios at Camp Gray, Saudi Arabia.

"Apparently, Jones is some kind of guru on the old Amtrac radios, and the Commanding Officer thinks Jones is the only person that can make them work. Jones fixed the encryption problem during exercises at Twentynine Palms and can do it again. The CO said he wanted Jones back with his unit in Saudi, and Jones volunteered to go.

"My SJA tells me I can dismiss desertion charges without prejudice and refile them anytime within five years. I decided if I was going to give Jones that opportunity, I owed it to the other Marines and gave all of them the chance to volunteer for combat duty in Iraq.

"Another thirty Marines volunteered to go to Saudi Arabia and signed the appropriate legal waivers. I put them on a plane an hour ago. I made it clear, if they do not perform or cause problems, they will be facing charges when they return."

"I like it!" The Commandant shouted approvingly. "Earl, you turned a problem into an asset! What do you think, Doug?'

"I think it was the right thing to do. I have no problem giving a Marine a second chance, and Fourth Tanks really needs Sergeant Jones's help," LtGen. Lenard answered immediately.

The Commandant paused but neither Reynolds nor Cahill chose to speak. The Commandant continued. "I have known General Reynolds and Colonel Cahill for years, in my opinion, both fine officers. For some reason, it seems to me that lately they have been fighting like schoolgirls. I am sick of it. Doug, do you think you could find a suitable job for Earl in Saudi?'

"I am sure I can and would love to have him here."

"What do you say, General Reynolds?"

"No objection."

"Earl?"

"Commandant, it would be my honor to serve with General Lenard in Saudi Arabia."

"All right, Gentlemen. Earl, you get things wrapped up in Yuma and get to Camp Gray as soon as possible. General Reynolds, you find a replacement for Earl in Yuma. Let me know immediately if Sgt. Jones can fix our radio problem with the Amtracs."

Chapter 89

After watching the C-141 leave for Camp Gray, Saudi Arabia, Capt. Beck drove his Range Rover to the law center and went directly to Maj. Hendrix's office. The door stood open, and she sat behind her desk. Just seeing her took Mike's breath away.

"May I come in? I need your signature on my checkout form."

"Of course, Mike,"

Mike stepped inside, carefully closed the door, and sat down. Cindy smiled and extended her hand for the form. She reviewed the form, signed it, and handed it back to Mike.

"I have been trying to call you."

"I know you have…I guess I should have called you back, but…Mike, I will always cherish the time we had together but…I don't feel like there is anything more to be said."

Mike was surprised by the intensity of his emotions. His eyes felt watery, and his voice got shaky. "Cindy, I made a mistake. A big mistake. I have been miserable. I love you and I want to marry you."

Cindy just smiled. She looked so beautiful. Mike swallowed hard and tried to talk again. "Look, Cindy, I can wait. I will wait for however long it takes. If you change your mind, please just call me. That's all I want to say…"

Cindy slowly stood and came around the desk. She shook her head, her lips in a straight line. Her face displayed as disapproving a look as Mike had ever seen on Cindy.

"Mike, just give me a hug and leave. Please."

They embraced tightly, their bodies joining together. Neither wanted to let go, but after a long time, Cindy gently pushed Mike away, then turned, and stared out her window. Mike had no choice but to leave.

By the time Capt. Beck completed the checkout procedure, it seemed late to start the drive back to Chicago. He checked into the Stardust Motel and walked across the street to the Hungry Hunter

Bar. At 1800, he ordered dinner at the bar but did not feel like eating. He then headed back to his motel room. He was dying inside.

It was a peculiar evening, Mike decided later. At 2200, he called Cindy's house. No answer, so he drove there, intending to stop, and try to talk to her one more time. The lights were on, but Mike hesitated and drove by. He circled the block, but when he returned the next-door neighbor pulled into the driveway. Mike drove his car by Cindy's house again and back to the Stardust. He felt like a stalker, ashamed of his actions. He knew that he had lost Cindy, and he knew why. He had enjoyed her body many times, but he didn't know her. She did not know him. No one got inside Mike Beck's mind.

At 2330, Mike crawled into the motel bed, and tried to sleep, but woke in an hour. He could hear the wind picking up outside, which probably meant a storm coming. Yuma might get some rain. There were no trees or tall buildings in Yuma to stop the wind. Some nights, like tonight, the wind beat relentlessly across the land.

Mike lay in the motel bed wide awake, trying to sleep until 0200, when he finally gave up. He jumped in the shower and let the hot water run off his head for a full ten minutes before soaping up. *I have to get away from this shit and go back to work in Chicago.*

He finished in the shower, dried off, and put on fresh clothes. Mentally, he still felt like crap, and physically he was tired, but at least he felt clean. He packed his bag and checked out with the night clerk.

Beck drove all the way to Oklahoma City without stopping, except for gas. He made it back to Chicago the next day and went straight to his office. He carried his travel suitcase up to his work condo—the bed in the room next to his office—and sat at his desk reading case notes, bar association magazines, and other publications that had arrived during his absence. In 30 minutes, his partner Sidney Johnson came rushing into his office, and closed the door.

"Mike, great to see you, but you are back a little early. The sabbatical does not end for another week."

"Sid, the people who rented my house won't be out for a couple of days. I will not be doing any work here, but I am going to catch up on case developments. I am sure that does not violate my deal with the Bar Association."

Now, Sid started to grin. "OK, Mike. No problem. Say, are you going to have any time on Sunday? I got this new case."

Sid's eyes were bright, and somehow the grin grew bigger. "Really great case! This case will keep you busy for the next five years."

"Sure, Sid. I will be here all day Sunday."

Sid stood up and started to leave. At the door he stopped and turned back to Mike.

"Mike, this case is huge! Fucking huge! More money than we ever dreamed of. See you Sunday morning. I can't wait to tell you about it."

About the Author

J. W. Stone is an exceptional author with 30 years of military service. He was with the Marines in Iraq during the Battle of Fallujah and developed a unique perspective on modern warfare. His writing brims with action, real characters, and a deep understanding of courage and commitment, both from the perspective of the grunts on the ground and the highest-ranking officers.